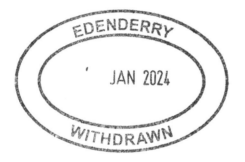

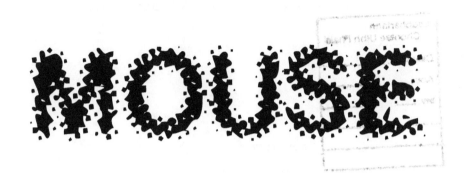

RICHARD
FORD BURLEY

PROSPECTIVE PRESS
TEEN

PROSPECTIVE PRESS LLC

1959 Peace Haven Rd, #246, Winston-Salem, NC 27106 U.S.A.

www.prospectivepress.com

Published in the United States of America by PROSPECTIVE PRESS LLC

⚡ TRADEMARK

MOUSE

Library of Congress Control Number: 2017941384

ISBN 978-1-943419-50-0

First PROSPECTIVE PRESS hardcover edition

Printed in the United States of America

First printing, August, 2017

1 3 5 7 9 10 8 6 4 2

The text of this book is typeset in Alegreya

Accent text is typeset in Acidic

MOUSE

For Ben

and for all the notes we'd send ourselves
if we could do things over again

The school bell rings, and within moments the muted swelling of voices and chairs erupts out of the classrooms. As everyone floods out into the swirls and eddies of third hall, Mouse clings to his books and stares down at the grey-green vinyl tiles. He gets tossed around and shoved into lockers while people wonder out loud why the idiot can't watch where he's going for a change. There are pairs of shoes he knows to avoid, the angry ones—a clean white pair of Nike trainers that are probably size nine, an absurdly-large pair of limited-edition black and neon orange Reeboks that are always so undone he wonders how the guy doesn't just walk right out of them. But for the most part people are pretty forgiving. They don't use the r-word, they just say "Careful, Mouse," and point him in the right direction again. It's better at this school than at the last one, he thinks.

A pair of purple Converse All-Stars—the high-tops with the Chuck Taylor signature and the logo on the side—grabs him by the arm, a cold white hand with purple nail polish pulling him aside, and he's at his locker—a half-drowned rat on a rock in the rapids. His savior is Bliss, always waiting next to his locker to toss him a lifeline. He nods a *thank you* as he fumbles with his lock.

He's always late for fourth period. The school was built for a small rural town, not the fast-growing suburbs that are creeping in from all sides. The halls are so busy between third and fourth that his usual mode of navigation, staring at the floor and hoping for the best, doesn't really cut it. It's not that he can't look up, but the thought of all those faces and all that information, the smiles and the frowns and the faraway looks, the poorly-hidden pimples and hickies under just-wrong-shade foundation, the fashion choices made by self-conscious adolescents specifically picked to send a message often unknown to their wearers. He gets it all at once. It's too much. He gets distracted and makes mistakes.

If the hall's mostly empty and he runs into someone, say Kyle from the student council, he'll take a glance up and know from the gel in Kyle's hair whether he showered that morning—he wears more when he hasn't, to make up for the bed head—and from the rumors going around the school he might guess that he was out with Christine from tenth grade later than he should've been the night before. They probably didn't get in trouble because Christine's mom does shift work at the county hospital and sometimes that means the night shift, and because Kyle's dad thinks that 'Boys will be boys' and if they won't, well, they probably should. Jackie—three lockers down—has a crush on Kyle, the way she's always looking at him except for when he's looking back, the way she delays herself at her locker busily doing nothing until he walks by so she's late, too. But when the tide comes in and there's dozens of Kyles and Jackies and Christines, all talking and laughing and broadcasting unaware on a hundred channels that he can't shut out; it's just too much.

So he stands there looking into his open locker, or rearranges his textbooks by color, or pulls out *Toradora!* Volume One and flips through, smiling to himself while Taiga takes things out on Ryuji again even though he's way nicer to her than he should be. These are faces he can stand to look at—faces simplified. Even when it's complicated it's easier. He can go back and try again, because it isn't real. Nothing's for keeps; it's safer.

鼠

The hallway is empty again. The walls are lined with lockers, an institutional shade of cream, repainted every few years to hide the wear and tear of forty years of student occupation. Bliss—with her black and purple hair, punk-rock shirt, pleated skirt, and knee-highs—is an apparition, a little too grunge for angelic, a little too perfect for punk, leaning nonchalant against her closed locker watching him.

Mouse's hair, too long and too short and a shade of blond so ashen it's almost grey, falls in front of his eyes as he stares into his locker, not really looking, listening without watching.

"You gonna stand there all day, Mouse?" she asks. It's not really his name, but it's what everyone calls him. He likes it. He likes it even more that, when it comes out of her mouth, it's a term of endearment. It's definitely better at this school than the last one.

He shakes his head and grabs the textbook from the shelf, hugs it to his chest with one arm while he closes and locks the locker with the other. He follows behind her, eyes glued to the ground.

鼠

He'd met her on his first day there, a week late into the term. He hadn't been ushered in front of the class or forced to introduce himself, that wasn't the way it worked. But he had been new and he had stuck out at what was really a much bigger school than he'd been used to, so the teacher of his homeroom class—tenth-grade chemistry, Mrs. Edelman—had said, "We've got a new student today," and had proceeded to direct everyone's attention to him. He'd sat in a desk near the back.

"His name is Simon and he just moved out here from the city, so everyone let's show him a bit of country kindness, hey?" She'd tilted her head a little to the side and clasped her hands in front of her, a relic left over from a time when the school had still been in the actual country.

Mrs. Edelman, blonde fading to grey, crows feet not unattractively embroidered at the corners of her eyes, looked as though she'd be equally at home behind the counter at the local diner as behind the black epoxy resin countertops that lined the chemistry room. "They're non-reactive," his last chemistry teacher had said to him once, "kind of like you."

For a while, when he was younger, they'd put him into a high-supervision class, drilled into him the meaning of a smile or a frown because they thought he didn't know. The last school had made him come in for an extra class at the end of the day, but at this one both cash and suburban pretension were in shorter supply, so because his grades were fine, he'd been branded normal and was generally to be treated as such by the powers-that-be.

He'd swallowed and unlocked his jaw. Taken a breath.

"Mouse," he'd said, looking down at his desk, cheeks reddening, hands folded in his lap under his desk. He'd been so quiet that Mrs. Edelman almost hadn't heard, but she had, and then had asked again. "Mouse," he'd repeated, not really any louder. There'd been a small giggle from one side of the class while the rest had sat in perplexed silence.

"Do you mean instead of Simon?" Her tone all sweetness except for the poorly-hidden confusion.

No one had ever called him Simon. His father might have, if he'd stuck around. But he was long gone into the wilderness of politics, ambassador to some place that had women who, if they weren't prettier than June, had at least been in the same time zone. Even June called him Mouse—June who'd forever insisted that, because it was just the two of them, he should call her by her first name. It was only later he'd realized that the other kids had a Mom and Dad, and that he alone had a June.

A few students had leaned over to whisper to each other. Mouse had scribbled a little note on a pad, torn it off and folded it up, passing it forward. This is how he talks, mostly. She'd gotten the file, he'd been sure. His teachers always had before. "Primarily non-verbal," it says, "anxiety and communication difficulty, nevertheless considerably bright."

Humor him, they could have added.

"So, Mouse, then?" He'd nodded, not looking up—he couldn't bear to do it, hadn't wanted to see—and she'd acquiesced. "Well, it's a little unorthodox, but if that's what you go by." She's the kind of person who stops without completing an *if-then* statement. "Mouse here has obviously missed a week, so can I have a volunteer to help out if he has any questions?" An enthusiastic, purple-nailed hand had shot up a few rows over and a seat behind, at the very back of the class.

Mouse had hazarded a look up in the pause that had followed.

He'd met a Cheshire Cat grin and nearly silver eyes, framed by black hair with purple streaks. He'd stared quickly back at his desk. After a definite hesitation—had Mrs. Edelman been hoping someone else would volunteer? He still wonders—the teacher had resigned herself. "Bliss," she'd said, in an embattled tone that suggested the decision had been made, but with reservations that were legion.

And then stranger still: she'd turned and started writing on the board when, after what could only have been a calculated delay, the Cheshire Cat had replied, "You can count on me, Commish"—from the sound of it while still grinning.

He'd later learn that Mrs. Edelman's insistence on a rule-based society had earned her the nickname of the "Chemistry Commissioner," a moniker that she held onto the way she held onto everything unpleasant in her life, the way a fire extinguisher holds on to carbon dioxide or a propane tank its combustible contents: under great pressure.

The class had seemed to tingle with static, until at last the commissioner's chalk had snapped. But she'd retained composure and, after a zenlike calming breath, had launched into a lesson on something. The periodic table and covalent bonding, it might have been, about how atoms want a complete shell and how they're not afraid to borrow, beg, or steal electrons to get it. Mouse had stolen another look over at the Cat—the girl—who by then had been scribbling madly into a notepad. Her grin had faded, ever so slightly, to a quiet smirk.

This is how he remembers meeting Bliss.

鼠

In third hall, the tide has ebbed once again. Bliss suddenly swivels about-face and Mouse nearly runs into her. He looks up at her just enough to see the familiar grin.

"You don't really want to go to business math." It's a statement. Bliss can have whole conversations with him this way, telling him his own thoughts, mostly being right.

He doesn't say no.

"Then, *to the batcave!*" she shouts and skips away down the hall.

There's a fire exit down by the library that hangs a sharp left out of sight of the security cameras. Bliss once figured out which way the camera faces, inside its little black-domed eye, and devised a route through the school that sneaks up on it and lets you slip out if you hug the walls. He follows her out into the chilly space between the doors. At some point a past student—gone long enough to have kids enrolled by now—had declared this space theirs, scrawled on the mortar between bricks in black Sharpie 'The BatCave, est. 1991.'

He's been at the school about a month. His grades are fine—his grades on anything that doesn't involve presentations or group work, that is. His English marks are a little low, but he's not missing English, and he's read *The Count of Monte Cristo* anyway. Well, he's seen the anime. Bliss, who hates the cold but loves to smoke, pulls out an e-cig and takes a deep breath. The end glows blue and she exhales a cloud of water vapor that hangs in the air like it can't decide whether to go up or down. It smells like chocolate and coffee.

"Flavor cartridges. You want?" He shakes his head. "It's a terrible habit anyway. Picked it up in the trenches." She's always saying things like that, like she's seen one too many World War Two films. She slides down the wall by the doors, knees together so she can hug them when she lands, then puts her chin on them and crunches into a tight little ball. She contracts, not even filling the space she occupies, shrinking into herself until she's barely there.

He sits down, too. He wants to say that he notices—that he sees she's all sharp angles and loud noises out there, but all small and quiet when she thinks she's alone—but he doesn't want to break the illusion, the feeling she seems to have that she's alone even when he's there with her. People don't like it when you turn their body language into words.

They sit quietly, while she smokes, and she's right. He writes her a note and watches her read it: *This is better than business math.*

She smiles and takes another drag.

鼠

It's October but they're still moving in; it's kind of how June works. They'd taken a car-load with them when they moved, whatever they could fit, and then had the rest sent as cheaply as possible in a slow-shipped storage pod. Somehow it had taken four weeks to show up, and now that it's arrived it's taking up three parking spots out front and making a great impression on the neighbors and shopkeepers, Mouse is sure.

Their new apartment is the top two floors of a narrow three-story plan with cracks in the plastered walls that make it look as though it wasn't so much built on top of the first floor corner store, as just dropped on it from some unspecified distance above. Thankfully, the place came furnished—the old guy who owns the shop and used to live above it has given up on stairs since he got his knees replaced, and every time they go in he tries to convince June to take over the store, too.

The boxes are full of everything from dishes and silverware to clothes and personal things. Mouse's few boxes of DVDs and graphic novels are there, along with a poster of Chihiro and No Face riding the train to the spirit world, and a small figurine of a red-haired Shana swinging her katana, trench coat flying out behind her. It's the only figurine he's ever bought and he's not likely to get another. Following June through the tightly-packed aisles of bikini-clad fantasy women had been several degrees of mortifying.

Mouse carries a box up the black metal stairs that go up the side like a fire escape to a big shared brick-and-concrete landing at the back, where the front door is. There are actually three apartments over three stores: theirs over the convenience store, the next over a tanning salon, and the last over an 'asian food' take-out place that's probably the closest thing the little town has to international cuisine. There's a waist-high wall around the edge of the terrace, intermittently adorned with flowerpots of pansies, and a dark-haired girl who sits and watches him ferry his cargo indoors. She's gone by the time he comes up with the last load.

"Grab us some plates, hun." June says as she's walking out the door, "I'm going to run downstairs and get some take-out. Something greasy to reward us for all our hard work." She grins conspiratorially and ducks out of sight. Mouse sighs. They've been unpacking for maybe an hour. Still, take-out's better than the alternatives—June's idea of a home-cooked dinner comes in a tray and has options labeled 1200, 1000, and 750 watts.

He fishes around in a box filled with crumpled newsprint and pulls out a couple of blue glass plates. They've had these for years.

The kitchen is lit only by a small bulb over the stove and a lamp that hangs over a table at one end. Sensing someone in the doorway he looks up, but there's no one there. Then, the dark-haired girl is standing behind him, holding another one of the plates up so that the light from the hanging lamp passes through it and casts an azure ring on half the kitchen.

"These are pretty."

At the first syllable the boy jumps and spins, clapping the plates together so loudly he nearly breaks them. The girl starts giggling uncontrollably.

She might be about thirteen, a little shorter than Mouse, who has always been a little short himself. She has long, jet-black hair and pale skin. She's in a yellow summer dress, tiny white socks, and black patent-leather shoes that have a single golden buckle on each that shines in the lamplight. A sea-green barrette with a silver flower holds back her hair. Even when she's there Mouse gets the feeling of being watched by a stranger he can't see. He hugs the plates to his chest until the laughter stops, until his heart slows down.

"You squeaked!" she says, with a smile. The plate goes back in the box. She's leaning to one side and a staring up in an attempt to see beyond his scraggly hair. "But you didn't run," she says. "That's a good start." There's another smile and a little scrutiny for a moment before she pushes up her lower lip and nods with the expression that means a person's made up their mind about something. She spins, making her sun dress fly out like a golden flower before flouncing away through the door with a quick shout of "Oyasumi, chicken!"

And then the room fills with absence.

His eyes linger on the doorway for a moment, arms still hugging the plates. He lowers them and looks down before holding one up to the light and watching the way the world goes blue.

A moment later June walks in and ruffles the boy's hair, disturbing his reverie, and plops a plastic bag labeled *Lucky Rangoon* on the kitchen counter.

鼠

"So I just met our neighbors," June says, finishing off an 'Unpacking the kitchen beer' and cracking open a 'Dinner beer.' They're sitting at the table, still surrounded by boxes. "Well, two doors down. The Kinoshitas. They run the take-out place downstairs." Mouse looks at her, then at the food. It's 'American Chinese.'

He doesn't even need to write a note, they've been this way so long. "Kinoshita-san—that's how I'd say it right?" He shakes his head in an embarrassed *no*. That's how you'd say it in an anime, or maybe in Japan, but this isn't Japan—he wouldn't know what Japan was like if he suddenly found himself in the middle of Tokyo—and who's to say their neighbors hadn't been here for generations anyway?

June looks a little crestfallen, but not enough to keep her down. She shrugs, takes a bite of fried meat on a stick and gesticulates with the rest, talking with her mouth full. "He says they do sushi, too, but only on Fridays. People around here aren't too keen on raw fish so he just makes what sells, which is mostly fake Chinese. Hey, I wonder if they'd like your rolled omelets." Mouse cooks when he can, and sometimes he likes to try to make the food he sees in anime. During the summer he'd made bento boxes for June to take to work with her. She takes a long draw from her bottle of beer and they sit in comfortable silence.

The boy pulls out his pad and writes a note: *Do they have a daughter?* He slides it over.

June's eyes light up. "Why? Did you meet a girl?" She grins at him and waggles her eyebrows. "Is she cute?"

Mouse sighs and sticks out his tongue, and June shrugs.

"Not that I know of, anyway." She takes a sip of her beer. "His son Kai's about your age, though. He was helping out behind the counter. Maybe you've run into him at school."

Mouse shrugs in response, and June takes another sip of beer.

"So how is it?" she asks. She means school. Chemistry, English, Lunch, Computer Science, and Business Math. The Chemistry Commissioner and the Cheshire Cat. He doesn't know for sure that she's been avoiding the topic on purpose, but he's been guessing as much. He wonders if the beer's helped.

What was it like? Within a day his name had been Mouse on all the attendance sheets. Bliss had introduced him to the 'Batcave Crowd'—a handful of them who fade in and out in the little fire escape hallway. A moth-eaten pair of Vans that often overlap with a petite pair of neon-green trainers, a pair of calloused feet in year-round Birkenstocks, always accompanied by the strumming of a gently out-of-tune guitar. A pair of worn but well-kept black leather shoes—square toed, with those annoying round black laces that always come undone—come to think of it, maybe that's Kai. He's the busy sort—comes and goes pretty quickly, saying things about clubs and sports and hall monitor duty. He told Bliss off for trying to sit next to him in Business Math the first week.

In general, people keep their distance, as they always tend to do, but the advent of Bliss and her adoption had already made things better at this school than at any of the others. He doesn't say all of this, just scribbles on his pad the word *good*. June reads it and looks at him, the time between her question and his short response too long for her tastes. He writes another word below it—*really*—and she smiles, drops the crab rangoon she's been gesticulating with, slides over, and gives him a greasy kiss on the top of his mop of hair.

"That's great, Mouse," she says, and holds him just a little longer.

Later, he wanders down to throw the garbage in the Dumpster out back. There's no one in sight as he climbs back up the stairs, but as he goes inside the girl is there, sitting unseen on the wall and watching him close the door.

語
鼠

The lunch bell chimes the next day, echoing in the spaces outdoors like the village timepiece. Students pour out of classrooms, headed for their lockers, and then the cafeteria. Mouse is following the back of Bliss's purple high-tops to the batcave when they run into the black leather shoes he'd been thinking about the night before.

"Kai!" she shouts as she puts her arms around his neck and swings around to face Mouse, grabbing him from behind. Mouse looks up and quickly looks back down, his suspicions confirmed. The pair of leather shoes is a serious-looking Japanese boy. He's wearing a white dress shirt with the sleeves rolled up, black slacks, and a super-thin black tie. The furrow in his brow is one of annoyance, but whether real or feigned Mouse can't tell.

"I haven't introduced you guys yet. Kai, this is Mouse. Mouse? Kai." Her smile shines. "Now you've met."

Kai looks as though his shirt itches. "Hi."

"Kai was the first person I met in this town. He was there when I landed." She grins at him and he rolls his eyes like it's an old joke.

Mouse fumbles for his pad, lunchbox flopping about in a plastic bag that hangs from his wrist, and eventually succeeds in writing a note of introduction.

I met your sister last night.

A sudden vacuum seems to form, as students walk out of the building, talking in the sun. It fills the distance between the note and its response.

Kai's face goes a few shades redder as he crumples the note and drops it to the ground. "What the hell is this? What the hell is wrong with this kid?" He's not talking to Mouse, but to Bliss. She looks confused as he storms off down the hall.

Bliss stares after him for a moment while Mouse stands immobile, paralyzed with confusion. He's said something wrong again, he knows it, but can't figure out what. She crouches down and picks up the crumpled note, carefully flattens it out on her knee before reading it. Then she folds it up and stands before handing it back to Mouse.

"He doesn't have a sister," she says, shaking her head. "Not since last year."

She tells him to go to the batcave and that she'll go and sort Kai out, tell him it was just a mistake. Mouse holds the note in both hands as she leaves, but makes no move to go.

鼠

She finds him sitting by himself outside under an ash tree that has a square wooden bench around it. The October chill hasn't quite set in, but he should probably be wearing a coat. He's eating a sandwich, his open lunchbox on his lap. She's standing on the next side around, behind and beside him, hanging a little from the tree. A many-zippered black leather jacket adds a little more punk than usual to her attire.

She leans over and looks down at him. The note that's caused all the fuss is in his lunchbox, next to a sugar-free 'fruit drink' and a little bag of almonds.

"Batcave not good enough for you?" she asks. It would sound confrontational, but her tone is gentle.

He shakes his head and pulls out his pad, dropping the sandwich into the box.

Too many people.

It's half an excuse.

She plops herself down next to him.

"Kai's a good guy, really. But Jesus, Mouse. Of all the things you could have said." She laughs sadly to herself. "It was kind of spectacular."

I'm sorry.

She sighs and puts her forehead on his shoulder. She talks without moving it.

"Anna was a year younger than us. But she looked younger than that, she was small for her age. The doctors never really figured out why. It was like somehow all her energy was being spent elsewhere. After a while she couldn't go to school anymore, so we used to hang out with her in her room when we got home. When she died last year, she nearly took us all with her. Kai's mom and dad split up. Kai and I split up. Kai didn't come to school, didn't go to work, didn't leave his room. It was like she'd been the only thing holding everyone together. Kai was even taking summer classes so he could get into a school with a good med program. It was like we were all living a dream that she'd keep on living if we just worked hard enough at it."

Her voice has fallen to a whisper by the time she stops. She lets out a wet sniffle. He pulls out a cloth handkerchief and hands it to her. It's one of those things he picked up from an anime again, a kind of odd attachment to an imagined past.

"Thanks," she says. When she hands it back it has perfect little crescent moons of mascara on it.

"Why did you think so, anyway? That you'd met Anna?" she asks.

He truncates his thoughts. That a girl had shown up in his apartment and disappeared, that he lives two doors down from Kai and his father, that he hadn't seen any other Japanese students at his school.

Girl at my apartment last night. Don't know her. K lives two doors over.

While Bliss is reading that one, he writes another.

I must've made a mistake.

She sighs. "I'll say." She shakes her head.

He writes her one more.

Tell Kai I'm sorry, too.

As she looks at it, the Cheshire Cat starts to resurface. She's smirking again by the time she looks up. "Oh, no," she says. "You're going to tell him yourself."

He shakes his head as he finishes his sandwich.

"Oh yes. And what's more," before he can react she's snatched his writing pad, "you're going to do it without this."

Panic.

鼠

He wants to run away, but she's leading him by the hand to the bat-cave, the pair of them rushing through the halls, her hand wrapped around his, his face going red. Before he knows it, they've barged in on Kai, sitting by himself in the hall. He's finished his lunch and is reading.

He looks up and Mouse audibly gulps. He's sweating. Where Bliss was holding his hand to drag him there, now he's holding her sleeve like a boy afraid of heights holds the railing on an observation deck. Don't look down.

Kai looks peevish at the interruption. "What?" he says.

Bliss's patience is like a cool breeze. "Mouse wants to say something."

Mouse *does not* want to say something; at most Mouse wants to *write* something. Preferably Mouse would like to *run away from here and never look back*, to curl up in a ball and put his hands over his ears. He takes a deep breath, but nothing comes out when he exhales. He tries again.

Kai's looking very confused at this point. Mouse's face goes three shades redder as he recognizes that he should have said something ten seconds before, but now that it's ten seconds of silence later, it's an even bigger deal than it was then and, please god, just let him say something out loud, anything at all. Anything. He feels cold.

"Gomennasai!" he squeaks.

There's an audible pause.

Kai looks at Bliss.

Another pause.

"Did he just apologize to me in Japanese?"

Oh, christ.

Did he? He was so frightened and anxious he just reached for the nearest thing in his head. He's seen apology scenes so often in anime and oh no oh no oh no. What must he seem like now? Oh god, is that someone walking by? Who else has been watching? The color drains from his face entirely until he's almost ashen. He thinks he might pass out. He's almost hiding behind Bliss's arm now, holding her sleeve like a talisman for protection. Maybe if he were a real mouse he could just climb up it and vanish entirely. Exit Mouse, sleeve left.

Three or four glacial ages pass in apocalyptic silence. The feeling of cold still sits on him like a weight on his chest.

"S—s—sorry." He manages, as an almost inaudible follow up.

And then, a miracle.

Kai bursts out laughing.

And he's not laughing *at him*.

Mouse can't make it out, but it's like he's laughing at something much, much bigger. Something on the scale of the universe itself.

Laughter like water in the desert fills the hall, until Kai's holding his sides with one arm and propping himself up with the other. Mouse desperately wants to know what Bliss's face looks like right now, to read her features and use them to Rosetta Stone his way through this, but all he can do is wait for Kai to heave himself to his feet.

"Where the hell did you *find* this kid?" He asks. Mouse hazards a look and can't comprehend what he sees. Kai has wet cheeks, like he's been crying, and his smile is not happy, but not sad. What, then? "Honest to god, Bliss." He puts his hand to his forehead, lowers his head, and looks at the ground. His skinny tie hangs down and waves from side to side and he shakes his head. "She was such a weeb," he says to his shoes. "She might've liked you."

He looks back up and pokes Mouse in the forehead, just hard enough that it forces him to make eye contact for half a second. Mouse squeezes his eyes shut, but not before he sees the intense sadness in those dark eyes, and the rueful smile that accompanies it, and the acceptance of the absurdity of the universe that underlies it all. Kai grabs his bag and starts to walk off, then stops and looks back over his shoulder.

"See you after class?" The question is directed at Bliss.

She nods, and he leaves.

Mouse is still clinging to her sleeve when she fishes out his notepad and hands it back to him. When he takes it he looks up at her face.

One time June took him to see the Grand Canyon. It had been the first time either of them had seen it, they'd driven out special, just to see it, as they moved between cities for the dozenth time. It was the first time Mouse had noticed how often June seemed to switch jobs. When you get there, there's this strange trick of perspective that happens when you approach the edge. All this time you've thought you were at ground level, but you reach the edge and it's like you're suddenly up in the sky, like you've climbed to some great height without realizing it, and there are other things up as high as you are, mountainous but way off in the distance. And all at once, you're somewhere you weren't before, and someone's swapped out your old reality for a new one, and your brain can hardly make sense of it.

That's how Mouse feels right then, because in her face he sees what he saw in June's face that day, and he feels it reflected inside himself.

It's like really seeing someone else for the very first time.

鼠

Later that night, he's unpacking another box when he finds a note on his desk. The handwriting is clean and in mechanical pencil on a little sheet of Totoro-themed paper.

ごめいわくをかけてすみません。

木下 杏奈

It takes him half an hour with a dictionary and Google Translate to decipher it.

Go meiwaku o-kakete sumimasen, it says. *Sorry for all the trouble.*

It's signed, *Kinoshita Anna.*

The outside of the apartment is quiet in the morning; the stores downstairs are still closed up. Sammy, the old guy running the convenience store, is rolling up the corrugated metal screen that covers the storefront from midnight to seven. The sun peeks between buildings, casting patterns of orange light and shadow onto the street as the buzzing sodium lights flicker out at the end of a long night's work.

She's waiting for him when he leaves the house: black patent leather shoes, shiny buckles, yellow sundress. October's chill has come in overnight and she's still dressed for summer. She has a sun hat, with a matching yellow ribbon, and its brim hangs down over her face as she stares at the ground, a pair of sullen footsteps following behind him on the pavement as he walks. He doesn't say anything.

"You're not ignoring me are you?"

Mouse shakes his head but doesn't slow down because he's going to be late. Plus there's an unfamiliar tugging somewhere inside him that wants to get there in time to see Bliss before chemistry starts. It's dragging him forward a little quicker than normal.

He wonders how long he's going to be followed.

"Everyone ignores me."

Mouse walks awkwardly trying to pull out his pad. Finally he's forced to give up walking and take it out.

Are you Kai's sister?

She nods in the affirmative. In the distance, there's a sound like tiny bells on barrettes.

"Sorry about yesterday. I didn't mean to get Kai mad at you."

Bells or maybe wind chimes.

Mouse takes a deep breath and tries not to relive the previous day's experience, but fails. There's something a little frustrating about the way memories that make you cringe refuse to stay quiet when you don't want to think about them.

It's okay, he writes. He's not handing the notes to her, just writing them and holding up the pad.

Her right hand holds her left in front of her in an anxious gesture, the toes of her shoes touching.

"I should have told you."

That you're a ghost?

"Yeah."

I wouldn't have believed you.

"I bet you would have."

He shrugs.

The wind blows a cloud shadow down the street. For a moment he seems alone. He starts walking again, trying his best to write notes as he goes.

What's it like?

She's walking next to him now. He doesn't even have to hold up the notes, she's just looking over as he writes. It's her turn to shrug.

"It's like the opposite of being hollow," she says. "Like, if you were a body and felt like you had no middle, you'd be hollow, right? But I'm *just* a middle. Sometimes when the wind blows I forget myself for a minute, like my brain's being scattered all over town, and then I notice myself again and I'm where I was, or else I'm somewhere new."

Mouse doesn't know what to say to this, and they keep walking in silence.

She stops all of a sudden, and it takes him a second to realize.

"Hey, uh." She stops and then starts again. "I mean, um. Since nobody else can see me, I was wondering if maybe you could, I mean if I could..." She trails off.

Mouse waits in the ensuing silence. She clears her throat and he has a moment to wonder if ghosts have throats before, fists balled at her sides, she says, "Can I? I mean, will you be—now it just sounds weird because I'm asking!" With a frown and a pout and a stomped foot, at last she says, "Friends!" She looks down. "I don't have any friends and it gets boring not having anyone to talk to, just watching people all day and so I thought maybe since you can see me and hear me then if you were my friend then—"

She's interrupted as he thrusts his pad between her eyes and the ground.

Sure. He even draws a happy face.

"Yay!" She lets out a peal of laughter and knocks the wind out of him with a hug that pins his arms to his sides. She doesn't feel like a ghost right then. She feels solid, warm. Her hair carries a drifting smell of lilacs in late spring, but it's still October and lilacs are nearly half a year away in all directions. She peeks up at him under his hair and smiles.

"I knew it. I knew you'd be my friend."

And then she's gone, back to the apartment or the take-out or wherever she haunts when he's not around. Scattered by wind.

He hears the bells that signal the start of class and sighs. He's going to be late.

※

Bliss finds him mid-period in the batcave, reading his chemistry textbook. His terror of showing up late and becoming the center of attention has overwhelmed any desire to learn through experimentation that PV always equals nRT. A bicycle pump will show you the same thing when it heats up as you use it. He thinks maybe he should get a bicycle, but he's never learned to ride one.

Today she's wearing a pair of black Docs with a dizzying array of zippers, buttons, and studs in chrome. In a larger size, he'd avoid those boots in the hallway, but they're not so intimidating in a size six. She tousles his hair and walks to the doorway, looks out the window, fishes her e-cig out of—wait, where had she been hiding that?— he wonders, momentarily tantalized by the short list of possibilities.

"Figured you'd be here," she says. "Running a little late, huh?"

He nods. He badly wants to tell her about Anna, about the sundress and the hat, about the smell of lilacs and the wind. He pulls out his pad.

Overslept, he writes.

She nods. There's a small breeze as she cracks the door to let the smell of mocha vapor out, and there's a faint sound of bells. Anna's standing behind her.

Mouse nearly jumps.

"She can't see me," says the ghost, wandering over.

Bliss looks out the window at the small corner of the field that's visible. There's a boys' PE class doing warmup laps. If they were going the other direction, clockwise instead of counter, they'd have seen her by now.

"Or hear me." Anna plops herself down on the floor next to Mouse.

What are you doing here? he writes.

Bliss leans over, sees him writing. "I knew you'd be here," she says. "Commish let me out because I promised to bring you back with me."

"I felt like it," says Anna. Two replies at once. Mouse picks his replies wisely.

I should be in class.

"You can come back in with me, Edelman won't raise a stink."

"Can I come, too?" She's hanging off his left arm, curled up in a ball.

I guess?

Bliss laughs. "Don't sound so enthusiastic, now."

Anna pouts. "That's what *I* was going to say. You should be honored. You're a very select group of people, you know. A card-carrying member of the spirit world wants to be your friend and this is how you react?"

He suppresses a smile and puts a hand on Anna's. It looks like he's just holding his arm. She goes quiet. Can ghosts blush?

Bliss closes the door and hides her vice so quickly that Mouse misses it. He writes another note.

Just don't expect me to talk in class.

Both his attendants get the message.

鼠

Against all expectations, class goes well. Anna peers closely at every-thing but refrains from making things move about the room on their own. She makes faces at Mouse when she thinks he's looking and he makes faces back when he thinks no one else is. It's strange, having a secret. Like carrying a live coal around in a pair of tongs, he wants to blow on it occasionally to see it glow. He's so used to feeling invisible himself that he doesn't notice that someone else is watching.

After Chemistry comes English, and then lunch, sitting back in the batcave. The year-round Birkenstocks-and-guitar guy is picking a quiet tune while the neon green trainers and Vans come round the corner holding hands to no one's surprise. Anna's playing hopscotch over splayed legs and lunch boxes, giving Mouse backstories for ev-eryone present.

The guitar guy is Charles. If he were talkative he'd have been a Chuck, maybe a Chaz, if he'd been a jock. But Charles is a silent, blond giant, with a few extra pounds and a gift for the guitar that leaves him sitting Buddha-like in an orange-and-yellow-flowered Hawaiian shirt, sunglassed and serene in any situation. The cute couple are Ginnie and Mason, and supposedly they've been going out and breaking up and going out again since middle school. They'll probably have broken up again by this time tomorrow, Anna's saying, which is why Charles is hanging around. He's a solid guy and good friend to both, but Anna's pretty sure he's got a crush on Ginnie.

Her narration cuts off the moment Kai walks around the corner and she's gone like white clouds of breath that vanish in October air. He sits down next to Bliss, who's been eating her lunch this whole time, folded up in an envelope of quiet. Mouse wonders if Anna's ever tried to talk to her brother or Bliss, and if so how it went.

He unpacks his lunch and looks over at Mouse. "So that's your mom, huh? Blonde, came in the night before last? You guys moved into Sammy's old place?"

Mouse nods. Scribbles, rips, and passes.

You can call her June. I do.

Kai nods and looks over. He's taken an interest in Mouse's lunch. The night before, Mouse had managed to unpack the rice cooker and tamagoyaki pan, so he'd made himself a rudimentary bento of rice balls and rolled omelet.

"She make that for you?"

Mouse shakes his head.

"I never—I didn't know you cooked." Bliss leans over, her quiet fading now that Kai's around.

He nods.

A little. June's...the kitchen isn't her thing.

Kai frowns, suspicious. Mouse can guess what he's thinking. Between the Japanese apology and the Japanese cuisine, he's sensing a trend. There's a light novel sticking out of Mouse's bag, too. Here it comes.

"You're not one of those Japan-obsessed people are you?"

The strange fetishization of a nation and its culture that oversimplifies and stereotypes it to fit its own ideals? The whitewashing of a complex geopolitical *other*, a kind of racism of optimism? Are you one of those?

No, Mouse writes.

Just anime.

Sometimes the books they're based on or the food.

But sometimes he wishes they would have firework festivals in real life like in the animes he likes, too, with well-lit evening food booths and colorful traditional clothing and sparklers held out over buckets of water, crouching in corners without the watchful eyes of parents or educational handlers. But no more than he wishes to be a part of a group of friends or to have exciting adventures like he sees in them as well. These things have always been fictional for him.

He wants to explain the simplicity of the characters, the complexity of the world. The way just looking at Kai or Bliss or anyone else in the hall is like sticking your head inside a running car engine to see how it works, when someone normal would just read the speedometer, or for that matter read the manual, watch a YouTube video, you know, something sane. He wants to explain that people don't come with manuals but that anime characters don't need them because they're easy. He wants to ask how everyone else deals with reality.

Instead, he writes: *The food is good. Want some?*

Bliss reaches over and snatches a small piece of omelet, pops it into her mouth.

"Hey, it's like your dad's!" she says to Kai, who then pretty much has to try some. He looks impressed.

"Pretty good," he says.

Mouse blushes a little. He doesn't really know how to react to compliments. He hasn't had a lot of practice.

Suddenly, the green trainers are leaning over him and picking out another piece of omelet. Red hair and freckles, followed by an exclamation of delight, "Damn, that *is* pretty good!"

Ginnie crouches down in front of him. She lifts his bangs to look under and he can't help it, he can't close his eyes fast enough. He imagines it's like being electrocuted; he sees it all in under a second, hears it like a building wall of static in his mind. He sees a dubious look on the surface of the most shining, blinding green eyes; he sees that she's curious, interested; beyond that, she's a little worried about breaking social taboos but a little excited by the prospect of it; he sees that she's often a little bored and seeking a thrill but that she's generally harmless to herself and others; that she's the kind of person who smiles a lot but cries easily and that she desperately, desperately wishes life were simple enough to be solved with single, grand gestures rather than the day-in-day-out course corrections that constitute the waking world; and beneath it all he sees something more—an intricate reweaving of times and places, of ordinary days and extraordinary ones, the sadness of the mundane, and a crystalline, blinding hope she places in the new. And below even that he sees something bigger, darker, deeper—

Mouse recoils violently, nearly dropping what's left of his lunch.

Even Mouse knows it was the wrong reaction. Everything's gone quiet and they're looking at him. The guitar has stopped. Mouse has his knees up to his nose and he can tell, even with his eyes closed tight, that they all have concerned looks. But he can't move, can't look. His stomach is a knot twisted to its snapping point, his heart is beating in his throat, he wants to throw up. Like a turtle curled up in its shell, he can't risk extending his legs even to run away. He imagines for a moment the impossibility of ever moving again, of being frozen like this forever; but he doesn't have to imagine, only remember the years of small rooms and soft voices, the gradual peeling open of a tulip flower cut too soon for the table.

And then there's a smell of lilacs and a cold shiver up his spine as he feels someone lift his hand, puppet-like, shaking a little at first, holding up the lunchbox to offer another piece of omelet to Ginnie. His jaw unclenches, and he says "Sorry, you scared me," in a voice that doesn't stammer or waver. He looks up a little, not at anyone, but not at his knees, and feels a cool calm like the bottom of a well in summer. It settles over him, then departs.

When the giant starts playing the guitar again, relief washes over Mouse like a wave, and Ginnie takes another piece of omelet and apologizes for frightening him and everything returns to a kind of equilibrium.

Kai's gone back to eating his lunch, but Bliss's silence has returned, quieter than even before Kai showed up. And Mouse knows that something has changed.

鼠

Comp Sci and Business Math pass by without incident, but Bliss is missing all afternoon. She's waiting for him at the entrance when the day ends.

"Mind if I walk you home? Kai's got baseball." She's not exactly lying, but there's something held back, like there's more to be said. Mouse nods because of course he'd like her company, but he begins to feel uneasy after five minutes of walking in silence.

"You weren't wrong, were you?" she says, at length. They're still walking, tracing his route of the morning in reverse, with a different accompaniment. The trees are deep shades of orange and red. "It wasn't a mistake."

Mouse keeps walking. He knows she's talking about Anna.

"Have you seen her again?"

Mouse nods.

"Was she there all day?"

Another nod.

"And when Ginnie...?"

He's been wondering, meaning to ask Anna but she hasn't been back since lunch. He takes out his note pad.

Maybe.

"I don't understand." Bliss is almost whispering at this point.

Me neither.

They walk the rest of the way in silence, and part ways at a fork in the road.

鼠

Anna doesn't show up that night, or any time the next day. Time passes like a series of vignettes—of classroom scenes, school bells, trees and harvested fields in the river's flood plain. On Friday, Sammy hangs up crepe-paper pumpkins and ghosts with little speech bubbles that say *Boo!* in the storefront downstairs. A crisp wind rolls through the town. Bliss and Mouse don't say anything all day, but she watches him, and every now and then he sneaks a glance back.

Saturday morning comes more eventfully.

Mouse opens his eyes gradually, as a little sunlight filters through the windows. He was having a wonderful dream, but he can't remember just what it was about. Then, a moment later, his eyes snap wide.

Anna is in his bed. With him. In his bed.

He launches himself upright and she opens one eye, stretches like a cat, and then creeps closer and snuggles in again. He sits motionless.

He takes a breath and manages a whisper. "A—Anna?"

"Mmhmm," she says. Lilacs. Strong and sweet, but cold. Can a smell be cold?

He doesn't have a pad nearby, couldn't make her read it if he did. He tries to wake her again, gently shaking her shoulder. Then, thinking about touching her shoulder and the way the strap of her sun dress is hanging, he blushes and stops.

"Just five more minutes, Kai," she mumbles.

Do ghosts even sleep? He wonders. He steels himself with as much propriety as he can manage and shakes her shoulder again.

She opens her eyes again, focuses. Blinks.

"Why am I—" she frowns "—in bed—" she sits bolt upright "—with you?" Storm clouds start to form, her look becoming an accusation that carries with it the potential for sudden and devastating physical violence.

Mouse does his best attempt to mime the phrase, 'How the hell should I know?' It involves a lot of hand-waving. She grabs a notepad from the side table and tosses it to him with a pen.

"Speak."

I have no idea. I woke up like this.

She eyes him with suspicion.

"Last thing I remember I was—oh." Her cheeks color slightly.

Then it was you. He wasn't sure it could have been anyone else.

"You looked like you weren't going to be able to make it out of there without a heart attack, so I just...kinda...possessed you...a little." Anna, it turns out, is a master thumb-twiddler.

He hands her another note.

Thanks.

She's a little surprised.

That was you before, too. When I was apologizing to Kai.

She rubs her eyes with the palms of her hands. "Yeah. Ugh. Sorry about the Japanese apology. I was going for English, honest." She's swung her bare feet around the side of the bed and is swinging them as they don't touch the floor. "It was my first time seeing him with real eyes and a real body since, well." She looks at her own hands. "Yeah. I panicked."

Mouse shakes his head. *It was better than I could have done by myself.*

"You got my note though."

It was a little cryptic. Nice paper.

"Ha! I thought you'd appreciate it. I saw your Miyazaki poster and thought 'Here's a guy I can get along with.'"

So you like anime, too?

"A little." She eyes him suspiciously. She's wandering around the room now looking at the figurine and the novels he's put out since he moved in. She pulls a harem anime off the shelf quickly—almost excitedly?—and then seems to stop herself before frowning and putting it down.

Hey, it's the only one of those I have.

"You're not into lolicon are you?"

It's his turn to frown.

"Not that there's anything *wrong* with it..." The way she says it makes him think she thinks the opposite. He changes the subject.

So you were in my bed because...?

"I don't know. How long has it been since I, uh..." She clears her throat instead of finishing the sentence.

Day and a half. Ish.

"Oooof. It was only a few hours the last time. Bodies are hard work. They're all solid and physical and heavy...and warm...and comfortable..." She's beet red at this point and she stops, realizing.

You fell asleep while possessing me?

"I fell asleep in—while—ah...yeah. Kinda...passed out." She's on his desk chair, staring at her toes. "I'm not very good at this ghost thing."

Mouse sighs, then shrugs. *I'm not very good at this human thing.* He holds up the pen and pad and waggles them for emphasis. She giggles.

He thinks for a minute and then writes a longer note than usual. *So I have to do some chores for June this morning, but how about this afternoon we go say hi to Bliss?* She'd given him her address and said to come by "Anytime," after all.

Anna's eyes widen and she waves her arms. "That's not a good idea. She wouldn't believe you. She'd just get angry like Kai did and then—"

He cuts her off with another note. *We talked while you were asleep. She believes me.*

Anna slumps in the chair. "I'm not sure I want to." She looks at her hands, now folded neatly in her lap. "Can't we just stay home and watch TV? We can even watch your stupid lolicon stuff, if you want."

~~I don't have any loli~~ He scribbles it out and starts again. *Why don't you want to go?*

She stands up and walks to the window, looking out on the fading colors of October. She tries to breathe on the window so she can draw in the condensation with her fingers but nothing happens. She looks unsurprised but still sad, rests her forehead on the window.

"I went before," she says. "It didn't go well."

鼠

In her memory, it's dark and rainy. The inside of a tidied bedroom on a grey day, the inside of an empty apartment, the backs of people milling about in dress clothes after a funeral.

"It was about a month after I died, I guess. It's hard to keep track of time because it's not like it's just *you're dead* and then *bam! you're a ghost looking at your body*. There are just these foggy moments like you're in a dream you're trying to wake up from but can't. There are things you try to remember and things you try to forget, and then there you are and it's April instead of March and the snow's pretty much gone and you've missed your own funeral, which, I guess is probably for the best. Everyone being sad that you're not there when you are, but of course you can't tell *them* that.

"People can't usually see ghosts. Animals and small children, sure, but even then it's not something they seem to enjoy. When the only reactions you get are barking, hissing, or crying, you start to hunger for a little more human interaction.

"You try to make contact. Maybe you start with subtle things, because you don't want to scare anybody. I mean ghosts are a big deal, right? So you push a pencil around on a table, or turn the TV off or on—electronics and ghosts seem to go pretty well together, actually, they're easier than physical objects.

"But here's the thing—people don't *want* to know about ghosts. In fact they'll do pretty much anything *not* to know about ghosts. They'll fail to notice dozens of things you've changed around the house, they'll call the TV repair guy, they'll replace the fuses, they'll put the posters back on the walls or pick up the pieces of broken dishes or replace the shattered windows and talk about humidity or wind or the house sinking unevenly. You finally go to leave a note, because how much more obvious do you have to friggin *be*? You're so *angry* that they haven't *noticed* you and you've been trying for so *long*, and you pick up the pencil, and—"

In her memory, Bliss is standing in the doorway to her darkened kitchen, watching a pencil stand impossibly on its point, about to write.

"And then you realize you're not communicating with them."

"You're terrorizing them."

"The missing things, the moved things, the broken things. You're not *talking* to them; you're *haunting* them. Because the only things you can do that they won't ignore are the things they absolutely can't ignore. And the things they can't ignore are awful."

Bliss watches as the pencil drops to the table, rolls off, and hits the floor. After a moment, she walks over and picks it up and stares at the paper on the table, but it's blank.

"So I can't go see her. Not now."

鼠

Days pass. Halloween comes and goes. Anna spends time here and there, following Mouse as he does chores, picks up groceries, gets a job restocking for Sammy, looking over his shoulders at school, but never again when Bliss or Kai are there. Some mornings he wakes up to the feeling of her disappearing, a vacancy left in the air that she'd filled just moments before.

They're back in Mouse's room on a Saturday morning. He's leaning up against the wall, she's sitting cross-legged next to him.

How long has it been? He asks.

"Last year March I died. I stopped trying to talk to them in May. Bliss broke up with Kai the next month. Mom left in August."

So you've been by yourself for more than a year?

She looks down at her hands, and June walks in. Anna's gone.

"Morning sunshine! Time to—oh! You're up?" June stands there in the doorway looking a little confused. It is Saturday after all.

I was just getting up. He'd already had the pad in his hands. There's a note on the bed where Anna was.

"I can see that." A small and pretty blonde with ice-blue eyes, June has always been younger than everyone else's parents. Too young, people used to say with their hesitations and tones of voice and body language, at parent-teacher interviews and therapy sessions, like they thought they were keeping it to themselves.

If you could see past Mouse's bangs you'd see his mother reflected there, in his eyes and in the little curl of the lips that sometimes makes people imagine June's thinking of something funny, though on Mouse it's more subdued, like he's remembering something warm.

"Got plans?" Her head's tilted at a familiar angle that gives her an air of confusion even when she's not.

He sighs and passes her another note.

Going to a friend's house this afternoon. After chores, he writes, then as an afterthought, *and homework.* He's decided to go alone if he has to.

She gathers her thoughts at the corner of her mouth and purses her lips. "Is this friend a girl?"

What is she, psychic?

Maybe.

"Oh, Mouse."

God, when did she learn that 'My baby's growing up' tone of voice?

I'll come make breakfast in a second.

"Okay," she says, smiling.

She walks off and Anna's back, watching her go. She has a look Mouse can't place, but she doesn't say anything and he doesn't ask.

鼠

He'd learned from an animated washed-up war god that if you stick tissues to the tile grout and leave them there all soaked in bleach, it gets rid of the mold better. That's this morning's job. After moving into his old place, Mouse isn't sure he'd ever want to eat anything from Sammy's corner store that didn't come in a hermetically-sealed package. Toothbrush in hand, he toils away for two hours until the sea-green tiles, tub, sink, and toilet shine like it's the mid-60s when, in defiance of taste and nature, they were first installed.

Anna disappears during breakfast and comes back near the end of his scrubbing spree, as he's peeling the bleach-soaked tissues from the worst intersections, revealing grout that's light grey rather than black. Finally, one might comfortably use the bathroom without a HazMat suit.

She stands there for so long, as though she wants to say something, that at last Mouse stands up from where he's been kneeling by the tub and looks at her. He can't write her a note wearing wet yellow rubber gloves, and he really doesn't want to say anything out loud, so he takes a deep breath and looks right at her.

She's gone.

He looks away and she's back. He tries again.

Gone.

He shifts his perspective maybe two degrees to one side and she's back. Yellow sun dress, today a matching ribbon in her hair. She tilts her head to one side, smiling sadly.

"I was wondering when you'd get it," she says.

He pulls off the gloves, sticky inside from sweaty palms, and fishes in his pocket for his pad and pen.

What's going on? Why can't I look at you?

"You just can't. Nobody can."

What do you mean?

"You can't look at me." In response to his confusion, she plops herself down on the edge of the tub. His ill-fitting black jeans are more worn than is fashionable anymore, his grey baggy sleeves are wet from where he's pushed them up with soggy gloves while cleaning. "This isn't new, Mouse. You've never looked at me before."

She points at the mirror. From where she's sitting they should both be able to see her in it, but the room is empty except for him. He puts his hand out and rests it on her head, still looking in the mirror. His hand is resting on nothing.

"You're different from other people. I've watched you. You don't look."

I can't. It's too much. He writes, thinking of Ginnie's green eyes and the biography behind them. *It's too loud to look at people most of the time.*

She nods. "But it's like the dial's turned up on everything else, too, isn't it? You see without ever looking. Little nezumi, a mouse with your eyes on the ground, never looking up—but never getting stepped on either." She sighs. "That's why no one else can see me. They only know how to see by looking."

Mouse is still confused.

"Think about it. Paranormal enthusiasts, ghost hunting TV shows, they go to the most haunted places. Why don't they ever find one?"

Well I would've said because ghosts aren't real.

"Well if you're going to be that way—" She sticks out her tongue.

Because they're not haunted places?

"Oh, hell no. The places they go are probably ghost hotels, grand central ghost stations. No," she says, "the reason they can't see them is because they're *looking for them.*"

I still don't understand. He's getting frustrated.

"Mouse, you just don't *look* at people. You go through life with your eyes on the ground. You tell people apart by their shoes and their hands. You've gotten so used to not looking at people you hardly even realize you're doing it. This is the first time you've ever tried to look at me. And you can't."

He looks at her, then away again. It's the same.

But I know what you look like, he scribbles. *I know what you're wearing.*

"Oh, little mouse." She stands up and takes him by the hand. "I don't know what you're seeing or how, but just look in the mirror. I don't look like anything anymore."

He's still confused. He wants to tell her what she looks like, her white hands and her summer dress, her violet eyes and the pretty yellow ribbon in her hair that's new to her wardrobe today. But he nods anyway, frowning, looking at his feet. Then, realizing he's looking at his feet and looking up, seeing her absence and looking away. He stands like a puppet with tangled strings, unsure where to face or what to do.

Anna sighs. "Come on, pack up. We're going to visit someone. And if you still want to go talk to Bliss afterward, I'll come with you."

He writes a one-word response: *Who?*

"Priest," she says.

What?

Anna's nervous hands are twisted around one of his, in front of her yellow dress. She says, "Priest. The reason I'm still here."

In a lot of animes there's a shrine. It's at the top of a tall set of stairs, through a torii gate with red pillars, with zig-zagging paper tassels and little wooden slot-topped boxes for donations in the new year or during festivals. Maybe there are shrine maidens or a Shinto priest, or even a local deity or two. Sometimes there's a slacker guru in an abandoned preparatory school wearing a Hawaiian shirt.

In this town, there's just a bar.

Anna leads Mouse into town, past the white picket-fences of the tidy suburbs. Past the local parish church and the little stone-walled graveyard. Past the weathered buildings of the town's old commercial center, light blue paint chipping off of aging wooden storefronts, relics of when the town used to focus on where you could walk to, instead of on the mall everyone drives to now.

They hang a left down a small alleyway, between red brick walls on a narrow cobbled path. They stop under a little awning, five steps down to a steel door with so many coats of black paint on it that it's a wonder it still opens. A crooked sign hangs on it that reads: *Open Daily 5-11*. Anna heaves the door inward.

Mouse doesn't know what he was expecting, but this wasn't it. It's a bar—dimly lit, but classy enough. All mahogany panels, brass foot rails, and little green glass lamps hanging low over the few booths that line the wall. Twisting brick pillars hold up low-vaulted ceilings that look like they could hold up a cathedral, and it occurs to Mouse to check out later what the storefront was for the floor above. He thinks maybe it's a shoe store. As he looks back at the doorway a small faded black and yellow metal sign gives the only hint of the basement's former life. It reads: *FALLOUT SHELTER*.

Why would a priest be in a place like this?

There's a man pulling down stools off the countertop and setting them on the floor one by one. He's maybe in his late thirties or early forties, dark jeans and black leather boots, loose white shirt rolled to the elbows and a dark grey vest. His hair's long enough to be tied back and his face is covered in a salt-and-pepper three-day-old stubble. He doesn't stop moving or even acknowledge them until he's done with the stools. Then he walks behind the bar and starts wiping it down with a rag so dirty it makes you wonder if it wouldn't be cleaner if he just stopped. He's chewing a toothpick at the corner of his mouth.

"We're closed," he says. The low rumble of his voice makes Mouse think of a thunderstorm June and he had walked home in one summer. They'd gotten soaked because June couldn't remember if umbrellas were a bad idea in a storm. His eyes are grey as a February sky, and one of them is cloudier than that. The skin around it is a spider-work of scars, and it stares into a perpetual middle distance. He looks at Mouse with both eyes, but only sees him with one.

Mouse stares at the bar top as a reflection skitters across it, but he doesn't speak. He wants Anna to explain what's going on.

"Say hello to Priest," she says. He goes to fetch his pad, but she stops him. "Not this time," she says. She holds his hand. "I'll be here, but you need to use your voice."

He almost hiccups, but holding Anna's hand he clears his throat. "H—Hi," he says, "M—Mr. Priest."

Mouse thinks he notices a pause in the thunderstorm that's brewing behind the bar. Hands as weathered as the old town storefronts use the same towel to wipe out a glass. He tosses some ice in and uses the soda fountain to fill it up with Coke.

"Take a seat." He drops a straw in and slides it over.

Mouse sits down in front of the Coke, Anna on the stool next to him. The bartender goes back to wiping down the surfaces, rearranging bottles. He takes a huge jug of unidentified green liquid and uses it to refill a smaller bottle, does the same with orange juice. He holds up a bottle of red syrup and swirls it around before deciding there's enough in that one before putting it back. Mouse sits in uncomfortable silence.

"What are you doing bringing strays in here, boy?"

Anna scowls, but says nothing.

Mouse grips his soda with both hands, talks to it instead of the thunderstorm.

"S—strays?"

"The shadow on the seat next to you. I assume you know it."

He swallows. "Anna," he says.

The man stops what he's doing, gets closer to Mouse. He slowly takes the soda and places it to one side. Then a massive sandpapery hand grabs his jaw and lifts his face so that he can't not see. Can't not be seen.

Mouse wants to struggle, but he fights it. He sees the wrinkles and the scars, the grey eye and clouds. He's sweating and about to jump out of his skin when something slams shut behind the face, like an old iron door on rusted hinges. Mouse blinks. He's staring at the man now, but there's nothing. No history, no fears, no dreams. It's like he's looking at a beautifully-carved block of wood: interesting, but hardly even there. Everything's gone quiet.

The hand releases his jaw with a low rumbling apology. "Should've closed up shop first. Didn't realize you were a sensitive."

Mouse is filled with a sudden excitement. He wants nothing more than to go back and stare at the man's face. His scars, his eyebrows, his *eyes*. He's never seen such quiet eyes and he wants, almost needs to see them again. He doesn't know what to say; doesn't know how to say it.

The man slides the soda back in front of him.

"This Anna," he motions at the stool where she's sitting, "she tell you to come here?"

Mouse nods.

The man squints for a second. "You have trouble talking, boy?"

The way a mob hit has trouble swimming in concrete shoes? Yeah, he's got trouble talking. He nods again, pulls out his pad. Anna doesn't stop him this time.

"That's not gonna work," the man says. He points at his eyes, the good one first. "This one doesn't read and this one doesn't see." Then the man reaches out and grabs him by the jaw again, but this time shoves his thumb onto Mouse's tongue—with Mouse frozen in surprise. There's a sound like static and a sharp pain in his face, and the man pulls away again.

"What the hell are you doing?" Mouse shouts, backing away and knocking the stool over behind him with a crash. He slaps his hands over his mouth, eyes wide.

Even Anna stares.

The man's gone back to cleaning. "Best get on and tell me what you need to, that'll wear off in a few minutes."

"I—" He's standing now. There's no tightness in his chest, but he does feel a little dizzy. He feels relaxed. Warm and fuzzy.

"I could've given you a few shots of whiskey, probably would've had the same effect. But there's that whole illegality thing and I hate that kind of attention." He leans on the bar with his forearms and looks at Mouse. "Might give you the same hangover though, just as a warning. So go on then and tell me. Why're you here?"

"I don't know," Mouse says. "Anna's a ghost. I met her this week." He thinks for a minute. He's never needed to think of words this fast. "We're friends?"

The bartender snorts, like it's a joke he's heard before, but doesn't say anything.

"She said I had to meet you. I think it's you." He asks Anna, "Priest?"

She nods, and the man does, too.

"She said you're the reason she's still here."

This raises an eyebrow. Priest scrutinizes the barstool when Anna's sitting. Then he nods.

"It's you, then. Started showing up last August."

Anna nods.

"She says you were always there to acknowledge her existence, that it kept her going. She says I can't see her, that she doesn't look like anything. But she does. I just can't see her when I look at her. If that makes any sense." There's something about saying things out loud, Mouse realizes, that makes things make less sense than they do in your head.

"So you can't see her when you look at her, but you know what she looks like, hmm?" He chuckles. "Neat trick."

Mouse frowns.

"Spirits don't look like anything," Priest says. "That's pretty much the definition if you can't be looked at."

"But how do you know she's here?"

He snorts again. "I didn't even know it was a *she* until you said so." He tilts his head to Anna's seat, "Apologies, miss."

"Tell him it's fine," she says.

"She says it's fine."

"And she can talk to you. Another trick." He thinks for a second. "What's she look like, then?"

As he tells the bartender about her sun dress and her white hands, her black shoes with the buckle, the yellow ribbon in her hair or the sea-green barrette that sometimes takes its place and her inquisitive, violet eyes, the man seems to visibly withdraw. Anna's starting to stare, but he keeps going.

"That's enough," Priest says, the low voice a warning, but Mouse wants to keep going, wants to use his new words to say everything about her so she knows she's not forgotten, to describe her in all the detail he can so she can tell he's really seen her.

"And she had a wide-brimmed sun hat last week," he says, "and she smells like lilacs for some reason." She's standing up now, but he can't stop.

"Enough, boy."

"And sometimes when she shows up you can hear bells in the distance, or maybe it's wind chimes. And—and she blushed one time when I held her hand! And—"

"Enough!" It's like a thunderclap, echoing through a small cave. Mouse jumps.

Anna's gone.

There's a moment as the silence settles in the room.

"By the field the scarecrow stands in, boy. Enough is enough when I say it's enough." He doesn't look angry, just tired. Mouse is just confused.

"I don't know how you know the things you know," he says. "I don't know how you're seeing what isn't there to be seen. But even I could see you were upsetting your 'friend.'" He shakes his head. "And to me she's just a bit of mental static on a barstool."

They sit in silence for a minute after Mouse picks up the barstool he'd knocked over five minutes previously.

"Spirits, if we can call them that, are nine parts emotion and one part everything else. They get too much and things happen. Sometimes things break, sometimes they scatter." He grunts. "What you just saw? That was her scattering. That was the best outcome." He stares hard at Mouse to emphasize his point, grey eye cold. "If the worst happens, and you'll know it if you see it, you get here fast, you understand?"

Mouse doesn't understand, but he nods.

"I need to talk to some folks. Go home. If you ever see her again, you'd best apologize." He waves his hand toward the door. Dismissed.

The bartender goes back to cleaning glasses. He scowls as the door to the cavern swings shut with a bang, and stares after the boy, the mystery, with his cloudy eye.

鼠

It's still Saturday afternoon but it feels like it should be night after his time underground. The sinking sun peeks over the crests of suburban roofs as he approaches Bliss's house. A patterned window cuts an oval through the front door, scattering quiet rainbows into the interior, where they dance on neat pairs of shoes in the entryway.

It's a small, cookie-cutter, split-level house at the end of a cul-de-sac. It's got a one-car garage underneath, red brick below and white siding above, and a bay window on one side. Mouse is standing at the door, hands in his pockets, trying to figure out what step two would be if step one were *ring the doorbell*. He hasn't committed to step one yet.

His voice has worn off—he tried it to be sure on the way over—and a small but persistent hum of discomfort is forming around the edges of his perception. He still can't understand everything that happened at the nameless bar, what the man with the cloudy eye and the quiet face—Priest, he supposes, though it doesn't seem to fit the man—what he'd said or meant. Who was he? What did he mean by "A sensitive"? But he has to talk to someone about it, and he can't think of anyone who'll believe him except Bliss.

Without a plan he rings the doorbell, waits.

And waits.

The doorbell made an audible noise, so he has to assume that no one's coming. Just as he starts to walk away the window over the garage flies open and he hears a familiar voice yell, "Wait wait wait! I'll be right there. Hold on!"

There's a flurry of movement and the curtains inside fly outside like a small hurricane is afflicting the residence, and after a series of crashes and thuds the front door swings open to reveal a damp and roughly-clothed Bliss with a towel wrapped around her head.

Mouse gives her a little wave in lieu of a hello.

She smiles widely. "Well don't just stand there," she says, and wanders away, leaving the door open. She's wearing an ill-fitting black tee-shirt and scruffy jean shorts, plodding barefoot away down the hall while pulling the towel from her head and rubbing her disheveled hair with it.

Aside from the hall, which leads away to a kitchen, the rest of the house seems to be composed of sets of three to five stairs, placed at improbable intervals and going to god knows where. Bliss is in the kitchen making coffee, her towel hanging over her neck to catch any stray drips.

"I was in the bath, sorry." She pours a cup, holds up the pot in offering, but Mouse shakes his head. She shrugs. "More for me." She puts it down and sits at the little wooden table in the kitchen, taking her coffee black as night. "Baths, Mouse. Let me tell you. If there's a god, the existence of hot, soapy baths are proof he loves us and wants us to be happy." She takes a long sip of coffee and closes her eyes. "And coffee. Anyway, at first I thought maybe you were one of those Jehovah's Witnesses, here to save my soul or whatever. Glad the water was starting to get cold, or I wouldn't have seen you walking down the driveway." She smiles.

Mouse smiles back. She looks so different. He's only ever seen her polished self—makeup and jewelry and armored leather. She looks at once smaller and more comfortable. Her tee-shirt is slipping off one shoulder revealing a tank-top strap, and she's got one leg up on the chair, hugging it with one hand, mug in the other.

He pulls out his pad and goes to write something and stops. Maybe he doesn't need to. If he can say hello to someone he doesn't even know, someone as scary as Priest, why can't he say the same to Bliss? He tries to remember how it felt, how wonderful and reckless it felt to just open his mouth and just *say* things. He tries not to think about how hard it is, about the lump in his throat or the clenching in his guts or anything else at all. Just the ease of speaking and the feeling of lightness in his chest. He looks down at his pad and pen. He thinks about looking up, but that's too much.

He takes a deep breath. What do people say after 'Hi'?

"How—how are you?" he manages. He's holding the pad so tight his thumb has gone white, his heart is starting to race. He takes another deep breath, looks halfway up to see Bliss beaming, and blushes.

"I. Am. Fabulous," she says. "Thank you." She leans back a little, taking a sip of her coffee. "How are you?"

He swallows, tries to respond. Nope, that's all for today folks. He shakes his head. Maybe he could have managed a 'Fine,' maybe he could have said that, but the truth is too many words. He smiles an apology back at her and writes a note. She takes it without a hint of judgment.

Things are strange.

She sighs. "Anna," she says, her smile fading.

He nods. He starts writing notes, trying to condense everything that happened: Anna haunting Bliss by accident because people don't want to see ghosts; his introduction to the, what, magician? Shaman? Wizard? Priest at the bar; seeing Anna, but not seeing her, but trying to explain; the shock in his jaw and the talking and the rumbling headache that has been building ever since; Anna disappearing. Bliss stays silent through most of it, asking questions to clarify when necessary, nodding or humming in assent when called for. She takes the notes and stacks them one by one, holding a quiet little deck of cards by the time he's done.

The last one reads: *Got any aspirin?* His head is now throbbing in time with his heartbeat, getting a little worse with each thump. *He said I might get a hangover, or something like one, and I think it's here.* It's like a thunderstorm is knocking at the front door of his brain.

Bliss gets up and fishes through a drawer, grabs a bottle of sports drink from the fridge and tells him to wash down the pills with it, saying something about electrolytes. He does as he's told.

"So she's not here right now?"

He shakes his head and the world keeps wobbling after he stops. It's hard to write when you're massaging your temples. Even if she hadn't scattered like that, he doesn't think she'd really have come. He shifts position, cradles his head with one hand and scrawls a note with the other.

So what do you think?

It's a big question and she dodges it with grace.

"I think my coffee's cold and my hair's going to stick like this," she says, standing up. The sound of the chair on the floor makes Mouse wince. "And I think you need to lie down before you fall off that chair." He'd argue the point, but by this point he's slumped so far down that he wouldn't so much fall off the chair as dribble out of it, pooling on the floor like a puddle of mercury. His eyes are mostly closed against even the dim shade of the November afternoon and the sound of his hair rustling as he nods is like sandpaper against his eardrums.

He lets her lead him by the hand to a soft and horizontal surface, and he hardly has time to wonder how he ended up in this position before he mercifully lapses into unconsciousness and everything goes dark.

鼠

In the dark, Mouse dreams of thunder.

He's standing by the side of the road in the rain. It's night, and the only light is coming from a sodium-orange streetlamp about twenty feet overhead. He's standing under it, soaked and looking about nervously. The world is limited by the light: a fifteen-foot cone of existence, surrounded by a sea of ink.

Something moves in the dark.

Then a voice sounds from outside, not friendly but not menacing.

"If you want to see what's in the dark," it says, "you have to step out of the light."

He's drawn to it, the curtain, the terminating line, the boundary. Shadows flit about in the dark beyond it, at the edge of perception. Shapes far enough from the light that all that can be seen is a moment's reflection.

Emotionless, he steps through into the dark, and he's looking back into the light where he's still standing. Behind and beside him in the cold, wet night the shapes and shadows are coalescing. They're colder than the rain, darker than the night.

The other him, the one still in the light looks up at him, through him, and away into the surrounding sea of writhing shadow.

He doesn't look, but he knows as the thunderstorm rages: he's surrounded.

鼠

Mouse wakes to the sound of rain beating on a window in the dark. A low rumble of thunder shakes the house as he tries to remember where he is. He's under a heavy blanket, held against a bed. The storm has escaped from his head and is doing laps around the town. Did he come to Bliss's house? Did he leave? Another roll of thunder, this one louder, rattles the windows and nudges him only a little more into consciousness. There's an outdoor light shining through vertical blinds, casting zebra-stripe contour lines on the room. Is it the light from his dream?

A large bed, a closet door, a desk? A guest bedroom?

There's a shape that hovers in the blackness of the doorway, hesitating, then comes over to the bed and slips silent under the covers next to him, but not touching. Facing away.

He lies with the weight of the comforter holding him to the bed, securing him to his dream, and mumbles, "Anna. Sorry." Speaking is easier in the dark, with her. Half-asleep he curls forward, forehead on the nape of her neck. "Priest said. Should apologize. Shouldn't upset you. Like that. Sorry."

She lies there in the dark, saying nothing.

He starts to drift back from half sleep to full, the headache rumbling inside echoing the storm. "Was it you?" He mumbles, thinks of cold shapes in the shadows. "Think you were there. See in the dark."

"Shh, now," she whispers. "Go back to sleep."

He feels so heavy he doesn't argue. He closes his eyes and lets the bed swallow him to more, this time unremembered, dreams.

鼠

He wakes with a start. Daylight is streaming through the window as he stares at an unfamiliar ceiling. He sits up, hauling the heavy cream- and navy-checkered comforter from where it pins him down. The room keeps moving a little when he stops, but compared with his headache the day before it's nothing. He's still at Bliss's house.

He gets up, discovering himself to be dressed in someone else's pajamas. His clothes of the day before are folded on the back of a chair.

The room isn't the bland undecorated spare he'd imagined—a vintage Godfather Part II poster and another of the Black Widow lend the room a lived-in, if tidied, feel. A signed baseball in a glass cube on the desk. A copy of *Ender's Game*.

The floor is carpeted in the room, but cold hardwood in the hall. He peeks his head out. There are noises coming from the right.

The smell of bacon hits his nose as he enters the kitchen, Bliss in jeans and a white tee-shirt, baseball cap holding her hair back, holding a spatula sideways in her teeth like some kind of kitchen pirate as she fishes for things in the fridge with both hands full. She sees him come through the doorway and waves a jug of milk at him. She says good morning but it comes out, "Oov oh-en." She puts it all down and takes the spatula out of her mouth before saying it again.

He smiles and lifts a hand in greeting at this, yet another incarnation of Bliss. Before yesterday he wouldn't have imagined that she owned any clothing so, well, normal. He looks around and finds his pad on the table.

Please explain..? He gives a sweeping gesture as he hands her the note, one that takes in what he's wearing, where he is, and everything else besides.

She laughs. "Must have been a hell of a headache—you were out cold. Your mom—June," she corrects, "called on your cell about ten, so I told her you were sick and asleep, and not to worry, that I'd bring you back tomorrow. She said okay, but she definitely giggled." She frowns. "Anyway she said something about working the night shift, so to be quiet when you get in? The pajamas are my brother's." Mouse stiffens, looks around. Brother? Bliss continues, "He's off at a fancy prep school and didn't take them with him, so he won't mind. You want some breakfast? You can have anything so long as it's bacon. Sunday is bacon day. My rule."

Mouse gets the sudden feeling that every rule in this house is hers, and wonders where her parents are. But more than that he's starving. He realizes he hasn't eaten since breakfast the day before. His stomach growls an answer before he has the chance, and he grins, sheepish, and nods.

"Right then. Café Bliss is open for business. Take a seat and I'll be right with you." She turns back to the sizzling pan on the stove, the azure propane flames occasionally licking up the side when they smell the grease in the air.

Thinking back, everything's a blur after he left the bar. He remembers coming to Bliss's house, she offered coffee. Did he have some? What did he tell her? There are whole patches missing in his memory, filled only with darkness and headache. And a dream. Anna in his bed. He shakes his head as if to reconnect something that's come loose, but all it does is make him a little queasy.

A plate of bacon drops onto the middle of the table, followed by two glasses of milk and a plate of buttered toast. Bliss plops herself down in front of him, taking a long swig of coffee. "Oh, shoot. Did you want some coffee? There's some in the pot."

Mouse waves for her to stay seated and fetches some himself. Normally he wouldn't drink coffee, but for some reason he feels like it's the right thing. Something to cut the grease, or maybe jog the memory. He sits back down and takes a sip, winces.

Bliss laughs. "There's sugar and milk if you want."

He shakes his head and takes another hot, bitter sip, making less of a face this time. He's craving the bitterness, thinks coffee should be bitter, that there's something honest about it, the way it sits heavy at the back of your throat, or crawls up your nose. Bliss is holding a piece of crispy bacon with her fingers, crunching off a bite at a time, watching him from under the brim of her cap.

There's such a disconnect, he thinks, between her outside and her inside, like once you get past the wall of clouds spinning around the center there's twenty miles of calm in all directions before the storm starts up again in the other direction.

He chews on a strip of bacon while writing.

Where are your parents?

"Hong Kong, probably," she slurps her coffee in between pieces of bacon. "They live there. But they go places on vacation without telling me, so really anywhere. New Zealand, Shanghai, who knows?"

I just spent the night at a girl's house? Alone? No wonder June had giggled. She'd probably assumed something wildly optimistic.

Bliss's eye go wide. "Your first time and you were unconscious? How scandalous!—Wait, that sounds wrong." But she's only mock-frowning and a second later she's the Cheshire Cat again, or maybe Groucho Marx, waggling her eyebrows lecherously, bacon for a cigar. "I'll have to make sure that one gets around the school myself. The rumor mill there is decidedly lacking."

Mouse reddens, then remembering the warm body in his bed, almost glows with silent embarrassment. She eyes him, suspicious of something, not saying what.

They eat in silence for a few minutes. There's a round window behind her chair, the sky an inverted robin's egg, a pale blue shell encasing the world.

Why are we friends? He asks. It sounds like an odd question, but the way they met was odd. He tries to clarify, thinking back to chemistry class three weeks—a month?—ago. Had it only been that long? He feels like he's known her forever. *Most people try to ignore me, not get to know me.*

She reads the note, screws it up into a little ball, and bounces it off his forehead. It lands in his coffee and she does a fist-pump of improbable victory with a laugh. She leans forward while he's fishing it out, putting the damp paper wad on his plate.

"Because I could just tell." She rests her chin on her hands, elbows propped on the table. "We're the same, you and me. Well—" she leans back, "I'm much more fabulous." She grins as Mouse shakes his head, smiling. "But I knew a future cave-dweller when I saw one."

The same, huh? *Well, I'm glad,* he writes.

She nods. "De nada. Besides," she whispers, *"you see dead people."* Eyes wide in her best Haley Joel Osment.

Yeah, where's Bruce Willis when you need him?

She rolls her eyes. Mouse smiles while she laughs, and for a moment they can almost pretend it was all a joke.

Then Anna's in the empty chair to the side of the table, arms crossed, eyebrow raised as if Mouse has maybe done something worthy of reproach. He freezes. Takes a sip of his coffee.

"Tell her I'm here," she says.

He looks over in her direction, then down at his note pad. He doesn't write anything.

"I'm here because you want me to be," she says. "And I said if we went to see Priest I'd show. So, tell her. It's your idea after all."

The kitchen is suddenly quiet as he writes. He hands the note to Bliss, and it simply reads:

We have a guest.

I t's so quiet in the kitchen you can hear the occasional ping of the cast-iron pan as the fat on it cools. A ray of sunlight shines through the round window and onto the table, giving Bliss a halo and illuminating dust motes as they meander. Mouse can hear his own heartbeat.

He sits across from her, Anna in the seat between them. The violet of her eyes seems more vibrant, her dress more white than yellow. Her hair is down and unadorned. Priest had said that spirits are nine tenths emotion. He wonders what Anna's feeling right now.

Bliss does her best impression of a casual person, leans back in her chair, takes a sip of her coffee. But her hand trembles a little as she puts down the cup, and she only leaves it there for a second before picking it up again and holding it under her nose, steam rising. A protective charm. A warding potion.

Anna says to say she's here. She's in the seat there. He crooks his thumb in her direction.

Bliss reads the note and nods, looks at the empty chair, then back to Mouse.

"Anna?" she says to Mouse. He notices that her voice finally matches her eyes, and wonders at the alignment. The Cheshire Cat is nowhere to be seen.

Anna nods. "Hi," she says.

She says hi. Mouse passing notes, feeling like a translator.

"Um, tell her," Bliss stops, starts again, "tell her that—"

Tell her yourself. Mouse writes. *She can see and hear you.* He smiles a little.

"Oh. Right." She faces the empty chair, not sure where to look while talking. "Mouse told me you're, that you've been here before. Last year."

Anna stares at the table. Mouse copies out her responses and delivers them.

"I'm sorry about the window," she says.

"I'm sorry I didn't notice you."

"I'm sorry I haunted you."

I think you're both sorry, Mouse interjects, by holding a note up and waving back and forth. Bliss is sniffling by now, but lets out a little laugh.

"Oh god, I'm going to start crying into my bacon," she says, grabbing a napkin.

Meanwhile Anna is visibly perturbed. She looks upset, not with Bliss, but with him. He writes a note to Bliss. *Sorry, I think I need to talk to her myself for a minute.* Bliss nods.

What is it?

"What is it? I disappear for almost a day and you don't even say hi."

What do you mean? I apologized last night. He leaves out 'in bed,' trying not to blush.

"I wasn't here last night."

Mouse blinks. But if she wasn't, then who—? He hazards a quick glance over at Bliss and turns a shade of crimson as he looks back.

I'm sorry. He writes. *I must have dreamed it. I thought I saw you last night, said sorry for scattering you like that.*

Anna screws up her eyebrows, nose and lips in a suspicious scowl, and then lets out an exasperated breath. "Fine. Apology accepted. You can make it up to me right now."

Mouse raises an eyebrow, unsure of where this is going. She continues, not waiting for a response: "This back and forth is frustrating. Can I borrow your body?"

Mouse pauses. He looks back at Bliss and hands her a note that says *hold on, negotiating something.*

From Bliss's perspective Mouse is writing out a series of notes in rapid succession, not even passing them but flipping pages in the spiral-bound booklet almost as soon as he's done each one. Finally he stops and sighs, defeated. He passes another note to Bliss.

We're going to try something. It might not work for long, and it's probably going to be a little weird. Probably weirder for me than you. But probably weird for you, too.

Bliss frowns, and then watches as Mouse looks at the empty chair, takes a deep breath, closes his eyes, and nods.

He stiffens a little, taking a short, sharp breath. Paying attention this time, it feels like jumping into a cold lake, but one that warms up within a split-second of the dive. He does his best to relax, not to fight, like breathing carefully to not blow away a dust mote under his nose. Immersed in the smell of lilacs, his body begins to move of its own accord. He looks up at Bliss.

"Been a while, oneesan," his voice is higher, airier. He claps his hands together and does a quarter bow.

Bliss's eye widen. "Anna? Are you, I mean, is it...?" She's at a loss for words.

"Borrowing it. He said it's okay. Ugh though," they look down at their arms and then back again, "bodies are super heavy. And oh my god." They take a deep breath. "Bacon."

Mouse/Anna grabs a piece from the plate in the middle of the table and takes a bite. They talk with their mouth full. "Oh my god, smelling and tasting. SMELLING AND TASTING, BLISS. Why didn't I do this sooner?" They stop and think for a second. "Oh yeah. Good reason. Fine, fair enough."

Bliss feels like she's interrupting. "Is Mouse, um, in there, too?"

They stop and think. "Yeah he's here. Oh this is so weird. It's like we're almost the same person. It's like we're overlapping or some-thing. Oh hey, I can see some of his memories, this is so surreal." She's narrating, waving around a piece of bacon while she talks, not looking anywhere in particular, and then her gaze snaps back to Bliss's. "Oh my god! What were you doing in his bed last night?" They nearly choke on a piece of bacon as Mouse recoils and their interests diverge.

It's Bliss's turn to blush.

Anna taps on their forehead, emphasizing her points. "Oh my god! Shut up. I don't care if you think she's pretty when she blushes," Anna says, looking up. "For a guy that talks so little your brain says *way* too much."

Bliss's eyes go wide but Anna takes no notice.

"I don't care if you can't help it, try harder, geez. And what is it with you and girls in bed? Are you some kind of perv? OH MY GOD! I did not want to think about that when the answers are RIGHT THERE—"

"...Girls?" Bliss squeaks at the use of the plural.

Anna realizes for the first time that she's been talking out loud—well, not that she's talking out loud, but that someone can hear her for a change—and slaps her hands over her mouth. She backtracks.

"Oh, no it's just that I, uh, well this one time, well a couple of times—"

"Anna!"

Mouse can feel her emotions now like a rising chaos, feel her being pulled in a million directions and tries to focus, bring order.

"It's not what you think!"

His/their mouth is still moving, but he's not paying any more attention, he's just trying to hold on, keep calm. He pictures holding Anna's hand but he can't tell now if it's his hand or hers.

"You're a ghost! What do I think?"

He imagines a balloon holding in a gallon of helium; a net holding back a million balloons.

"I don't know but I can explain!"

The doorbell erupts at a stunning volume and Mouse loses focus at last. He jerks, slumps down in his chair, and catches himself on the table just as he's about to fall. He puts his head down on his arm and groans. Anna's gone again.

Bliss sits in silence for almost a full ten seconds before putting down her coffee cup, standing, straightening her tee-shirt, and walking to the door.

Ginnie's standing on the doorstep.

"I brought coffee!" she says, as though she's already had a few cups herself, and bounces past Bliss into the house.

Bliss closes the door and follows her back in.

"Mason again, huh?"

Ginnie turns, purses her lips. "Who needs guys anyway, am I right?" She's striding backward toward the kitchen, still talking. "Of all the insensitive creatures on the planet, I swear. Boys! What good do they even serve? I say we get rid of the lot of—" She turns as she enters the kitchen and stops. Mouse has turned around in the chair. He waves, smiles weakly.

Ginnie stops talking. That in itself is something profound, but then she turns back to Bliss. Then back to Mouse. Then back to Bliss.

"Oh my god, are you two—"

"No." Bliss says, relieving her friend of the coffees and putting them on the table.

"But those are pajamas—"

Bliss looks at her friend, deadpan, "Yes they are. Mouse stayed the night. Do not infer anything else from this situation. He stayed in Rain's room."

Ginnie grins, willfully ignorant of the implied threat of violence behind the words. "Yeah, but where did *you* stay? What with the weather and all."

Bliss gives her a *yeah, right* look that's remarkably convincing given the circumstances, before turning away and smoldering, picking a convenient moment to be suddenly in the middle of scraping congealing bacon grease out of the frying pan.

Ginnie's standing behind Mouse's chair. As they both look at Bliss, she bends over so her mouth is right by his ear and whispers "She hates thunderstorms, if you're wondering."

Mouse coughs and turns a few shades of scarlet, not having fully recovered from inhaling bacon crumbs earlier. Ginnie laughs, delighted. He regains his composure after a slurp of coffee and hands their latest guest a note.

Have some bacon, it says.

She plops herself down, with a characteristic flounce, in the chair where Anna had been sitting. Anna's probably passed out from the exertion. He wishes she were still here, if only for moral support. He wonders when she'll reappear.

She grabs a piece of toast and leans back, then looks Mouse over, while talking to Bliss. "I mean he doesn't say much, but he's pretty cute. Some people would say that's a good combination."

Mouse doesn't know how to react to a statement that's such equal parts compliment and insult. Bliss is washing the pan with vigor but doesn't miss a beat. "So what did Mason say this time?"

Ginnie waves with the toast. "It doesn't matter, does it? He's just an ass and we're through. Everything ends, right Mousey?"

"He grabbed your butt in public again, didn't he?" Bliss asks, and then sighs.

"Nah," she smiles through her toast. "I like it when he does that." She winks at Mouse, who does his best not to react.

"Grabbed somebody else's?" Scrub, scrub.

"Nope." Toast. Coffee.

"Invited you to church again?" Scrub.

"Ugh. Gag me, no. No he's not that dumb." Bacon and toast in a little sandwich.

"Complimented your sister?" Bliss leans over and takes a sip of her coffee and looks at Mouse. "She says her sister's got a bigger rack." She makes exaggerated cupping motions in front of her chest. "She's really self-conscious about it."

Mouse's eyes widen. What sort of rabbit hole has he fallen down? The Cheshire Cat is back and he's sitting at the table with the Mad Hatter.

Ginnie crosses her arms and pouts. "No." She scowls. "And anyway size isn't that important. Right, Mousey?" She leans forward, elbows on the table intentionally close together.

He takes a sip of his coffee, looks down, looks *farther* down, says nothing.

"Safe answer." Bliss says, back to scrubbing and not looking again. "Watch out for this one. She's a wolf in sheep's clothing. Trail of broken hearts follows her around every time she and Mason take a three day vacation."

Ginnie flops back in the chair with a huff. "I'm not *that* bad."

"No? We can call up witnesses if you like. What about Martin last June? Frank in April? What was his name in January? Year older than us? Nice guy, certainly not cut out to handle you."

"Peter," she says, frowning. "He *was* nice."

"Peter. We could call them up and ask. Or we could call Charles."

"Don't start." She's chewing on the side of her coffee cup.

"Don't worry, I'd kill you if you tried anything on Charles. He's a sweetheart and deserves better."

"Maybe I should go apologize to Mason."

"I thought you said it was something he said." Bliss isn't looking, but Mouse can hear her smiling.

"Well maybe it was something he said *back...*"

Bliss doesn't even say anything, just makes a noise that sounds about as far from surprised as a noise can sound.

"I just wanted to know if he was going to be applying to the same colleges as I am."

Bliss dries her hands on a towel and carries her coffee back to the table, sitting. Mouse wonders how she can switch gears so quickly. He's still lost in the conversation Anna and she were having five minutes earlier.

"Colleges? As in, the things we won't be applying to for two years?"

"A girl's gotta have a plan, Bliss."

"And what did he say?"

"So get this," she pauses for effect. "He says he might not even be *going* to college."

There's a loud pause in the conversation.

Mouse writes a note, passes it to Ginnie: *So?*

"What do you mean 'So?'?" she asks, exploding. "What am I supposed to do if he doesn't go? I don't want to stick around here my whole life."

Mouse writes another note, passing this one to Bliss. *I'm confused.*

"You're not the only one," she says. "So let me get this straight, just for the record. You asked him where he's going, because, I'm going out on a limb here, that might affect where you want to go. He says he might stay here—and run his dad's hardware store?"

Ginnie nods.

"And so because you're upset that you might break up in say, three years, because *you* might go away to college, and he might *not*, you broke up with him...*now*."

Ginnie nods again. "Exactly." Totally unrepentant.

"I don't even...okay, well," Bliss is half nodding, half shaking her head. "Good, then. I guess."

Mouse passes a note. *Is it okay if I have a shower here?*

Bliss nods. "Towels in the linen closet at the end of the hall. Turn the taps slowly, they're temperamental."

Mouse gets up to leave.

"What, you're not going to go help him?" Ginnie says with a wink.

"Oh, I think I've got my hands full here, don't you?" Their red-haired guest can't even pretend to miss the implied threat this time, and acquiesces.

"Oh, you're no fun," she says, but as he's walking down the hall he hears her yell out from the kitchen, "but leave the door unlocked in case Bliss wants to sneak a—OW!"

鼠

His clothes are neatly folded on a chair in what he now knows as Rain's room. Bliss and Rain. She'd said her parents were hippies. He grabs the clothes and a towel and wanders back across the hall to the bathroom, wondering about the process by which he ended up in pajamas the night before. He hopes he put them on himself.

The water is hot and fills the bathroom with rolling plumes of steam as he undresses, but as he takes off his shirt he catches a glimpse of himself in the mirror. Something's different. He can't put his finger on it. Does he have more freckles than he used to? He wipes away the fog on the mirror with the towel and leans in for a closer look.

Yes, this is new.

Looking closer, he realizes there are fine white lines, thin as a needle point, tracing patterns over his right shoulder, down his chest, and onto his stomach, like a spiderweb of abstract design. But there's a pattern to it—symbols and writings in spirals and curls. He twists and tries to see his back, and it's stretching across part of it, too. What the hell?

He pokes it, tries rubbing at it. It's like a fishbone-white tattoo. It doesn't hurt, at least.

When he gets in the shower it becomes more obvious. As his skin reddens from the heat, the lines stay white, until the pattern, almost invisible on his normally pale skin, looks like someone's drawn all over him with a superfine silver Sharpie. It doesn't come off when he scrubs, just stands out more against his reddened shoulder.

He finishes up and dries off, running the fan and cracking the window to try to clear the mirror up a bit more while he dresses. By the time he can see in the mirror again it's faded back to near-invisibility.

鼠

Ginnie's not around when he returns, clothed, wet towel in hand. Bliss is at the table, flipping through the torn-off notes Mouse has written her. She doesn't seem to notice as he walks in, so he sits down.

He writes her a note.

As if my life couldn't get any weirder.

Bliss looks up. "What?"

He sighs, writes another. *I've gotten tattoos in the night, apparently.*

Bliss screws up her eyebrows in physical repetition of her earlier sentiment.

Look, hold on. He stands up, walks over, and pulls up his shirt. The marks go down his right side under his arm as well.

Bliss leans in close. "What the hell?"

He steps back and shrugs, as if to say *beats me.*

"Take off your shirt," she says, and he does as he's told, pulling it over his head and letting it hang, inside out, from his left arm. It's colder out here than in the steamy bathroom, and the lines are almost invisible, but he blushes a little at the touch of her cold hands on his shoulder and back which probably makes them more visible.

She maneuvers him over to the stream of sunlight coming in the window.

"They're not white," she says. "They're iridescent. Like seashells." She maneuvers him in the light. "What the hell? Do you think this has something to do with Anna?"

Suddenly, a cough from the doorway frames them in a tableau. Mouse with his shirt off, Bliss with her hands on his back and shoulder, leaning in close. They both look up to see Ginnie holding a finger to her cheek in a gesture of mock innocence, then grinning.

"Forgot my bag?" It's hanging from the chair.

Bliss closes her eyes, exhales. "How long were you standing there?"

Ginnie lets the smile drop and purses her lips. "Long enough to not think the obvious." She sits down instead of grabbing her bag. "What do you mean about Anna?"

鼠

"Anna's dead."

"Yes."

"But she's still around."

"Yes."

"And Mousey here can talk to her."

"Technically, anyone can talk to her. Mouse is the only one who can hear her replies."

"And she can possess him."

"Mmmhmm."

"And now he's got shiny math tattoos."

They do look a little like equations, just not in any numeric system they're familiar with.

"That's the long and short of it."

"And you totally weren't taking advantage of that fact to get all touchy-feely with him with his shirt off."

Bliss walks over to the coffee maker, picking a convenient moment to be in the middle of refilling the tank and making a pot. Mouse puts his head down on his arms on the table.

"You two. I just don't know." Serious for a moment. "This is the weirdest crap I ever heard."

Mouse passes her a note. *Try living it.*

"Fair's fair. Well, I guess if it doesn't hurt and there aren't any immediately obvious side-effects...maybe it'll go away as quick as it came?" She shrugs. This feels like a perfectly Ginnie solution, but they can't disagree.

"Well what else are we going to do? Go see a doctor?" Bliss is sitting back down again, while the coffee gurgles and wheezes to life.

Mouse looks up. Maybe not a doctor, but how about a priest? *Grab your things.*

鼠

"You did WHAT?" The thick-painted black door shakes on its hinges as Bliss and Ginnie wait outside the bar, sitting on the steps under the awning. When the three had tried to walk in, Priest had waved the other two away with a simple, "One at a time, folks," after which the door would no longer open. As far as they can tell there are no locks.

If Mouse is speaking, it's too quiet to hear, but the occasional impassioned responses from the bartender leave them worried. Inside, Mouse is standing shirtless while Priest repurposes a hanging table lamp as an examining tool.

His voice has dropped low.

"Scarecrow's eyes, kid. I only know so many people who could do this at all, and you did it by accident?" He's chewing on another toothpick while peering at the mother-of-pearl tracery on the boy's skin. "It's heavy duty alchemy and you just up and 'Whoops!' did it."

Mouse frowns, thinks about what he wants to say, and lets it fall out of his mouth. "Wh—what does that mean?" He hasn't done the lightning bolt to the head trick this time, but it's easier to speak in here, with just the quiet face of the bartender.

"Your spirit friend—Anna you said?—that's her." He taps the patterns on the boy's chest. "I sure hope you like her though, kid. You're going to be stuck with her for, uh..." He turns Mouse sideways and peers again at one of the symbols. He lets out a breathy whistle. "A while, anyhow."

Mouse just looks at him.

"How do I put this? In a sense, you've adopted her. Spirits are like people, but they're missing a couple of the key ingredients—form, image, reflection. You just gave her a little of each, by drawing her on yours. If you imagine a boat in a river dropping anchor to keep from being swept away, the anchor?" He snorts. "That's you."

He blows air through his nose appreciatively, steps back and shakes his head. "Put your shirt on," he says, walking back to the bar. "She's your familiar, now."

He reaches under it and pulls out a bottle so old and scratched up it could say anything on the side. He grabs two glasses and pours an inch into each, liquid the color of straw. "The question is, what did you pay? Nothing's free, you know."

He slides a glass over to Mouse's side of the bar.

"Here, drink," he says. "I don't care how old you are, we're both going to need one."

Mouse takes the glass, smells it. It smells of leather, hay, wood, fire.

"Cheers, kid." They clink glasses and Mouse takes a swig. He swallows. His throat is on *fire*. Do people seriously drink this stuff for fun? He coughs, sputters, shudders, puts the glass back down.

"Thanks," he whispers, hoarse. Priest laughs a viking laugh, a chesty sound that shakes the door again.

"Right. Now call her up," he says.

Mouse looks at him in confusion.

"Your—*Anna*." He catches himself. "Summon her."

Mouse just raises his eyebrows.

"Oh, for crying out loud. Look. You remember her."

Mouse nods.

"Well, she's somewhere in there. Just remember where you put her and go get her. Close your eyes if it helps. Having another swig of this rotgut might help, too." He grins. "Made it myself."

Mouse swallows, picks up the glass, and has another sip, the sour heat giving a rough texture to his tongue and causing the blood to rush to his head. He closes his eyes and thinks of Anna. Calls up her name, her face, her clothes. The sound of the bells he hears now and then when she's around. Nothing. He thinks for a minute, remembers walking to school with her. Tries not to cringe at the embarrassment of waking up in bed with her. Breathes in deep the smell of lilacs.

There. It's like running his hand over smooth silk and feeling a loose thread, woven in by amateur hands. Now what? He reaches out with his mind and tugs on it a little.

Fire.

And then the fire is in his head and it's in his chest. He's doubled over, falling over, eyes wide and tearing up, staring at the bartender who's walked around the bar to where Mouse is curled up on the floor. He crouches down and speaks through the boy's pain, through the fire.

"This is the first lesson. All Knowledge comes from Fire. Focus; don't let it consume you. With time you'll be able to walk around the fire instead of through it. Now what's her name?"

Mouse twitches on the floor. "Anna," he croaks.

"Her whole name. As much of it as you know."

"Anna Kinoshita," he says.

"Now repeat after me. 'Anna Kinoshita, I grant you image in the middle distance.' An incantation is a contract with the universe. The middle distance is here, and you want to see her. 'I grant you image in the middle distance.' Say it."

His jaw is locked, stomach clenched. "Hurts!"

"Say it!"

Mouse repeats it, but nothing happens.

"Say your name! Say 'I, whatever-your-newbie-name-is, grant you image in the middle distance.'"

Mouse curls tighter into a ball. "I, M—Mouse, grant you im—image in the m—middle distance." He spits out the last word. He's starting to feel the fire coursing down his legs. It's in his spine, his lungs, his fingers.

"Not your nickname, your name! Your real name. You're letting it use you. Take control!" Priest is barking orders now like a first responder at the scene of a disaster. "Say it like a command!"

Mouse thinks he imagines the bartender's bad eye glowing, imagines a blurry world lit by blue fire—confused, like double-exposed film. He clenches his fists. Focuses the fire like he focused Anna's emotions that day in the kitchen.

A tickle of frost courses out from somewhere dark inside him, a wave of nausea hardening into a tapestry of icy threads like marionette strings, moving his mouth and saying the words.

"Anna Kinoshita, I, Simon Anacreon, grant you image in the middle distance."

The pain begins to ease, but his mouth keeps moving of its own accord, an alien force puppeteering his actions.

"In the name of the one who stood, stands, and will stand, I call you forth and grant you form of my form."

Ancient words, spilling forth from a long-forgotten memory. The ice creeps out into his lungs, his heart, his blood. A shadow in the dark whispers to him from beyond a streetlamp's terminating circle. Back in the room, another circle, one of light and arcane symbols, shimmers around Mouse's twisted form on the ground.

"I bind you with the universal root to the incomprehensible air and grant you reflection in the seventh spirit."

He's hauled himself up to his knees now, feels a pressure on his shoulders like a hundred tons and yet somehow lifts it. He calls the massive weight into a thimbleful of space before him, makes a dark star in his own orbit.

He sees it all in an instant: the blackness, the wet streets and cobblestones from that night, himself in two places—in the light, and again in the shadows of the periphery. He sees the web of connections that link an old man on a dusty road with a silent, mop-headed child, wide-eyed in the back of a car between towns. He sees familiar faces he's never seen before, comrades in arms against a shivering horror from the spaces in between. He sees the confusion of the times to come, and then the nothingness that stretches after—vast, like a starless sky. He sees it all like a sleight of hand trick, like pulling a coin from behind a bashful child's ear.

He is calm and cold. He is someone else.

"I move upon the surface of the waters," he says. "I call you."

Then they're gone, the ice and the fire, the pain and the memory drifting away like smoke from a spent match. The room is just a room, and Anna is sitting in front of him, looking confused. Mouse slumps down where he's kneeling on the floor, palms hitting the worn wooden floor, slipping to an elbow, catching his breath.

Priest sits down on a bar stool and stares at him, hard.

They sit in tableau until Priest breaks the silence.

"Where did you learn those words?" He's speaking to Mouse, but he's looking at Anna.

He's *looking at* Anna.

Anna looks back. "You can see me?"

"And hear you." He walks over and puts a tentative hand out toward Anna, and it comes to a rest on her head. And touch you, he thinks. He pulls his hand back, just a little too quickly to avoid betraying the appearance of calm, and walks back to the bar.

Mouse wants to ask, but he just can't find the energy. He wants to crawl into bed, to sleep for an eternity. He feels heavier, like someone's turned up gravity. He presses his forehead against the cool floor. It feels wonderful.

Priest picks up the rest of Mouse's drink off the bar and knocks it back himself in one gulp. He grabs the bottle and splashes more in the glass, then drinks that, too. This should not have happened. It should have ended with a minor light show and an exhausted kid telling him about the brief and ephemeral return of his invisible friend. Instead the world had been shifted on its damnable foundations. Not much. Not enough to do any damage. But enough to attract attention. He rubs his hand against one of the columns that support the ceiling. His wards are down. Hell, everyone's might be.

And he should not be able to touch the kid's familiar.

Anna stands up, walks over and crouches down by Mouse. "You okay?" she whispers, putting her hand on his head. He grabs it and looks up, nodding. She stands and helps him to his feet.

She frowns, rubbing her bare arms. "Nezumi," she says. "I'm cold." She looks around the bar as if seeing it for the first time. Mouse shrugs out of his coat and drops it over her shoulders without a word. She clutches it around her and looks at the bartender, who's watching this all unfold with quiet detachment. She looks at Mouse again, a sudden tremble of fear in her voice. "I'm cold, and I'm hungry, and the bar smells of smoke, Mouse." She looks around, confused. "It *smells*."

Mouse looks at her, through her, and nods. He steps forward and puts his arms around her. He's not a big guy, but Anna's even smaller, and he envelops her in the embrace. He whispers to her. *Gome. Sorry.*

The older man is leaning back, elbows propped against the bar, white sleeves rolled up. He's undone the buttons of his dark grey bartender's vest. He lets a breath whistle out between his teeth.

Mouse looks over but doesn't say anything. When those words had spilled into him from the broken dream, he'd felt their power, their *rightness*. For a moment, he'd seen things in a way that felt so familiar and yet new. He'd known what needed to be done, seen the way it was all going to unfold, and had cast the first of the dice in what he knew would be a long and dangerous game. But it's all evaporating into the mists like so many nightmares, and he can't find the words to say, to explain.

There's an audible gasp from the doorway. The door to the bar has loosened on its hinges, and now Bliss and Ginnie are standing there, watching.

Mouse turns to welcome them in, but his legs start to give out, and Anna catches him, his arm over her shoulders. He goes to apologize, but can't make his mouth work.

"He says sorry about the fuss," Anna says.

Mouse looks at her, she looks back. They don't need the notepad anymore.

They look up at Bliss and Ginnie.

"Anna?" Bliss says, her voice tiny.

"Hi. Yeah." She smiles, almost embarrassed by the attention, feeling a little naked. "It's me."

"No, I'm sorry, I mean your hair, and you're so—" She nearly says 'pretty,' but stops herself. In her most recent memories, Anna was still sickly, her skin sallow, eyes raccoon-ringed with purple. Her arms had been perpetually stained and bruised, her eyes faraway, like they were watching from a distant shore. She'd always been in bed or a wheelchair, or going from one to the other. But standing here, Anna is healthy, vibrant, strong enough to carry Mouse, eyes so bright she could be seeing the world for two. She's *alive*. Or something more.

And then of course there's her hair. Anna catches sight of it as it hangs down to her collarbone: a silvery blonde so light it's practically white. She catches another apology drifting over from Mouse and looks at him, exhausted and hanging over her. She sighs.

"I'll get mad at you for this later, deal?"

Mouse nods, smiling.

Before any more questions can be asked, they start walking out. Ginnie and Bliss part like the waters as Anna sees him up the steps to the door. She turns to face Priest, still sitting at the bar. "He says we'll answer whatever questions we can tomorrow, is that okay?"

The bartender shakes his head. "I've only got one question, and if he can't answer it now, he won't be able to tomorrow."

"What is it?"

"What did you pay?"

Anna looks at Mouse and he shakes his head.

"Thanks for the drink," she says for him, and they walk out into the afternoon. Bliss stares hard at the bartender, looks like she's about to say something, then turns and follows.

M ouse is curled up on his bed. Sometime in the night an ice dam had burst in the back of his mind, flooding his dreams with an ancient cold that had threatened to drown him in his sleep; but the worst of it had passed, and the receding waters had left him washed up on the banks of his sub-conscious like driftwood after a storm.

After half-carrying him home in near silence, the girls had discovered the apartment empty. Ginnie had said it was all a little too much for her, and had gone off to find Mason and maybe apologize. Bliss had stayed with Anna into the early hours of the morning, the two conspiring ways to explain his condition to June, though in the end she hadn't come home.

Bliss had fallen asleep in front of the television and had wandered home when she woke up at six A.M. to go get ready for school. Anna had stayed behind all day, unsure of how to fill the time that she had once spent insubstantial, drifting. She'd tidied the apartment, checked in on Mouse, picked through his collection of light novels and read them in rapid succession, savoring the feeling of paper in her hands.

As evening draws near, she finds herself in the kitchen, picking up a freshly-clean plate and drying it. It's one of the blue ones through which she'd first seen Mouse. Her nezumi. Simon. The name feels as familiar as her own now, and she wonders, staring through the plate, catching sight of her own reflection in it, what else has changed about her. In the blue world beyond she sees Bliss pass the kitchen window and hears her come in. It isn't until she smells the food that Anna remembers her hunger.

"I brought take-out." Bliss puts it on the table.

"Ugh, thank you. I don't know if I'm supposed to be eating now or not, but I'm going to."

They've discovered things about Anna's condition. She's solid and can be seen by anyone, including herself in the mirror. She can smell and taste and breathe, but she can also hold her breath for a really long time, maybe forever—they'd given up after she made it five minutes without any sign of distress. She bleeds when pricked, but has no pulse they've been able to detect. They've also discovered that she can jump between rooms like she'd been able to before, but that when she gets tired she doesn't disappear or scatter—she just falls asleep. She doesn't know what she is, but right now, she's hungry.

They don't notice the shadow lingering at the front window as they unpack the food, or the sound of the door as it opens and shuts. When Anna looks up from her chop suey, Kai is standing in the doorway.

鼠

"Hey," he says. If Anna did have a heartbeat it would have stopped.

Bliss jumps and spins around.

"Jesus, Kai! Don't scare me like that."

"Sorry." He walks into the kitchen, extending his hand. "I'm Kai, I live two doors over. It's Izzy, right?"

Anna nearly chokes on her food, but manages to take his hand. "Hi," she says.

He looks at her. He's the same as ever, still guarded, stern. She looks at Bliss, who interjects.

"Yeah, Kai was working at the take-out just now. I told him how you'd be in town for a while, and about June being your dad's old neighbor and stuff." Her eyes are wide, imploring Anna to go along with it.

"Ah, yeah." She stops. "Family friends and stuff." She looks down at the ground.

A shadow of recognition flits across his face. "Have we, I mean—have you come to town before maybe? You look familiar somehow."

"Oh! Um," she stops. "Yeah. I used to live around here, but, uh, I don't anymore." Not exactly a lie.

"Right, well. Maybe I've seen you around then." He turns to Bliss, and Anna notices he has something in his other hand. "You forgot your soup."

Bliss sighs. "Aw, thanks."

"You'd forget your head if it wasn't screwed on so tight."

"Did I say thanks? I meant shut up." She smiles and takes the soup.

He laughs and walks toward the door. "You're welcome."

"Hey has June come by—Mouse's mom? It's just that he's sick and we can't find her."

Kai's face darkens. "Yeah. I've seen her. She'll be by later, I guess."

Anna and Bliss exchange looks, but don't say anything.

"Anyway, I gotta get back to work. Nice to meet you." He waves and walks out the door.

They hold their breath until he's passed by the window again, then Anna quietly locks the door before walking back to the table and slumping down on it.

She makes it as far as picking up her soda before bursting into tears.

"I'm so sorry Anna," Bliss says. "I told him that Mouse was sick, and added that old neighbor stuff just in case he saw you through the window. I never expected him to come by." She hands Anna a napkin, which she uses to dry her eyes as she calms down.

"I guess I cry now, too." She sniffs. "Add that to the list. But why didn't he know it was me?"

Bliss shakes her head. "I suspected it might be the same as before—if someone can avoid knowing it's you, I think they will."

"Guess I'm still dead."

"Dead plus."

"Dead Two: Son of Dead."

"That's the one." Bliss half-crouches so she's about the same height as Anna sitting, and puts her arms around her. "But you're here, now. And whatever that means, I'm here for you."

Another sniffle escapes as Anna buries her head in her friend's shoulder. Then she puts her head up.

"He's awake."

She wipes her eyes and stands up, grabs the kettle from under the sink. She fills it and sets it on the stove. By the time Mouse darkens the doorway to the kitchen, she's pouring the boiling water into the teapot. Bliss watches as he sits down at the table and Anna brings him the pot and a mug.

"You're welcome," she says. "But don't expect me to do it every time you ask."

He smiles, still half asleep, and nods as Anna sits back down at the little kitchen table.

As he's pouring the tea, Bliss notices lines on his arm where his sleeve is rolled up. She reaches out, and then stops as he waves her off with his other hand. He rolls up the sleeve to show that the faint mother of pearl lines that had once only graced his shoulder and back now stretch to his right wrist, and have darkened to an iridescent abalone. They're peeking up a little around his collarbone, too.

Anna looks at him, then at Bliss, then grabs a notepad from the table and tosses it to him. "Say it out loud or write it, Nezumi. We're not the only ones here."

Mouse flushes, glances up in apology at Bliss. He takes a deep breath, tries to speak, but then he makes eye contact with her and stutters, distracted. He looks back down at the pad.

"You and me, we're gonna work on that." Anna says, handing him a pen. "But for now, write."

Mouse nods. Scribbles away, handing Bliss a note.

You have questions, but I only have some of the answers. Anna knows almost as much as I do.

"Which is totally helpful," she says, "because I don't know anything."

You know a lot.

Bliss thinks for a moment. "Is Anna alive?"

Mouse nods, writes. *Yes.*

"Alive with no heartbeat," Anna says.

Only humans need heartbeats, Mouse responds.

"Are you saying she's not human?"

Mouse nods. *She's better.*

"What do you mean, better?"

Mouse stops and thinks. *I'm not sure yet.* He starts writing a longer note, then stops, looking at Anna.

"Fine, fine," she says, "but just this once."

Bliss looks a little confused, but rolls with it.

"I'm not going to pretend to understand it, I'm just going to describe it as Mouse understands it."

Bliss blinks. "Wait, have you been reading his mind?"

"Uh, it's like that but not. But sure, we'll call it that for now. I mean. Ugh. How do I explain this?" She stares at Mouse, frustrated. "We're sharing. Even though I'm over here and he's over there. Like this." She slaps her own cheeks, hard.

Mouse jumps in his seat, brings his hands to his cheeks, eyes watering.

"Didn't hurt me a bit." Anna grins.

Bliss's eyes widen. Mouse is rubbing his cheeks and glaring across the table at his familiar.

"It worked, didn't it?" She turns back to Bliss. "Anyway, ignore him. He's the one who wanted me to explain this. So yeah. The guy back in the bar, that's Priest. Not sure if it's a name or a title, but my guess is it's a little of both. He was trying to show Mouse here how to summon me, seeing as how he'd already written me up as a contracted spirit. Remind me never to possess someone without doing research first." She sighs, takes a swig of cola. Mouse sticks out his tongue and so does Anna. "Oh ew. Ew ew. Tea and cola. No. Oh damn it, this is going to be awkward. We're going to have to practice not sharing."

Mouse sighs loudly, but Anna continues. "Anyway, so he gets halfway through the summoning process and it's like he remembers something, like a long time ago someone knew something was going to happen and told him he'd need to do this, but that he'd forgotten. And so instead of stopping at summoning me, he did...well, this."

Mouse nods, scrawls something down: *Made her a Pyx.*

"She's a Pyx?"

Mouse nods. *Not just air anymore. A vessel.*

"And before you can ask, he doesn't know." Anna sighs.

"Know what?"

"How he did it. How he knew how to do it. How he knows that I'm called a Pyx now instead of a Sprite, which, apparently, is what I was."

"This doesn't make any sense."

"Nope. None."

"But you were just a ghost."

"No such thing as ghosts, turns out."

"What?"

"Right? Turns out if you die, you're dead. You go where dead people go. But sometimes, you don't die. You become something else. Maybe you've got something you still need to do, or something you're pissed off about. Or someone you need to protect." Anna trails off.

They sit around the table in awkward silence for a minute before Mouse takes another sip of his tea and Anna sticks her tongue out. "Nezumi, stop. For the love of god. I wish I hadn't made you that tea."

He rolls his eyes and hands a note to Bliss. *She was the one who woke me up with the taste of chop suey in my mouth.*

Bliss grins.

"Oh crap. There's one more thing. There's a distance limit. It's not tiny, but I can't go that far from him. Gotta stay in the same zip code type thing."

Bliss feels like she should be taking notes. "What happens if you don't?"

"It's not that something happens. I just can't. It's physically impossible."

Bliss shakes her head. "This is just—" She puts her chin on her hands and her elbows on the table. "How are you both so calm?"

Mouse writes a note, hands it to her.

We believe in the universe we're presented with.

Anna nods. "And so things are the way they are now."

"One more thing, though."

Mouse nods, an invitation to continue.

"What do you mean when you said a long time ago someone

knew something was going to happen? What kind of something are we talking about?"

Anna suddenly looks nervous, Mouse is staring at the pad, not writing anything.

"Should I—"

"No." Mouse says, a whisper. He chews the end of the pen, then writes for what seems like an eternity, crossing things out, starting over again. Finally he hands Bliss a note. It says:

I don't know what it is, but something is coming. And I'm going to need you, and Anna, and Kai. Everybody. I'm going to need you all to trust me. And that's going to be a challenge for Kai.

"For Kai?"

And maybe for Anna, too.

As if in reaction, the front door unlocks and opens, and they can hear June come in, talking to someone. There's some quiet laughter followed by the sound of a quick kiss before the door shuts, and Mr. Kinoshita walks by the window, straightening his collar as he heads to the stairs.

When June sticks her head into the kitchen she sees three bodies and two sets of eyes staring at her. She looks only a little surprised and doesn't miss a beat. She walks over and tousles Mouse's hair.

"Well, hello," she says to the girls. "We haven't met. I'm June."

語

After brief introductions they move up to Mouse's room. Anna and Bliss are on the bed, Mouse is leaning against the desk with his hands in his pockets.

"Well that explains Kai," Bliss says.

June hadn't said anything about Anna and Kai's dad, and they hadn't asked about him either. Things had been pretty clear.

"You knew," Anna says to Mouse.

He nods. He half knew.

"I kind of knew, too, didn't I?"

He nods again.

"It's been more than a year since mom left."

Silence fills the room.

"What do we do?" Bliss asks, at last.

Anna shakes her head. "Nothing. I mean there's nothing we should do, right?" She sniffles. "Dad's a nice guy, June seems pretty sweet. Not really our business."

"No," Bliss says, gently.

Tears drip into Anna's lap and Bliss hugs her.

"Mouse, hun, could you go get—" Bliss looks over and he's wiping his eyes on his sleeve. "Oh, the two of you," she says.

He holds up his hands in a silent protest. Not me, he's saying. He grabs a box of tissues from behind him and passes it over.

"You're really that close now, huh?"

Mouse shrugs. He doesn't know how close they are, he just did what he knew needed to be done, even if he can't remember exactly why anymore.

"I'm going to start feeling left out if you're not careful," Bliss says. She's smiling, but she's only half-joking.

He writes a note. *If she stays with you, it might diminish the effect a little.* Both the link, he thinks, and maybe the way Bliss is looking at them right then.

Anna looks up from blowing her nose. "Could I really stay with you?"

Bliss smiles. "Of course!"

"And have bacon on Sundays?"

Bliss grins.

"No offense, Nezumi, but you can't beat bacon."

He holds his hands up as if to admit the superiority of bacon.

"What about Kai?"

"He's not staying with me," Bliss says.

Anna lightly taps her on the head. "You know what I mean."

A half-hearted smile. "I guess we wait and see."

鼠

That night, as Anna and Bliss walk across town, the constant clutter of two sets of thoughts dims to a quiet hum in Mouse's head. They can still reach each other if they try, but otherwise Mouse only catches snippets of Anna here and there. A warm glow when Bliss makes her feel at home, a dull ache when she thinks of Kai, her father, and June.

The two of them show up at school together the next day, Bliss and 'Izzy,' who's coming as a transfer student thanks to some forged signatures and what Bliss refers to as "Connections." He doesn't ask. Anna complains about the homework, but learns she can just pick Mouse's brain for the answer if she's desperate. Things settle into a pattern approaching normalcy.

Looking back, they should have been using the time to prepare.

鼠

Mouse lies on his back on the bed, staring at the ceiling. The first light December snow is falling outside, drifting down over the town, putting soft edges on everything it touches. But the silence it carries with it brings ghosts when he closes his eyes, and he forces them open until he can't avoid it anymore and drifts off into a dreamless sleep. He wakes to a muffled thud from below.

It's still dark and he checks the clock: three A.M. June's out, though whether she's at the hospital or two doors down he's forgotten. There's a rumble and a crash from the hallway below, then a flurry of angry whispers. He presses his ear against the bedroom door.

"Argo!" A woman's voice? "Your elbows for pity's sake..."

The third step from the bottom squeaks.

He closes his eyes and calls out to Anna.

鼠

Bliss wakes up with a start—someone's knocking, then opening the door.

"Bliss! It's about Mouse. I have to go."

"What? What time is it?" She sounds groggy and half-dazed.

"Someone's there. At his apartment. Come along as soon as you can."

And then Bliss is alone in her room again: Anna's gone.

鼠

The snowflakes pass like stars as Anna runs across town. The furthest she can skip is room-to-room, but she makes use of it as best she can—two steps on the ground at a run, a flash forward fifteen feet, another few steps, repeat, winking in and out of existence like a dancer under a strobe light. Her footsteps in the thin snow are sporadic—under a streetlight, passing a driveway, running down the deserted main street.

She's on her way.

"Wait for me, Mouse."

鼠

Moving as quietly as he can, he's maneuvered furniture across the door. His chair and a few still-packed boxes of books and DVDs, a garbage can now filled with his backpack and textbooks. When the footsteps hit the landing he decides to forego the element of surprise and, grabbing the end of his mattress, heaves it up on top of the rest with a crash, just as the doorknob turns.

Mild curses come from the hall and a loud bang erupts as the pile of stuff shifts and falls back against the door. He doesn't have long.

He pulls out his phone and stares at it, wondering. Can you text 911? He doesn't have time to try as the door shakes with another bang.

The window is one of those faux balconies that's really just a line of railing across a door-sized window. He slides it open and his breath clouds out into the cold. He tears out the screen and looks down. He's two stories up over the landing at the back of the building. It's still a long way, but for once he's really glad his room is over the door instead of the street.

The next bang shifts the mattress up to vertical and then over, crashing not back to the door but down into the room. Mouse grabs hold of the railing and lowers himself out, sliding down so he's hanging from the bottom of the window. His feet kick at the open air but can't find anywhere to rest. He'd been really hoping the ground would be closer, somehow. He fumbles, tries to reach the kitchen windowsill with his bare feet.

A final crash and they're in his room, and a woman's face, familiar yet unfamiliar, is sticking out the window, looking down at him.

"Argo!" she snaps, and a huge mass of man materializes in the room, punching through the railing like it's not even there. He tries to catch Mouse by the arm, but Mouse succeeds in twisting in time to avoid it.

Unfortunately, he doesn't succeed in grabbing anything else, and falls, imagining broken bones or worse.

He lands with a softer thump than he'd expected, finding himself cradled in the arms of his familiar.

"I told you to wait for me."

He smiles, sheepish. "*Gome.*"

"*Baka.* Jumping out windows. Jeez." She puts him down and stares up at the uninvited guests, who return their gaze before disappearing inside.

"Quick, they're coming."

Anna puts Mouse down and stands, suddenly beautiful, haloed by snow, near-white hair lit by the full moon. She looks down at him and smiles, blushing a little.

"Thanks, but this kinda isn't the time."

He doesn't have the opportunity to respond.

The woman strides through the door and out onto the terrace. Face-to-face she's quite tall, with raven-dark hair and eyes. She's dressed in clothes that almost look military—short black coat with cargo pockets and lapels. Her hair's pulled back in a tight braid. Mouse thinks she looks maybe college-age. And she definitely looks familiar, but he can't place where from. Her partner appears next, wearing the same outfit. His arms are bigger than Mouse's thighs and he has no neck to speak of. He's also got about as much facial expression as he has hair, which is to say none.

"I need you to come with us, Simon."

Why does she know his name?

Anna looks at Mouse and then positions herself between him and their company.

"Yeah, no."

The woman frowns. "Argo," she says, like an order.

Mouse feels a wave of something pass by, remembers something in the shadows. Anna gets the message and jumps back in time to avoid the giant's flickering movement forward. He leaves a wisp of something, a swirl of energy, as he strobes forward—he's a familiar. That means the woman must be—

Anna grabs Mouse and jumps. The world blurs and they're on top of the roof. Another leap and they're out in front of the shops, down three stories to street level in the blink of an eye. Mouse doesn't have time to be amazed, though—the woman's familiar has followed them. Under the streetlights Mouse notices something—the man has no shadow. Anna, on the other hand—

"Look out!" Anna shouts.

Mouse turns and narrowly dodges a giant hand as it swings through the air with ease, much to Mouse's dismay. He'd been hoping that the mountainous man had at least given up some agility for his size and strength.

"Don't count me out yet," Anna says.

When next blow comes, she intercedes. The massive fist crashes into her small forearm with a dull scuffing noise and implausibly comes to a stop like it's hit a brick wall, causing their assailant to look perplexed. Anna takes advantage and lands a powerful punch in the middle of his chest, sending him flying back through the air and into a lamppost, which lists at an unlikely angle when he rights himself. He tilts his head to one side and stares at them.

Anna cracks her knuckles and sets her jaw.

The two rush at each other as Mouse stands by in blinkered silence. As quick as the other familiar is, he can't match Anna's speed, and every hit he lands seems to have less effect. He catches her off guard and slams a left hook into her, but all it does is send her skidding back a couple of feet before she rebounds and throws herself at him. Another flurry of punches is followed by a kick that sends her opponent flying again, landing in a heap and sliding a track through the snow before coming to a rest at the feet of his master, who has walked down the stairs to join them in the intervening time.

The woman raises an eyebrow, almost in appreciation. Anna isn't sure how to react, and circles back around so she's between Mouse and the intruders again. Then the woman looks past her, past Mouse, and nods.

And suddenly Mouse is being lifted from behind by his shirt, kicking his legs and grabbing at his neck where the collar's digging in and cutting off his breathing. He can smell leather and old smoke. He reaches behind him and bats at the dark hand holding him up. Anna runs toward him but the giant familiar is between them again. As Mouse starts to black out he touches the arm of his assailant—skin and bone. He's reminded of the feel of Priest's hands, his thumb on Mouse's tongue, the physicality of that interaction and the shock.

A feeling of cold, like ice in his chest, creeps up his spine and into his skull. For just a moment, he's back in the dream, under the streetlight, the voice from the shadows echoing from all around him, a giant icy hand clutching at his heart and making it race. He bites down on his fear and focuses.

There's a crackle and the faint smell of burning and he's back on the ground, hands to his throat, gasping for air.

"Sonofa*bitch*!" He swivels to see the figure behind him cradling his arm, glaring. The man is about six feet tall and wearing a long, dark trench coat. He's got a shaved head hidden under a black baseball cap. He clenches his hand into a fist and then relaxes it, then reaches into his coat and pulls out a gun. "Can I just shoot him, Helene? I know that wasn't the plan, but *please* let me shoot him."

Mouse stands transfixed. No one's ever pointed a gun at him before.

It's scarier than he imagined it would be.

"Let me tell you something, kid. Guns are unfair." The man takes a step toward him, so close it would be impossible to miss. "It doesn't matter who you are, a bullet will kill you the same if you're a king or a ten-penny thug." The man's not smiling; Mouse can't tell from his face if he even knows how. "They're not artful, not showy like Kung Fu or shiny blades or explosives. But I'll tell you what." He leans in close so the gun's cold weight is pressing against Mouse's cheek.

"I'm not an artful man."

Mouse moves without thinking, calm like the winter night. He watches himself as he squeezes a single finger between the gun barrel and his cheek and moves it aside. He looks up at the man's face.

They're both so surprised that they stand there in freeze-frame for an entire second, the man's gun now pointed at an angle away from Mouse, being held there by a single audacious finger.

Then Mouse repeats the electric shock trick.

Three things happen simultaneously because of this, and because of a simple fact of human anatomy—electricity makes muscles contract.

One, there is an incredible noise, so loud it nearly blinds Mouse, and he slams his hands over his ears as the world is enveloped in deafening silence. Two, in the momentary confusion Anna manages to squeak by her assailant, grab Mouse and get to the curb, where; three, Bliss has just pulled up in a beat-up silver hatchback and is motioning frantically for them to get in.

Anna throws him into the car, dives into the passenger seat, and they peel away from the curb leaving a streak of rubber as they go.

The man with the gun cradles his hand again, giving the woman—Helene—a pained and sheepish look. "I wasn't *really* gonna shoot him."

Her gaze follows the car as it drives off.

The large man walks over to their trench coated companion and gently takes the gun from his hand, squeezes the barrel between his palms until it's flat, and hands it back.

Helene suppresses a smile as he pouts at his ruined toy.

"It's definitely him, Vallis. Let's go."

As they walk off into the night, a curtain slides back into place in a window over the stores.

鼠

Inside the speeding car, and fueled by adrenaline, Anna's mind has drifted a long way from Mouse's, who's still recovering in the backseat.

"Great timing!" she says, excited. "When did you take driving lessons?"

Bliss is focused into a frown of concentration, foot down as they fly through the town in the hours that only night-shift workers and insomniacs see. "Who says I've taken lessons?" As if to demonstrate, the car lurches to a crawl to take a corner and then heaves itself into a sprint again. "Where am I going?"

"To the bar. Even if Priest isn't there it's solid and defensible."

"Right. Who were those guys?" Bliss looks over her shoulder when Anna says she doesn't know.

Mouse shakes his head, still tender from the gunshot. There are about a thousand things he wants to say but he can't slow his mind down enough to express it all. The icy calm he'd felt before had been blown away by the gunshot, and it's since been replaced with nothing but chaos. He's snatching at thoughts flying by, but they get away before he can claim them. He snags one at last—it's a part of a memory, an intuition; it's only partial, but Anna gets a glimpse of it and turns around in her seat.

"That's why you made me like this, right? To fight these guys."

Mouse tries to respond. Shakes his head. Focuses as best he can. To fight, yes, but—

He pulls out a pad and scribbles on it, passes it up front.

Not them. Anna reads it aloud.

"What do you mean?" Bliss asks.

He wants to say that he thinks they're just incidental, a sideshow. That the main act is still coming, but he can't remember any of the details. All he has are fragments of memories from a dream of a streetlight's circle and the shadows beyond. Something much worse is coming. He shakes his head again, trying to physically rattle the broken pieces of memory into place.

I think they're a part of what's going on, I'm just not sure what part yet.

Bliss frowns as the car shudders to a stop out by the bar. She turns off the engine and silence fills the space and thickens the air.

"We need to get inside," Anna says, "before they—"

She's interrupted by a polite tapping on the window. The large familiar is looking in the passenger side, devoid of expression. The raven-haired woman and the talkative gunman are walking around to the driver's side from in front, lit at thigh-height by the headlights.

Mouse writes another note, passes it up to Anna, and gets out of the car.

Stay inside, it says.

鼠

The car on the curb, the bar behind them. Mouse is standing in the street like it's a showdown in a spaghetti western. But he's got no spurs on his heels, no gun at his side, and his bare feet sting in the cold. He'd make a lousy cowboy, he thinks, and shoves his hands in his pockets to keep them from shaking. The woman steps forward.

"I apologize for Vallis. He's a little lacking in the tact department."

Mouse says nothing. Maybe if he waits long enough he won't have to.

The woman looks at him. "Not going to say anything?"

Mouse *can't* say anything, his heart's racing too fast, ears still ringing from the gunshot. His stomach's just a twist of nausea that the rest of this body is crowding around. Saying anything would be impossible, but he doesn't want to admit any weakness, either. He pulls out his pad, forces his hands to stop shaking long enough to write a note. He walks up and hands it to her.

Words are powerful. What do you want, Helene?

The name, her name.

The gunman had said it. It's there in the splintered memories, too, somewhere. He thinks of the figure in the shadows from his dreams. Feels a tug in his chest, a nausea like pulling on stitches.

She nods appreciatively. "Come with us."

Why? His heart in his throat.

"You should know why."

Pretend I don't.

He stares at her nose, tries to bluff his way through. He's glad it's cold out, or he'd be sweating enough to give the game away. She stares at him, as if trying to decide something.

"The darkness is coming. Are you ready?" She looks at him the way a painter looks at her creation as it nears completion; it's a look that asks *What more does this need?* or maybe *Is it done yet?*

The words resonate in Mouse's memory, echo in the icy halls of the past that lie unvisited in his head. There's a darkness that's coming, into which no one can see. He knows what he should do, wishes he knew why.

I'm staying here. I need to. But you're welcome at my side.

She reads the note and laughs under her breath. It's a bitter sound. "How do you do that? Stay the same when everything around you changes?"

Mouse gives her a questioning look.

"You always—" She looks away, staring at nothing. "You have always known just the wrong thing to say." She shakes her head and swivels, walking away down the street. She pauses a few steps away. "I'm satisfied for now, but I'm not giving up on you yet, Diviner. We'll meet again in the new year. If you're not prepared by February, I won't be so lenient." With that, she and her companions slip silent into the night that lies beyond the streetlamps.

Mouse climbs back into the car and slumps down in the seat, folds in on himself—at once and without warning terribly, terribly sad.

He can't even say why.

Anna puts her hand on Bliss's shoulder. "Let's go home," is all she says.

Bliss looks at the exhausted form crumpled in the back of the car, and then back to Anna, before turning the key in the ignition and pulling away.

By the time they get back to the apartment, the police have arrived. Strobe lights paint the storefronts with blue stripes in flickering waves and a man wraps a perimeter of traffic cones and yellow tape around the damaged lamp post. It's going to be a long night.

The sun peeks above the horizon, a thumbnail of crimson painting the eastern sides of the town with a reddish hue. In the apartment, Mouse is sitting at the kitchen table opposite a police officer who's just standing up, holding a pile of notes.

"Mind if I hold on to these, son?" It's not really a question.

Mouse nods, sipping at the cup of tea he's been nursing since they arrived back to find the police walking through the apartment. June had been there before they arrived, and Anna's hiding in the car.

June walks by the kitchen, looks over at Mouse and smiles in reassurance. She's showing another officer around the apartment. She says she'd been two doors over at "Greg's"—Kai and Anna's dad's first name, Mouse supposes—and had woken to the sound of the gunshot. She'd thought it was a bunch of kids with fireworks, she says.

Not much damage has been done to the place. A bowl on a table near the front door—the one June uses as a dumping ground for junk-mail and keys—is in pieces on the floor, and a few drawers have been hauled open, left askew, and rifled through here and there. The lock on the front door won't need replacing, but the frame is a write-off. The deadbolt took the plate and frame with it when the door was heaved inward. To Mouse, it all looks very suspicious. Aside from the crash of the bowl—the big guy, Argo she called him, probably knocked into it by accident—Mouse hadn't heard anything. Someone had gone to the trouble of making it look like a burglary after the fact.

"I don't think anything's missing," he hears June saying, "but we're still unpacking—you know how it is when you move." From the sound of the officer's response she's given him one of her *silly-me* smiles;

one that says that even if everything were unpacked and away, she probably still wouldn't know if anything was missing. In the other room, he can hear the officer who interviewed him talking with Bliss. Beforehand, in the car, they'd agreed that Bliss had come to help when Mouse had texted that he'd heard someone in the house. Anna—"Izzy"—not officially in existence as far as the police are concerned, is out of sight and out of mind, as the saying goes.

Mouse is staring into nowhere, trying to sort through the night's events, and figure out Helene's part in it. He's so lost in thought that he nearly spills his tea when Bliss puts her hand on his shoulder. He hadn't even heard her come in the room.

"I'm going to head home," she says. "You okay?"

Mouse nods, puts his hand on top of hers without thinking, then jerks it away when he notices the intimacy of skin-on-skin. She grabs his hand before he pulls it away too far and gives it a squeeze. "I'll see you at school," she says, and slips out of the house.

School. Right.

He stands up and walks to the bottom of the stairs. June is showing the last of the police out, who are calling her "Miss" and assuring her that they'll do everything in their power to catch whoever's responsible. Mouse sighs and climbs the stairs. Shower and breakfast, then off to school.

From the top of the stairs he hears the door close as best it can. The apartment is silent. He peeks down, unseen, and looks at June. She sits down on the floor, back to the door, eyes closed, before pulling out her phone and tapping out a text to someone. It dings a response and she taps at it again. She's deep in conversation when Mouse slips away to shower and get ready for the day.

Things calm down after that, and they live their lives as high school students as best they can toward the new year, Helene's words echoing in Mouse's head in the moments of quiet. This isn't over, they say, this is just beginning. Be prepared.

But Mouse doesn't know how to prepare, or even how to learn. Priest's bar has been locked up tight every time they've been back, and no amount of library work or Google-fu seems to dig up so much as a clue. Meanwhile, June's relationship with Greg is keeping her away from the apartment so much that Mouse hardly sees her, which bothers him more than he expected it to. It's putting Kai in an ever-worsening mood as well, and Anna—as Izzy—tries daily to comfort both without bursting into tears at the sight of her estranged brother. Only Bliss seems to have things under control, somehow able to be the only peace in the maelstrom.

One day, nearing Christmas break, Mouse finds himself in the batcave, alone except for Ginnie, who's lying on her back, quietly smirking into a novel. Bliss has some kind of art project to work on, Kai is doing the student council thing, and Anna's trying to help him out with it. Mouse has gotten used to the hum of her thoughts across the school, but every now and then he'll show up when she needs him without asking, or vice versa. Sometimes people wonder about them, and he catches the odd glance, but for the most part he's finally become what makes him most comfortable: invisible.

Except, it seems, to Ginnie.

"So, how's it feel?" she asks. She's finished with her book and is now propped up on one elbow, studying him.

Mouse is perplexed, and pulls out his pad.

How does what feel?

Ginnie grins, and he looks down, remembering eyes like green fire.

"Being popular," she says. He can't tell if she's serious; he's not sure she can either.

He doesn't respond, just gives her a dubious look.

She laughs. "Oh come on, you're *totally* popular. Look at you— quiet, cute, and not one but *two* girls hanging off your shoulders? Well, three if you count me." She grins and leans forward. "I'd totally jump you. You're all like *rawr*, strong and silent."

Is she joking? Silent he'll buy, but strong? Definitely joking. Probably.

She leans back again and lies back down, still grinning. "But don't tell Mason. He's the jealous type." She giggles at a joke only she understands, arms behind her head like she's staring at the sky and not at a thirty-year-old drop-ceiling that's probably concealing asbestos.

He tosses her a note.

I don't think—that's not how things are.

She reads it and rolls back onto her side, staring at him, eyes searching. "No? I've known Bliss for a while. She's different around you." She has a faraway look on her face. "A lot of people are different around you. You have that effect on people."

He thinks for a moment, then passes her another note.

Thanks, I think.

"You do," she says, looking him over the way an art collector looks over a museum piece—maybe it's not for sale, the look says, but then again for the right price... "But the notepad thing perplexes me." She hauls herself back up into a sitting position and slides over to sit next to him, cross-legged and staring. "What's so tough about talking anyway?"

It's not like I've never talked.

"So?"

He remembers talking to Priest, or when Anna has talked through him. He thinks about all the times he's tried to talk and the words have stuck in his throat, or that he's said the wrong thing, or that he's been terrified and overwhelmed by just being there about to speak. He shakes his head.

I get distracted. The world is so full. It's like being in the loudest room ever and trying to have a conversation. I think sometimes maybe I am talking, it's just that no one can hear what I'm saying but me.

She takes that note as he writes another.

And then when they do hear me, things go wrong. No one understands, people get hurt.

"Mouse, babe—can I call you babe? You're kind of a babe—Mouse, babe—"

Please don't. He holds up the pad.

She giggles, but then gets quiet. "Meaning's hard for everybody, Mouse. Everybody says things they don't mean, or doesn't say the things they do mean. Or means one thing, but then gets understood another way. That last one's my own personal specialty." She's got her hands on her ankles and she's looking down at them, not saying anything for a good ten or twenty seconds. Then she swivels and flops her back against the wall next to Mouse, kicking her legs out straight and facing the same way as him.

"All I'm saying is, maybe it's not that weird. And if it *is* harder for you than for everybody else, well, maybe that means you should try more, not less."

Mouse nods, wondering if their conversation's more about him, or her.

For five minutes they both just sit there, side-by-side in the bat-cave, not saying anything, but comfortable with it. At length, he wonders how Bliss is doing, and packs up his things and stands. Before he goes, he stops and looks down at Ginnie, who's produced another book from somewhere and is already a few dozen pages in.

He takes a deep breath, swallows. "Th—thank you." He takes another breath in, another out. "For the talk. A—and," he thinks for a second, "the company."

Ginnie looks up and grins and he can't help but catch a glimpse of shining green eyes. He thinks they look more familiar now, less frightening but still mysterious. She looks back down at her book. "Anytime," she says. "I'd tell you to stay out of trouble, but I think we both know you're incapable of that." She flips the page. "We have that in common, at least."

Mouse walks away wondering just how much of that conversation he really understood, but doesn't have time to dwell on it. He makes it about ten steps down the hall before a wall of panic starts flashing neon in his mind: Anna. Help. Now.

He runs.

鼠

The school has a dedicated room for student council use. It's a little closet of a room, but they use it for office work and for selling tickets for dances and shows and sports. As he rounds the corner, he sees Kai running away down the other hall, the door ajar and the light still on. He slips inside, closes the door behind him.

Anna is sitting on a chair, hugging her knees. Waves of emotion wash over him, fill the air between them—shock, frustration, sadness. He rolls up his sleeve, revealing the binding marks that trace their way up his arm in iridescent purples and blacks. He steps forward, takes a breath, takes her hand and places it against his forearm, trying to bring order out of chaos. His calm is her calm. Her sorrow is his. She takes a sharp breath in, like being doused with cold water, then lets it out gently. She looks up at him.

"Thanks," she says.

He already knows what's happened. She's been working closer and closer with her brother, wanting to be near him, help him out. Mouse'd heard rumors about them, but hadn't done anything because he thought they'd go away on their own. Turns out not.

"He tried t—to k—kiss—"

Mouse holds her hand in both of his, crouches down. She grabs onto him like a lifeline and sobs. Kai had taken it the wrong way, but it was hard to blame him. Mouse was sure on some level Kai knew that he loved Anna, even if he didn't know it was her. But she was also a pretty girl who wanted to spend all her time with him. They should have seen this coming, but neither of them had wanted to.

Sniffling into his hair, she keeps talking. "You need to go. He left here so angry. He's trying to find you. He thinks it's all your fault. Your mom and his dad, and now he thinks you and me..."

Mouse sighs. That night, Helene had called him "Diviner," but it didn't take any kind of mystical foresight to see what had to happen next. It was going to hurt, too.

Anna backs up, sensing his thoughts. "No, you can't. He's the star of the boxing club and he's started Muay Thai lessons. He'll take you to pieces."

Mouse nods. He knows. That's why when the door flies open to reveal the furious brother, he stands calm and smiles. Rolling down his sleeve, he takes a breath and says one word aloud, "Outside."

鼠

A small crowd is beginning to gather in the field just off school property, around the two contenders, coats off in the snow. Not enough for the teachers to notice, not yet, but it's growing fast. Anna wants to intervene but every time she makes a move to, Mouse holds up his hand to stop her. This is the way things have to be, he thinks, and though she disagrees, she respects it.

Students he's never seen before are gathering, too, and before they know it a low chant of "Fight! Fight! Fight!" has begun.

"I hear they're fighting over the new girl."

"I heard it was about Mouse's mom."

"Kai's gonna pummel him."

Other whispers from the crowd.

And then Kai is diving at him, throwing punches. Mouse brings his arms up to cover his face, his thin sleeves adding little padding to cushion the blows. He tries a feeble duck and swing, and catches Kai in the side, but it doesn't have much effect and in the next second he receives a punch to the ear that makes his head ring out in pain. Anna tries to dive in again, but this time he holds her back with an act of will. He's holding all the pain in himself, not sending it to her, but if she gets any closer there'll be no helping it.

Mouse hits the ground with a crunch of snow, but hauls himself back up. He takes a deep breath, straightens his spine, and motions for Kai to begin once more.

This time Kai fakes to the left with a punch, and then lashes out with his foot, catching Mouse under the arm and in the ribs with his snow-wet patent leather. Mouse goes over again, but harder this time. Something in the snow—the wet stalks of uncut field grass or maybe a hidden twig from an autumn storm—scratches the side of his face and he comes up bleeding.

Kai is breathing heavily now, his anger surfacing.

"This is your fault," he says, and punches Mouse square in the chest. "What is it with you?" Another punch catching Mouse's shoulder as he feebly tries to block. "What's with your whole stupid family?" He punctuates his accusations with blows, his opponent dodging and blocking where possible.

Kai kicks him in the ribs again and the crowd lets out a collective "Ooh" of sympathetic pain. That one had really hurt.

But Mouse gets up again. And he will continue to. He'll keep getting up as long as this takes.

Kai's just getting angrier and angrier. "Why don't you *say* something?" He shouts. He grabs Mouse, who's growing less able to block, less able to respond to the punches and the kicks, by the front of his shirt. He throws him at the ground, and then he's down on top of him, pummeling him.

"I don't have *anything*! Why do you get *everything*?" It's like a dam has burst inside him, and it's all pouring out through his fists. Through the fog of his blurred vision Mouse thinks he can see Kai crying. "First my dad, and now Izzy, too?"

But it's not Izzy, and it's not Greg. It's not even Bliss, who he kind-of lost before Mouse even came to town. Mouse remembers Kai laughing in the hallway in the autumn, laughing at something as big and absurd as the universe itself, remembers the glimpse of sadness in his eyes and the way he kept his shoulders straight as he walked away.

He can't take any more punches. Mouse's face feels like ground beef and probably looks worse. He wrestles an arm free and tries to catch the next punch, holding it back with all his might. He grabs Kai's shirt with his other arm and pulls him in close. He's got to say it now, growl out what whispers he can.

"Her name's—not—Izzy." He chokes as a bead of blood drips down the back of his nose and into his throat. "Look." His head falls back to the side. "Look," he says. "Her name," he gags through half a cough, "is *Anna*."

Kai's rage and sadness fall back for a split second as he turns to look in the same direction as Mouse. Anna's standing at the edge of the circle, tears streaming down her face, mouthing the words 'Please stop,' over and over.

Kai freezes in recognition. He drops Mouse and looks at his hands, red with blood. He stands frozen, half over the well-beaten Mouse, half toward his undead sister. He doesn't know what to say—what can he say?—but as he steps toward her, a shadow moves out of the crowd and slugs him so hard in the nose that he hits the snow with a muffled thump and rolls onto his side holding his face.

Bliss looks over them both.

"What. The *hell*. Is *wrong* with you two?"

Mouse closes his eyes.

Long after the fight, a number of those who'd watched would swear—though no one would ever really believe them—that as they were walking away they'd heard something like laughter from the crumpled and bloodied form lying in the snow.

Snowflakes melt when they land on Mouse's swollen cheeks, facing up at the winter-white sky, framed by snow and hair and speckles of blood. His eyes are closed, but he's smiling.

鼠

"A three day suspension? For fighting?" June's yelling into the phone. They'd finally managed to get hold of her when Kai came home and had to tell his father about the fight, and she'd come right over. Mouse is sitting in the kitchen listening to her yell at the principal while she rolls her eyes sympathetically for Mouse's benefit.

"Have you even *seen* my son? By all reports it was hardly a fight and more of a beating." She pours herself a cup of coffee as she talks. "Yes, I understand it's not about who won the fight. Yes," she takes a sip. "Two black eyes? Really?"

She looks over at Mouse, eyebrows arched. He'd taken the blame for Bliss's punch, because at that point he was already up the creek anyway. He shrugs for June's benefit. She makes the universal sign for 'We're going to have a talk about this' and goes back to talking on the phone.

"Well, fine. Fine. I'll send him again on Friday to get whatever he needs for the break. All right. All right." Another sip of coffee. "Yep. Oh I'll give him a talking to, but I'm betting the bruises will do enough of that. Yep. Right. Friday. Yep. Thank you. Have a good night. Good-bye."

She presses the off button and sighs. "Jesus, Mary, and Joseph, Mouse." She slumps down at the table with him and examines his face. He's a raccoon with a swollen cheek, the red line where he hit something in the snow adding another color to the purples and blues. His shirt's done all the way up and the sleeves are still down. "Did he only get you in the face? Take off your shirt."

Mouse shakes his head, puts his hands up as if to say it's fine, but as he does he winces and she insists. He tries to stand, to back away in the hopes of postponing it, but he can't avoid it any longer. Well, this should be interesting, he thinks, and takes off his shirt.

Purple lines scrawl from his collarbone down his arm, the bruises on his shoulders and ribs almost obscuring them at times, except for their characteristic abalone sheen.

It is to Mouse's ultimate surprise, then, when June ignores them in favor of the bruises.

"Oh, honey. What on earth?" She peers at the ribs, puts her hand on his breastbone and presses a little. Maybe she can't see it? "That hurt?" He shakes his head. "How about breathing, that okay?" He nods. She lets out her breath. "Thank god. Looks like you've managed to avoid breaking any ribs—but you wouldn't know it to look at you. What on earth were you and Kai fighting about?"

Mouse looks away, and June flinches as if stung.

"Oh." She sits back down. "God, really?" She puts her hands to her mouth and looks down. When she looks back up she takes his hands. "Mouse, hun. I'm *so* sorry."

Mouse shakes his head, looks around. His pad is in his shirt pocket, on the ground. He takes a deep breath. "N—not." He swallows, tries to remember talking to Ginnie in the hallway. "Not just you."

Her eyebrows shoot up in surprise. "I'll get your pad."

He shakes his head. "Practice," he says. "I—I want to practice."

He closes his eyes, doesn't look at anything, doesn't think about anything but the shape of the words. "You were just," he reaches for words, puts them in order—a catalyst? He thinks for a moment. "Trigger. There's also—" Anna? "—Izzy." It's getting more and more complicated. What does June know about Anna, how can he explain without explaining her? He sighs, shakes his head. "Pad."

June squeezes his hand and puts the pad into the other.

God, that's even slower than writing.

She laughs, hands him back his shirt. "You need to know that Greg and I, we never meant to make things hard for you or Kai."

Mouse nods. *It was bound to happen. I think things will be better now.*

She snorts and takes a sip of her coffee. "Hurr. Man fight. Man bond with other man. Smash. Now brothers."

Mouse chuckles. *Something like that.*

"What about the girl?" June raises an eyebrow, mouth hidden behind her coffee cup.

That's more complicated.

June nods. "Is that her?"

Mouse frowns. Is what—oh. She's looking at the marks on his arm.

Wait, what?

"Your arm," she says. "The incunary."

Mouse's poker face evaporates.

June sighs. "Give me your arm." He does as he's told, and she inspects the markings, trying not to press on any bruises. "Turn," she says, and he swivels in the chair. When he turns back she's squinting at him, pursing her lips. "Well, call her down."

Mouse starts writing *What do you mean?* but he's interrupted.

"She's in your room. Gosh, kiddo. I mean really. I'm not blind. Or deaf."

Mouse blushes, silently calls for Anna to come down from the room, where she's been hiding since the fight. He repeats himself when she insists that it's a terrible idea. The words "She knows *everything*" carried with them. Anna creeps down the stairs and peeks into the kitchen.

June smiles at her. "Oh, it's *you*."

Anna walks in and sits down at the table, too.

"I thought it was going to be the pretty one with the purple hair."

"Hey she's—" he stops before he can say 'pretty, too'. They both blush.

June stands up. "Oh my god, you two are too cute." She finishes her coffee and walks over to get a refill. "I remember my first familiar." She looks over her shoulder. "Of course I didn't *incarnate him*. Sometimes I wonder. Fighting over girls. Fighting over me? You're just like—" She sits back down, shakes her head. "Well anyway, I was hoping you wouldn't have a gift for it, but I guess *that's* out the window."

Mouse doesn't know what to say. Or rather, he doesn't know what to say *first*. How does she know about all of this? What does she mean by a gift? *Her* first familiar? Her *first* familiar? Anna looks at him and says, "Calm down, I'll ask." Mouse closes his eyes and nods.

"Actually, before you do, can I ask a few things? He's still in a heap of trouble for fighting, and I did promise the principal I'd give him a good talking-to." June grins over her coffee. Anna stays silent.

"Right, so, 'Izzy.'" She takes a sip. "Not your real name. Who were you before you croaked?"

Anna's visibly taken aback.

"You're a familiar. Once upon a time you were alive. Was it recently?"

"Um, yes. I'm Kai's sister. I'm Anna."

June's eyes widen. "The plot thickens!"

Anna nods. "I think Kai knows now."

"God. Well. Don't tell your father and I won't. Greg's a lovely man, really kind, nice smile, pretty eyes, *great* shoulders..." She coughs and clears her throat. "But he's not ready for this."

Anna turns to Mouse. "Please stop your mom from talking about my dad like that. It's weirding me out."

June laughs and Mouse just sighs.

"So who taught you?" June says. "I didn't know there were any of us in town until the break-in."

Mouse shrugs. "Nobody, really," Anna says for him. "We didn't really know there *was* an 'Any of us'."

June frowns. "Nobody taught you how to see them?"

Mouse shakes his head.

"Or how to make a pact?"

"It was an accident."

She rubs the bridge of her nose. "What about the incarnating?"

"Priest," Anna says. "At least that's what we called him. He tried to show Mouse how to summon me, but this happened instead."

June goes quiet.

"This priest—"

"We think it's his name."

She purses her lips. "It's not a name, it's a callsign. What did he look like? Did he have an eyepatch?"

Mouse shakes his head. "But he did have a damaged eye," Anna says.

June grits her teeth. "Where is he now?"

Anna shakes her head. "He skipped town after Mouse, uh, 'Incarnated' me."

"And the incarnation was supposed to be a simple summoning."

"If that's what you call it."

"Jesus, Mouse."

Mouse looks down. "Sorry," he whispers.

She grabs his hands again. "Hey. You've got nothing to be sorry for, okay? You're my son. If you didn't know about this stuff, it's because I thought I could hide you from it. I'm the one who should be sorry."

Mouse nods.

"But Jesus, kiddo. No wonder the Trust came for you. They probably think you're fit to be the next Hermes after that stunt. Here I thought they were after me." She stands up and starts pacing. "God damn it, I told them I was retired. That alone should make you off limits."

They sit in silence while June stands there in the kitchen, fuming into her coffee cup. Somehow being angry makes her look even younger. She takes a breath.

"I guess I'd better tell you all of it. Can I get you a coffee, Anna? Tea? This is going to take a little while."

鼠

"If you want it told right we should probably just call up your grand-dad. He's always been a better storyteller, but I'll do the best I can.

"Thousands of years ago, there was this great knowledge that was handed down to humanity. Back then we were like little kids. We weren't entirely helpless, the fact that we'd gotten as far as we had—no longer just finding our food but growing it on purpose, beginning to build towns, even trading with each other when some of us had more and some of us had less—it showed we could work together. Things were looking up, at least to those looking down on us from above.

"And so the heavens sent us someone, someone just a little more than human, someone who had knowledge of the way the universe worked. He told us a universal truth, the only universal truth—*as above, so below*. It was simple—the way the heavens worked was the way the Earth worked, the way our minds worked was the way our hearts worked. Just by looking closely, we could see how to do things that had seemed impossible before.

"We learned faster after that.

"We made charcoal to heat our fires hotter, we stopped using stone tools in favor of metal—first bronze, then steel. We remade the world to suit us—redirected rivers, built towers into the sky. We mastered writing and inscribed our oldest stories on clay, then reeds, then animal skins and paper. We remembered the hard times, the di-sasters, and turned them into myths—floods, droughts, famines. We told stories of the one who had brought us this knowledge, over and over, until eventually we'd forgotten his name. Those who remem-ber—that's where the Trust gets its name—'Those entrusted with the memory'—they call him Hermes, but that's probably not it either.

"But you've seen people, we're not really good with self-control. 'Humans are quick and clever, but rarely wise.' That's what your granddad says. Once we had the ability to rule over one another, we made ourselves kings and tyrants, waged wars against each other, made our steel into weapons, our writing into unjust laws, we built walls that divided us from each other, instead of bridges that could have brought us together. And at the same time, there was rebellion in the heavens. They were fighting about us.

"It was a war between those who wanted to go back to zero, to erase humanity like bugs from a garden, wash us away, embarrassed at their mistake, and those who were sure that doing so would only make things worse. They'd realized that their own division was due to the division they'd caused, because their greatest teaching worked the same in reverse—as below, so above. They eventually understood that if they wiped us out, something similar would happen to them.

"And so they agreed to embrace division, and they sent more and more bearers of wisdom to the Earth. If you want to balance a set of scales you need to break up the uneven bits and redistribute them. They sent us truth after truth until it couldn't be said anymore that one group was right and another was wrong, until everyone had their own truth and could be happy with it by themselves, and for the most part live in peace. And up in the heavens they forgot themselves like we did on Earth. And we forgot the heavens, too.

"But a few up there still remembered what had been sacrificed to build the new balance, and so they sent a messenger to teach some of us how to take care of it, to stop things from going back to the terrible way things were. He showed them that there were still ways of seeing, ways of acting on things that were beyond what everyone had thought before. His name was Simon, too.

"And that was how the Trust got started. Some had more talent than others, but they were all able to do things that defied common explanation. People called them different things over the centuries— witch, magus, sorcerer—but they weren't really any of those. They were just people using another kind of knowledge that they'd been entrusted with, along with warnings about what had happened the last time humans had been given new knowledge.

"And so we've interfered over the years. Choosing kings and overthrowing governments, holding back scientific advancement and speeding it up. Trying our best to preserve the balance that keeps heaven and earth in one piece. And let me tell you, the more we learn, the harder that gets.

"I don't think they ever thought we'd make it this far."

June leans back in her seat and takes a sip from her mug.

"Balancing things is only ever temporary. Every solution just buys time until the next problem. But in the hundred generations since we started, people have lived and died and been happy—happier than they would've been if we hadn't been trying to keep things in order. Your granddad once said he thought we'd be out of a job in 1962 when both sides nearly bombed the hell out of each other over Cuba. He was there, you know, when everyone had their fingers on the big red nuclear buttons. He said the real thing of it was, at that point, that there was nothing we could do. The world didn't end that night, not because of us, but because regular, ordinary humans decided it wouldn't."

She puts her mug down, staring off into the past. "That's why he retired, why he didn't want me to ever join up. But I was a little brat with more ability than I knew what to do with. I was drafted young—younger than you—as part of the Cold War cleanup, but things got a little out of hand..." She trails off. "And now I'm retired, too. I thought they'd come to bring me back, but I'm guessing now they came to recruit you."

Mouse and Anna look at each other, then back to June. Anna speaks.

"Did Mouse's father know, about all of this?"

June sighs. "I told him."

The unspoken part of her response hangs heavy in the air.

"Oh."

"There was a lot about me he didn't know," she laughs sadly, "including how young I was." She looks away again, seeing a different history, one that can't be related to anyone through words. "He was gone before he even knew I was pregnant. I tried to tell him later, but he never wrote back. Never answered any calls."

"I thought Mouse's dad was some ambassador."

"Embassy worker, yeah. Still Cold War cleanup, but the more official kind. Last I heard, he was in Kazakhstan cutting ribbons on rocket launches. I try not to look him up, but the Internet's right there, you know?"

They sit there in silence, trying to process it all.

June puts her head down on the table and groans. "Some days I wish I hadn't given up smoking."

Before Mouse can think of anything to say to June, there's a knock at the door and she hauls herself to her feet to go answer it. There's a little conversation at the door and Mouse catches a "No no, come in." A few seconds later she returns to the kitchen followed by both Bliss and a hesitant and raccoon-eyed Kai. Anna stands up and everyone in the room freezes, except for June, who walks to the fridge.

If someone had said something—anything, really—they could have talked about it right there in the kitchen. Nobody does, though, and so no one knows how to start.

June offers drinks to the newcomers, her nurse's calm and casual smile smoothing the corners of the tension in the room, but still no one knows how to act. She sighs. "Let's all go sit in the living room then." She looks at them all not moving. "Go on. I'll bring in drinks and snacks. There aren't enough seats in here and we might as well be comfortable." Bliss pushes Kai out of the kitchen and stays behind to help, and a moment later Anna and Mouse wander into the hall.

Kai's already in the living room waiting. As Anna's about to go in, Mouse thinks maybe she'd like to talk to Kai alone and hangs back, but she turns to face him and shakes her head. It's going to be tough. She leans forward and rests her forehead on Mouse's chest. He can't think of anything to do, so he ruffles her hair. She sighs, and walks into the room, with Mouse following close behind her.

Lying in bed that night, sore in every position he can get into, their long conversation replays itself in Mouse's mind. What Kai had found the hardest thing to deal with had been not recognizing his own sister. Beyond the fact that Anna was somehow back from the dead, beyond the fact that Mouse was from some kind of ancient line of magic users, beyond the fact that there was a secret global organization pulling the strings to try to keep peace and balance in the world, it was that one lack of personal recognition that had hit him the hardest. He hadn't been able to see Anna even when she'd been right in front of him.

He'd also expressed regret about beating Mouse to a pulp, which had been appreciated.

But the whole time, even now lying in bed, Mouse had been thinking about family.

Kai had gotten his sister back, and now they could talk together about how June and Greg are a real thing that's really happening. There's something about experiencing the fact that adults go on dates that's more revealing than just knowing it. That parents and children aren't so different as they'd thought. It's unnerving.

And the thing with Mouse's father. June *never* mentions him, and there she'd been just sitting at the table and saying she randomly Googles him from time to time. And the Trust, and June's and his granddad's work for them, traveling all over the world, and then retiring to a basically normal life, all before his life had even started. It had hit him all at once, sitting there in the living room while Anna and Kai and Bliss had talked about magic and ghosts and history, while June had been making a fresh pot of coffee and dropping a plate of cookies and snacks and just being her regular self...there's so much. So much life lived, so much beneath the surface, so many stories behind everything he knows that he can't even think of the questions to ask. He'd just wanted to say, "Tell me everything I don't know. Tell me all the stories. Tell me what it was like. Tell me who you are." If she could have told, if he could have asked, "Tell me who I am."

But instead, he hadn't said a word.

Answers are easy, he thinks, it's the questions that are hard.

Anna has gone back to Bliss's house, Kai has gone back home, and as Mouse lies there, he can still hear June wandering about in the kitchen, cleaning and tidying things late into the night. It's the kind of thing she does before a move, or before switching jobs, and Mouse considers trying to go help. But he doesn't know what he'd say, and even though he's uncomfortable from the bruises he's too tired to get up.

Downstairs, June is going through another pile of boxes, setting some aside, putting the contents of others away. When she comes across a box labeled *just in case* she stops, pulls it open. It's full of knick-knacks and curiosities, and at the bottom are some black clothes. June traces her fingers over the heavy seams, then puts them aside. She pulls out a stack of blank playing cards and a old leather-bound notebook, and puts the rest under the sink.

Upstairs, Mouse dreams of things he's never seen—of his family's past, of the silent movements behind great events, of rocket launches on the Kazakh steppes, and the faceless man his mother once loved. The morning will come too soon.

"Rise and shine, honey."

Mouse awakens to the sight of June leaning over his bed. It's still dark out, and being the first day of the winter break he has no idea why he's suddenly, mercilessly awake. He sits up and looks at her. She's dressed in the same military-esque fatigues worn by Helene and the others.

She tosses him an old notebook, wrapped in brown leather. The cover is blank, and the inside is filled with handwritten diagrams, drawings, and notes in his mother's hand.

"Starting today I'm going to teach you all the things I should have taught you years ago." She grimaces. "If they're going to try to pull that recruitment crap on you, I want you to be able to at least give them a black eye for their trouble."

She motions for him to follow her downstairs, and he groggily obliges, padding barefoot down the stairs in a white tee-shirt and plaid pants, carrying the old notebook in both hands.

In the kitchen, June has put a mug out on the table. "Lesson one," she says. "Boil some water for tea."

Mouse walks over to the kettle and she stops him, rotates him by the shoulders, and puts him in front of the mug. It has water in it, but it's cold.

"It's basic alchemy. The root of the tree is fire. Here." She hands him a note card with something drawn on it. "Memorize it."

Mouse looks at the card, then at her stern expression, finding himself wondering who this woman is, and what she's done with June.

The drawing on the card looks like a triangle with some circles and other triangles inside it. An equilateral triangle inside a circle, a circle at the middle of each side with a triangle inside each one of those, and circles with triangles at each of those sides, reducing forever and ever until they're just little clouds of points.

It's a fractal.

It's also the first picture in the book.

"The picture on the card isn't as important as the way it looks in your head," she says. "But for now, just put the mug in the middle of it."

Mouse does as he's told.

"Now I want you to focus on moving heat around. The basic principle of the Knowledge is something called correlative exchange. Basically, if you're going to put heat somewhere, you have to take it from somewhere else, or give something in exchange to create new heat. You get what I mean?"

Mouse's eyes light up and he pulls out his pad. June keeps talking as he writes.

"This is something you're going to need to do without thinking about it, so from today on, you're going to do this half-asleep for the first fifteen minutes you're awake—without any coffee or food—until you can boil a cup of water in your sleep."

Mouse pretends he hasn't heard that bit and hands her the note. *After I incarnated Anna, Priest asked me "what did you pay?" Is that the same thing?*

"Yeeahh..." She stops and thinks, with head tilted to one side. "And also no?"

Mouse almost chuckles with relief at the way her eyebrows are knitting together, trying to find the words to explain. This is the June he knows. She looks up and to the side, thinking.

"To conjure a familiar, you can give it some of your image—it doesn't take much. But incarnation..." She shakes her head and tries for serious again. "The principle still applies, but I don't know *where* you got the power for that."

Mouse shrugs. He doesn't know either.

"Anyway we're not going to do any of that shortcut crap that Leonard—that *Priest*, sorry—was trying to get you to do." She rolls her eyes as she says his callsign. "None of that incantation stuff. If you're as liable to incarnate your familiar as summon her, we're going to have to start with baby steps. So—" she smiles "—boil the water."

Mouse sighs, and focuses on the drawing. It feels more familiar the longer he stares at it, but he has no idea what to do with it. He looks back at June.

"Explore the image in your head. Think about the difference between what makes something hot and what makes something cold. Remember, heat's just a kind of movement. Try to shift some of the heat from the room into the mug."

She turns and puts the coffee maker on.

"Take your time and think about it. It'll be here tomorrow, too."

Mouse stares at it for ten whole minutes, thinking about heat and movement. Finally, he thinks he can imagine some of the heat of the room finding its way into the water. He stares at it and focuses, imagining a ring of movement closing in toward the mug from all sides.

With a loud *ping!* the mug jumps six inches into the air, then lands back on the table with a solid crack, spilling its contents onto Mouse's lap and the floor.

He jumps up and June stifles a giggle. She walks over with a towel, righting the miraculously intact mug and soaking up the still-cold water. Mouse looks a little embarrassed and she smiles as she tousles his bed-head hair. "A little less literally next time, okay?"

Mouse nods as June takes the mug and refills it, putting it in front of him. But after five minutes, he can't come up with a different way of thinking about it. "Time's up for today," she says, and puts a finger on the edge of the mug. Mouse almost thinks he feels the tiniest shift in the temperature of the air, and the water starts to boil.

He blinks.

June smiles at him. "Just wanted to let you know it wasn't a trick. Your granddad made me do this every day for a year."

Wow, Mouse thinks, Granddad was a hardass.

"Right," she says, dropping a tea bag in the boiling water. "Have some tea and wake up, then grab your gym clothes and an orange to eat on the way. We're going out for a bit."

鼠

In Bliss's brother's room, Anna lurches into consciousness with a start and grabs her clothes. She doesn't even stop to wake Bliss. The birds are starting to sing the morning into being as she bolts out of the house.

Out in the streets, she's skipping from lamppost to lamppost, navigating her way across the town. She passes his apartment, but she's drawn further. He's not at home, she thinks. Where is he?

She follows the feeling of him past town and to the bridge over the river. He's in pain; why? He's not panicking. The closer she gets the more curious she becomes. Across the river she recognizes where she's going—the hospital.

Down the street, through the parking lot, a side door with a passcode. She flickers past it and into the hall. One door, two doors, a left turn.

She bursts in just in time to see Mouse hit the blue floor padding with a loud slap, having been thrown halfway across the room. She dives in and grabs him, throws up her hands and prepares herself to fight. Then stops, confused.

"June?"

鼠

There's a fitness center that the hospital staff have access to, and at this time of day—Mouse notices with horror that it's only just turned five-thirty in the morning—no one uses it. Anna sits on a bench at the side, eating an orange while she watches June throwing her son around. She winces when he hits the ground with a louder thump than usual.

"Hey, be careful how you land, Nezumi." She talks around a mouthful of orange. "I felt that one."

He gets up and walks over, then takes a piece of fruit out of her hand and eats it wordlessly before walking back to be thrown again. If he's going to taste the orange, he might as well eat some of it, he thinks.

"Well, fine then," Anna says, mock pouting.

June throws him again. "No, you have to roll into the landing, hun." He looks up, then lies back down and holds up his hand.

"Five minutes," June says, walking over to Anna. "Sorry again for getting you up. All the way across town and you still felt it?"

"I'll ignore it next time," she says, chewing. "So you're going to beef him up before he gets his butt handed to him again?"

"He can't just rely on you all the time."

Anna grins. "Sure he can. Mouse rebuilt me pretty tough."

June raises her eyebrows and calls out to Mouse without looking away from Anna. "Hun, take a seat over here. Your familiar and I are going to have a round." She looks down. "Shoes off, though."

Anna shrugs. She's had to borrow clothes from Bliss, but everything she incarnated with—the sun dress, hairband, and shoes—aren't so much clothing as a part of her. She squints at the shoes and they vanish. "Better?"

June nods, and they take their positions. Anna bows. She's wearing jeans and an old black tee-shirt with a glittery motorcycle helmet on it, her long silvery hair tied back in a ponytail. June is in her all-blacks. She bows, too.

Anna runs at her.

June seems only to make a slight gesture, and Anna lands abruptly on her side behind her, looking surprised. Mouse blinks to make sure he didn't miss something.

Anna gets up and tries again.

June's arm comes up, and she swivels, barely touching her assailant, allowing Anna's own weight to carry her into a heap on the floor.

"There's no rush," June says. "Think before you attack."

Anna scowls. This time she launches herself again, but a split second before arriving at her opponent, she vanishes and reappears behind her. Without looking, June ducks and spins, foot out, and Anna backflips away just in time to avoid being tripped.

"Better!" June says, smiling. "Again!"

Anna flies at her, flashing from side to side in blocked attack after blocked attack. It's only when she goes in for a roundhouse from the left that at once becomes a roundhouse from behind that June isn't quite fast enough and staggers two steps to the side. Anna knows well enough to stop at this point.

June smiles. "You've got potential. Did you train?"

Anna finds she's exhausted, and she leans forward. "A little. When I could." She remembers childhood karate lessons with Kai before she got too sick to go, and shakes her head to clear the memory.

"You've got good form," June nods over at Mouse, "you could learn a thing or two from this one."

Mouse smiles wryly.

"But you both need to work on your stamina. And remember that it's not enough to be able to take down a normal human." She puts an arm up and does a strange circular motion above her. Mouse feels something shift in the air. "Try again. Just a kick. Not too hard."

Anna frowns, prepares a kick and lets it loose.

The moment her foot should make contact with June it stops like it's hit a brick wall. Anna's foot bounces back and she staggers and falls, staring at a small, spinning disc of shapes and sigils that hangs in the air.

June waves her hand and drops the barrier before helping Anna up. "The redirection of force is a pretty simple matter, if you know what you're doing." She looks over at Mouse. "Did you feel it when I did that?"

Mouse is rubbing his ankle, but that's not what she means. It's the feeling of static in the air, a shifting haze like the shimmer above the asphalt on a hot day. He nods.

"You'll need to warn her if you feel anything like that. These people aren't above dirty tricks and it's your job to spot them." She looks back at Anna. "We're going to be doing this daily from now on. You should join us."

Anna looks at Mouse, still purple in places from his fight with Kai, and nods.

"Right, that's it for today, kids, I've got a shift in fifteen minutes. Go home and have a shower. If you get bored, try to boil some water."

Mouse sighs, but nods. It's going to be a long winter.

鼠

On the 28th of January, he and June share a birthday—he turns sixteen, and she turns, "None of your business." She lets him sleep until
six before putting him through his paces. Just once in the past week
he's managed to make the water steam a little, which he puts down
to a fortuitously-timed sneeze while concentrating, but which also
caused the mug to shatter about ten seconds later.

Anna's not faring too much better, but for different reasons.

She and Mouse are standing outside her old place, large flakes
of snow drifting out of the grey-white sky. There's a crash and a loud
round of cheers and laughter from beyond the door.

Last ones to the party, Mouse thinks over to his familiar.

"I know." Anna looks at her feet. They're all celebrating together
this year. Greg's birthday was apparently the week before, so he and
Kai and June and Mouse and Bliss are all there. Anna's coming as
Izzy, even though everyone but Greg knows who she is. She's managed to avoid him so far, but obviously that can't last. It's going to be
unnerving, seeing him again, but she thinks she can handle it. "I'll
be okay." She looks at Mouse, thinking about how far they've come
already. "Thanks."

He nods, sending her way whatever reassuring vibes he can.

They walk in and everyone's smiling and laughing. There's a well-
decked tree still standing in the corner, and Kai is scrubbing something sticky off the linoleum floor.

"Come in, come in!" Greg gets up to let them in. "Happy birthday,
Mouse. And you must be Izzy, come in!" He smiles a warm and gentle smile. He looks older than she remembers, and Mouse feels her
suddenly fighting back tears. He's got wrinkles around his eyes and
a little more stubble, but he looks happy in a way he never did during
the last years of Anna's life.

"Hi," Anna says.

The wave of emotion nearly flattens Mouse, but he takes it all in,
nods a quick hello, and then excuses himself, making motions that
he's forgotten something and will be right back.

He dives out the door, and, while Anna smiles and says hello all around, back in the apartment Mouse closes the front door and leans back against it. Hot tears stream down his face and he crumples down to the floor.

After a few minutes, Anna calms down and it passes, and he gets up and washes his face in the kitchen sink before looking around. What can he say he went back for?

A sudden thump from the floor above draws him from the cupboard where he's found a bottle of fizzy wine June had left over from New Year's. Someone's upstairs. Someone's in his room.

He flips the bottle around, and, brandishing it like a club, creeps up the stairs. The light is off in his bedroom, and the door is closed. Just the way he left it. But there's a scraping sound and another muffled thump from within, and he creeps closer.

There's a split second where he wonders what the hell he's doing, going in by himself, bottle for a billy club, before he throws the door open and flips on the switch, flooding the room with light.

The window is open, the screen down on the floor, and little wet animal footprints are everywhere. The room looks like a tornado hit it.

The footprints lead from the window to the door, then back to the window, then start to fade out as they trace around the room. They go to the closet, then back to the window a third time, then to the bed, and end, faint, in a pile of sheets and laundry in the corner of the room, which Mouse has a sinking feeling he didn't leave that way. The sheets are off his bed.

He creeps closer, and, holding up the wine bottle with one hand, and very slowly pulls the top sheet back.

A raccoon?

In the little pile of sheets, curled up and passed out, is something very like a raccoon—maybe a little smaller and more rusty-colored than he'd expected. But then, he's never actually seen a raccoon up this close before. Its whiskers are twitching in its sleep, and it looks like it hurt its paw breaking in.

He realizes he's still holding the bottle aloft and puts it down. He sighs, looking down. Why now? He leaves the room and comes back with a large plastic tub—a huge blue one they use for the Christmas decorations that are still set out. He lines it with old towels and punches some holes in the lid while mentally apologizing to June. Now the fun part.

He very carefully pets the raccoon's nose with one finger.

No response.

He shakes the pile a little.

Nothing.

Reassured, he picks up his new houseguest and places it gently into the tub. It's still asleep, but it's definitely breathing. He shakes his head. It looks tiny in its new surroundings. He grabs a bandage from the bathroom and sticks it on its paw, then pulls a corner of the towel over it like a blanket. He adds a little bowl of water in case it gets thirsty before putting on the lid and dropping a couple of textbooks on top just in case.

Only then does he close the window and put the screen back up, and spend a minute cleaning up the footprints. He'll deal with the rest later.

He gets the feeling, from Anna, no doubt, that he's being missed. He looks at his phone—8:15. He's been gone for half an hour. Crap. He grabs the bottle and closes the door to his bedroom before running out the front door.

鼠

"You were gone a while," June says. "Everything all right?"

Mouse nods, holds up the bottle of bubbly apologetically.

June shakes her head. "We were just about to have some dinner."

He sits down and Anna leans over, whispering. "What was that all about?"

Mouse shakes his head. He'll explain later. She wouldn't believe it anyway. He doesn't believe it. Raccoon burglar.

Anna catches snippets—at this distance they can exchange words without even meaning to. At 'raccoon burglar' she raises an eyebrow, but doesn't say anything.

After they eat, things settle down a little. As a pretense to slip away from the adults for a while, Kai offers to give Anna and Mouse a tour, since they've never been over. Bliss comes along, too. The apartment is laid out basically the same as Mouse's, he realizes, but it's a little wider, the surfaces are all newer, and the decor is, well, better.

At the top of the stairs they hang a left and crash in Kai's room for a bit.

"I feel bad leaving them alone down there, but I kinda don't, too," Kai says. The room is a little bigger than Mouse's and hardly looks lived in. The word spartan comes to mind. He flops down on the bed. "Part of me thinks they'll appreciate it," he sighs. "And the same part of me wants to go back downstairs and stop them from appreciating it."

Anna sits on the bed next to her brother.

"So the hair's pretty cool," he says, holding up a bit of it.

She swipes it back out of his hands, then holds it up and stares at it. "I know, right? Mouse likes it." She grins at him and Mouse gets looks from the other two. Mouse thinks back to what Ginnie was saying. She didn't think that Bliss and Anna...? He waves away the thought but it lingers in the background. He looks at Anna's smiling face framed by silvery hair, and he's got to admit, he does like it. Anna senses this and smiles more.

"Well, you chose it," she says. "Right?"

Mouse isn't sure he did, or at least, isn't sure that the him that's around right now did. Maybe he did. He gets a chill whenever he thinks too hard about the moment when he incarnated Anna. He's really starting to feel like it's not just individual things he can't remember about the incident, but a whole other him. A smarter, more powerful him. A colder one. He's been having the dream more and more often these last few weeks. He remembers Priest's question and wonders himself. What *did* he pay?

At the question, Mouse shrugs, and Anna's smile twists into a pout. She bounces up from the bed and jabs him in the side before walking out of the room, muttering "Baka" under her breath. He follows her, leaving Bliss and Kai alone in his room, both feeling left out by the amount of silent communication the other pair seems to possess.

On the landing, Anna stops outside a closed door. In Mouse's apartment, it'd be his own room, but here the door has a little name-plate on it: Anna. She opens it slowly and they go in. A peal of laughter erupts from June downstairs as Greg says something funny. Mouse watches as Anna walks around her old room.

Something catches her eye on the bedside table and she picks it up and walks over to Mouse. It's a sea-green barrette with a little sil-ver flower, like the one he first saw her with.

"Here," she says, reaching up and pinning his bangs out of his face with it, then grinning at the results. "Perfect. Now we match."

"Looks good on you," Kai says, deadpan. He and Bliss are standing in the door. Mouse blushes and pulls it out of his hair, shoving it in his pocket. Anna pouts a little, then looks around the room a little more.

"You didn't change anything," she says, picking up an old picture of herself with Kai and their parents. In it, she's smaller, more frail. She has dark rings under her eyes and she's hanging over Kai's back like he's giving her a piggyback ride. They look happy.

"A few things," Kai replies. "Got rid of the medical stuff. Put away some of your figurines. Tidied up a bit."

Put away some of her figurines? Mouse holds back a feeling of surprise as he realizes that there are dozens of anime figurines on every horizontal surface. There are posters on the wall over the bed with names like Supercell and Egoist emblazoned across them. The lamp on the bedside table is in the shape of a Japanese lantern. There are dozens of light novels and DVD box sets on shelves, and a hand-ful of stuffed Totoros and other fantastic beasts on the bed. A couple of bokken lean up against the wall in the corner by the door. Mouse looks at the complete box set of Ouran High School Host Club and raises his eyebrows at her, trying not to think of the word *weeaboo*.

Her face visibly colors. "It was...I was going through a phase..."

"Banana," Kai says offhand, grabbing one of the wooden swords and poking at an oversized Totoro on the bed.

Mouse gives him a questioning look.

"Yellow on the outside, but totally white on the inside?"

"*You're* the banana, *jerk*," Anna retorts, unskillfully. "I was just trying to reclaim some of our heritage."

"This—" he holds up a big-eyed little doll wearing a black and white maid's outfit "—is not our heritage."

"Yeah, well, at least I was trying."

He picks up a plush, tiger-striped fox-thing from the bed and gives it a squeeze. "You were trying way too hard." He tosses it over to Anna. "There are easier ways you know, like maybe reading a book about Japan or something."

She sticks her tongue out and hands the plush to Mouse. "This is Teto."

He takes it from her and stares at it for a little while, visibly unsure of what to do with it. Bliss laughs and takes it from his hands.

"He's adorable," she says.

Anna picks up another one—one that looks a little like a raccoon. "And this is Yasaburou. He's a tanuki." She grins.

Kai rolls his eyes as Mouse almost jumps in recognition. "Tanuki!" He says, out loud.

The other three stare at him. He tries to explain, but stumbles over his words and resorts to writing it out on a note.

What took me so long earlier. I thought it was a raccoon but it wasn't. It's one of these.

"Wait, wait." Bliss says, incredulous. "You're saying you saw a tanuki?"

Not saw. Found. In the house.

"Raccoon burglar? Is *that* what you meant by that?"

Kai looks at Anna with the same look he was just giving Mouse. "Did you guys sneak some wine when I wasn't looking?"

Anna scowls. Mouse responds.

It's in my room. In a tub. I put holes in the lid.

Anna grabs his hand and walks him down the stairs before Kai or Bliss can say anything. Bliss frowns and follows last.

Kai yells through to the living room as they pull on their shoes. "Back in a minute!" And they fly out the door.

Climbing the stairs to Mouse's room, he tries to calm them down, because it might still be sleeping. He opens the door quietly and peers in.

The textbooks are on the floor, the lid is open, and, in place of the small, furry animal in a tub, there's now a human asleep on his bed, hand cradled at her side, long dark hair spilling over the side of the mattress, the quilt pulled half over her. Mouse walks over and looks down at his guest.

It's Helene.

She's hurt.

Also—naked.

She half-opens her eyes and squints up at him, more exhausted than embarrassed.

"You said I was welcome at your side." She half smiles, a twinkle of mischief hidden at the corners of her eyes. "Thought I might take you up on the offer."

鼠

Kai and Mouse are sitting at the top of the stairs.

The girls are still in the room, Bliss wrapping Helene's hand with bandages and getting her dressed in some clothes stolen from June's closet while Anna stands guard. After they'd all stood there in shock for a moment, Mouse had noticed that she was bleeding around a now very small-looking bandage. The girls hadn't taken well to the way Mouse and Kai were staring at their quilt-clad guest—and at the way she was smirking back—and had shooed them out into the hallway.

"Naked girl in your bed, man."

Kai's examining the bokken he took from Anna's room.

Mouse nods.

"I mean, pretty hot naked girl in your bed."

Mouse scribbles on his pad.

Yeah. Still not as cool as I'd hoped.

"Still better than a tanuki."

Mouse nods, considering.

Never been attacked in the middle of the night by a tanuki though.

"Point."

They sit there for another few moments.

Kai twirls the wooden sword on its point.

"How old you think she is?"

Mouse thinks. He remembers how familiar it felt talking to her. *Helene.* Just thinking about it he can feel the threads around the cold blank spaces in his head beginning to fray. Like an itch he can't help but scratch, he starts to pull on a thread, and a chill runs through him. He thinks of the way the words flowed up from inside him when he tried to summon Anna, that feeling of remembering something forgotten when he shocked Vallis. The alien feeling of something old.

鼠

He closes his eyes for only a second and he's back in the dream, without even falling asleep this time. He's alone in the street, and Kai, the stairs, his apartment, are all blown away like so much dust. This feels real—as real as the world—but looks abstracted, like seeing through a stained-glass window, or a bug's faceted eye.

The rain pelts down in the dark, and the shapes beyond the streetlamp's cone of orange light writhe. He can feel them more than see them—reptilian, cephalopodic, insectile. Legs and carapaces and scales and eyes. But in the dark there's something familiar, too. A cold, like ice, that he feels in his chest.

"You can't fight what you can't see," comes a voice, right at the edge of the night.

He walks toward it, toward the ink-black curtain where the rain falls from nowhere into the light.

"But are you prepared to fight at all?"

Something moves beyond the wall, something serpentine, enormous in its silence, and Mouse jumps back. The voice is behind him now.

"The light provides only the illusion of safety. It provides you with ignorance, the ability to ignore them."

As if on cue, a dark shape, a *thing*, like a wingless dragonfly in shades of midnight, flying despite its winglessness, darts through the light and back out again into invisibility, tracing a trail of droplets, like black oily dew, hanging in the air where it flew. Mouse reaches out and touches one without thinking.

Nausea. Despair. Terror. Rage. They eat away at his senses, try to swallow him up. The voice brings him back with a snap.

"All the subtleties of a fine wine," says the voice, "if you could grow vines on nothing but pestilence and human misery." The voice shifts direction again, footsteps circling on cobblestones, and Mouse spins to follow. "They wait at the edges. They feed on our diseases and horrors. They are as old as humanity itself."

A pair of eyes shine in the darkness, not quite human, but not far off.

"They have a terrible patience. They wait for the right moment to strike."

Mouse retreats to the center of the light, avoids the droplets that pass by, weightless.

"And so, therefore, do we."

There's a pause, and Mouse feels cold eyes on him from outside. The voice is behind him. Not in the darkness, but in the light. If he turned, he could see it, but he can't.

"You and I."

The voice seems suddenly older, more tired.

"And I'm sorry, but that moment is now."

A spike of pain lances through his chest, colder than any of the times before, but more alive, iced lightning arcing through his chest. A single wordless command unbinds the thing inside him, and he's thrown out of the dream in a cold sweat.

鼠

"How old do you think she is?" Kai's asking. Didn't this just happen? The world seems stilted, rippled, warped.

The pain in his chest carries through from the dream, numbing as it spreads, as it seeps out from within him, a vast intelligence. A knowledge.

Same as me, he thinks.

Older than she looks, he writes.

Kai gives him a strange look and then the door opens and their guest emerges, flanked by Anna and Bliss. Kai stands, but Mouse remains sitting, looking away. The marionette threads are already tightening inside him. He can feel the chill of the dark like it's a living thing. He sees the things moving beyond the streetlamp coming closer. Helene interrupts his thoughts.

"You can call off your dogs, Diviner. I'm no danger to you."

Mouse can feel Anna restraining herself and he sends her a mental thank you, but doesn't turn to face her. He closes his eyes. The growing cold within him contains so much knowledge. Not just the power to incarnate Anna or to shock an assailant, but memories, calculations, histories, futures. The streetlamp in his dream is flickering off, but the world isn't getting darker. His eyes are adjusting to the night and he feels like he can see a wide and teeming world coming into view.

In the distance, at the back of his skull, there's a rising panic building, a vestige of small self-preservation calling for pause, but it's being smothered—even as it builds—by the solid, crushing weight of the glacial intelligence bearing down on him from somewhere Other.

"Why are you here, Helene?" he says aloud. Slowly, clearly, but aloud.

He gets a feeling of unease from Anna, and wonders just how alien the sound of his voice must be, but he continues.

"You should know," she says.

He knows in the cold, creeping into his bones, in the recesses of his mind, that there's something missing from the equation, something else to explain why she's here. He feels like he's waking up, like he's stretching his mind after a long slumber. He stands positioned between the key players, sees the board as it's laid out. Pieces falling into place.

"A preemptive strike," he says.

"A test of our defenses," she says.

He can feel her guarded bravado drop a notch, something softens with a judgment passed. What had she called the rhinoceros that served as her familiar?

"Where's Argo?" he asks. That was it. "And your talkative friend?" He knows the man's name is Vallis.

"Scattered. Argo's off reassembling himself. And Vallis is on cleanup duty."

"They're not planning on joining you here, I hope."

He feels detached from his tongue, the cold in his chest spreading into his head like icicles in time-lapse, building a frozen wall between him and the world, pushing him into the background.

"Not yet."

"Good." His mouth is moving without him. All of him is moving on its own.

No, not on its own. It's him doing it, but it also isn't him, somehow. He feels his body stand and face her. He's numb. He can't even move himself to feel fear. It's like when he was possessed by Anna, but worse. That had been diving into a swimming pool. This was being a single fish in a planetary ocean. A rogue comet drifting timeless between stars.

He takes hold of her injured hand, looks in her eyes. "It's been too long."

Helene looks away. He expected her to.

Mouse wants to look over at the others, at Anna, Bliss, Kai. He can feel Anna quietly frightened by the exchange taking place in front of them, but nobody can interrupt. They're all too surprised, spellbound by the transformation.

He can feel power running through him, coming from beyond that dark place, humming past the bandage and into the wound like electricity. When he lets go, Helene purses her lips and undoes the bandage to reveal no trace of injury.

"It'll take a while for you to recharge, but at least you won't be dealing with that," he says.

Her guard totally down, she rubs where it used to hurt, looks at him.

"You're so young," she says.

"You were always older."

"It's more of a difference when you're sixteen."

"You came to wish me a happy birthday, then?" Even his voice is different, like a stone weathered smooth. He chuckles.

She smiles, and the cold in his chest doesn't feel so cold anymore. He feels a longing for this familiarity, as though he's known her forever, and badly wants to know her again. He can talk; he feels calm, sure of himself. The cold in his chest is fading, the way the ache from jumping in a springtime lake fades with a few minutes' swimming.

Maybe, he thinks, he can stay like this. He can talk, he can look people in the eye, he can relax. He can start again with Helene, try to make up for two thousand years of distance, rebuild it all from scratch. It'll all be like it was, like it was supposed to be before the universe intervened.

The world starts to become distant, like he's sinking in a calming sea, and then—

Fire.

"Get *away* from him!" Anna shouts, her touch like flame on his arm, pushing back the cold. She knocks Helene away and pushes him up against a wall, hands on his shoulders, looking him in the eye. He just stares at her, makes no move to talk, or to even look away. He can feel the heat of her hands, the warmth of her breath. He can hear Kai and Bliss holding down Helene as she struggles to free herself.

Anna's scared. He can see it and feel it. What is she scared of? He can't remember why, feels like he should know.

"*Come back*, Nezumi," she says. "This isn't *you*. You aren't *you*."

His whole body is pins and needles as the heat spreads from her hands. The cold is suddenly sharp again, like a bucket of ice water. The parts that aren't frozen are on fire. He panics, struggles, but she's much stronger than he is and she holds him down until the cold is out of his head, until it's back in his chest, held at bay. Until he's sunk down, back against the wall, knees to his chin, held tight by his familiar, by his friend, in her arms.

He can't speak, eyes wide and tearing up. He puts his arms around her, speaks confusion into her shoulder, "What?" is all he can muster.

The view from the stairs would make an imperfect mirror of them. Helene, upset, is staring at him from across the hall, held down by Kai and Bliss; Mouse and Anna opposite.

He doesn't know why, but he's crying. Something important has been lost.

And everything is falling apart.

M ouse is barricaded in his room. Bliss is standing on the outside of the door. He'd run inside the moment Anna had looked away, wrestling free and slamming the door, somehow locking it. Anna had tried to jump inside, but had found herself unable to get in. As Bliss listens, she hears the faint sounds of sobbing, interspersed with the sound of things being thrown across the room.

"Mouse?" she tries talking through the door. "It's just me. I sent Anna and Kai downstairs. Can I come in?"

She pushes the door open a crack, enough to see him sitting on the bed, arms hugging himself, rocking back and forth. The lights are out, but in the moonlight she can see the reflections of tears on his face. He looks at her, not seeing. The look on his face—she'll never forget it—terror, sadness, shame. He realizes she's there and quickly turns his face away. The door slams shut, propelled by an unseen force.

She fetches June.

鼠

June's sitting in Greg's living room chatting with a glass of wine in hand, but stands up the moment Bliss enters. She's seen that face before, on teachers, psychologists, handlers.

"We need your help. It's Mouse. He's...we can't talk to him. We don't know what to do." The living room where Bliss had spent so many hours now seems alien and unfamiliar, made somehow different by the urgency of the situation.

"Can I help?" Greg asks. He's a little tipsy from the wine, but genuinely concerned. June's face shows the sinking feeling of an old familiar pain, but she smiles through it.

"No," she says with a kindness learned from patience. "I'll be back, though."

Bliss stops her before she opens the door to the apartment, trying to explain outdoors in the cold what she couldn't in front of Kai's father. About Helene and Mouse, and the way Mouse was, and how he is right now. They look up, and his window is dark. They can make out his silhouette staring out at the horizon.

June thanks her, and walks in.

Helene is in the kitchen with Anna and Kai, the latter of whom is now tapping the front of his toe impatiently with the bokken. June takes one look at her and throws a barrier up in the doorway before moving on. Patterns of iridescent letters and shapes luminesce into life and rotate silently in the space, like satellites in eccentric orbits. June climbs the stairs.

鼠

It's dark outside. Inside, too. And the moon.

He tries to close his eyes but there's too much. He tries to slow his mind down, but he can't. It started running the moment he saw Helene's agonized face across the hallway, saw what was locked inside him, saw all the things he could have been, but isn't. It's still running; he's still running away.

A knock from the door.

Mouse is staring out the window, blinking away tears.

Anna had been right. He wasn't him. Isn't. It's too confusing, he can't make sense of it. He's him, the same him he's always been, but back in the hall he'd been him, too—a calmer, smoother, easier him. A him who could just say what he meant and look around him and not see everything at once. A better him, he thinks.

And the memories. They come and go, flashes of things he's never seen before, people he doesn't know, but now, maybe, he has seen them, does know them. He's lived them. He doesn't know who he is, and now, fully ashamed, knows perfectly how different he is from everyone else. How faulted. How disabled. How *retarded*. He crouches down and buries his face in his knees as the door opens.

It's June. He knows it's her without looking. The way of walking, the way her weight always rests on the pads of her feet like a cat. She crouches next to him, quieter than usual. Cautious.

"Hey, hun," she says.

He doesn't respond. He can't. He wants to look at her, wants to say something. He's so angry at himself for not being able to. He hugs his knees tighter.

She puts her hand on his head and smoothes his hair.

"You're going to be okay," she says. "We're going to fix this."

But she can't fix it, he thinks, he can't unknow all the things he's learning. Like waves on a shore, every few heartbeats brings another swell from that dark place inside him. Only now, it's not so dark. In the distance, the pitch black night outside the streetlamp is beginning to brighten, and the shapes that moved out of sight are coming into view.

She sits with him for five or ten minutes, and then silently gets up and leaves the room. He can hear a whisper in the hallway as the door closes, and she heads down the stairs.

鼠

The barrier to the kitchen comes down and Helene looks up from where she's been sitting, guarded by the familiar and the kid with the wooden sword.

The blonde, the boy's mother, the one who'd put up the barrier before, walks in and throws—literally throws her—out of the kitchen and into the side of the stairs. Pain radiates out and shoots up her neck from where her back hits the wall. Helene holds back her instincts tight—even weakened as she is she knows she doesn't want to use the Knowledge here. If she's learned nothing else over all these years, it's that you don't get what you want by destroying potential allies. Unfortunately, in this lifetime she hasn't spent much time learning to fistfight. She pulls herself back up and tries for a left hook, but the blonde grabs her and redirects, folding her arm behind her, pushing her to the ground, knee in the small of her back.

"What have you people done to my son?"

A silver-white glow surrounds her that even the uninitiated could see. The familiar keeps her distance, waves of power summoned in anger radiating out with no specific focus.

"He's not—your son," Helene croaks out. A twist, more pain. "He's not—*just*—your son."

The blonde puts more weight into the hold, pushes down on her, and it takes every ounce of her self-control not to lash out.

"Sixteen years," the boy's mother says. "Sixteen years he's been working. Every. Goddamn. Day." She gets up, throws her against another wall, eyes like silver fire. "Therapist after therapist, school after school, he's been trying to fit in. Trying to be a normal kid." She's holding Helene by the front of her shirt. "He hasn't been like this—" like what? Rocking back and forth, terrified and angry and paralyzed "—Christ, he hasn't been this bad since he was *eight years old*. Just what did you *do?*" She punctuates the final phrase with another slam against the wall that rattles Helene's teeth in her skull and makes her nauseated. "I'm *retired*. And my son. Is. *Off. Limits.* You should *know* this. He's not joining the Trust."

That's what she thinks? Helene is starting to understand. Her mind scrambles for a way to explain.

The blonde pulls up a fist for another punch.

"Qasr Antwr!" she says, her desire to explain more carefully overridden by her desire to keep all of her teeth. She pronounces it *kasser anteer*.

The fist freezes in the air as if stuck.

"What did you say?"

Helene takes a breath, closes her eyes.

"I'm not with the Trust. I'm Qasr Antwr."

June throws her back into the kitchen and points at a chair.

"Sit," she says. "Speak."

Bliss hears the fight from upstairs, the crashing, the shouted words. She tries to slip into Mouse's room again, and this time he lets her.

He's not rocking anymore, just sitting facing the window, hugging his knees, every muscle tense. She sits down next to him, looks out the window, too. The moon shines quietly in the sky.

"So your mom's pretty scary when she's angry," her words at once gentle and conspiratorial.

Mouse doesn't respond, just stares out the window. She's not even sure he can hear her. It's starting to snow outside.

"We're all worried about you," she says. No response.

"Please don't be mad at Anna. She was just trying to help. You were acting so strangely. It scared her."

She puts her hand on his arm. He's cold as ice. She grabs the quilt off the bed and pulls it over both of their shoulders. Slides up alongside him.

"There, at least we won't be cold."

She puts her arm around him and just sits—the quiet boy who'd brought back her friend from the dead, who'd built a bridge for them both back to Kai. Who'd be so very important in her future.

"You may not believe me," she whispers. "But you're going to get through this. I promise."

They sit like this for five or ten minutes, just quietly being, while the moon shines down through snow that drifts past like salt flakes in a shallow sea. She imagines being like this outside, silent for an age, slowly buried as the quiet drifts build up around them. It's an act of commitment, an act of patience. An invitation to someone distant and frightened to return on his own time. She realizes then that he's crying, and, like another kind of act, an act of alchemy, Mouse's marble form, all taut muscles and unmoving fear, turns to sand. Somewhere inside him a wall crumbles, and he leans into her and sobs.

鼠

"What's Qasr Antwr?" Anna asks.

Helene is sitting, bruised but intact, in a chair at the kitchen table. June is facing her, and Anna and Kai are leaning against a countertop and the side of the fridge. Kai's still tapping his toe with the bokken, and Anna's arms are crossed, silvery-blonde hair hanging down behind her. Mouse's friends.

"That's what I'd like to know," June says, still staring at Helene. "When I was on cleanup duty out east I heard rumors, but I thought they were a fairy tale made up by Hermes Castlereagh—" she shakes her head, backs up for Kai and Anna "—the current massive ego at the top of the Trust's food chain—to cover for whenever they screwed the pooch. A fictional scapegoat for when bad plans went worse." She frowns. "And yet, here you sit."

Helene nods. "What do you know about us?"

June shakes her head. "No way, sister. That's not how this is going to work. *I'm* going to ask *you* questions and *you're* going to *answer* them. And if I really like your answers, maybe—just maybe—I won't start thinking of ways to smuggle your body into the hospital incinerator."

"Simon wouldn't like that," she says.

"Okay, *yeah.*" June leans in close. "Let's start *there*: how the hell do you know my son?"

Helene sighs. "I don't know your son," she says. "I know who your son is."

"That's not cryptic or anything," Kai says with a snort.

Helene scowls at the interruption. "Qasr Antwr is *old*. As old as the Trust. Older. We have an unbroken lineage." She takes a breath, as if the explanation were always to some degree tiresome. "The Trust is corrupt. They have good intentions, but every few centuries or so they forget themselves in their own ambition. I—*we* take care of that. The Trust as you know it is dedicated to the memory of the one who taught us everything. Qasr Antwr is dedicated to the man himself."

"Hermes Trimegistus," June fills in.

"Simon Magus," Helene corrects.

June raises her eyebrows, and Helene continues.

"Hermes is a myth. A title that the successive heads of the Trust have given themselves over the years. No one—not the Trust or anyone else—knows who first presented the Knowledge to the world, but we know who rescued us from ourselves, who gave us a purpose. I know him. I've known him every time I've seen him for nearly two thousand years."

June leans back in her chair, skeptical. "You're telling me you're Helen, you're *that* Helen."

"I prefer the pronunciation Helene, but I've been called other things. The First Thought. The Lost Sheep. I quite liked Sophia."

"The goddess Wisdom herself is sitting in my kitchen." June almost snorts.

"I'm not..." She sighs, as if looking for words. "Not what I once was," she says, with a quiet smile.

"And you're saying my son, my Mouse, is the reincarnation of—what, the reincarnation of Simon Magus? Your husband. From two thousand years ago."

"Partner. Other half." She says it with a touch of regret, then sighs again, her furrowed brows relaxing. "And not exactly." She searches for an explanation. "As for me, yes, I reincarnate. Every time I die, I'm born again as a child. I have no memory of myself until I reach a certain age, perhaps twelve or thirteen, and then it starts returning, little by little, until I seek out Qasr Antwr and rejoin them. This has been going on for...longer than I care to remember." She slumps just a little in her chair, closes her eyes for a moment. "It's not like that for Simon. Simon doesn't reincarnate, because he never really dies."

"But Mouse—"

"Your son isn't the reincarnation of Simon. He's a part of him, a fragment. And a very important one. He might even be the last." She sits up in her chair. "Before those ignorant...*people*—" she looks like it's not the word she means "—had him executed, Simon Magus spread himself out across all of time, seeing it all at once, choosing pivotal moments to intercede, choosing places and times to be." She taps the table with her finger. "Here and now, a little bit at a time, your son is Simon Magus. My Simon." She leans back again. "Will it be for all of his life? I don't know. Why your son? I don't even know why he chose here and now. But I'm willing to bet it has something to do with a darkness that's coming. That he warned us about a long time ago."

June thinks about this for a moment. "Say I believe you—and I don't know if I do, but let's just say so for now...how many times has this happened?"

"Since he first found me two thousand years ago? Eleven, no—twelve. Including now."

"That's insane," June says. "Even if it worked across such huge timescales, the correlative exchange would end up being—"

"Catastrophic."

June turns to the doorway where a figure from her past stands in a thick winter coat that hangs open to reveal a white shirt and grey vest beneath. Grizzled cheeks, sightless eye, he's chewing on a toothpick at one corner of his mouth. It's Priest.

鼠

"Leonard, you son of a bitch."

Before anyone can move, June's hopped out of her chair, grabbed the wooden sword from Kai's hand and swung it at the intruder. She stops herself a hair's breadth from his nose. He doesn't flinch.

"Hey, Junebug. Long time no see." He isn't smiling.

She lowers the bokken, then leans so close in that Kai and Anna think she's about to kiss him. He almost seems to think so, too, from the look on his face when she slaps him across the cheek.

"What the hell have you got to do with this? Are you with her? And on what godforsaken planet do you *live* that you try to teach *my son* the Old Knowledge without *my express consent?*"

He rubs his cheek, chuckling to himself.

"I'm touched." He chuckles and flicks the toothpick like a cigarette into the garbage in the corner, before producing another and gnawing on it.

She holds up the bokken again and he raises his hands in surrender. "I'm with her." He points at Helene. "And before you hit me again, I didn't know the kid was *your* kid. When the hell'd you change your name to Anacreon, anyway?"

"It was my mother's. I was trying to get off the radar."

"Well it worked."

June tosses the bokken back to Kai.

"So you guys know each other?" Anna says.

June and Priest look at each other.

"Wait, he's not your ex is he?"

June goes a few shades of pink. *"Absolutely not."*

Priest's answer, given at the same time, is exactly the opposite.

He laughs as she turns on him. "Aw come on, Junebug, you're going to tell me—hey!" He laughs again as he dodges a swipe.

"Don't call me that."

"Still mad, huh?"

Anna and Kai exchange glances.

Kai squints at him, then at June.

"He's not Mouse's *dad*, is he?"

June's eyes nearly pop out of her head.

"Hey, whoa. No. Absolutely not, kid." Priest's hands go up in the universal gesture of *not me.* "Number one, I'd know if I had a kid. And number two he's too young anyway. I can't have a kid as young as him with a girl I haven't seen in, what, more than sixteen years now." He starts to laugh at the idea, but trails off when he feels the eyes of the room on him. When June coughs in response, the room goes quieter than quiet.

Priest clears his throat, repeats himself to June. "Because I'd *know* if I had a kid, right?"

No one says anything until Anna breaks the tension.

"He's sixteen," she says. "Mouse is. Today."

June walks to the cupboard and pulls out a bottle of whiskey. She hands it to Priest. He takes it absently.

"Now hold on—"

"I don't know," June interrupts.

"You don't know if he's *my kid?"*

She turns on him then. "Now let's get something straight. Even if he's related to you, and I'm pretty certain he's not enough of a self-interested jerk to be related to you, but even *if* he were, he *still* wouldn't be 'your kid.' Mouse is *my* son, no one else's."

He almost falls into one of the chairs. Helene sits back, almost forgotten for the time being.

He pulls the cork and takes a swig straight from the bottle.

"Scarecrow's eyes, Junebug."

"And anyway, he's probably David's. Almost certainly."

"Ugh, the suit?" He takes another long swig.

June shoots him a look that only needs something combustible to start a fire, but it bounces off harmlessly.

"'The suit,' as you call him, was a better, more decent guy than you'll ever be."

Priest snorts. "Yeah, then where's he now?"

"Where's *he*? Where were *you*?" She shoots back. "It's not like I didn't *try* to say goodbye."

The words hang in the air until Helene plucks them back out.

"The partners reunited. Fitting, I suppose, since it's partially my fault you were separated."

June looks at Priest, who nods. "Qasr Antwr assigns Helene a pair of guardians at age five that keep her safe until she remembers who she is."

"You've been with them since then? Since before then? And you couldn't even swing a—a what—a 'Seeya, toots'? Couldn't make something up? Leonard I don't even know where to begin with—"

"Hurry!" Bliss is standing in the doorway to the increasingly crowded kitchen, her eyes wild with panic. "It's Mouse, and—" She gasps for air, shakes her head. "Whatever you're planning on doing, you need to do it now!"

鼠

The room is lit by a pale blue glow, which is radiating out from Mouse.

He's hovering three feet off the ground, unconscious, head back, mouth hanging open, eyes rolled back in his skull. "We were just sitting there by the window, and then he freaked out and—"

Anna lets out a yelp of pain and doubles over. The glow has spread from Mouse to her, and Kai is holding her up.

"Get her downstairs now!" Priest shouts. "The last thing we need is that kind of feedback."

Kai looks to June for confirmation and she nods. Anna doesn't want to go but she's in no state to refuse.

"You might want to go, too, Junebug," Priest says. "This isn't going to be pretty."

She clenches her fists. "If you think for one second I'm going to let you near my son, you've got another thing coming."

He turns to face her, serious. "I promise I will do everything in my power to keep him safe. Have I ever broken a promise to you?"

June looks back at Mouse, hanging there limp in the air.

"Fine. But I'm staying."

"Good," Helene says. "We'll need your help anyway, since I'm not up to fighting strength yet. Right now we need to reset his grounding points before he comes unglued."

She steps forward and opens Mouse's shirt, placing a hand over his solar plexus. "Priest, I need a second-order Sulaymani here, now. You," she looks back a June, "a 4th-order Claviculum through his second astral to feed some energy into him."

June hesitates.

"You think I'm joking? The universe is trying to draw the correlative from your son instead of from Simon, and he doesn't have it to give. If we don't do something now, we'll lose them both, and maybe the girl downstairs, too."

June rolls up her sleeves and steps in.

鼠

The journey there is easy. Light floods his eyes, and everything is silent.

Mouse is alone.

He can feel the ground beneath his feet, smooth—like worn stone, pure white and featureless. He's not breathing. He checks for a pulse, but he knows he doesn't have one. Everything is quiet. Everything is calm.

And then he's not alone.

"Hello."

The man is a little taller than he is, head wrapped in a black tur-
ban with a band of cloth below his eyes as well. He's in a flowing robe
of a type Mouse has never seen before. He pulls down the cloth so that
it hangs below his chin, revealing a face that's old and worn, sandy
and toughened by sun.

He's smiling.

"We haven't properly met."

Mouse nods. "Under the streetlamp," he says. In this strange
calm talking is no issue. "You were in the dark."

"One must step out of the light to see in the dark."

"They don't want me to."

"Your friends?"

Mouse nods. "They want me safe."

The man smiles sadly. "But you know better."

"No one is safe."

The man nods. "You are less of me than any other," he says. "And
also more. Across the ages I will never again be so."

Mouse nods this time. He knows, but he doesn't know everything. And he won't, not yet.

"You stand at the crossroads, the place of all places that I couldn't
see. That's why they're moving now. That's why you and I have a
choice to make. And I do so hate making choices without knowing
all the variables."

Mouse feels a gentle tugging in his chest, pulling him backward.

The man rubs his chest. "I feel it, too. Why should it be you?"

Mouse thinks of home, of June and of his friends. He thinks of
sitting in the batcave and eating lunch, of walking home after school,
of Bliss taking his hand or waking up next to Anna. Of sharing bacon
with Ginnie. Of fighting with Kai.

"Ah, but I have many lifetimes of homes and friends and memories. Why should yours take precedence over mine?"

Mouse thinks. He can't think of a reason, has nothing to base a
decision on.

"And that's where we stand, positioned on the edge. Do we jump right, or left, not knowing what lies beneath on either side? And why should it be you?"

The tugging is stronger now, almost painful. A line of thin, white fire through his heart and spine, tracing its way back to the beginning of all things.

"What did you give?" Mouse asks. "To do all this? What was the price?"

The man smiles a lonely smile. "You've met her," he says.

Mouse thinks he understands.

"Then it should be me," he says. The man raises his eyebrows, in surprise. "Think about why you made me this way. You know why," Mouse concludes.

The man nods his head, sighs.

"I do indeed. I just wanted to make sure you did, too."

Mouse nods.

"Then godspeed you." The man places a hand on his chest. "Take what knowledge you need. And tread lightly." He gives a gentle shove, and Mouse falls away.

The journey back is far more painful.

鼠

"Something's interfering with the process!"

The air in the room has begun to spin around, throwing papers from the desk, pulling posters from the walls. Bliss is curled up on the bed in the corner, trying to stay out of the way. Eyes wide and watching everything.

Sigils and seals flash in purples and blues above and below Mouse's body, windows of light closing as fast as they can open them.

"Is it the familiar?" Priest says.

"No," says June, "that's an isolated factor." She motions toward the borders of the inscription. "See the terminations?"

"Then what?" Priest's hands work quickly over the body, looking for something, anything. His eyes snap open. "Hermes' balls, the tracker!"

Helene's hand reaches forward and into Mouse's mouth. "You left it in there?"

"How did you think I knew where he lived?"

There's a crackle of static amid the sound of rising winds and Helene pulls her hand back in pain. "Gods."

She looks up at the other two. "This is going to be it. When I fragment the sign, all of these will collapse in on themselves. We'll either be successful or we won't, but either way it's going to be a big release of power. Brace yourselves."

June and Priest nod. Bliss holds her breath.

Helene reaches forward and there's a huge blast of light, brighter than anything she's ever seen. June, Priest, and Helene dive back, arms covering their eyes, but faintly in the light Bliss can see Mouse start to fall and she dives toward him. Then there's nothing but white.

鼠

In the kitchen, Anna's been clinging to the edge of the sink for dear life. At this distance, the pain has been commuted to intense nausea, wave after wave passing over her, the world casting itself back and forth like the apartment's a ship on a god-awful stormy sea. Kai's been trying to steady her, his hand on her back.

"It's going to be okay," he says. "Mouse is going to be fine. You're going to be fine."

She nods, then pulls herself over the sink and burps. She hiccups and groans and sinks back down to the ground, still holding on to the sink. She feels as though the world itself is coming apart at the seams.

There's a sound like a massive rubber band snapping from upstairs.

Anna looks toward the kitchen door, tries to stand.

"Hey, now," Kai says, "hold on."

Anna swallows, shakes her head. "No, but I have to go. He's calling."

She makes it to her feet before the wave of light comes cascading down the stairs. Every surface of the kitchen is suddenly white, every stitch of fabric they're wearing, every strand of hair on their heads.

It's like the world has been reduced to a line drawing in the faintest greyscale.

Anna drags herself to the door and starts climbing the stairs even as Kai tries to stop her. By the time they reach the door to the bedroom, the light has faded.

It's like they're arranged in a tableau—June, Priest, and Helene standing aside, and at the center, limp in Bliss's arms, is Mouse, unmoving, eyes closed.

"You weren't kidding." Priest turns to Helene, but she shakes her head, looking serious.

"The seal's still there. I didn't get the chance." She looks at June. "We were too slow."

"Mouse?" Bliss is talking to him, so soft that no one can hear her, his body and hers a perfect pieta as she cradles his head. "He's not breathing." She looks up, tears running down her face, eyes imploring. "This shouldn't be happening. June," she starts, but can't think of anything to say.

June steps forward and crouches down over her son. She reaches forward and brushes a stray lock of hair from his face. No one can say anything.

No one, that is, except Anna.

"Get out of the *way!*" She yells, and lurches forward. She elbows June sideways, bends down, grabs Mouse by the back of the head, and plants her lips firmly on his.

You could hear a pin drop.

Then there's a sudden shift in the room, like it's been turned 90 degrees and back again relative to the world, and Mouse's eyes fly open.

Anna pulls back, and Mouse gasps for air.

Anna's eyes meet Bliss's and they both look away.

"A failsafe." June looks at Mouse, unsure of how to feel. He's alive, but who is he? Her son, or...?

Helene is shaking her head. "Amazing. He planned for all of it."

June looks from her son to Helene and back to the form of her son, who's stopped gasping for breath and is now looking around the room, eyes bright.

"The correlative should have killed him, had to—so he let it, and hid a failsafe in his familiar. In two thousand years, I've never seen it done." Helene seems almost giddy.

The form still half-cradled in Bliss's lap grabs her shoulder and gives it a little squeeze. She backs up and lets him stand, and he offers a hand to help her do the same.

Everyone waits to see what he'll say.

He smiles, holds up his hands and makes a motion.

Pen and paper?

It's Mouse. He's back.

鼠

I'm sorry, Helene, the note says. *It had to be me this time.*

They're standing in the snow on the doorstep, just the two of them. He asked everyone for this time alone, and after some suspicion and lingering doubt Anna allowed it.

"You met him then."

Mouse nods. *Am him. Just not all of him. Not the part you wanted.*

"Why?"

Did he ever tell you about the things he saw?

Helene shakes her head. "He said he couldn't."

It'd change things going into the equation.

"Yes."

This time it's different. There is no equation.

Helene leans back against the wall, a calm showing every one of her two thousand years. "What do you mean?"

It takes some time to write a response, but she waits with patience. She's had a great deal of practice.

Thanks to the coming darkness, the next three or four months are a black box. No one can see into it, and everything that comes out is fragmented by possibility. In some versions, nothing comes out, which is impossible, but there it is. He's tried to control the variables as much as he can, limited what any of us know—including himself, or me—in order to limit the possible outcomes, but he can't get close enough to the crux of it to tell what needs to hap-

pen. This town is the epicenter, and for the next eight months this is it. It's us.

Helene frowns, and Mouse thinks she looks beautiful doing so. He wonders how much of that is him and how much his past. There's been a lot of overlap today.

"That's why they're moving now."

Because he's blind.

"There are other ways to see."

Mouse smiles. *You know that's not true for him.* She knows the paradox of a seeing everything at once is how limiting and monolithic it can be.

"But for you?"

He made me this way for a reason. You, too.

Helene only nods.

He wants to say that he's sorry. Sorry that the other him made her take the long road through time while he stepped aside and lived it all at once. He wants to say that some of the threads that wind their way out of the black box ahead find their way back to her, or that they might do if only this, and if only that—but there are too many ifs, and he's not the one responsible, not the one she needs to hear it from. She's stranded in his absence, separated from her other half, and he's the only one who can see her for who and what she is.

"It's a gift," she says, drawing him out of his reflection, "the time in each life before I remember who I really am. For those years, I'm nobody special," she laughs a little, "and I usually spend them wishing I was. And then fifty lifetimes start pushing their way through the cracks, and I find myself missing him, and hating him, and wanting him back. I think there used to be more to me than this."

She steps forward to the edge and looks out on the curving back alleys all coated in snow. She looks back over her shoulder at Mouse, the boy who would have to do the work of a greater man than himself. "I'm almost glad you're not him. For your sake." A light wind whips her hair to one side, pulls her final word away as she says it, "Almost."

They stand in silence for a minute before Mouse notices a pair of shadows at the top of the stairs. Her guardians—Priest and Vallis. Helene's leaving. He writes a final note.

He trusts you, it reads. *I do, too. I don't remember much of it, but I re-member that.*

She looks at the last note for longer than it takes to read it, then folds it carefully and puts it in the pocket of the old coat June has lent her, to go with the borrowed clothes.

"Stay safe, Diviner."

She starts to walk away, but he grabs her by the hand and pulls her close, wrapping her in a full-bodied hug. He's a poor substitute for the real thing and he knows it, but even for the extra inches she has on him, she feels smaller than she had before, more fragile.

When she pulls away, she does it slowly, being careful not to look at him as she goes.

He waits until her footprints are filling up again with snow before going back inside.

鼠

His eyes scan the apartment as he walks in. Anna's sitting at the bottom of the stairs waiting for him. She's even closer now, and she can feel all the things he's not saying, all the remembered feelings that are his own and somehow aren't. She stands on the bottom step and hugs him, unabashed. There'll be time for embarrassment later.

Down the hall, Kai and Bliss have dozed off at opposite ends of the couch, and June has at some point put blankets over both of them.

In the kitchen, June's nursing some old wounds over a cup of something warm, and as Mouse and Anna go to sit down with her, she leans forward and wraps her arms around both of them. Maybe later they'll talk in hushed tones over tea, or in loud ones over something stronger, about her past with Priest—or Leonard—and David. But for tonight, there's just sitting and being together, before, as dawn cracks the sky, June wanders away next door to find Greg dozing by the television, thanking him silently for his superhuman patience.

And in a bar on the other side of town, Vallis spreads out books and papers over tabletops and corkboards, while Priest pours a 7:00

A.M. whiskey and puts it down in front of Helene. She looks up at him with wordless thanks and settles down to business. It's time for battle plans.

I t begins in March.

Mouse is eating his breakfast while the TV news rattles away about the latest police action or Hollywood divorce, starving after another hard workout with June. It's become their daily routine. Sometimes he even lands a punch.

"...Jones of Dearborn is the sole winner of last night's Megaprize lottery..."

He picks up a mug of tea that's gone cold and holds his hand over it until it's steaming. June's taken the microwave and kettle and put them in storage, so now if Mouse wants warm food, he has to do it for himself. Some days, when June isn't looking, he boils water in a pot on the stove, but after that night in January, he's found it more like getting back on a bike than learning to ride from scratch, as the saying goes. Some fragments of the Knowledge seem to have remained, even as the presence of his other self has vanished without a trace. Studying June's notes is more like reading an old, familiar book than one he's never read.

"...parents say they still haven't heard from the three teens, and a search is currently underway."

The last headline catches Mouse's attention, and he turns up the TV. The local reporter is standing in front of his high school.

"Authorities were alerted to the disappearances late last night when parents reported that all three students had failed to return home after an extracurricular meeting at this area high school. The cars in which they were traveling were later found by location services, abandoned together by the side of Riverside Drive, mere feet from the Highway 23 bridge." The camera cuts to a row of three cars, surrounded by yellow tape, parked by the bridge. "The police say they are following up on leads, and are asking for anyone with information on the whereabouts of the three students to contact them at the number below."

Turn on the TV. He sends the thought across town to Anna. Since his birthday they've been practicing doing things on purpose, including talking over a distance.

Already watching, comes the response. *Is this it?*

Mouse takes a sip of his tea and stares at the screen as the segment ends with photos of the three boys.

It might be. Keep your eyes and ears open.

These days, anything could be a sign of what's to come. He finishes his tea.

鼠

Two days pass. Bliss is sitting in her kitchen, staring off into space in the typical portrait of morning, hands around a cup of tea. She jumps when Anna pops her head around the corner.

"Hey," she says. "I'm going to skip breakfast and go watch Kai's boxing practice this morning. See you there?"

Bliss nods.

"You okay?" Anna squints at her. "You look a little pale."

"Ah...yeah. Fine." She smiles weakly. "Just feeling a little off this morning. I'll see you there."

Anna frowns. "All right, well. See you later."

"You, too."

Bliss purses her lips as she listens for the sound of the door opening and shutting in the background. She looks down at the cup of tea, now gone cold, and closes her eyes. A moment later it begins to steam.

鼠

There's something jarring about the days when, despite everything weird in his life, Mouse still finds himself sitting in class. Mrs. Dinshaw's Bio class to be exact. They're watching Neil deGrasse Tyson explain evolution, using a really big tree as a metaphor. He wonders what the astrophysicist would think about magic. I mean, if it happens, it must be explainable by science. Maybe by quantum physics or string theory or something. Definitely above Mouse's pay grade, regardless. Maybe he'll look into it when he gets to university.

If he gets to university. If any of them do.

He sighs and is about to put his head down when a note appears on his desk. Bliss doesn't look, so as not to raise suspicion, but her hand is darting back to her desk. Mrs. Dinshaw hates it when students pass notes.

I need to talk to you, says the note, *without Anna around.*

Mouse frowns. He's not sure why she wants to talk without Anna around, but doing so is going to be a challenge. She's by his side more and more these days, at the morning practices with June, between classes, after school. Thankfully he's getting better at only communicating what he means to; six weeks ago he'd have already heard a rapid 'Without me around?' pop into his head.

Another note: *Skip next period with me?*

She sneaks a look back at him and he nods. He can afford to dodge a math class—after alchemical conjuring, trinomial factoring seems pretty simple, and Mr. Wigmore doesn't take attendance.

He crumples the note and drops it into his bag.

鼠

The spring thaw has come early, and the snow on the school's roof is melting so fast that the drips from the icicles hanging from its gutters are doing a pretty good job of making it look like it's raining.

Mouse is standing just outside the fire exit by the batcave, in the two feet between the doors and the curtain of drips. The air isn't much warmer than it was in October, but after winter it feels nice to get some air. A shiver runs through him and he gets a ping of curiosity from Anna—why's he outside? He takes a deep breath and walks back in.

Just getting a little air before math. It's nice out.

Are you skipping class again?

Busted.

No?

A sigh. Amazing how a sigh can be sent person to person like that.

Fine. See you at lunch.

He sends warm thoughts in her direction, and detects a faint *Baka* in response.

He sits cross-legged in the fire escape for a moment, making himself aware of everything around him, then dims the part of his mind that sends and receives. On his arm, the tied-off curlicues of script at the edges of the design fade from purplish back to almost white. Privacy mode: on.

Bliss rounds the corner. She's wearing a pair of ripped black jeans and a black Ramones tee-shirt. Mouse hadn't even known there'd been a band called the Ramones until he'd met her. She's back in the purple Cons that she'd worn when they first met, and the streaks in her hair seem more vibrant today than usual. He remembers that first day in class when she volunteered to look out for him, and wonders at how much things have changed. How much he's changed. She looks the same as then, but infinitely more familiar now. She looks tough, like she's ready to kick ass and take names.

She looks great, he thinks.

She smiles, demure. "Anna will get jealous if you keep looking at me like that," she says.

Mouse swallows and drops his gaze, blushing, grateful for privacy mode.

She sits down across from him, sliding down the wall, with a coffee in each hand. She passes him one.

"Grabbed these from the caf on the way over."

He nods, accepts it, then sets it down next to him and pulls out his notepad.

So what's up?

Bliss nods and stares at her coffee cup in silence. She brings it up to take a sip, then hesitates and lowers it and holds it in her lap. She draws her knees up and puts her arms half around them. The coffee isn't there to be drunk, he suddenly thinks, it's so she has something to do with her hands. He's seen June do the same thing before telling him they need to move again. What's going on?

"So..." She stops, sighs, lets out a disgusted "Ugh" noise and starts again. "Look, I don't want this to be melodramatic, but I need to know. And you can't ask me why. Because reasons, okay?"

Mouse frowns, but nods.

"It's about you, and me, and Anna...and about the future. I mean our future."

Mouse is confused. What is she asking?

He scribbles a note in return.

Are you asking—wait what are you asking, exactly?

She opens her mouth and then shuts it. Then opens it again to speak. "Like, okay—" she takes a sip of her coffee, chews on the edge of the cup a bit "—so you and Anna, you've got this telepathy thing going on, and you've got this future together, so I don't want to talk about this with her around because—"

Mouse waves his hands at that last statement, in a *whoa, hold on* kind of gesture.

What do you mean a "future together"—you mean she's going to ask me out or something?

Bliss looks suddenly unsure of herself. "What? What do you—?" She blinks. "This isn't what I was going to say but, I mean it's just that Kai and I, we were pretty sure that you and Anna...by now..." She trails off, looking at his face. "Really? I mean you're really not?"

Mouse blinks a few times, then looks down as he writes a note.

Not...dating?

Bliss looks down at the note, talks without looking up. "Mm. I meant, maybe not so formally...as that."

Wait hold on. You and Kai thought Anna and I were, like, hooking up when nobody was looking?

Bliss clears her throat and takes a sip of her coffee, eyebrows raised, looking away. Her silence is a response in itself. He doesn't even know how to respond to the question. He supposes it makes a kind of sense. He starts writing a response.

She starts an, "It's just that—" but he interrupts with a waving request that she wait until he's done writing, which takes a while and involves what seems like a lot of crossing out and scribbling. He finally hands her the note and she reads it.

I guess now that I think about it I can see why you might think that. But it's not like that. I mean it's not that it wouldn't be nice. She's cute, and funny, and stuff...But it's not where we are, and I don't think it's where we where I can be right now. Besides...

There's something else completely scribbled out at the end, so much she can't read it, and she wonders if maybe...but he's put dots to let her know he's still writing, and by the time she's finished reading he's handing her another note.

I've never had a girlfriend, or, I mean. This me. I haven't even kissed a girl or anything. Well, there was that thing with Anna when I nearly died, but I really don't think that counts since it was more like CPR and anyway...

A third note:

But part of me remembers Helene, what things used to be like, with the other me, and I get these feelings. And maybe I'm an idiot, too, because I didn't know that Anna felt like that or anything. And then with the world coming to an end or whatever the hell is happening...

And finally:

I guess I missed it huh? Is she mad? Did she say something?

Bliss shakes her head and says a gentle, "No." She looks over her knees at him and sighs. She's a mystery to him, he just can't figure out her expressions. She just looks at him for a minute until he writes another note and just holds it up.

What?

"Nothing. It's funny." But she's not laughing. She looks a little sad, if anything.

No, really, but what?

"I wasn't even really asking about that. And now I don't even know how to get to where I was going with it because this is just..." She shakes her head.

Mouse starts to write but she cuts him off by putting down her coffee and sliding over. She puts her hand on his pad, leaning so close he catches the scent of something sweet. It must be just whatever she washes her hair with, he supposes. But it smells nice.

"Enough," she says. "Don't worry about me. I had something to tell you, and I still do, but it'll have to be later. I just don't have the energy right now." She sighs and puts her forehead against his shoulder, then looks up.

He turns his head to face her. He's about to ask anyway—about what it is, when she might be able to talk about it, if there's anything he can do to help—but her face is right there and their eyes lock and somehow it isn't scary at all. Her eyes are warm and kind and familiar, and he doesn't feel any panic or self-consciousness or worry. Looking into them, he no longer feels like the geography of the world has changed, but rather like he's remembering his place in it.

So when he leans forward and kisses her, his heart doesn't race. It doesn't feel like whatever a first kiss should feel like. It feels comfortable, habitual. Like coming home.

It occurs to him that he shouldn't be kissing her at precisely the moment when Anna comes flying around the corner. She stops cold.

Bliss shoots up, flustered. "Ann—Izzy!"

Anna takes a step backward.

"This—I can explain this."

"I was trying to tell you..." she manages to say, staring at their feet. "And you weren't listening." Tears are starting to form at the edges of her eyes. "So I came to find you, and, hey—" she half laughs but it sticks in her throat "—here you are." She clears her throat. "It's totally fine."

Bliss steps forward. "I'm sorry, this is my fault, I was just—"

"No, it's fine!" She takes another step backward, wringing her hands. She looks away. "It's, uh. I'm sorry. I didn't mean to interrupt."

"Izzy," she shakes her head, "Anna—wait, let me explain."

"No, it's— it's fine. I just had a thing...and. I have to go."

"Anna it's not like—"

"Yamenasai!" she shouts. A tear rolls down her cheek as she looks at Bliss, then at Mouse. "Please! Just stop. I don't need your excuses. It's fine." She turns on her heel, then vanishes into thin air.

Bliss exhales sharply and looks down at her feet.
"Balls."

語

She's not responding to me, I don't know where she is. He hands Bliss the note without looking while they walk. School ended half an hour ago. They've been searching for her since the moment she left.

"Kai says she's not at his place," Bliss says, ending a call with a quick tap. "And she's not picking up the cellphone I got her."

I shouldn't have kissed you.

"It's not like I stopped you."

He looks at her, nods and sighs.

We have to find her.

"And say what?"

I haven't gotten that far.

As they pass the bridge something catches their attention. There's a group of high school students standing in a cluster, and someone's yelling.

"Marcus, stop! What are you doing?"

Bliss and Mouse look over in time to see a wave of dark purple energy drive one of the students back, his feet going out from under him, landing in a pile ten feet away. He doesn't get up.

"What did you do that for?" A girl shouts and runs over to the injured boy.

As they get closer, they can hear someone talking; he sounds like he's giving a sermon. "...think of it, Lucy. We'll never be bullied, beaten, harassed again. We're the ones with power now. They offered this to us as a gift, and we need to take it!"

Mouse recognizes him. He's one of the boys who went missing.

"*He* knows, ask *him!*" The boy has dark hair and thick-rimmed glasses, he's wearing a too-big spring jacket that's probably a hand-me-down from an older sibling. He's smiling and pointing at Mouse.

"He knows the power of the ancients. They told me." He looks right at Mouse. "They want to meet you, Simon."

The boy's friends are looking now, two of them are the other missing boys, who are staring at him with the same creepy look, but two more, another boy and a girl, are looking over nervously.

Mouse looks at Bliss, writes a note. She nods.

"What's going on?" she asks. "And what did you do to him?"

"Don't play dumb, little kitty. We know you know. They *told* us you know."

One of the other boys tilts his head at an unnerving angle, somehow reptilian.

"Know what? What are you talking about?"

His eyes narrow. "Liar. They said you'd lie about it." He looks at Mouse. "You're the talk of the school, Simon. But they don't know what we know, do they? That power has its virtues." He pushes past the others and comes closer. "New kid like you, nervous, quiet kid. Can't even string three words together in a sentence." He smiles. "And you've got a girlfriend." He turns to stare at Bliss with a wicked smile on his lips. "The much admired, much desired Bliss."

Bliss tenses up.

"Pretty girl like you. And not with that Japanese prick anymore. But what are you doing with this guy?"

"Stop," is all she says.

But he doesn't. He turns back to Mouse. "*I've* never had a girlfriend, have I, Pat?"

One of the others, the one with the head tilt, answers, "Nope."

"How about you, Arnold?"

The other twists his face into a parody of a smile. "Nuh uh."

"That was fine. We accepted it. We knew what we were. Nobodies." He gets so close that Mouse can feel the power rising off him like static, making his skin crawl.

Arnold and Pat walk over to Bliss, and Mouse instinctively shifts his weight.

"But you, Simon. You *should* be nobody. Do you want to tell us why you're not?"

Simon looks at the ground. He's angry, his heart's racing, but he still can't say anything back. It's a variation on a scene that's played out a dozen times before at different schools, but never at this one. And never for this reason.

"No? Then I'll say it for you: power." He looks at Bliss, through her. "Ladies like power, don't they?" He looks back. "Isn't that why you have not one girlfriend, but two?" He leans in so close that Mouse can smell his breath. He doesn't smell human. He smells of stale air, rotting wood, wet dust.

"Come on, Marcus." The girl behind them—short, brown hair, freckles, and glasses. Her voice has a tremor in it, but she's standing firm. "You're being weird."

Marcus takes no notice. His eyes flicker over to Bliss and then back to Mouse. "How about you share a little, hmm?"

He reaches out to grab Bliss and Mouse reacts. It may only have been three months, but it was three months every day with June as his teacher and Anna as his sparring partner. He grabs the boy's wrist, twists and tucks, grabs his elbow and kicks him in the back of the knee, following forward with all his weight. In under a second, the other boy is flat on his face in the dirt, Mouse on top of him, knee in the small of his back.

For a second Mouse doesn't recognize the sound coming from beneath him, and then, laughter?

The boy starts to push back against Mouse's hold, putting what must be excruciating pressure on his own shoulder and elbow. In his shock, Mouse holds on tight until, all at once, there's a series of cracks that send a shudder through him, like the sickening crunch of crushing a bug with just the palm of your hand. The boy's just snapped his own ligaments.

And he's giggling.

Worse, Mouse has realized something else, too. The boy's cold. His wrist doesn't seem to have a pulse in it. There's no regular rise and fall of his chest. He's dead.

He freezes with recognition—all three of them are already dead.

Mouse gets up and stands back, repulsed.

The boy stands, too, arm dangling limp at his side. He grins. "See? Power."

The girl who spoke out and the boy with her start to back up to where the other boy is just starting to sit up. This catches the attention of Pat and Arnold, who turn and start to advance on them.

"Hey," Bliss says. "Leave them out of this."

"Leave them...out? What, you want us to keep all this power for ourselves?" He starts back toward Mouse. "We're not selfish like you."

Then something inside the boy changes. His broken arm seems to get longer, impossibly stretching, skin darkening to a shade like rotten eggplant, veins bulging like greyish mold. The rest of him follows suit—he's seven feet tall now, eight. His eyes expand, huge and all black, ears ragged, smile widening until the skin at the edges splits revealing row after row of sawlike teeth. The fingers of the broken arm knit together until they're one long jagged scythe and the other grows in muscle and sinew until each finger is a shining, claw-tipped weapon. No longer human, they're being physically *unmade*, being warped into something perverse.

Marcus's voice is now like a rumble. Behind him there's nothing human left about the other two either, loping in an asymmetric shambling crouch toward the others.

"Look at what they gave us." A madness in its eyes. "Power. It's *ours*."

Mouse grabs a card from his pocket. He's been tracing out alchemical signs in his spare time, trying to work on ideas as they surface. He fingers the design and wills energy into it, and the world changes, dims, almost stops. He's got maybe ten seconds.

He grabs hold of Bliss's hand and drags her around until they're between the creatures and the other students. Things shift back and the world reanimates.

Mouse puts a hand up, as if to say *stay behind me* as he reaches into his pocket and pulls out another card. This one had taken him a week and he hasn't had time to test it out, but the principles are right. There's a metal rail at the edge of the bridge, and he turns and slaps the card against it. The air around it chills until frost is covering all the surfaces for fifteen feet in all directions, but the bar itself glows white hot, changes shape, and then drops to the ground, dissipating its heat back into the surrounding air. He picks up his creation and points it at the creatures. It's a leaf-bladed spear with a small crossbar and a couple of rings reminiscent of a Japanese monk's staff.

Success.

He levels it at the things. A warning—stay back.

Pat and Arnold seem to laugh in oily gurgles to one another and take a few steps forward.

Mouse is getting tired, and fast. He's never even tried to throw this much power around at once, and now he's down to his last trick. He grabs the final card and checks it—he can't help but feel like he's forgetting something. But he doesn't have time, so he wraps it around the spear and goes for it. He focuses everything he's got, draws all the power he can from the sky and from the ground and from whatever he can reach with his mind. He plants the foot of the spear in the dirt and points the blade at the two closest creatures, and then releases the energy with an act of will.

The sky darkens. Arcs of lightning pulse through the air and into the two things. They convulse, letting out inhuman shrieks, like a legion of beasts all screaming in unison. They shudder and belch and contort into distended quivering masses, burning from the inside out as sky and earth meet within them. The pulses stop and the creatures that were once living beings named Pat and Arnold collapse into heaps of sodden ash, stink-ridden steam rising from the corpses.

It might have been overkill.

Mouse drops to one knee, hand spasming, locked clawlike around the still-humming spear. Everything spins and lurches from one side to the other. The heaving world combines with the unholy stench of cooked monster and the way every nerve fiber in his body is screaming, and he can't help it—he spills the contents of his stomach onto the street until his throat is raw and his chest is hollow. He can barely breathe or even think.

And there's still one left.

The one that used to be named Marcus, all shark-teeth and greasy scales, lets out a multi-tonal, alien scream, and lunges forward, faster than should even be possible. Mouse can see it pouncing, as the world dims around the edges of his vision. He can't move. He should have waited, should have let all three get in range first.

He loses balance and topples sideways in a heap, watching in slow motion as the creature's hooked blade of an arm descends. His eyes close.

鼠

The blow never comes.

"Get him up!" He hears a voice shout. "Get him back!"

He forces his eyes open. Anna's holding the arm-scythe with her bare hands, wrestling with it. The creature lets out a hideous cackle and swipes at her with its other clawed hand, tearing the front of her shirt as she throws the other arm up and heaves herself backward out of the way.

She clenches her fists and lunges at it as Bliss grabs Mouse under his armpits and drags him backward. The spear rattles on the ground as he drags it with him, the muscles in his hand still cramped around it.

"Yesss," the creature says, holding the final sibilance a little too long. "Strength. Power." Grinning wide and salivating, it lashes out and catches Anna from behind, pulls her in close, smells her like some kind of delicacy. She twists and pulls something out from behind her, tucked in her waistband—a kitchen knife—and neatly slices a chunk out of the creature's arm before squirming free and standing at sparring distance, knife out.

Mouse rolls onto his side and heaves himself upright, so his back is propped up against the side of the bridge. Looking down, he sees his hand for the first time. It's blistered and charred in patches. No wonder it won't let go of the staff. He's going to need to get that fixed, he thinks absently. He looks up to see the terrified faces of the other students, unable to draw their eyes away from the fight, where Anna is holding her own. Bliss, on the other hand, is looking at him.

He takes a deep breath.

"Need to...give this." He holds out the spear and manages to wrench his hand open. He swears something inside it creaks and grinds as it reluctantly obeys. "To Anna."

The creature has lost interest in them for the time being, and is focusing all its attentions on Anna, the pair circling one another, trying to get in a fatal slash or thrust. She's a better fighter than Mouse, and faster than the thing she's facing, but a largish sushi knife is no match for the creature's reach. The spear tip itself is the same length as her knife, but there's another six feet besides. Bliss takes it from his hands and nods, a determined look on her face.

He tugs at her sleeve as she gets up. "No...hero...stuff." She looks down at him, then back to Anna. She doesn't respond, and for the first time in the fight, Mouse is afraid.

"Hey! Over here!" Bliss wishes she could have thought of something better to get its attention, but the thing is between her and Anna. She rattles the spear and points it toward the thing's face. It turns, considers, and then turns back to Anna. Bliss grits her teeth. Fine, then, she thinks.

She holds it over her shoulder and leans back. "Going to turn your back on me, huh?" She yells. "Varsity track and field javelin champion," she says, winding up and taking a step. "Two—" step "—years—" lunge "—running!" The last word comes out explosively as the spear leaves her grip and flies through the air. The creature turns in time to see the projectile strike it square in the mouth, the tip bursting out the back of its neck. It reels, and falls.

Anna sees Bliss over the body of the creature and stands in shock for half a second before running over and giving Bliss a high five.

"That was *amazing!*" she says.

Bliss decides she won't tell Anna that she was trying to get the spear *over* the creature, and gives her a hug. They look at each other and start giggling, giddy from the adrenaline. Anna wants to say something about the kiss, but there's nothing really to say and she guesses this isn't really the time.

And then her eyes go wide as Bliss lurches forward, a red spire blossoming from her abdomen. She looks down in surprise, hardly realizing what's happening before the creature's scythe arm, now segmented like an armored tentacle, lifts and tosses her over the edge of the bridge and out of sight, down to the river below.

For a full two seconds, Anna's world stops.

Then Anna screams, her shock and horror crystallizing into wordless rage, and she's on top of the creature, hacking piece after piece from its regenerating hide. It lurches to its feet regardless, as she rides its shoulders driving her knife into its skull over and over. Now blind, it staggers, arms whipping about its head trying to dislodge its assailant, but every time it brings a limb close, Anna moves, impossibly fast, severing tendons, lacerating its hide. The blade, though small, glows with a pale purple light that leaves the creature's flesh smoking wherever it hits.

The thing falls to its knees before it finally gets purchase on Anna's leg and flings her from its mutilated, oozing head. It leans forward, trying to push itself back to standing, steps forward to where Anna stands with knife in hand and white with fury.

And then a part of the creature's middle disappears. And another. It takes Anna a moment to realize that each disappearance is accompanied by the sound of a loud bang, and she turns behind her.

Vallis is walking up, holding a rather large, shiny, pump-action gun of some kind, launching round after energetic round into the creature until it crumples into a heap. He walks past her, ignoring her entirely, until he's standing over what's left of the thing. Somehow, it's still moving, its vocalizations reduced to leaky gurgles and pops. From somewhere inside, it releases a sound very much like the word *power*, before Vallis vaporizes its head from point-blank range.

Anna runs to the edge of the bridge and looks down, but all that's there are the icy black waters of the thaw-swollen river. No trace of Bliss remains.

鼠

Mouse opens his eyes, and Anna's standing over him.

"*Gome*," he says. "Passed out." He tries to focus his eyes closer but can't. "Bliss," he says.

Anna crouches down and wraps her arms around him. She's sobbing.

He reaches up and rubs her back, confused. There was fighting. He'd been fighting. His hand hurts. Why does his hand hurt? He closes his eyes again. Being awake is hard.

He gets sudden images flashing before his eyes—the creatures, the spear, the lightning. He sucks in breath and his eyes snap open. The fight.

He forces his mouth to move. "Win? Did we win?"

Anna pulls back, puts her forehead on his, nods, suppressing her tears for a moment.

"Good, good..." Oblivion beckons, but he can't help the nagging feeling something is wrong. If they won why is Anna crying? Why is everyone standing around? He sees a figure behind Anna.

"Vallis?" he manages.

The trench coat looks at him, shakes his head, and walks off.

Mouse looks at Anna, confused. "Where's Bliss?"

Anna looks down, then back at Mouse, shakes her head. "She's..." She swallows, can't finish the sentence.

Mouse grunts and sits up. Demands that his mouth obey him for a change. "Anna, where's Bliss?"

Anna looks away, tears creeping down her cheek once more.

"Anna—"

"Right here."

The voice comes from behind Anna, and she swivels around to stare.

Bliss is standing there, soaked to the bone, leaning on the spear. Her shirt is stained with blood. She looks exhausted, but alive.

Anna jumps to her feet. "Bliss!" she shouts and wraps her arms around her. "But you—you're...?"

Bliss nods. She pulls the shirt up to show a stomach unscathed by injury.

"But how?"

Bliss frowns and crouches down in front of Mouse, ignoring the question.

"Hey," Mouse manages. "You're wet."

She smiles and puts a cold hand on his. It's hot to the touch; he's running a fever.

"You're going to be okay," she says.

He nods, closing his eyes.

"Mouse?" He doesn't respond.

He doesn't stir when she shakes his shoulder either.

"Vallis!" she shouts over her shoulder. "We need to get him to Priest."

The trench coat shrugs. "Hey, don't think just because I fished you out of a river we're going steady now—"

"New York!" she snaps. "Sarajevo! Paris! You hear me? Now follow the protocols and let's get moving."

Vallis's face changes, jaw hanging open. "How do you—?"

"Because it's *me*," she says. "Now do it."

"But how—"

"Because it's *him*! Don't ask questions, Guardian, you know how this works. This is to be kept in strictest confidence, and I may need your assistance later. I'm electing you, understood?"

He stands straighter, somehow, and puts away the gun. "Mistress," he says with deference.

Vallis walks over to the four teens, still crouched and lying, unbelieving, just feet from the corpses of the monsters that were once their friends. They've been so wholly unprepared for the reality they've seen, they haven't even been able to respond. He leans over them.

"If you had any idea, you'd thank me for this," he says, and reaches toward them. In his dark hand is a small white device that lets off a cool light. Before they can say anything, their eyes are closing. Tomorrow, they'll wake up in their beds, having only the faintest recollection of the horrors they've seen, like a terrible nightmare they've all woken up from. It's for the best.

He straightens. "We're set here." He points to a black van at the far end of the bridge. "Take that. I'll do the rest."

Bliss nods. "Thank you, Guardian. Remember: not a word." She turns to Anna. "I'll explain things to you the best I can later, but right now we need Priest's help."

Anna nods, unsure, but more focused on Mouse than on her friend's survival and suddenly strange behavior. As she leans forward, Bliss puts a cold hand on the back of her neck and she stiffens, freezes in place. Bliss walks past her to Mouse and crouches down, puts a finger between his eyebrows and smiles a little sadly before standing back up and walking to where she was. She puts a hand back on Anna's neck again and the familiar twitches, then stands up straight, confused.

"Is something wrong?" Bliss says, her eyes searching.

Anna looks around, like she's lost something, and then shakes her head. "No, it's fine. I thought for a second...no, it's nothing. Come on, I think Mouse has a fever and I can't wake him up. We should get him some help."

Bliss nods. "Is June at the hospital or—you know what, never mind. We'll take him to Priest. He and Helene will be able to help." She shouts over to Vallis. "Hey, mister, can we borrow your van? It's kind of an emergency."

Vallis is crouching over the body of the last beast, frowning. He looks up and nods.

Bliss turns to Anna. "I think that's a yes. Let's go before he changes his mind."

鼠

The van shudders to a stop in front of the bar, but they have to wait until no one's around before they surreptitiously unload their injured cargo into the blind alley where the pub's entrance lies.

They wait behind the van's shaded windows while a couple wanders by—a woman visibly pregnant, a man doting on her every whim—oblivious to the horrors Bliss and Anna have seen this afternoon. Anna has the sudden urge to kick open the door and yell at them, to snap them out of their daydreaming lives, to wake them up to the world they really live in and tell them to *run*, to *get somewhere safe*—but, she thinks, there probably *isn't* anywhere that's really safe. Is there even any point in telling people about a threat they can't do anything about? The thought just makes her feel even worse, like it's just her and Mouse and Bliss and Kai that have been thrown into this strange world, like the biggest problems have fallen on the smallest shoulders, and the adults are just there for backup.

Anna had always been sick, had always been dying. Right from the first thing she can remember, her mother and father and Kai had been carrying her around like she was made of eggshells or tissue paper, worrying that she'd crack or tear at the slightest bump. But from her perspective she had been tougher then than she is now—she had never been afraid. They say fear is only something that attends the possibility of death, that when it becomes a certainty, it becomes less scary somehow. She had never been going to make it to eighteen, never been going to have to worry about what to do with her life, about who to care about or imagine a future with. Never had to worry about others, except what it might be like for them, for her to leave them behind. Death had never been a possibility for her, only an inevitability, and when it came, it came peacefully. For a while.

Now she's looking into the back seat at the boy who accidentally brought her back to life, or something like it, who she's just seen turn two freakish monsters into heaps of ash by harnessing actual, honest-to-god lightning bolts, maybe not a reincarnation but a part of a being powerful enough to actually reshape the world. And he's just lying there, asleep or passed out or delirious and feverish in the back seat. And she wants him to be okay so much that it hurts, wants to live forever so she can keep him safe. Now more than ever before she's afraid for what's coming next.

She looks back at the couple outside, finally passing out of sight, and suddenly wants them never to wake up, to go on living their daydreams forever. To be happy and worry about what color shoes to wear or what neighborhood to live in, or what to name the baby when it arrives. Normal things that seem so distant now. She wants to fight to protect them, to protect everyone, so at least she can have that.

She looks at Bliss, who's staring out the front of the van, chin placed between her hands on the top of the steering wheel. She looks so calm. Anna wonders what she's thinking.

"Coast's clear," Bliss says, sitting up, still looking out the front window. "Let's get him inside."

鼠

"What happened?" Helene barges into the back room where Priest has helped them lift Mouse onto a bench and cover him with blankets.

"Three...things," Bliss says. "Used to be students at the high school. They were acting creepy and then they just, changed. Big, scaly, asymmetrical?"

"Azazim," Helene says.

"Sure," Bliss says.

She points to the spear where they left it in the corner. "Mouse took out two of them with that thing and—I can't believe I'm saying this—with that thing and lightning bolts. The third one nearly got us," Bliss nods over at Anna, "but your friend, what was his name? Big, black trench coat, probably names his guns?"

"Vallis," Priest says, offhand, inspecting Mouse.

"—Vallis. Took out the third one with some kind of magic shotgun or something. He lent us his van to get here, while he cleans up the mess."

Anna squeezes a few words in. "There were other students who saw everything, but he said he'd take care of that. He didn't mean—"

"No, no." Priest looks up. "He'll just wipe their memories. He may be a real talker and a bit of a gun nut, but he's a hell of a one-man cleanup crew. Any witnesses will be a little confused for a couple of days, but they won't be scarred for life, and we won't have to explain the *azazim h'adam*, or for that matter—" he looks over at the spear "—you said lightning?"

Anna nods and Priest whistles through his teeth. "Let me guess, he didn't draw any circles on the ground beforehand or anything?" They shake their heads. "Well, that explains things." He taps on Mouse's forehead and Anna thinks she hears him mutter the word *amateur*.

Anna tries to explain. "I was just coming to find him, after..." After what? She feels like maybe they were fighting? Over what? She stops for a moment. What had she been going to say? She shakes her head. "Anyway, there were these lightning bolts, and then he fell over, but he only got two of the things. And then Bliss took one out with the spear and then..." She stops again. She can't remember what happened after that. They were fighting, and then—what? "Vallis took out the third one, I guess."

Bliss nods. "Yeah, he went all 'Here comes the cavalry' on it, at the end. But Anna, you were amazing fighting it like that with just a knife."

Anna frowns, trying to remember. "Yeah, I guess." She has flashes of striking at the beast, stabbing it, but it's all patchwork, with bits missing in between. She'll have to ask Mouse, when he wakes up. Assuming he does wake up.

"Is he going to be okay?" she asks. "And what were those things? You called them azazim?" Priest holds up his hand for silence while working on Mouse, small flashes of light tracing their way over the inert body in intricate patterns.

Helene nods. "*Azazim h'adam*. Azaz if there's only one. It's an old name, means something like 'rebellious men.' A sprite stitched back into its own dead body. It's a kind of necromancy that's been banned for centuries, and for good reason."

"Wait, you mean somebody killed them? And then brought them back to life?"

Priest grunts. "If you can call that life. Nothing like giving the finger to mother nature."

"But Mouse brought *me* back," Anna says. "Is that going to happen to me?"

Helene shakes her head. "No, Mouse didn't break any Laws with you, he just found loopholes and exploited them. Necromancy is arguably easier, sure, that's what draws people to it, but the products are unstable, the violations are severe and the repercussions are... well, I assume you saw."

"They went crazy, became monsters."

"They became exactly what they were: violations of the natural order." Helene frowns. "It takes a corruption of the will—they have to want it, at least some part of them, for it to work." She shivers. "You can't force someone to become one of those things. You have to recruit them into it."

"The one kept referring to it as a gift, something he wanted to share with everyone."

Priest makes a disgusted noise. "I tangled with one of those when I was younger, before you were born, Helene, this time anyway, me and Junebug, back in Scotland. Stupid kid with a talent for the Knowledge tried to bring his girlfriend back. She talked like that, about sharing her disgusting wonderfulness with the world." He pauses, thinking back. "We set her on fire in the end. Not before she killed him, of course. Poor, stupid kid."

"The question is, who's our necromancer?" She sighs. "I'm going to go look up the usual suspects. See if they have any leads." She moves to the door, and Bliss stops her.

"Wait!" Bliss grabs her by the hand, and Helene looks at her curiously. "They knew about Mouse. About Mouse and Anna." She looks over at him, lying on the bench. "They said that whoever had done that to them really wanted to meet him."

Helene stares hard at her, then nods. "That might narrow the list, thank you." She stops to look at Mouse, then at Priest, then, after he nods the all clear, she walks out.

"Vallis might be able to figure it out," Priest says to Anna and Bliss. "For now, we need to make sure Mouse makes it home. You did right to bring him here—I've stabilized him. But now we should get him to bed." He stops to consider. "Maybe *you* should get him there. I don't think Junebug's gonna be too happy with me. Especially with the lightning thing."

Bliss nods, and they work together to get Mouse ready for the trip home.

鼠

It's dark outside as Helene emerges from the bar, a stoic expression on her face. Bliss had slipped something into her hand when she'd stopped her back inside. She walks to the nearest streetlight and unfolds a letter, too big to have been ripped from one of Mouse's pads. It's several pages long, and as she reads it her expression shifts from curiosity to confusion to bewilderment.

"The hell...?" she says, under her breath, turning to go back. Then she stops and thinks differently of it, turning away. She stands under the streetlamp and stares at the letter again, before folding it carefully, sticking it into the pocket of her coat, and walking off into the night.

It's pitch black until Helene lights a Zippo, casting a faint orange flicker over the shadows in the room. She's not alone.

She turns to her right and a heap of rags flies at her, something small and lithe beneath, with tiny shining claws glinting in the firelight. Helene drops the lighter and pulls two curved blades from sheaths within her cloak. The ragged form hits her, and they roll in the dark, until they stop against a wall. In the shadows, Helene has one blade at the creature's throat, the other pinning one of its hands to the ground in the small sickle of space where her kukri blade curves.

She breathes heavily as she says to the other, "Bid me parley or I take your head."

The little imp giggles and a tiny voice responds. "Fine, fine. Granted."

Helene lets it up, and the small figure wanders to a dark spot on the wall and throws a switch. A dim light fills the room from gas lamps that ignite around its periphery. It's like a curiosity shop of garbage and gold, newspapers and treasures stowed around and under and behind each other.

"How have you been, Helene?" The small figure is female, with porcelain doll features—if one were to make a porcelain doll with a wicked grin and tiny claws and long, ragged, pointed ears. She softens her smile and a snaggletooth pokes out one side of her mouth. "Or is it even Helene these days? It's so hard to keep track." She sits on a pile of rags that gives way to hold her just as a throne holds a queen. "I marvel at you, Magus's skipping stone, skipped all the way down here to my collection of lost and forgotten things. You could stay, you know. You'd fit right in."

"I have a question for you, timekeeper."

The imp giggles.

"I know! And I keep telling you the answer, too!"

Helene scowls. "So I have been here before."

"You will have been. You will have been over and over and over!" She cackles and grins in a high-pitched voice. "But will it even be you? You're the reason I built this little cache here. For such a dull little town the convergences here are fascinating!" She flops down in her rags and tilts her head back so far it looks as though it's almost fallen off. "Oh but whose fault is that?" Her head snaps back up and she grins again.

"You cryptic little beast."

"Oh you're just jealous."

"Of you?" Helene scoffs.

The imp giggles again, slides a hand under the her ragged cloak to reveal a long, slender white leg. She runs a clawed finger up her own thigh.

"He stayed with me once, you know. I like that moment a lot. I go there over and over. Any moment can be every moment for me you know." She stops and smiles at Helene. "You only wish you could have him the way I do, because I have him forever and ever."

"What you have is a snowglobe."

The imp sighs. "Limited human. So linear. Still, *you* seem to get a little more *variety*, I'll concede. Even if you have to wait so very long in between." She pouts the last few words out, a small finger pressed to her chin in a parody of a parody of childhood—a wretched Droste effect.

"You aren't cute at all."

"I wouldn't want *you* to think so. Still, *he* thought I was." She sighs and drops the mocking tone for only half a second, looking off into nowhere, her tone warming. "He actually thought so, the fool."

"You wish," Helene says and snorts.

"Oh what would you know, *human!*" the creature says, snapping at her, the last word meant as an insult. Then she relaxes back into her smooth, controlled smirk. "I've seen him this time. I wonder if he remembers me."

"He's different this time."

"Oh I know. He's *so* different." She leans forward. "Do you want to know how different he is?" She smiles and her irises, emeralds so dark they're almost black, shine in the gaslight. She whispers. *"He surprised me."*

Helene raises her eyebrows, leans back.

"Or he will surprise me." The imp furrows her brows. "Or he is surprising me. You humans, I don't even know how to relate. Why must you live in such a bizarre set of straight lines?"

"But he doesn't."

"Neither do you. You just don't know it, my little skipping stone. He really did a number on you when he left, didn't he? You used to be, how should I put this?" She taps her forehead. "More intuitive." She sighs. "Well, no matter." She gets up and wanders off into a dark corner of the room, before returning a moment later.

"This is it, right?" She holds up a few pieces of paper. It's the same letter that Bliss gave her. She peers at it in the dark. "She finally gave it to you, not that it'll help."

"But how—"

"I granted you an audience, darling, not Solomon's Key. If you're too thick to get it, go ask yourself for the answers until you figure it out." She waves her hand dismissively. "I prefer her to you. She at least has manners."

Helene grits her teeth, wanting to spit out another comeback, to goad more information out of this little being that sees her whole life all at once, who *must* have all the answers, but refuses to tell them. But this is all she's going to get, so she stands, bows a little, and says "Thank you, timekeeper."

The imp turns away from her, an imperious queen dismissing a subject from her sight. But as Helene's walking away the little voice follows her.

"He did, you know."

Helene stops and replies without looking.

"I know."

"If you get the chance to tell him," she says, but then stops and laughs a little to herself. "But you won't. I suppose I'll have to tell him myself."

"Goodbye, Ver."

"For now."

Helene walks out, leaving the imp to stare with dark eyes into the shadows that reflect them.

"Come back soon," she says.

鼠

Mouse wakes up to sunlight shining on his face. He's in his own bed.

"You're an idiot."

He rolls over and Anna is lying next to him, on top of the covers. She's on her side, staring at him. He tries to sit up, startled, but sore all over and still half asleep, the covers hold him down.

"That's what Priest said to tell you. That, and that you need to use limiting circles when drawing on celestial powers. You know, things like *lightning*."

Mouse sighs. He knew he'd forgotten something. A limiting circle works like a spray nozzle on a hose. You can still shoot water out of a hose without one, but it takes a hell of a lot more water to do it. He'd just done the magical equivalent of blowing out a candle by screaming at it. No wonder he feels like crap.

"And you're also an idiot for trying to take on those things without me."

She's only six inches away from his face.

I was looking for you at the time, he thinks to her.

"Well you should have looked harder." She sits up. "It's not like I was trying to hide from—" she winces, and puts a hand to her head. Something hasn't felt right since the fight. "Wait," she says. "Was I?"

She gets up and walks to the window, looks out. A pair of birds are nesting in a nearby tree, and one flies off as she watches.

"How much do you remember about yesterday?" she asks.

I was walking home with Bliss after school, and then—

"Yeah, but where was I?"

Mouse frowns. *What do you mean?*

"I always walk home with you. Why wasn't I there?"

Mouse doesn't know.

"There are missed calls from Bliss on my phone from yesterday. Why would she try to call me?" She doesn't wait for an answer. She repeats herself, "Why wasn't I there?"

He sits up in bed, and puts a hand to his head. Maybe the lightning had fried some of his brain cells, but Anna's, too? *We should ask Bliss*, he thinks.

"I'm not sure we should," she says, so quietly Mouse can't even really hear her.

What's that?

She shakes her head. "I'm sure it's nothing."

Before Mouse can ask again, June knocks and walks into the room.

"Hey, kiddo. How're you feeling?"

Not wanting to be a bother, he grabs a pad and pen from the bedside table. *Okay*, he writes. *Sore.*

"Anna told me what you did yesterday. I don't know whether I'm proud of you or pissed. Lightning without a limiting circle! Use your head next time." Her voice almost falters over the last two words as she says them. That there will be a next time is a certainty, and they've all had to accept it. She looks over at the spear in the corner, picks it up. "Where did you get the idea for this?"

Mouse shrugs. *I think the other me left some ideas behind before the darkness shut him out.*

June shakes her head while tossing the spear from hand to hand, appraising it. It comes apart into three sections that somehow snap back together almost seamlessly. She seems impressed as she puts it back in the corner.

"Right, well. There's coffee downstairs, and you look like you might need a cup." She sniffs at the air, which Mouse has to admit smells a little like overdone barbecue. "After that, take a shower." She looks at Anna, then back at Mouse with a smirk. "One at a time, though."

Mouse turns red and Anna looks out the window as the birds becomes suddenly interesting. Had Anna been there all night? Oh god, what did June think? While Anna looks away, June looks at Mouse and mimes the phrase, *we're going to have a talk about this*, before walking out. Anna volunteers to shower first and exits without making eye contact.

鼠

There have been more disappearances while he was asleep. A girl who volunteered at the hospital never made it home after her shift, and a boy from her class who she'd been seen walking home with from time to time was missing, too. A few adults have been reported missing, too, mostly people who lived alone, so exactly when they'd been taken was up in the air. The folks on TV have been trying to be calm about it, but there's something so peculiar about the way people have been vanishing that it puts everyone on edge. The newscasters look like they're about ready to bolt when they cut to a commercial and Anna turns off the TV. Mouse's wet hair hangs down in front of his face in ratty ringlets as he picks at his food, deep in thought.

"A lot of them are happening around the bridge," June says. There are actually two bridges across the river in town, but the other one is so rarely used and almost out of town that 'The bridge' has come to mean the one to the hospital. The one where they fought. June is cleaning a frying pan while Mouse and Anna finish a late breakfast. "I'm going to have a look on my way to work."

Mouse puts down his fork and writes her a note, which Anna passes along.

Take Priest with you.

"Leonard? Why?" she says. "No."

Then we'll check it out. It's dangerous to go alone.

She sighs. "The great Simon Magus looking out for his old Ma, huh?"

Mouse nods, serious.

"Fine," she says, acceding, "I'll swing by and grab him, if he can be parted from your—that is, from Helene." She ducks down a little to try to see past his bangs. "Okay with you?"

Mouse nods again.

"Now come on, you've already missed first period. If you're quick, I'll give you a lift."

Mouse looks like he wants to say something but doesn't, and June walks out to get ready to go.

鼠

The car doors close with a clunk and June waves as she drives off. Once again the mundanity of life strikes him as jarring. On the way into the school he grabs Anna by the arm and pulls her aside in the deserted hall. She already knows what he's thinking, but he puts it into words for her anyway.

What are we even doing?

"What do you mean?"

Why are we at school? More of those things could show up at any minute.

Anna looks at him, her expression unclear. "So far as we know, there aren't any more yet."

But there have been disappearances, we should be out looking for them.

"That's what June and Priest are doing."

*Then we should be helping them, not hanging around here like everything's okay. Everything's **not** okay. How can we be just doing this, just going to school like normal when some crazy-evil freaks are out there turning people into monsters? You saw those things, what they were after, what they were going to do—to those other kids, to Bliss—*

"To you?" Anna looks at him like she can't decide whether to yell at him or cry, which makes him all the more confused when she wraps her arms around him and whispers into his shirt. "*Baka.* Everybody just wants you to stay safe for as long as you can. We want you to...I don't know, have a little more normal in your life. I mean it's crazy enough that we're fighting the evil dead out there, but you...you're part of some crazy, *bigger* you, too."

She looks up at him, then looks down and rests her forehead on his chest while she talks. "I'm *dead*, Mouse," she says. The words hang in the air for a moment before she continues. "Nothing's ever going to be normal for me again. I *had* my normal. June and Priest and the rest of the adults—this *is* their normal. But you...we're, *I'm* worried. That it's going to happen again. That you're going to become that *other* you again and forget all about us—"

But that can't happen, at least not during—

"You didn't see yourself summoning that lightning," she says. "The expression on your face? Just..." She trails off. "Just let someone else handle things for now, okay?" She pulls back and looks up at him. "Please, Nezumi? I just...I want you to stay you."

The sight of her face, her eyes wet with tears, starts to remind him of—he puts his hand to his head as a little bolt of white pain shoots through it.

Anna looks at him. "Okay?"

He nods. He's not sure what it was but it's gone now.

He hugs her back and agrees to go to class.

The rest of the day passes in montage, and the following night, and the rest of the week. Sitting at his desk, exchanging glances with Bliss or Anna in the batcave, zoning out during dinner. He tosses and turns at night, wondering when the next attack will come. The disappearances seem to stop, and Mouse's whole world falls into a kind of desperately numb stasis.

鼠

A spear thrust and a shout—Mouse is training early in the morning. It's been two weeks since the last disappearance. No more creatures have appeared, and the town feels like it's sleepwalking its way out of some kind of unspoken calamity.

"Stop there. Hold it." June walks over to him as he holds the weapon up in the air at an angle. "It's just like with grappling, you need to remember to keep your stance wide. See how easy it is to push you over if I get hold of your spear?" She steps in past the point and uses it as a lever—not knocking him over, just showing him that she could. He plants his feet farther apart and she pushes again. "Better."

He puts down the spear point and sighs.

"Remember, with a spear once they're past the tip your enemy can grab it, so you either need to pull it back with your right hand or step back with them when they advance."

Mouse remembers; she's told him a few times already.

"Now, let's see you work on your focus."

He nods. With the butt-end of the spear, he spins a quick circle around himself on the floor that, with a little will, leaves behind a faint glow. Next, he pulls a card with a design drawn carefully on it and holds it around the shaft. The lights dim slightly as he focuses, and a small ball of white light appears just past the spear's point. He holds his focus to the count of ten, fifteen, twenty, twenty-five—until June claps and shouts. "Good!"

He lets the ball of lightning dissolve into the air and exhales as the lights brighten again. It's hard work, but with a limiting circle it's a lot less work than it would be—and a lot less likely to kill him.

"A couple of those will take out an azaz, no problem." June smiles, straightens and bows—a gesture Mouse returns before relaxing and looking over at the empty bench.

Anna's not here today. Since Kai found out about her she's been trying to be his supportive kid sister again, and sometimes that means following him to boxing practice in the morning. Of course school practices don't start quite as early as those with June, and he thinks over to her to see if she's even awake yet. As he reaches the bench and trades his spear for a towel he realizes that she's showering and snaps that mental door shut so fast that it probably makes a noticeable bang on her end.

June walks over to the bench and tosses an orange to Mouse, snapping him out of his reverie. "How many of those can you shoot off in ten seconds?"

Mouse catches the orange and holds up three fingers.

"Aim for five."

He nods, bends down and snaps the spear into its three sections before stuffing it into a small duffel, which he slings over his shoulder. It's warm enough now that even at this time of day he doesn't mind walking. He waves goodbye and sets out while June heads on to her shift.

鼠

Mouse walks down to the bridge as the dawn starts to shine over the far hills, turning everything in the town a shade of yellow that will fade to grey as the sun climbs above the clouds. As he nears the bridge, he puts his hand into the bag and onto the spear, trying not to be tense, telling himself that it could have happened anywhere and that it had just happened to be here. He's not very convincing.

He walks across in silence, alert, taking careful steps and breathing slowly, extending his senses—nothing. Not a peep. So why does he feel as though—

"Simon."

He nearly jumps out of his skin. He spins, and the disassembled spear snaps itself together in his hand. It's Helene, standing right behind him.

One corner of her lips twists in a suppressed smile, and she raises an eyebrow at the sight of the spear before he sighs, lowers it and continues walking. She walks next to him.

"It's unusual to see you without your familiar."

He looks at her and shrugs.

"How has your training progressed?"

He looks around—no one for miles. How did Helene even get here? He wonders if she does this a lot, follows him around without his knowing. He stops, draws a limiting circle and lets off a blast into the nearest shrub. It causes its still-green branches to pop and burst, casting small fragments of wood and leaf around the area. He walks over and steps on a smoldering twig.

"If we were up against Abu, lesser god of plants, we'd have little to fear," she says. He can't tell for sure if she's joking, but he feels like maybe she is.

He takes apart the spear before stowing it in his bag and starting home again.

"I've been meaning to ask you something for a while now." He looks at her and his expression invites her to continue. "About Bliss. Who is she?"

He looks at her, then sighs, stops walking again, and fishes in his pockets for a pad and pen.

What?

"The girl hanging around with you all the time. Not your familiar, the other one."

I know who Bliss is. What about her?

"Who is she?"

What are you asking? She's Bliss. She's my friend. The first person I met at school.

"How much do you know about her?"

He just underlines the first words of the same note, repeating the question:

What are you asking?

"Is she from around here? Have you met her family, for instance?"

No. They travel a lot, her brother's at some prep school overseas.

"Which one?"

I don't know.

"Did he come home for Christmas?"

No, I guess he didn't. What are you getting at?

"Where was she born? How long has she lived here?"

I don't know. She dated Kai for a while, knew Anna before she died.

Helene nods, thinking to herself.

"How much do you remember from the day you fought here, on the bridge?"

Not much after I became the human bug zapper.

"How about before?"

He stops and thinks. They had been on their way home from school. No, it had just been him and Bliss. Where had Anna been? She was there for the fight. Why wasn't she—

A pain fills his head with white light and he presses a palm to his temple and winces. What was that?

Helene nods. "Just as I thought. Hold on."

She holds up a hand and whispers a quick incantation. Mouse puts his hands up as if to say, *Hey, wait,* but before he can get the message across something that feels surprisingly like a ping-pong ball hits him in the forehead and sets his teeth on edge, like he's bitten down on an electric toothbrush. He drops his bag and staggers backward, then drops to one knee, holding his skull.

As the vibration eases, so, too, does the white light in his head. As it recedes, it reveals memories: kissing Bliss, Anna running away, looking for her.

Mouse just looks up at Helene, in shock.

"Memory blocking. Simple and effective, but easily undone if you have the know-how."

Mouse scribbles quickly in his pad.

And you think Bliss did this?

"Your sidekick wouldn't know how, and it sure wasn't done by one of those violations—they wouldn't have been half so careful about it. This was surgical." She tosses him a small stone. "A little will should activate it—use it on your familiar."

Mouse shakes his head, stepping back. *But Bliss—she doesn't even know how to use the Knowledge.*

"Someone this skilled would know how to hide it."

But that's crazy. Why would she do that? Why do any of it?

But there are the missed calls on Anna's phone, the little headaches when he tried to think about it. And he's felt as though Bliss has been standoffish since the attack. He looks up at Helene and then back down again at the pavement. Would she? Why?

Helene looks down at him and then strides away, leaving him to stand up and dust himself off. She turns around and walks backward for a moment, far enough away that she has to raise her voice, but not far enough that she needs to shout. The expression on her face is unreadable: frustrated? Impressed? She almost laughs.

"Because it's what *I* would do, Simon. It's exactly what I would do."

鼠

He runs home and showers before throwing everything into a bag and rushing to school. He gets there in time to see everyone coming out of the small gym and heading to the locker rooms. Anna waves as she's going in and he sits on a small bench in the hall waiting for her to pretend to need to change. She doesn't even really need to shower, she just likes to. He stops himself opening that mental door again and reddens at the thought.

He looks down at the little stone Helene gave him. It's like a little rounded piece of quartz, white and smooth with tiny shining hairs running through it, like spider silk caught in clear amber. Does he really want to give it to her? He thinks about kissing Bliss, wonders how he could have forgotten it, forgotten Anna's reaction.

Kai comes out first from the locker room on the other side of the hall. "Hey, how's it going?"

He sits down next to Mouse, who holds up a hand and waves it in the universal symbol for, *Enh, pretty good.*

They sit in silence for a second, before Kai clears his throat and starts to speak again. "So I need to ask you about—"

"Mouse!" Anna comes out of the changing room and bounces over, ruffling his hair with both hands. "You need to spar with Kai," she says, emphasizing every second word. "Your spear's all well and good, but niisan can really throw a punch. He'll teach you a thing or two." She throws a thrust and a hook with accompanying cartoon sound effects. Then she stops, putting a finger on her chin. "But maybe I'll lend him my bokken, just so you don't skewer him."

"Thanks for the vote of confidence," Kai says, and Anna just grins.

"Whatcha got there?" Anna says, looking at the stone.

Mouse shoves it in his pocket and puts up a hand. *Later,* he thinks, and she squints at him, then shrugs, letting it go.

Bliss comes out with a towel still around her neck, drying her hair, and Anna explains that she'd come in with her and Kai had given them both a workout. Mouse looks hard at Bliss, so much that she stops and reddens a little. "What...?" she says. "I mean, hi."

Anna flicks him in the side of the head and he scowls at her. *It's not what you think.* He sighs. *It might be what you think.*

Anna scowls back at him.

I'll explain later, when she's not around.

Anna's eyebrows go up.

"Would you two stop?" Kai says.

Anna laughs. "*Gome, Niisan*. I forget sometimes you can't hear us." Bliss purses her lips and eyes them both before declaring her intent to attend at least one class this morning. Kai shakes his head.

"Go to all your classes for once, delinquent."

Bliss salutes and wanders off as the five minute bell rings. Both Kai's question and Anna's memories will have to wait.

鼠

They're sitting in Wigmore's math class when it happens.

A cellphone rings.

Wigmore scowls in its direction, as Kitty Munroe, a girl Mouse more knows *of* than actually *knows*, dives through her bag apologizing. She pulls it out to turn it off, but then stops, staring at the screen while it keeps ringing.

"Well, Ms. Munroe?" says the teacher, impatient at the prolonged interruption.

Kitty's face is pale. "I— I have to take this," she says, and runs into the hall.

Whispers from the seats behind her:

"Didn't the screen say 'Dad'?"

"I thought her dad died last year."

Mr. Wigmore claps his hands to silence the class. "Settle down, let's not extend the interruption—"

But then another phone rings. And another.

"Let me remind you all that your phones are required to be off in class!"

"It was!" comes a response. "Mine, too!"

A small symphony of ringtones, every call from a dead relative, friend, or acquaintance.

Every call a warning.

A sea of ashen faces fill the room as they answer the calls while their teacher tries to stop them, until his phone, too, rings. An ascending chirping from Mouse's pocket: unknown number. He looks at Bliss, the only person whose phone hasn't rung, and answers.

"They're coming for you, Diviner. They're coming for everyone, but they're *really* coming for you." He recognizes the voice. It's the boy from before. The dead one. Marcus.

"Time for everyone to die."

The building goes silent as every phone cuts off at once, as the lights go out, as the heavy metal *chunk* of the emergency lights all coming on at once echoes in the rooms and halls.

And then the panic starts to set in.

There aren't a lot of windows in the school. It was built as a tribute to the marvels of concrete, back when the psychological effects of ugliness and sunlight deprivation hadn't been properly considered. Even in the middle of the day it'd be as black as night in the math class without the emergency lights, their dim yellow glow casting unfamiliar shadows in the room. Students start to whisper to one another, all afraid that too loud a voice will somehow break the fragile stability of the class. If just one student had screamed, had panicked and shouted—but not one did.

Mr. Wigmore stands at the front staring at his phone, in a kind of daze. Then he puts it away and looks over the class.

"Phones away, please," he says. The class continues to hum with mutters and whispers. He repeats himself, louder: "Phones away. Eyes on me."

The students all look at him, and true silence fills the room.

"I understand that what's taken place just now must be unsettling for all of you. I have to admit it's been a little unsettling for me, too." His hand goes to his pocketed phone as he talks. "I'd like you all to treat this in the same manner as our safe schools drill that you learned at the beginning of the year, and to stay in your seats for the time being. Stay calm, and feel free to talk amongst yourselves."

Bliss swivels in her seat and stares at Mouse. "Who called you?" she asks in low tones.

He scribbles a note in the dim light. *Azaz kid, Marcus.*

"What did he say?"

They're coming for me. For everyone.

A knock at the door makes the class jump, but Wigmore sticks his head out into the hall, and converses with someone for a minute before closing the door again.

"All right, everyone. The administration has decided that, because of the unusual circumstances, classes will be suspended for the day. Please avoid going to your lockers unless it is absolutely necessary—I'm sure your belongings will all be waiting for you there tomorrow morning. Please leave by the nearest exit and go straight to the sidewalk and head home. Those of you needing rides should gather in the west field, where Mrs. Stephanek will be waiting for you." He waits for the class to react. "That's it, guys. Go on home and I'll see you tomorrow."

It's almost miraculous how calm everyone is able to stay, as they get up and leave the school.

Bliss follows Mouse to his locker so he can retrieve his duffel, and after a moment Kai and Anna meet them there. They walk down the hall, not talking. It isn't until they're on their way out of the darkened and nearly empty school that they see a cluster of students standing at the exit, looking out.

Bliss taps one of them on the shoulder. It's the girl from the other day, short brown hair, freckles, and glasses. The same look on her face Mouse remembers: fear, but resolution. The girl from the same group of students Marcus and the other two had tried to attack, who had tried to stand up to the dead boys before they changed their shapes. She looks at Bliss as if recognizing her, and then puts a hand to her head as if in pain. She shakes it off, looking a little confused. Mouse frowns, remembering the small white stone in his pocket.

"What's going on?" Bliss asks.

The girl looks out the door and then steps aside. "Have a look for yourself."

The world outside is eerily dark, lit only by the headlights of idling school buses and teachers' cars, all packed to the brim with nervous students. No streetlamps light the streets, and even the usual orange nighttime glow, reflected back by the clouds, is absent.

All of which is made the more unnerving by the fact that it's only just turned noon.

᠍᠍᠍᠍᠍

The power's out across town, except for the hospital and the few homes that had their own little generators installed after last year's ice storm. A few cars pass theirs, lighting the streets with headlights as their drivers scurry home in the pitch-black afternoon. Even the stars seem to have gone, and the sporadic drops of rain the windshield wipers scrape off the glass even seem to be darker, somehow muddy.

Kai gazes up through the passenger window while Bliss drives. "This can't be real," he says.

Mouse nudges Anna, asks her to relay a message for him.

"Mouse wants to know if we can take a detour. He's got a theory and wants to test it out."

Bliss looks over her shoulder.

"Kennedy between Tenth Line and Miller Road," Anna says.

Bliss nods and hangs a left at the next intersection.

"What are you thinking?" Kai asks.

Anna looks at Mouse, who's looking out the window and lost in thought. She looks at her brother and answers for him. "It's just a hunch, but it would explain the blackout as well as the night."

They pull onto Kennedy and Mouse waves for them to stop just before a railway crossing. Before Bliss has even put it into park Mouse has wandered across the empty street, looking up.

They're in a large transmission corridor, one that runs right through town and brings power to it and points beyond, to other parts of the state. Or, it did. There, about seventy-five feet in the air, between two of the steel-girder space-invaders that hold them up, the cables simply stop. Two hundred feet to the right they seem to begin again in the air over a field. The rail line just ends in the grass a hundred feet from the road. And in the distance Mouse can see something even stranger.

"Is that the hospital?" Kai asks.

Bliss nods. They've all left the car and followed Mouse into the field. The hospital should be on the other side of town.

"Recursive spatial loop," Anna says, receiving the information from Mouse. She looks up. "A pocket universe."

"So the power cables don't go anywhere," Kai says, "except here. And the sky?"

"There's probably nothing above a few hundred feet up there." Anna stares up at the sky. "Except maybe the dirt beneath our feet."

"So the rain is—"

"Ugh," Bliss says, wiping a drip of muddy water from her forehead. "Ground water."

There's a giggle from the point where the rail line ends, and Anna realizes Mouse has kept walking this whole time. She flickers forward just in time to see what he sees—there's a small figure sitting on the tracks, a girl with ragged pointy ears and a snaggle-toothed smile.

Bliss and Kai run up behind them.

"What's going on, Mouse? Who's this?"

Mouse looks like he wants to say something, but can't find the words.

The small figure laughs and stands up. She's wrapped in nothing but rags, but somehow she carries a regal air about her. She walks up to Mouse. Anna tries to stand between them, but suddenly finds herself behind them, ten feet away. The girl tries to take Mouse's free hand, but he pulls it away after giving it a brief squeeze.

"I'm flattered you remember," she says. "You haven't recognized me before."

"Verthandi," he whispers, looking down.

"The old you must have thought the knowledge worth keeping. How delightfully sentimental."

"Stay away from him!"

The command comes from the other side of town. It's Helene.

"Oh, my. Still jealous are we?"

"Is this your doing?" Helene strides across the dividing line, and there's a faint rippling as she walks across town with a single step.

There must be a little resistance around the edges, Mouse thinks, at least to prevent the sky from falling.

"My? My, my, little human. My doing? Oh, no." She grins wide, revealing pointed teeth. "I'm just here to watch." She tilts her head to one side, staring at Mouse. "You've been a subject of interest with my sisters and I, Diviner—in the past, when I had sisters. And you—" she looks back at Helene "—have been a point of much contention."

Helene almost growls.

"Or should I say, *you* have." She looks past Mouse, past Anna, and squarely at Bliss.

Bliss frowns, but says nothing.

"Do you think you should tell them?" The imp's eyes widen in a mockery of childlike wonderment. "I wonder, I wonder. How would that affect things?"

"Don't interfere, your ladyship," Bliss says.

"Oh, but that's the point of contention."

"But—"

"You swore!" No one sees her move, no one sees her cover the distance between Mouse and Bliss. Instead, everyone's heads turn at the sound of her small hand striking Bliss's cheek so hard that she nearly drops to one knee. The imp lowers her voice. "You swore you wouldn't knot my threads any further child, and now *she* knows, and *he* doesn't, and you're not even following your *own* advice. How many times—"

"I didn't have any *choice!* You *know* I didn't. I tried *everything...*" Bliss's voice has grown so small it's almost childlike, but the world has fallen so still in the windless, self-entombed town that she could be shouting from the top of an embankment.

That's when Verthandi, the Second of the Three Fates, the Embodiment of the Eternal Present, reaches out a gentle hand and wipes a single tear from Bliss's cheek. "And now what will you do? How will you fix this?"

The Fate looks around at Anna and waves a hand. "She stole something from you, little Pyx. Have it back."

The stone in Mouse's pocket vanishes and Anna grabs her head and her eyes widen as the memories return.

Then Verthandi stares at Mouse and smiles. "I almost hope you don't figure it out, Diviner." She's standing next to him again, but he doesn't recoil. "Or perhaps Diviner is the wrong term for this version of you. My limited little Mouse. All intuition and no knowledge." She grins. "My sisters would wonder why I like you so much."

Mouse bows ever so slightly. "Ladyship," he says. Her eyes light up as though it were the most gracious of all compliments.

"But!" She looks around at the bewildered faces. "This is only the opening act! I'll leave it to you to sort out the rest." She holds out a hand to Bliss. In it is a copy of the letter. "Anything to add?" Bliss takes it and shoves it in her pocket without saying a word.

Verthandi sighs, then looks straight at Mouse again, and points to the field across town, and the glowing beacon in the night that is the hospital. A purple flash lights up the darkness, followed by a white one. Her voice, almost a whisper, carries across the field to him. "Run, little Mouse. The night is still young."

And then once again, without any intervening steps, she's gone.

All eyes turn to Bliss, shoulders slumped, staring at the ground. "I—"

"There'll be time for explanations later." Helene says, looking at everyone. "For now..." she looks toward the hospital and the fight that's beginning in the distance.

Anna ignores Helene and glares at Mouse. Without saying a word, she slugs him in the shoulder—hard—then walks over to Bliss. "I don't know why you did it, or even what you've done. But as far as I'm concerned we're still friends."

Bliss can't even make eye contact. She stares at the ground and nods.

There's a rumble in the distance, and all eyes look off toward the hospital, where flash after flash in the dark call them into action.

Anna grabs Bliss by the hand.

"Let's go."

鼠

"Aren't you glad I stopped by?" A stream of noxious black oozes from the body of a fallen azaz, as Priest flicks some more of the same off a silvery glowing sword. A rotating circle of white sigils flares up in the air as another beast tries to break through June's barrier.

"Shut up and fight, Leonard, I'm still not talking to you." She weaves a lance of white light and impales a more insectile creature, which screams and collapses. "I should've known you only showed up because you had a thing for nurses."

Priest lets out a deep belly laugh. "Hey now, sweetness—"

"Don't start with me, you old lech." But she's smiling.

He grins back at her, then turns and uses a small buckler to parry a black-clawed strike that makes it past the wards before using his sword to hack off the offending limb. June is about to fire another insult at her ex when a ball of white light strikes the rest of the creature from behind and leaves it twitching on the ground, a smoking hole where its chest used to be. It's Mouse.

June beams with pride. "Nice one!"

They enter the fray.

There are too many of the abominations to count, wave after wave lurching out of the black field and toward the hospital in a dizzying array of misshapen combinations—reptile, insect, cephalopod. Claws and teeth and pincers and tentacles attached as if at random to three or four or more legs, as if assembled in the dark by some blind and menaced Dr. Moreau.

Anna pulls out the knife she used in the fight on the bridge. It glows with a faint white light as she flickers from creature to creature, cutting tendons here, muscles there. A larger shape follows in her wake. Helene's familiar, Argo, has appeared at some point as well, and is taking a less subtle approach—he slams one of his mammoth fists into what might be called the face of one of the injured things, and it leaves a trail of dust rising as it skids across the dirt.

Kai drops behind June's barrier and pulls a gently curved sword out of the duffel bag he's been carrying around.

"Is that Greg's?" she asks.

"Gramps's—his dad's," Kai responds, holding it like a baseball bat. He swings at an incoming tentacle and connects, but the blade barely penetrates.

June reaches over and traces a finger along the weapon's spine, leaving a pale glow behind it that gradually seeps through to the edge itself.

"That should help," she says, smiling. "Not just anything can get through demon flesh."

Kai swipes at another to much greater effect. "I'll keep that in mind."

June nods and folds a glowing-sigil barrier around one of the creatures, squeezing until—after a series of sickening cracks—it stops thrashing and goes limp.

"Anyone ever tell you how beautiful you look when you destroy violations of the natural order?" Priest is grinning at her.

"Shut *up*, Leonard."

"What are they after?" Anna shouts.

Bliss points up at the hospital, its windows glowing in the cavernous dark, a stark contrast to the rest of the town. Elsewhere, the few beacons of light in the distance have begun to wink out.

"Fear," Bliss says. "They want everyone in the dark and afraid."

And then the monsters just stop, like they've been put on hold. Mouse drops another one with a blast to a disgusting head-tentacle combo, but even then they stand stiff, like mannequins; a Lovecraftian statue garden in the blackened field. In the absence of movement, the sound of muddy groundwater-rain becomes almost deafening.

And then slow applause.

"Oh, excellent. Excellent!"

A shiver goes up Mouse's spine and he spins like he knows what's coming.

A blast very much like lightning, but somehow darker, flashes sideways through the air and slams into Mouse. He manages to get his spear between himself and the attack, splitting it into two blistering, branching arcs, but even so the force sends him reeling back. The ground smokes on either side of him and he wonders what would have happened if he hadn't turned just then.

Bliss stares at him, and he can see in her face just how close a call it was.

"Fantastic!" shouts the voice.

June throws up a new series of wards in the direction of the voice, their slow, glowing gyrations lighting the field, littered by the corpses of azazim and their still-standing, stiff and unmoving counterparts. In the faint glow, two figures emerge from the starless night.

At first glance they seem preternaturally beautiful—tall and thin in immaculate, crisp black robes, their white faces seem to shine like finely crafted porcelain. But as they approach, their expressions don't change, and it becomes apparent that that's precisely what they are—porcelain, or something like it. Both have the same beautiful face, one on the verge of tears and one smiling beatifically. It's the smiling one that's speaking.

"Oh, my. You're everything we hoped you'd be, Diviner. And look at all your friends!'

Bliss walks up behind Helene and whispers in her ear. "We need to go. *Now.*"

"But—"

"They're out of our league."

Helene opens her mouth to ask a question and Bliss cuts her off.

"If we don't get gone, then yes."

"But what happens to you?"

Bliss is silent for a moment. "Just do it."

Helene looks up as the sad one approaches June's barriers and inspects them for a moment.

"Everyone *fall back!*" Helene shouts. "*Now!*"

Mouse looks over as the figure reaches out and starts deconstructing June's wards, like they're made of little glowing threads. They come apart, segment by segment, fading into the dark as June's eyes widen.

"Don't ask questions, just run!" June shouts, throwing up ward after ward as the threads of each one come undone faster than the last. They've waited too long.

Priest chimes in. "You heard her, MOVE!"

He steps in next to June and smiles at her. He puts his hand on her shoulder, closes his eyes, and a glow encompasses them. The rate at which the wards are coming apart slows, but only for a few moments.

A big black van pulls up behind them and the door swings open. It's Vallis. Kai tries to tell Anna to get in, but Mouse refuses to go, and so does she.

Helene snaps, voice like a gunshot, "Do your duty, familiars!"

Argo flickers for a moment, and then appears behind Kai, grabs him, and jumps to the van.

Anna turns to look at June and Priest, and June turns to face her. She takes a long look at Mouse, looks back to Anna, and nods once. The look in her eyes will haunt Anna in the times to come.

Anna jumps, grabs Mouse, and skips across the field in a couple of flashes until they both land in the van. She holds him down as Helene and Bliss pile in.

"Come on!" Kai shouts, but June and Priest don't turn around. It's taking them all they have to just keep the barrier up against the unstoppable tidal wave of *undoing* behind the tragic mask. Vallis slams the door.

"They aren't coming."

"Hey, wait—" Kai begins, but Vallis's foot is down and the tarmac is flying beneath them.

Mouse breaks free and screams wordlessly, lunging for the back window in time to see the last light of his mother's wards flicker out, before they swerve round the hospital and speed off into the night. Anna dives over the back seat and wraps her arms around him as he struggles, then stops, and then collapses into sobs. Wave after wave of anguish pass wordlessly between them.

They both know there's no going back.

In the front seat Bliss stares down at the letter, calm, quiet, and cold. Everything will end tonight, just like it always has. She pulls out a pen and writes.

A hooded figure sprints down an alleyway, dodging piles of rubble and diving into a doorway, back flat against it, unbreathing. The narrow strip of sky between the buildings is a dark canvas lit only by faint orange stars, and against it an even darker shadow flits by. Here, in the unending city, the alleyways are like narrow canyons that splinter their way through the landscape, both safer and more dangerous for their obscuring depths. A hollow, scraping noise makes the figure tense up, weapon at the ready, until a tumbleweed of trash clatters its way by, blown by the sulfurous wind that hooks its way around the corners. Just empty cans and scattered plastics. It could as easily have been the *azazim h'adam*, out for an evening snack.

After an eternal minute, the figure lets out a breath and turns to the door. A small circle of symbols appears in the air over it and then disappears, and the door unlocks.

The space inside is coal-dust black as the figure closes the door on the world outside, and then light streams through a crack that widens to a second doorway. She steps inside and lowers her hood to reveal a young face and silvery hair. It's Anna.

The room inside is lit only by candles, and it's more than a little shabby. It's the industrial basement of an old city townhouse, windowless, with bare metal beams at regular intervals, only just supporting the weight of the derelict building above. The rusted-out corpse of a boiler sits inert against a wall, a sleeping dragon from another age, next to a pair of solid-looking doors that go to the toilet and the makeshift kitchen, respectively. There's a coarse-blanketed, sagging cot in one corner, and a table with a few folding chairs in the middle of the room, where two people, a man and a girl, are sitting.

Anna looks over. "Is this her?"

The man nods, but doesn't look up from where his eyes are seemingly focused on a spot in the middle of the table. He's in his mid twenties but looks older, dressed in the same ragged way as Anna. His hair looks like it was something like blond once, but now it just looks dirty, with grey in it like it's been showered with dust. His stony face is covered with three days' worth of stubble, and worry has worn lines like rain marks in a graveyard statue. The thick line of a scar parts his hair where the top half of his left ear used to be, and a burn mark stretches up his neck to his jaw from beneath his shirt.

The girl sitting next to him is young, how young is hard to tell. Like the man sitting next to her, she looks like she hasn't bathed in months, or for that matter, eaten a decent meal. Her hair is dark and her eyes are almost silver. Her hands are folded on the table in front of her in a strangely adult pose.

"How old are you?" Anna asks.

"Nine or ten," she says, "no one tries to keep track these days except old people like you. Like me, too, I guess. It's weird remembering this young, too, I'm sure of it. I know what the Knowledge is, but I don't have much in the way of memories of, you know, other ones; the other me."

"And the last three cities?" Vallis had taught them what to ask, years ago.

She rolls her eyes. "Damn protocols. New York last time, September 2001. Before that, a long one. Sarajevo in June 1914. Before that it was a run-down little townhouse on the outskirts of Paris in February 1848." She scowls at Anna like just looking at her gives her a bad taste in her mouth. "I don't remember everything yet, but it's coming back in bits and pieces."

"Nine-Eleven, Franz Ferdinand, and, 1848...help me out with this one."

"The February Revolutions," says the girl.

"The February whats? God, Western Civ was a long time ago." She's getting a headache just thinking about it. "Anyone ever tell you your timing sucks?"

"Story of my life, apparently."

Anna frowns. "What are we calling you this time around? Still Helene?"

The girl shrugs. "Doesn't feel right. I guess just call me what my parents called me." She rubs her temples as if the whole ordeal were tiresome. "My parents *this time*. It's the only name that feels like me right now."

Anna stares at her. She suddenly feels like she knows her name already. The eyes, the hair, the attitude—but it couldn't be.

The man sitting at the table doesn't move anything but his lips.

"Bliss," he says.

Anna tries not to slam the door behind them. The 'kitchen'—such that it is—is lit by three candles, jammed into old bottles that have held dozens more before them. An industrial sink lies on one side with a steel barrel of water next to it, and a sturdy workbench sits on the opposite side. A cast-iron pan sits atop an old hibachi full of the ashen remains of the smooth black firestones they use for cooking. Times have been tough since the Fall.

"Did you know?"

The man looks down, not responding.

"Mouse." She puts her hands on his broad shoulders. They used to be smaller; now they're all tight-knotted muscle from nearly a decade of pitched battle. "Did you know it was her?"

She gave me a message before...I didn't understand it.

"But she—" she stops, lowers her voice and starts again. "But she *died*. She died when Helene died. In the Fall."

For years I've wondered what Verthandi was doing there that night.

Anna stops and thinks for a moment. "Then the correlative exchange—?"

Mouse nods.

"And the darkness itself?"

Another nod.

"Christ. It never made sense. No matter how many times I went over it, it never did."

They stand in silence until Anna looks up at Mouse's weathered face.

"How many times, do you think?"

Have we done this? I don't know.

"Do you think she knows?"

Not yet.

"We need to find Verthandi."

She'll find us. When it suits her.

"And if she doesn't?"

But Anna knows the answer, and they stand in silence for a moment before she grabs a fresh black firestone from the counter and tosses it into the hibachi, where it bursts into smokeless flames. She sighs and leans down to open a crate by the bench, pulling out a couple of cans.

"Right then." She holds up the cans. "Do you think she'd prefer beans, or beans?"

鼠

A steel door creaks open on its hinges on the roof of an old high-rise apartment and Mouse, Anna, and Bliss slip out. This is what passes for day since the planet folded back on itself. In the distance above, where the sky should be, lies another city, as ruined as the one they're in. In point of fact, it's the same city. Ever since the Fall, the rules of the world no longer hold true the way they once did. If you walk back the way you came, you wind up somewhere you've never been. Location is now a vector.

A smoggy mist hovers in grimy orange patches, lighting the city just enough for shadows to stretch in unpredictable angles of deep, inky black. An acrid tarry breeze gives the air the smell of sweaty asphalt on a hot day, and in the distance of the city above and below garbage-can fires create an abyssal starscape. If you could see far enough, you'd see humans gathered around them, too abject to even generate enough fear to feed the azazim who patrol the streets looking for a meal of human terror. This truly is the end of the world.

"How did it happen?" Bliss asks. "I should know, but..." she shakes her head. "It's not back yet."

"The Antiochus Algorithm," Anna says. "An alchemical weapon of mass destruction."

"But that was just a theory—"

"About how a flood could cover the planet, for instance, when there's not enough water in the world to do it. Or to separate the day from the night, the land from the sea. The fire of creation itself." Anna doesn't look at the girl, just stares out into the hellscape. "They used it to reimagine the world, and this is what they made." She snorts. "It's a joke, just for us."

"What do you mean?"

Anna gestures as she recites the phrase, "As above, so below." She shakes her head. "Of course above and below don't have meaning anymore, which is the punchline."

"But where could they even get a power source to drive something like that? And how could the Trust let it happen?"

Anna just looks at Mouse, and he shakes his head.

"As far as we can tell, no one else in the city has the Knowledge. It's like when they remade the universe, they left everyone in the Trust outside."

"Or maybe we're just the only ones *inside*," Bliss says.

Mouse shakes his head again at that. Anna explains. "We spent the first year wandering. After a while the city repeats the same patterns over and over, but the people always change. If it's not *the* entire world, it's *an* entire world, with what seems like a population to match. In some parts they've even started worshipping the azazim, placating them by torturing their own friends, family, children..." Some had done worse, and stranger, things still.

The masked necromancers had taken so much that day—first June and Priest, then Kai, Bliss, and Helene in their final attempt to stop them. After that the world had changed, the vast wheels of the Algorithm contracting the world into the hellscape it became. Even Vallis had gone down, guns blazing, in the weeks that followed. And then the azazim had started in on humanity itself, farming its terror for their consumption.

"As for the power to do it," she says and looks at Mouse.

"The darkness," he says. Until today, they'd had no idea what it even was, or why no diviner, not even Simon Magus himself, could see into it. But if it is what Mouse is starting to think it is, he's beginning to get an idea how it could have provided enough raw power to undo the world. And why it was so *dark*.

He sighs. For now there's nothing to be done, so he puts his hand on Bliss's tiny shoulder and points to a glowing speck in the distance. It's time for a raid.

鼠

"It's bait," Anna says, "but it's edible." She's peering out from behind a pile of rubble in an alleyway that dumps out into a large intersection. She closes her eyes and can imagine the way it would have been— packed with cars under a blue sky, honking horns at each other for crossing before there was space for them, pedestrians weaving between whenever there was a chance, hurrying about their busy lives during the half hour or hour they got for lunch each day. Instead, when she opens her eyes, there's a pile of canned goods sitting in the center of the intersection, and eager shadows twitch and writhe in the darkness past the burnt-out shell of a convenience store, shards of broken glass lining the window like teeth in a giant, freakish mouth. "On second thought, it's bait *because* it's edible."

"Mom and Dad just bartered with other survivors," Bliss says.

"It's a good idea for mundanes." Anna looks at Mouse, whose attention is focused on the toothy storefront. "But someone needs to throw a little back into the supply chain when it starts to get scarce."

"Rain stole from traps a couple of times."

The name sounds familiar, and she tries to think back. "Your brother?"

Bliss nods. "Twin brother, yeah. He died in the fire with my parents."

Anna's not sure how to react. Death is commonplace in this world, but to lose her whole family at once like that is still harsh.

"It's fine," Bliss says. "It's...I've been on my own for a while now."

Mouse closes his eyes as though in prayer, then looks at Anna before standing up, spear in hand, and striding into the middle of the intersection.

"There's three in the square. A fourth on the rooftop opposite as backup. Two, maybe three more in the shop that might or might not be interested in a fight."

"You guys are pretty close." Bliss says.

"I'm his familiar, so yes."

"Wait, so you're...how old are you?"

"Old as he is, just about." Anna, still fourteen everywhere except her eyes, watches Mouse's casual progress toward the trap.

"Did you die in the Fall?" A child's curiosity combined with an ages-old instinct to gather information, piece it back together, to recover not one lifetime, but dozens.

Anna shakes her head. "No. A couple years before. Mouse brought me back." She almost laughs, wistful. "Kind of by accident."

Bliss sighs. "And you've just been by his side since."

Anna remembers who she's talking to and looks down. "Ah, yeah. Sorry."

The girl shakes her head. "No, it's...don't worry about it. We never get to, you know, line up like that. I remember that much."

Anna looks at the girl and sees her old friend suddenly, kissing a teenaged Mouse in a school hallway, inspiring an echo of jealousy that feels inappropriate in the present. She looks up and sees the older Mouse, her Mouse, scarred and silent and strong, bending down to pick up a can of peas and spring the trap, and looks back at the girl. There are a dozen things she could say, but what comes out is just, "Get ready."

Mouse stands in the intersection, staring at the can's ingredients, as if trying to decide between the regular and the low sodium variety. Then he tenses up and strikes the ground with the butt of his spear, sending out an expanding wave of light that ripples over the surface of everything it touches. Three shapes surround him, their distorted forms made visible by the unbinding—azazim. Their shields unraveled, they crouch to pounce.

"Wait here," Anna says. "When the coast looks clear, grab what you can and run back."

Anna flickers, and then she's cleaving through one of the monsters from head to chest with a white-bladed katana that still bears traces of June's enchantment a decade on. Mouse's eyes are closed, but he's spinning, light on his feet, his spear tip drawing arcs in the air that slice through demon flesh like razorwire whips. Each move somehow anticipating where the creatures will be next, their strikes accompanied by unearthly screams.

When the first three are down, Bliss makes a run for the pile, burlap sack in hand, throwing cans in without even checking to see what's inside. If it's sealed it's edible, unless the ends are bowed out. Rain taught her that.

The ground shakes as a mass of scales and teeth lands beside Mouse. Bliss looks up to see Anna removing one of its limbs with near surgical precision while Mouse, nonchalant, turns his back and walks over to the pile of cans. He looks down at Bliss, still throwing cans into the bag, and then over at the storefront. Without looking back he says, "Enough. Run."

She does as she's told.

A flood of black ichor streams from the broken windows of the storefront as she retreats. It isn't until it's almost surrounded Mouse that she realizes that it's not liquid at all, but tens of thousands of tiny insectile shapes. They pile atop one another until they're a vaguely humanoid mass of writhing, clicking horror.

Anna finishes the other, but doesn't advance. Instead, she walks back to Bliss's position and crouches down next to her. She doesn't even watch, instead looking in the bag with a casual, "What did you get?"

Bliss can't look away.

It starts slowly. Mouse takes two steps backward and sweeps a sideways semicircle with the point of his spear. Every move he makes leaves white lines, drawing a faint glow on the ground and in the air around. Another step, another circle, an arch above, inscribing an alien architecture on the ugly darkness that surrounds him. Even if his eyes are open he isn't looking—he doesn't need to. He knows this dance like he's done it a thousand times and with a thousand different partners. He spins and ducks, jumps and swirls, weaving a deadly graceful tapestry as the beast attacks.

At first the swarm strikes as one—a massive buzzing fist slamming down against a fragile looking spear, but Mouse's movements wave it away like a minor nuisance. It splits and tries again, divides over and over, trying a thousand separate attacks, each smaller than the last, trying to find a way past his defenses until they're a thin sphere of vibrating carapaces completely blocking Mouse from view.

"Anna, look!" Bliss's concern shakes her compatriot from her appraisal of the canned goods.

She shifts her focus, raising her eyebrows, then smiles. "Oh, I love this part."

Bliss almost looks away in surprise.

At one moment in time, Mouse is encased in a solid sphere of writhing black; at the next, it falls away, forming a piled-up ring of ash that glows in the slow wind like embers from a fire. The sphere Mouse has woven of ten thousand iridescent threads has expanded by only an inch, but in doing so, it has bisected each and every bug at once. Mouse lets the circles fade, then steps past the remains and walks over.

He looks past Bliss at Anna, who nods in reply. "We should take this and go before backup arrives." She hauls the sack of cans over her shoulder and starts to run down the alley away from the intersection.

Bliss looks up at Mouse. She wants to celebrate, give him a hug or a high five, tell him some kind of congratulation, but he's wrapped in a shell of quiet and calm, and she doesn't know how to get past it. Everything she can think of sounds trite in her head, like saying, *good game*, or *way to go, champ!* So instead, as he walks past, she grabs his hand and gives it a squeeze.

He stops, blinks, looks down at her, and pauses.

"Take this," he says. He gives her the spear.

Then, in a single fluid motion, he grabs her around the waist, twists and throws her up onto his back, his arms crooked behind her knees, her free arm around his shoulders. Together, they break into a run to follow Anna away and into the city beyond.

用

"Right, try the next one."

Anna and Bliss are in the old townhouse basement, standing in front of a piece of wood carved and burned with curls and symbols. It's going on three months since Bliss's first raid, and her memories are still only hers. She can remember echoes of Helene, but in the same way she can remember just pieces of the Knowledge—as though someone told them to her once, or she read them in a book. Familiar when mentioned, but distant, disconnected.

Bliss puts a can down in the middle of the plank, in the spot where all the carvings seem to point.

"What've you got?"

Bliss puts a hand on either side and pushes a little will into the mechanics of the carvings, trying to see what's inside the can. The raids have become so successful that the shadows running the world have started poisoning the food supply. Last week three people in Potter's Block, one of the semi-nomadic bands of survivors that wander this part of the world, fell to the effects of what they're starting to call the Madness. Like every insult suffered by the survivors of the Fall, it's more dangerous as a psychological weapon than as an extermination tactic. The symptoms progress overnight from a low-grade fever to a violent psychosis. Only one of the three had been infected; that one took the other two with him.

"Baked beans. Clean," Bliss says. She can feel the energy feeding back to her hands, leaving a strange sweet smell in her nose. Tainted cans feel sour somehow, and smoky at the back of her throat. Mouse had designed the testing block the week before, in order to make the process faster, and Bliss had been keen to do something to help. So while Mouse is out doing a local run to Hanlontown, throwing some much needed clean food into the general supply, Anna's helping her learn.

Anna repeats the process herself, then smiles. "Ten out of ten. Looks like you might just know what you're doing."

Bliss beams. "Don't say it like it's such a surprise, geez."

Anna's smile widens to a grin. It's been almost like old times, but this time she's opening her home to Bliss. The memory prompts a sudden craving.

"Hey have you ever had bacon?"

Bliss purses her lips. "Animal, vegetable, or mineral?"

"Oh my *god*, Bliss. Animal. Like, thin strips of fatty, salty pork." Bliss doesn't look convinced.

"You're really selling it, there." She makes a face and Anna just sighs.

"Yeah, but it was good because it was *fried*. It's...okay, before the Fall, before all food came in, ugh." She picks up the can of beans and tosses it into an old milk crate full of the same. "Do you remember any of that?"

Bliss shakes her head. "Names and dates are one thing, but smells and tastes and personal experiences...not so much."

"Well, before that," Anna closes her eyes and takes a deep breath. From the expression on her face you'd think she could almost smell it. "Before that, when the world was still on its feet and all we worried about were stupid little things, back then Sunday was bacon day, for me and...my best friend." She looks down. "And we'd have it, and coffee, and sit around talking about boys, and TV, and school, and...god, I miss school." She laughs to herself. "Never thought I'd say that."

Bliss puts another can on the plank, getting ready for another go. "Dad taught math before the Fall, he said. He used to try to teach me, but there wasn't much point beyond basic trade and barter stuff. Maybe if we'd been scrappers—"

"Be glad you weren't." Junkyard Dogs and Scrappers were supposedly resistance fighters who made weapons out of whatever scrap metal and plastic and glass they could find. Only supposedly, though, because in ten years Anna and Mouse had never seen a group of humans last more than a few weeks from the day they started fighting back against the azazim.

"At least we'd have been *fighting*. You and Mouse—"

"—are just about the only people qualified." She chews her lip. "And every close call seems to get closer."

Bliss looks at the floor, sullen, and Anna puts a hand on her shoulder.

"You know the type of creeper with the scissor arm? Arm like a flattened out lobster claw, razor sharp and quick as hell. That was his ear gone." She draws a line across the side of her head with her finger. "Should've been his head. The burns were from earlier. A big tentacled thing with acid. That was new." She sighs. "You have to understand, we do what we can because we have to, because it's the only way we can live with ourselves after all this—*Jesus* what now?" She looks up and over at the door, then curses under her breath as a loud thump against it causes Bliss to jump.

Anna throws the door wide and lets two people stagger in— Mouse, using his spear as a walking staff, and a stranger, arm over Mouse's shoulder and trailing a small river of blood.

鼠

"Put your hands here and lean in, and don't pull them away unless I say, okay?" Anna's folded some clean rags over the stranger's injury—a ragged hole below his ribcage—and is holding Bliss's hands down over the top. Anna looks over at Mouse, who's sitting on the floor, propped up against a wall, face ashen from overreaching during the escape. "What did I say about privacy mode? *Baka.*" He closes his eyes and shrugs in a way that seems to say he didn't think it was worth bothering her. "He's not going to be good for much," she says and sighs. "Just press down and keep the pressure on until I get back. If I don't burn away that blood right now the creepers will get their hellhounds out and they'll follow it right back to us."

And after grabbing a handful of firestones from the kitchen, she's out the door, leaving Bliss to hold the poor stranger's insides in, while Mouse gives the basement floor a thousand-yard stare.

Her patient, if that's what you can call him, is maybe in his late twenties. He has long blond dreadlocks and a beard, and like everyone here, his eyes are older than they should be. He's passed out at some point since they arrived, and is now just lying on his back, occasionally wincing in his sleep when his body takes a deeper breath than usual. His weapon, a long machete made of salvaged steel, ragwrapped handle and sheathed in old hand-sewn red leather, lies on the ground beside him.

The bleeding seems to have slowed. Given that he's still breathing, Bliss wonders if maybe it's a good sign. She thinks for a moment back to a time when Rain had cut his leg and her parents had washed it out with a mixture of boiled water and moonshine. If they didn't disinfect the wound it'd fester, but she's pretty sure they don't have any alcohol, and even if they did she's stuck here applying pressure. Anna's still not back and she feels like she should be doing something. What if...

She tries focusing like she did when trying to read the can, picturing in her head the shapes that are carved on the board over on the table, sending her will and her senses out, looking for corruption—not in a can this time, but in the wound. It's a lot harder to focus without the written forms, and it takes a lot more effort, but she's starting to get a picture. She closes her eyes and concentrates.

The man's injury isn't too deep; it's like she can see it in her mind. But there's something lodged in the bottom of it, a piece of tooth, or bone maybe? It sits wedged, grey and rotten in his flesh, giving her the same sense of sour and smoke as with the tainted cans. The edges of the cut are the shade of a peach, healthy, and she discovers suddenly that she can feel them actually *trying* to heal, to push the fragment of corruption out, to close up the vacant spaces where air shouldn't reach. But at the rate they're going it'll take days, weeks even.

Instinct launches her, propels her until she's throwing her whole self into helping the stranger's effort, millimeter by millimeter knitting cells back together and pinching the dark wedge out and into the open air. The muscles and blood vessels all knowing where they ought to be, wanting nothing but to be back where they were; she shows them the way, pushes it all together again until there's nothing left to heal and all the work is done.

And then her eyes fly open. All she can see are stars, fireworks in her field of view. Her mouth opens to breathe, but nothing works—has she been breathing? Had she forgotten?—every muscle is tense and the world won't come back, it's all just colors rippling before her unseeing eyes. She pulls back, fights the panic and the ache in her lungs and calms herself. And then the distance closes and the colors fade, and the world slides back into place, washing over her like a cool breeze. Air, like cold mountain water floods her lungs and brings her back into the present.

She blinks, focuses her eyes. The world is spinning, but slower with every breath.

She looks about, regains her bearings. Their guest is still lying before her, Mouse is passed out against the wall, oblivious. She twists and grabs the rags from the man's wounds and smiles before pulling herself to her feet.

Five minutes later, Anna returns, wrapped in a light blanket of ash to find Bliss curled up next to Mouse, both fast asleep. Their guest is sleeping, too, his wound replaced by healthy skin. Next to his body is a wad of bloody rags and a single inch of black, bony claw.

鼠

Bliss opens the door to the roof and peeks out. Their guest, back against the low wall and smoking a hand-rolled cigarette, is sitting on the rooftop. After a minute he notices her and waves her over.

"You smoke?" he asks, his voice a calm baritone that sounds like plucking a heavy string.

"I'm ten," she says, looking down at him.

"Not what I asked." He pulls a small tin out of his pocket and offers her one, which she takes more out of curiosity than anything else. He pulls out a lighter and tosses it to her, and she lights it up, trying to look cool.

It works for about three seconds before she starts coughing and hacking all over the place, and their guest laughs.

"Awful, right?" He looks at the twisted thing in his hands and then takes a long drag off it. "You know how you can tell it's no good for you?"

"The fact that it makes you cough and tastes like hell?" She makes a face like she's trying to spit out the flavor.

"The fact that they're still around." He tosses the stub over the side of the building with a flick of his thumb. "Think about it, you ever seen a tobacco plant?"

She sits down next to him. "I've never seen any plants, except in books."

He pulls out another and lights it up. "Makes you wonder what's in 'em."

"And what's in the cans."

He closes his eyes. "Good point," he says, and they sit in silence for a minute.

"Mouse and Anna tell me you're the one who patched me up good as new. That true?"

"Mm." She nods, and a gust of wind pulls her hair away from her face as he stares at her.

"Saints' Row really is the real deal." He takes another puff.

"That's what they call this place." It's only half a question.

"Yeah," he says. "And thanks, by the way."

"Sure."

The wind blows by again and she makes another sputtering attempt.

"Are you a scrapper?" He's what she imagined one would look like, weapon now strapped to his back, yellow dreads tied back in a knot behind him.

He smiles somewhere under his beard and shakes his head. "It's Bliss, right?"

"Yeah, and you are?"

"Charles," he says. He leans his head back so he's looking up at where the stars should be, and stares off into a place in the past only he can see. "No such thing as a scrapper. Just saints here in Holyland and mundanes like me everywhere else. Me and Mouse and Anna," he stops as if he's trying to find the right words. "We go way back," he says.

鼠

"You can't seriously be considering it."

Anna's been pissed ever since Charles suggested that Bliss do a ridealong on a relief run to Hanlontown and the Creed Cell. The three adults are standing on the roof, trying to have the argument out of earshot of the girl sleeping below.

"Hanlontown's one thing, but the Creedies are *bleeders.*" Near the beginning, when what was left of the human race had begun to organize itself into communities, some people had noticed the way the azazim were drawn to blood. They'd started offering it to their new keepers in the hopes of keeping them at bay. Anna wonders aloud why should they stick their necks out for people who won't even look after their own.

"All the more reason to make sure their kids have something to eat," Charles says. Mouse's words echo the same sentiment in her head. She knows his compassion is well-placed, but if he thinks for one second she's going to let—

Mouse interrupts with a hand on her shoulder.

We know how it's going to turn out for her, even if we don't know how she'll get there. She'll be fine.

"And you, will you be fine? And don't give me any of that whatever-will-be crap." Mouse sighs and she turns to Charles. "One hair on his head—one—and I'll beat your sorry butt into next week, you understand?"

Charles nods, serious and calm. She and Mouse have seen what that calm is capable of; nobody makes it ten years into the Fall without a few regrets.

"Fine," she says, turning back to Mouse, "but no privacy mode. I know you don't want me to worry, but I mean it this time."

"You could always come with, keep an eye on things," Charles says, but he knows she won't, not after the last time she'd been there. Even without a heartbeat a Pyx bleeds, and can do so for as long as its bond is alive. Anna was adamant she would never go back.

Without thinking about it, Mouse puts his arms around her, and she closes her eyes.

Be safe, she thinks to him.

I promise.

Behind them and unseen, Bliss's shadow slips away from the stairwell doorway and back into her bed three flights below.

鼠

In the darkness she panics and runs. Escaping through the tunnels alone Bliss trips and falls, scraping her cheek on rough, thankfully dry brick. She's too exhausted to continue running, let alone summon a light, and so she curls up against a wall in the blackness that's now cold and absolute. She wishes it were a dream, just a nightmare she could wake up from, but it's not. How had it gone so wrong?

First to the Creed Cell, and then on to find out what was left of Hanlontown after the raid. That had been the plan. Mouse had led them through the tunnels beneath the city to avoid detection. The sound of their footsteps as they splashed through the abandoned subways and sewers had echoed down and back again, making it sound as though there were a half dozen others down there with them, stepping when they stepped, breathing when they breathed. Light skittered away almost as fast as the glowing globe hovering at the end of Mouse's spear could generate it, drunk up by dark and hungry pools of stagnant water. Bliss had had the feeling of being watched from every service tunnel exit and every station platform they'd passed. Some think the underground world holds some grand secret, others that it's just another trick—another way of lighting the lamp of hope, and then dashing it against the rocks. She'd heard stories about the ones who'd dared to try their way through the tunnels and never returned. And now she's one of them.

But for Mouse, it's just a minor inconvenience.

"Dead end?" Bliss asks, as they reach a brick wall.

Mouse shakes his head, then holds up his hand, pulling each finger down in turn, counting from five to one.

Then the brick wall is an open passage and he strides through. She and Charles follow, and then ten seconds later it's sealed up again. The tunnels are filled with gates like that, shifting and maze-like, navigable only to those with a degree of power and intuition that surpasses the mundane.

They'd arrived at a ladder, hoops of slimy steel rebar ascending into the distance above, and slipped into the darkness when Mouse had extinguished his light to climb. Bliss's heart had raced Mouse to the top, until with a heave, his silhouette had appeared, framed by the orange halo of an open manhole.

鼠

As nomad encampments go, Bliss had thought the Creed Cell's current site was unusually habitable—the streets had been cleared of trash, any broken windows had been covered with scavenged plywood or metal, there were no oilcan fires or bodies in the street. In fact, there had been nothing in the street, including people.

But there'd been the smell, faintly metallic at first, then darker and more rotten the longer she'd paid attention to it. The smell of blood, new and old, wafting on the breeze.

Mouse had crouched down and pulled off a backpack full of cans, building a small pyramid of tuna, beans, carrots, and corn. Bliss had been transfixed by the sight of an old storefront where two figures, a small boy, maybe six, and a girl about her age, hung around the edge of a doorway and stared at them—the cans, not their deliverers. It wasn't until Mouse had finished, stood, and turned around, that Bliss had noticed they'd been met with force.

"Didn't think we'd see your face around here again, jihadi."

Six fighters with makeshift spears stood around them. An old man, grizzled with hair cropped short, deep lines in his face and clothed in a robe of black rags, led them.

Charles answered for Mouse. "I asked him to, Kern, for your children's sake."

The man lifted his hand and the spearpoints had lifted, too.

"And for that you have my respect," he'd said.

And then he'd wiped his forehead with his sleeve, sweating despite the chill in the air, and shown them to the barracks.

The plan had been to spend the night, then head back through the tunnels to find what was left of Hanlontown. They hadn't gotten that far.

"Bliss. *Wake up*, girl."

Charles is standing over her, Mouse by the curtain that passes for a door, listening to a voice on the other side whispering to him. Maybe it's the girl from the storefront, the one she'd seen the day before, or someone else grateful for the food.

Punch drunk from sleep, she blinks her eyes to clear them of the fog. "What's going on?"

"Kern's gone off the deep end." There's a scream from outside, though if it's from pain or rage she can't tell. The way it cuts off sends a chill up Bliss's spine. Then the smell of smoke starts to build, until it hangs heavy in the air and covers the smell of blood. "He was always severe," Charles says, "but not like this. Mouse thinks it's the Madness, but everyone's still following his orders."

"He's feeding us to them," Bliss can hear the voice whisper, "you have to *go*." And then there's a prolonged silence, followed by the hard sound of jackboots on wooden floors.

Spear-bearers burst through the doorway, waving their weapons and pinning them all in place.

"*You*," says the captain of the guard, accusing. "It must be *you* they want." He stares back and forth from Mouse to Charles to Bliss and back. "General Kern's already fed them two of our own and I won't have him feed any more. Thank blood he's asked for *you* now."

"This is crazy," Charles says. "If the Madness hasn't seized him, some *other* madness must have."

The captain sneers at him. "I've no time to hear the general insulted by a deserter. Tell me, how is it that you're alive when the rest of Hanlontown is lost?"

Lost. Bliss's heart sinks and she can only imagine what Charles is feeling.

Charles balls his hands into fists. Mouse sighs and looks at him, who returns the gaze with fire. As they're being ushered out the door, he makes his move.

Mouse's spear snaps across the room into his hand and he disarms two of the guards, knocking them out with the butt of the weapon. Charles produces his machete from somewhere and neatly slices the captain's spear in two, leaving the disarmed man to raise his hands in surrender. Charles punches him in the nose and he goes down.

"We need to go, *now*."

鼠

They're twenty feet from the manhole when the general alarm goes up—the azazim have breached the encampment borders.

"Stop them!" The captain is shouting from the barracks windows pointing at the three of them in the street.

Mouse hooks his spear into the cover and pries it open as the street fills with people. Not just young men with weapons, but old men, women, and children, the hidden populous laid bare by the attack.

"You first," Charles says to Bliss. She doesn't ask questions, and starts to climb down. But as she's halfway to the bottom, she realizes no one else is above her.

"Charles! Mouse!"

"Sorry, kid!" Calls a voice. It's Charles. "Stay calm and use your intuition. You'll find your way." She looks up in time to see his face, taut beneath his beard, in a grim smile that means violence. He seals the manhole above her. She climbs back up and tries to push it open, but it's too heavy.

"Mouse! Charles! Damn it, let me out. Let me help."

But there's no response, except the sounds of footsteps running past and panicked shouts, echoing through the one-inch hole for prying the manhole open.

She's about to call out again when everything above her goes silent, followed by the lumbering, irregular footfalls of azazim.

She freezes on the ladder as what sounds like heavy breathing, a shuffling, wet sound, passes over the cover and pauses. It's so close she can smell it, like old dust and steam and rotten wood, a sulfurous breath drifting down into the sewer from only inches away. She desperately wants to escape, to climb down into the blackness below, but doesn't dare move, even to breathe. Her heart is slamming against the inside of her chest so hard that she's sure the thing above her, only an inch and a half of steel between them, will hear.

Then, after an age, the sound of heavy, dragging feet passes on.

She doesn't take a breath until she reaches the bottom, and when she does she runs until she can't—can't stand, can't breathe, can't even make a light to see by. Blind, she trips and falls and feels her way over to a wall, dry and rough brick beside and below her, the sound of her own helplessness the loudest thing for miles. Curled up in the blanket of utter darkness, sore from the fall and from the newfound separation from her friends, she hugs her knees and waits out the anger, the frustration, the shame. Eyes open or shut, her mind wanders to worrying about Mouse and Charles—wondering about what she'll tell Anna, about whether she'll even find her way home—until at last, exhausted and alone, she finds her way not home, but into a ragged and dreamless sleep.

The first thing she notices is the color blue. Even in their safe house the color palette of the world has been limited to shades of rust and darkness. She's never even seen the color with these eyes, not outside a dull and faded picture book, but something in the depths of her memory recognizes it for what it is—a deep evening sky. The stars are just beginning to peek through the endless ceiling, little white points of light representing whole other worlds, collections of worlds, so far away you couldn't even imagine it if you tried. Rain had always loved the books on planets and stars, but Bliss hadn't ever been able to picture it beyond the oil drum fires and the orange haze. Now that she sees them, she wonders what it's like to be there, to look at your own home from so far away that all of it, the whole world and everyone in it, amounts only to a tiny speck.

She peels herself away from the sky to look around. She's standing on a footpath, on a hill covered in tall yellow grass that sways in the wind. Grass? No, wheat. She remembers wheat and dirt and farms. Who had lived on a farm once? Had it been her? A thatch-roofed hall stands at the top, ringed with what look like round shields. Their metal bosses still shine, even in the evening light.

She spins, looks behind her, only to see more fields, more sky, stretching as far as the eye can see. The subterranean labyrinth of the endless city's underside is gone like an exhaled breath of smoke, drifting away into the breeze.

"Hello?" she calls out, but no one responds.

She'd been in the tunnels. She had awoken in darkness and managed to light her way, cobbling together a weak copy of Mouse's spell. Some passages had felt familiar, and others hadn't. She remembered Charles saying something about intuition and decided she'd have to follow hers. And then around one corner or another she'd taken a step forward and found herself in this place. There is no door, no obvious way in. Or back.

The cool wind on her cheek smells sweet as it carries familiar scents from the building—the smell of something baking. Drawn forward by memories, she walks to the giant hall and knocks. After a moment the door swings inward. A small face peeks around at her, then disappears out of sight.

The inside is cavernous, and filled with children, none of whom sits idle. The youngest are playing, running, building things with wooden blocks and dowels, while the older among them are cleaning, repairing clocks and kettles and assorted machines, painting pictures or sitting and writing—in one far corner a child of twelve plays a piano while another pair of children dance. One blond boy is playing with a wooden sword and shield.

"What do you think?"

The voice comes from behind her, and she turns to see a snaggle-toothed grin and a large, maroon dress. She's a young woman, dressed in something out of a Paris salon that, combined with her pointed ears, makes her look something like a fairy.

"Oh, my my. It's *you* again." She folds her hands in front of her.

Bliss stares at her. She looks familiar, but she can't place her.

"My name is Verthandi, Second of the Three Fates, the Embodiment of the Eternal Present. You can call me Lady Ver, or, if you prefer, your ladyship." The way she says it makes Bliss doubt that her own personal preference has much to do with it.

"What the hell is—I mean, that is, *your ladyship*—what is this place?"

Verthandi smiles. "Why it's my home for wayward children. Strays like yourself."

"Strays..." She looks at the children, notes there are no parents, no adults of any kind. "Orphans?"

"Quite right, child. That abortion of a world doesn't deserve these children, and they certainly don't deserve *it*." She peers more closely at Bliss. "But I don't know about you. Do you deserve it or not? Still, you found your way here again." She stops and thinks. "You, of course, don't remember me. I have to say I'm always a little insulted."

"Have we met?"

"Oh!" She mocks being hit in the heart. "The tragedy of being forgotten. Still, we haven't met with you in this body, yet, I suppose. From your perspective, at least."

"You look, I don't know, familiar, I guess? I couldn't remember much of anything, before at least, but just now..." She closes her eyes and thinks. "That smell. Cinnamon buns?"

Verthandi smiles quietly. "Careful, little one."

But Bliss isn't listening; she's remembering. "And outside, that was...I know this place. I *know* this place! I've been here befor—"

And then there's pain. Catastrophic pain, like nothing Bliss has ever felt. It rings inside her head and rattles around like a hive of angry bees, stinging her from the inside, like a gunshot in an echo chamber, each repetition louder and faster until the cacophony is nothing but a blinding wall of agony.

She can't even scream, can't react. She falls to the floor and writhes, eyes wide and watering, not thinking or even breathing— and then a cool hand on her forehead washes it away as though it had never been.

Verthandi is crouched down beside her.

"I did say to be careful, child. But you've never been one to listen, have you?"

Bliss blinks away the cold tears her eyes had been preparing. "What...was that?"

"That was you trying to remember your past, and finding eternity instead. This place isn't like the world you hail from—there you can't remember anything, and you're safer for it. But here, oh the things you could see if I let you try. To be quite honest, I'd advise against it."

"But I should be *able* to remember by now. I'm *Helene*. The First Thought and the One the Great Diviner Lost. Once the goddess Sophia, now the Caretaker of History. If I'm old enough to *know* all that, why can't I *remember* any of it?"

Verthandi stands and offers her a hand. "Because you are, and yet you aren't."

Bliss frowns and gets up on her own. "What's that supposed to mean?"

Verthandi lowers her hand, looking bored. "Oh, ask your Mouse," she says, then sighs. "But he won't tell you either, I suppose."

Bliss frowns again at this. "Do you know him?"

"I have done, and I will." Bliss suddenly thinks Verthandi's smile makes her look as if she's just eaten something delicious. The Embodiment of the Eternal Present wipes the expression off her face when she catches Bliss looking. "And so have you."

Bliss scowls. "Nothing you're saying makes any sense. Who are you? How should I know you? What's going on?"

"All valid questions, but not interesting ones. Not the one you really need to ask." Verthandi looks over Bliss again, and seems to come to a decision. "No, you don't quite belong here, not yet, and I couldn't keep you here for more than a few days before I accidentally let my guard down and let you implode your poor sweet little head again. Just looking at you here makes me tired. There's nothing of the child about you, and, even if you can't remember, you are responsible for all of this."

"For what?" Bliss has never been more confused in her life, but Verthandi keeps monologuing.

"Oh yes, go on back. Ask your little Mouse what I'm talking about, if you like. He won't tell you. He never has before, at least." She flicks her wrist and in an instant the two are back on the hill where she appeared.

Bliss staggers at the sudden change, but manages a response. "Wait, what do you mean I'm responsible? For what?"

Verthandi smiles sadly. "For the end of the *world*, child." She sighs at this, and continues. "But I'll help you out when you come to do it again. I always do, I suppose."

"What the hell are you talking about? How can I be responsible for the end of the world? I wasn't even *there*. Was it Helene? Will I remember—"

"Oh, child. Keep asking questions and you'll get there eventually. Now run along home. I'll drop you close, just climb the nearest ladder and you'll be fine."

"Look, lady—I mean, your *ladyship*, you can't just send me away without—

"—an explanation." But the world has shifted, and the end of her sentence echoes in the dark and empty tunnel. She curls her hands into fists and then relaxes them, breathing out and letting her shoulders droop.

She climbs the ladder, there just as was promised, and heads for home.

鼠

Bliss stands outside the doorway, alone with her own thoughts. What will she say to Anna? She's been thinking about it the whole way there, but she can't begin to explain. She hadn't *wanted* to let them go alone; she couldn't stop them.

She steps into the breezeway and takes a deep breath. She's about to push her way through the inner door when a booming laugh echoes from within. Startled, she shoves the door open, and there's Charles, sitting on the cot, arm in a sling and a grin on his face. Anna's sitting on the table nearby listening to him tell a bombastic story.

As soon as she hears the door click, Anna flies across the room and wraps her in a wide hug.

"Oh, thank whatever heaven is left. You're *safe*."

Bliss lets herself be hugged. She wants to ask what happened, how they got there, what happened to Charles's arm, and the Creed Cell, and—

"Where's Mouse?" she asks, noticing his absence with worry.

The look on her face must be something awful, because Anna rushes to reassure her. "He's fine. He's in the tunnels looking for you." She closes her eyes and opens them again. "He says he'll be back in a few minutes. Where have you *been*?"

Bliss explains, about the darkness and her night alone and Verthandi. At the mention of how they closed the manhole cover on her—without giving her directions or explaining anything about how the tunnels work—Anna throws a look that could sear flesh at Charles, who just smiles and shrugs. At the mention of Verthandi—and especially her maroon dress—Bliss thinks she sees a twinkle in his eye, but he still says nothing.

"Verthandi—that's what she said her name was—she said all these things that made no sense, like how she knows, or she did know Mouse. Or will know. She said...a lot of things."

Anna twists her mouth into a frown. "She does say a lot of things."

"Do you all know her?"

"We've all met her. That's almost the same thing."

Bliss gets the feeling that it isn't even close.

A moment later, Mouse slips through the door. He looks down at her, his shadowed eyes betraying nothing beneath the surface. And then he leans forward and hugs her, so tight she's actually surprised. He almost picks her up.

"See?" she hears Charles say. "It all worked out in the—"

Bliss doesn't see him do it, but she's pretty sure Mouse silences him with nothing but a look. Mouse holds her for a moment longer—just long enough that she realizes just how much warmer it is, here with Mouse and Anna, than in the cold and dark of the tunnels—and then he lets her go.

"She met Verthandi," Anna says.

Mouse looks at her, then nods slowly. Something has changed in the room, and now he's looking at Charles, dark clouds beginning to build behind his eyes. Bliss isn't sure what's happening; she looks on in confused silence.

"Yeah, you were right." Charles stands up, dusting off his trouser legs with his one good arm. "Guess I'd better be on my way."

"You don't have to go," Anna says. It's almost like a question she's asking Mouse, rather than something she's saying to Charles. But he waves a hand and nods in Mouse's direction, who may not be saying anything aloud, but whose body language is speaking a few very angry volumes.

"Yeah, I think I do." He grabs his machete and slings it over his shoulder, smiling the whole way. As he passes Bliss he looks down at her and tells her not to worry. "I've got a standing invitation for a place to stay," he says, and winks before turning and grabbing the door handle.

Mouse stops him with a hand on his shoulder, and the smile that was on his face fades a little. It makes him look older, sadder.

"It was still the right thing to do." He says it like a man who knows he's hurt a friend.

Mouse sighs, and lets the clouds recede as two words roll off his tongue, "I know."

With that, Charles walks out, and leaves the three of them alone again; alone but together.

They won't have any more visitors.

鼠

"Hey, Mouse?" It's what passes for night in their underground apartment, and Bliss is lying on the cot, smoking one of the last cigarettes Charles left behind. The ember glows like an orange eye in the darkness. She knows Mouse doesn't approve, but he doesn't say anything. Since the Fall, not a lot of people have lived long enough to die of lung cancer.

He also won't say anything about Charles, even though she gets the feeling that somehow they were fighting over her. It's been almost a year since that day, and she's never gotten any straight answers out of them. They talked about the battle, they had managed to fight their way through the azazim and taken the survivors—those who were willing to leave the Creed Cell's leadership, which was more than a few—to meet up with what was left of the Hanlontown nomads. The reports of their demise had been greatly exaggerated; people get good at running, given enough practice. But beyond that, and apologizing for sending her down to the tunnels alone, Mouse won't say a word. When she asks Anna, she just shakes her head and looks away.

Afterward, Bliss became reluctant to go down into the tunnels, leaving Anna to do the relief runs to Cannery and the new Hanlontown settlement. She'd offered to drive—there are still cars around if you can find the gas, and Rain had given her a few lessons—but Mouse wouldn't have any of it. It would draw too much attention. Anna had tried to protest, but Mouse had pacified her with unspoken words and she'd accepted it. Bliss had felt bad, but it had given her something that she'd never had before—time alone with Mouse.

In his quiet way, he'd told her stories of the world since the Fall, a game of twenty questions with occasional course corrections. There had been so much chaos in the first few years, right after she'd been born, that any human survival had seemed a miracle. It wasn't until they'd seen the feeding mills, where those still capable of feeling genuine terror were dragged for harvest, that they'd realized that human survival wasn't a miracle—it was just another part of this horrific new world's terrible design.

He'd told her about the life he'd led with Anna, how she'd patched him back together after everyone he'd known had died. How she'd served as his translator, his advocate, his companion through the years of terror. How she'd defended him from the accusations of other survivors when they found out what he could do, and from his own accusations when he realized his limits. She'd helped him perfect their strategies, build their support networks, create a kind of resistance. She'd been his whole world, and then Bliss had appeared.

"Mouse?" He doesn't respond as she puts out the cigarette, so she floats a little glowing orb over in his direction. She's been practicing twice as hard since the Creed Cell fell, even working on shields to make herself useful for battle. The light meanders like a bubble on a breeze until it comes to a stop right in front of him. He's sitting with his knees up and back to the wall, eyes open. She lets the light fizzle out.

"Verthandi said something, when I met her."

There's a lot of space in the room. Talking to Mouse always feels like that, she thinks.

"She said this is all my fault, that I caused the end of the world. She wouldn't say any more, and I thought she was just messing with my head, but I've been thinking about it a lot lately. You were actually there, you and Anna. Did I...?" She stops, unsure of how to say it. "Did I do something? Did I, I guess I mean did Helene do something, something that, I don't know, helped to make the world this way?"

There's no response from the room, and for a moment she wonders if he'd really been asleep, even with his eyes open. Then she feels the cot sag as he sits on the edge of it. She doesn't reach out to touch him, and he doesn't move or speak. They stay this way for a couple of minutes, just knowing the other is there. But it's cold, and maybe he feels her shiver through the bedsprings, or maybe he just feels it himself, but at length he stands, grabs the sheets and tucks her in. She feels his stubble as he kisses her forehead gently.

"Everything ends," he whispers, and she wonders if she's imagining the tightness in his throat that makes it sound like he's trying not to cry. "Remember that."

In the dark, she can't tell whether he's nearby or not, but she falls asleep before Anna returns. She doesn't ask about it again.

鼠

Bliss dives through the door and seals it with a rapid incantation that flashes bright and then fades into invisibility. She's older, taller than Anna now, and her dark hair is pulled back in an efficient pony tail. She leans back against the door and catches her breath.

"What is it?" Anna comes through from the kitchen holding a pot of canned boiled cabbage.

"They're doing a sweep."

"What?"

"A messenger just came by from Cannery. People around here aren't afraid anymore. They keep talking about you two. You've given them hope."

Mouse is kneeling on the floor, meditating with his spear laid out before him. "You, too," he says. In the past twelve months she's been helping out with the raids again, making herself more than useful. Instrumental.

"Thanks," she says, and means it. "But more hope means less fear, and less fear means hungry beasties."

"Where have they started?" Anna puts the cabbage down on the table.

"Four Corners, heading toward Cannery and then this way, looks like. They're rounding everyone up, taking them to the mills for harvest."

Anna looks down at Mouse. "Rear flank divide and conquer? Give everyone time to pack and go? We'll need to get there fast."

Mouse nods and stands up, spear in hand. He looks at them and says, "Tunnels."

Bliss takes a breath and bites her lip, but she doesn't say anything. For the first time in nearly two years, she's going underground.

They fly through the tunnels. There's no time for Bliss to worry that she'll slip into Verthandi's orphanage again by accident, no time to think about the dark, or the things she might have done. Two rights and a left, and they're under Cannery. Another hundred yards and they'll be at Four Corners, if they don't slow down. Mouse leads the way again, the ever-present globe of light leading the way past brick arches and under concrete ceilings, dodging sewer streams and the paradox of old but never-used subway rails. They haul themselves up onto a disused station platform and dive for a round opening in the wall.

Then the scenery changes, and where a tunnel used to be there's nothing but a brick wall, a subterranean cul-de-sac.

"Damn it!" Anna swears. "This shouldn't be here. It'll be five minutes before—"

Mouse cuts Anna off with a held-up hand. He looks back the way they came, listening.

"Trap," he says.

The air in the tunnel has gone completely still, and from behind them comes the irregular smack-slither-click of azazim locomotion.

A short shriek echoes down the tunnel when an oversized hardened claw scrapes against a metal bulkhead. It doesn't sound like animals coming, more like a horde of broken machines—at least, until the speaking starts.

"We've been watching you, Simon." Words like grease slide along the walls from the darkness and back again. "We've been waiting to see what you had in you. Hoping, really." The rolling, plodding, slithering steps splash as they pass through some not-distant puddle of sewer water. "Imagine the meal if we could take the Great Diviner himself, and make *him* fear for the future."

A figure slides into view at the edge of the world bounded by Mouse's light, surrounded on all sides by a teeming horde of eerily silent azazim. A smiling mask, all porcelain and hollow eyes, a mannequin wrapped in black. "But we can't have you interfering this much with our perfect world now, not when the cycle's nearly complete. Our friends here are hungry, and we can't have *that*, can we?"

Bliss tries to work out just what it is that bothers her so much about the figure's voice, then it hits her: it sounds friendly. Calm, jovial. *Nice.* This isn't like the captain of the guard in the Creed Cell, all sharp angles, barking out orders with determination bred from fear. This man, this *thing*, it's having a nice day. It hurts people just because it can. Because it *likes to.*

A beast launches itself toward them, but Anna flickers forward, sword drawn, and in under a second it lies crumpled in a smoldering heap. She returns to Mouse's side, her face a mask of grim determination.

"And as for *you*, young miss, don't you worry. We wouldn't want to harm *you*." It tilts its head to the side as it stares at Bliss. "After all, you're the one who makes this all possible, aren't you?"

Fragments of her conversation with Verthandi resurface in her mind, like bodies—buried in swampy, too-shallow graves—after a heavy rain. "What do you mean?" she asks.

It giggles from behind the mask.

"You will always make the same choices. It's so beautiful, it's such a shame you can't see it." It leans forward. "Why do you think you can't remember?"

"Don't listen to it," Anna says. "It's just trying to get inside your head."

The mask continues as though it hasn't heard.

"I'll tell you why: you're *nothing*. You're an echo. You're a broken cog. You're a scratch in the record of eternity that gets deeper every time the needle gets caught. You think you're Helene? You're nothing but a copy. A *bad* copy, a fork in the road." It giggles. "Yes, *yes*. That's it. You're the road less traveled. You've made *all* the difference."

Bliss is suddenly certain that if there truly is a face behind that mask, if there's anything behind there but malice and glee, that it's smiling.

"Enough." Mouse levels his spear.

Their adversary leans toward one of the creatures, conspiratorial like an actor's aside. "Oh, by the eyes of the great scarecrow himself, he's deigned to speak to us." It leans forward again. "How utterly delightful to hear your voice before you die."

Then it holds out its hand toward them and issues a command. "Kill them."

Anna takes out the first two in a matter of seconds before falling back behind a barrier Mouse erects. Sparks fly as three more crash against the shield and push, even as it tears into their claws and scales. A dark pulse arcs against the barrier and even vaporizes one of the monsters' limbs, but they keep pressing forward.

Bliss shakes her head to clear it. She doesn't have time to wonder what the thing was talking about. She needs to focus here, now. "How long?" she asks. "How long before it opens up again?"

"One minute, if I haven't totally screwed up. Then, we'll do a standard shielded retreat, okay?" Some days Anna looks like a child, Bliss thinks, but not today.

Bliss nods and starts preparing a barrier spell of her own. She'll put hers up a few yards back and Mouse will retreat behind it and replace it with one of his, and they'll repeat the sequence until they're clear, until they're in the tunnel and the passage has closed and they can run. So far she can only make a shield last for ten or fifteen seconds at the level Mouse can hold one at, and it takes her a while to prepare, but they've had a lot of time to practice.

"Ready?"

"Yeah."

"In three, two, one, go!" The spell is cast and the barriers switch. As they back up, the creatures throw themselves against Bliss's shield, and enough force seeps through to push her back a few inches, but she holds it until the next switch.

"Go!" Anna shouts, and they swap again. They're right up against the wall, now. Bliss starts preparing for the next staged retreat.

They don't make it.

"In three, two—" Anna says, but 'one' never comes.

Bliss looks up to a sound of throttled pain.

The wall has opened early, and from the previously empty passageway a single arrow has flown, piercing Mouse's back. The arrow's head shines dark with blood where it protrudes from between his ribs, black feathers shining on the shaft that's lodged in his back. Anna flickers to his side as he drops to one knee and Bliss throws up her barrier behind them in time to catch two more of the whistling projectiles, which bounce off with relative ease. Another—no, *two* more masked faces emerge from the otherwise empty darkness.

The mask of tragedy reaches out and starts unraveling Bliss's defenses, thread by thread. She feels like her heart is being drawn out through her fingertips and gasps for breath. The third has a face as emotionless and impassive as stone, and carries a bow with another arrow notched and ready to fly.

Mouse is still holding the others at bay, but there's so much blood that it's pooling at his feet. Anna seems to be getting fainter, somehow. Bliss steps sideways toward them, desperate to know what to do next, but when she looks down, it's Anna looking up at her.

Anna touches the wound, holds up the blood. Mouse's blood. Her hand is going translucent beneath it. The azazim are still pounding against Mouse's shield and the sad mask is still unraveling Bliss's spell. But despite it all, in the midst of the growing turmoil, it's almost as though everything has gone deadly still.

"He's dying," Anna says. "We're dying."

"There's no time for that," Bliss says. "You'll get out of this. We'll get out of this. We'll escape, we'll find Charles, and I'll fix Mouse up and we'll put you back together—"

"No," Anna says, smiling a sad smile, "maybe next time." She's starting to flicker like a candle-cast shadow against a wall. She puts her hand on Mouse's shoulder, puts her head on it, too, and whispers to him in lovers' tones.

"Stupid," Mouse grunts. "Should've. Sooner." He looks up at Bliss, his sad eyes desperate to say more. "Not, your fault," he says. "Everything, ends." He swallows, trying to speak through gritted teeth. "Al—gorithm" he says, panting between syllables and words, "for Ark—angel."

"What?"

"Tell me," he says, taking a deep breath, "use it."

"What do you—*no*—" she can see him gathering energy, raising his right hand toward her. "No, you *can't*. You *can't do this, Mouse.* When I'm gone the shields will—*tell him*, Anna *he can't*—"

He smiles a terrible, sad smile.

And then, with a flick of his wrist, she vanishes.

As the wards drop and the shadows gather, he reaches up and gives Anna something. He doesn't need to; she knows it's been in his pocket for years. A sea-green barrette with a silver flower. Anna leans over him and kisses the top of his head.

"Goodbye, Nezumi."

"Oyasumi," he sighs into the night.

Then there's darkness, and the silent flight of arrows is followed by the sound of claws.

鼠

Bliss wakes to clean sheets and a pillow wet with tears. She's in a small, chilly room, no wider than the bed is long, with a low ceiling and exposed wooden beams. The light coming in the window is a faint blue, and she knows where she is.

The door opens into a long quiet hallway, the wood floor not polished so much as worn smooth with untold years of human traffic.

Bare-footed and now wearing some kind of nightgown, she pads down to one end where a door lies ajar, with a soft line of orange glow describing its shape. When she opens it, she finds Verthandi alone, not dressed in finery, but just a slip, and sitting not on the elegant chair by the fire, so inviting in the cold, but on a small wooden stool with three legs, knees up with her arms around them.

"I hate that part," says the demigod quietly, all pretense to nobility dropped. "Of all the moments I have, that is the one I like the least."

"Are there others?" Bliss feels like she's intruding.

Verthandi smiles, wistful. "There are always others." She stands up. "Welcome back. I want to show you something. Come with me."

In one corner of the room is a small door to a stairway down. It winds its way in blackness through the spaces between rooms in this impossible building. The windows they pass all show the same view, despite the descent, as though every window were the same window—not a building but a universe, if a smaller and less awful one than that from which she's come.

"He sends you to me," she says. "He knows what it means, that you have no memories, that the world is twisted like this. I can never tell him, but he always figures it out anyway. And yet he entrusts you to me. I love that about him. Loved that."

At the bottom of the stairs is a doorway to a dark room lit by gas lights around its periphery. It's filled with furniture covered in sheets, piled with trinkets and clocks and little automata. Verthandi sits on a pile of rags, regal in the dusty squalor.

Bliss looks around, picking up trinkets and putting them back. "Why don't I remember?"

Verthandi folds her hands in her lap. "Still not quite the right question."

Bliss thinks again, and asks, "Who am I?"

Verthandi's eyes light up. "Ah. Do you really want to know? You may regret it."

Bliss doesn't say anything, just stares into the gaslit shadows, silence acting for consent.

"You're a broken toy, child. The universe is shattered, and you're its fractured center. You don't remember your lives as Helene because you aren't her, and won't ever be. They hijacked you, broke you, remade the world around you." She wanders to one corner and fetches something, brings it back and hands it to Bliss. It's a letter, a series of letters.

"What's this?"

"It's in your writing."

"But I never—"

"Ah but you did. And you will."

"I don't understand."

"Just read."

鼠

Bliss sits on one of the pieces of furniture draped in cloth and reads.

"Dear Bliss,

"Ver has told me that I won't remember if I do this, so I'm making a note for her to give to you. She can't do much, she says, but she can do that. As she explains it, the reason you can't remember writing this is because we're stuck in a loop in time, doing the same things over and over again, for eternity. That's how an infinite recursion loop works—you can't actually get into one or out of one, so you're always either in one for eternity, or never in one. And since we're in one, we're in one eternally, which is too much for any mind or body, so the memories, well it's like you don't have any. Sorry if this is complicated. If it hurts when you think about it, you're probably thinking about it right. The goal is to get out of the loop, or, that is, to never have been in one in the first place.

I know.

"You've probably heard Mouse and Anna talking about the darkness. Do you remember Mouse? Not the fighter you grew up with, but the quiet new kid at the high school. Have you even been to school? I guess not. I'm writing this for a future me who isn't going to remember being me, because you won't have been me yet. God, this is weird.

"The darkness is the time loop. For once in your life it's all about you, and you're going to wish it wasn't. You're going to go back in time and try to stop things. Verthandi will send you, if you ask, and if you don't ask, the masks will send you instead. They shouldn't be able to, they shouldn't have that kind of power, but because of the infinite regressive power of the loop they can run an Antiochus Algorithm when they shouldn't be able to. It's messed up because every repeat of the loop is caused by the previous one. It's a paradox: it literally can't have started, which means it always was. We should never have even been there the first time, but we were.

"Ver tells me that one of the times before, Mouse told her that the old him, Simon, who you can't remember either if you're anything like me, said there were possibilities on the other side of the Darkness. That means there has to be a way to get out of the loop, which is the point of this letter. Keep trying new things, and write down what you're going to try. Remember to give this note to Ver before, well, you'll know when. Good luck."

There's a line across the page in another ink but the same hand.

"Bliss,

"I should have taken better notes, I'm sorry. It starts really early. Mouse doesn't even move to town for two years. I've tried telling people—Anna won't listen, before or after—

Something's crossed out.

—(you'll find out), and Ver told us we shouldn't tell Helene, but I think it's because she's got some kind of grudge. I tried telling some of the others but they don't believe us. I don't know what to try. I don't know how it ends."

More lines, more notes. She flips through to see how far it goes, then flips back and continues reading. A name catches her eye.

"Bliss,

"Charles is here! Do you remember him? You have to, you're me. He's quieter, and he's definitely not a fighter yet (maybe he won't ever be?). He's great to have around, but be nice and don't tell him. Maybe then, he and Mouse won't fight."

She skims the rest of the note but there's nothing more about him. She keeps reading.

"Bliss,

"We have to move faster. June and Priest died this time fighting outside the hospital to buy us time to escape. Work on your barriers, you know how quickly they come down. Maybe if you can keep those two alive longer? Give it a shot."

"Bliss,

"It must be something that happens at the last moment before the Algorithm is activated that sets it all in motion, which sucks because I can't write a note right then (I imagine I'll be a little busy). Kept

June and Priest alive this time, but since you're reading this obviously that didn't help. I think Helene dies. We're born right when the world is warped, so that's when she must end up dying. If she doesn't, we don't get born, and we can't be sent back. By that logic, well, I guess you're pretty aware that we die at the end each time, too, otherwise we'd be the same age as Mouse. Maybe I'm glad I don't remember."

The ink changes again and it continues without a dividing line.

"Bliss,

"I'm standing in front of Verthandi right now. She says Helene has to die. She says she showed up and killed her to preserve the timeline, yelled something about additional paradoxes, and seemed pissed about having to do it, so I guess leave Helene out of it. She says I can't kill Mouse or Anna either (not that we would), but she says it doesn't help and that we just end up less able to work toward fixing things. I asked her what we should do, and she said that's something her sister Skuld (?) would know, and since the loop is an eternal present (??) she doesn't have sisters right now (???). I'm so confused."

"Bliss,

"I don't know if it's even possible. I tried telling Helene and even gave her a copy of the note (Ver got mad but got over it), but she hasn't gotten back to me and I don't know that she will in time. God, the only good thing about this entire godforsaken mess is the bit where you get to kiss him...Consider not wiping his memory afterward this time.

"PS—Helene's too slow. Give it to her sooner."

She gets more despondent with every continuation. How long has this been happening? She skips ahead through several pages.

> "Bliss,
>
> > "I don't know what to write. This is just a record of another loop. It's all gone the same as last time I think."

A series of shorter notes follow:

> "Ditto."

> "One more."

> "Another."

The last one is long again, and it looks as though it was written in a steadier hand, like she'd taken time to write it.

> "Dear Bliss," it reads, "everything ends. It's just something stupid Ginnie says sometimes. You haven't met her yet, but you'll like her. You would like her. You probably won't get the chance to meet her, or, hell, I guess even read this, because I have a feeling it'll work. I'm going to tell Mouse just that: that everything ends, and that he has to kill us when he meets us in the future, in our past, when we're still a kid. Then we won't be able to go back and the whole thing will just end. I'm sorry, but as I said, it won't happen, I won't write this, and you won't read it either. I guess I'm just writing because I feel guilty. I'd feel worse about telling him to kill you, but it's me, too, so. Sorry, I guess. Bye, me. It's been fun."

Bliss looks up at Verthandi, then back down at the letter, awe-struck and confused. "But I *did* read it," she says, demanding an answer from the paper echo of herself. A tear runs down her cheek, dripping onto the paper. "And he *didn't*." She stands up and looks at Verthandi. "And he *knew*. That's why h—he said—" But she can't continue and just starts crying, childlike and adrift in her grief, until Verthandi wraps her arms around her.

The old one sighs.

"You didn't get the chance to tell him, you know. You told Charles, left him a note knowing he'd make it, and Charles told him. But, Mouse didn't have the heart to end your life, and so Charles tried to send you to me, to have me do it. Not that I have any interest in seeing you dead, but then, he didn't know that."

"That's what...but, but *why*, then? Why couldn't they just...or why wouldn't you? If it would mean an end to *this*?" She buries her face in Verthandi's shoulder. "Isn't it worth it?"

"Oh, little one, now you truly belong in my sanctuary. Usually so full of bravado. For once, I'm a little sad I can't keep you."

"What do I *do*?" she sobs into Verthandi's shoulder.

"If I knew, child, I would tell you. All I know is that it has to be you."

Bliss thinks back and remembers Mouse's last words, the last words of the last people in this world to care about her. She thinks about all the different times she must have tried, all the different ways she must have failed. She grits her teeth and pulls back, clears her throat and it almost sounds like a growl. She's going to see them again. A little different, maybe, but she'll see them again soon.

"Arkangel," she says, swallowing. "That was his answer." She takes a deep breath. "He said it right before he died, right before he sent me to you. I don't know what it means, but I have two years to figure it out when I get there, right?" She rolls the letters and wraps her fist around them, looking down. "I'll figure it out," she says. "I have to."

Verthandi watches her, lips pursed, saying nothing. Evaluating.

"Good," she says at length.

Bliss blinks, wiping her eyes with her fingertips, her cheeks with the palms of her hands. "What?"

"For a moment I was starting to feel sorry for you." She steps back. "You were starting to remind me of Helene, and she's become so dull of late."

Bliss wants to ask about their history, but can't find a way to word it. "But not now?" she asks instead.

"Not now." Verthandi smiles. "You've reminded me of all your potential."

Bliss twists her lips, unsure of the compliment.

"Thanks?"

Verthandi waves a hand. "Of course. Now, will you be off? Back again to set things right?"

Bliss nods. "Everything ends," she says. "Everything has to end sometime."

"Every ending is a beginning, child." She says it like it's not just a truism. She says, "Good luck."

Then Verthandi puts her hands on Bliss's shoulders and, with a few words of incantation and an act of ancient will, Bliss vanishes with a sound of breaking glass and static.

Alone again, Verthandi stares out at the clutter in the room and sits back down, pondering the new information. "Oh, little Mouse. That's twice you've surprised me," she says, and the corners of her lips turn up in a mischievous smile. "What a wonderful gift."

Bliss is staring at the sky. She holds up a hand at arm's length and stares at it silhouetted against the bright, expansive field of blue. The breeze is cool on her cheeks and balances out the sun, which she's never seen with these eyes, at least not that she remembers.

"Heey!" A shout from the distance, coming closer.

She can feel the footsteps thumping toward her, then suddenly there's a boy leaning over her. Dark hair and eyes, white short-sleeved dress shirt and a black tie. He's panting.

"Hey, are you okay?"

Bliss sits up and looks around. She's in a field of tall, yellow grass by a river. In the distance, a road climbs a tree-lined hill. After the unending rust and smoke in the city of the Fall, it looks like paradise itself.

She scratches her head. "Uh, yeah. Why wouldn't I be?"

The boy looks embarrassed. "I just," he almost laughs. "You're never going to believe this. I could have sworn I saw you—" he shakes his head "—wow, it sounds even crazier than I thought it would."

"Saw me what?" She's suppressing a grin, and wondering why she never mentioned this boy to herself in the letter.

"Ah...fall out of the sky?" He manages at last.

His expression is so earnest that Bliss can't help but laugh.

"And you ran over to help me?"

"Well, I, uh, yeah?" His hand goes to the back of his head and he grins sheepishly.

"That's totally sweet of you." She stands up and sweeps the grass from her nightgown, ignoring how peculiar she must look. She sticks out her hand. "I'm Bliss."

He takes it.

"Kai," he says.

"I'm new in town. Wanna show me around?"

鼠

He does, in fact, want to show her around, and spends the next week looking for the right way to accept the invitation. When Sunday arrives, she finds him in the middle of town.

"Over here!" Bliss shouts when she spots them. Kai and the girl in the wheelchair with the wide-brimmed hat, his sister.

"Hey!" Kai waves and crosses the sleepy town square. As they pull up, she sees how frail the girl is, her arms seem to be bruised in patches. "Hey, sorry for being late. This is my sister, she wanted to meet you."

The girl looks up and smiles sleepily at her, and Bliss's heart skips a beat.

"Anna..." Her hair is long and dark, her eyes are ringed with purple, and she's even smaller than the Anna Bliss had known, but it's definitely her. To become a Pyx...the realization sinks in.

The girl tilts her head. "Hmm? Hi." She blinks slowly. "Gome," her voice is softer, too, smaller. "I fell asleep on the way over. Are you Bliss? Oniichan was telling me all about you. I think he has a—"

Kai interrupts by leaning around the brim of Anna's hat and giving her a look.

"—a nice day planned for us." She giggles at the obvious course correction.

Bliss realizes she's still staring and forces a smile. "Ah, hi! Yeah. Yes, Bliss, that's me." So awkward.

Anna looks down, and then back. "They don't hurt," she says. "Most people get that look when they see me for the first time. It's okay, really."

Bliss looks away. "Sorry, though."

Anna shakes her head and holds out a hand. "I'm tougher than I look. Nice to meet you."

"My pleasure," she says.

鼠

It's a year later and the rain is falling on the line of parked cars outside, little funeral flags all sodden and limp.

"Oneesan," Bliss says to herself, "that's what you called me. That's twice you took me in and made me family."

She's standing in front of the polished wooden casket, and flowers are lying on top of it. Everyone else has gone out front and is either milling about under the awning or else climbing into the cars and sitting listening to the rain, waiting for the slow drive to the cemetery. Someone should already have moved the casket to the hearse by now, but lines of communication must have gotten crossed somewhere and no one's come for it yet. Kai's in a car with his father already, but Bliss just couldn't leave her alone like that. She'd saved her life too many times for that. Or she might do.

"I had another family, one you're never going to meet. I wish you could have met Rain. He was my brother. We were the same age, but he acted a lot like Kai, actually, always sticking his nose where it didn't belong. In all the right ways, though." She smiles a little and puts her hand on the cold, smooth wood. "I'll see you again, Anna. I promise."

Some faceless men in suits shuffle in, then, and Bliss makes her way to the door.

鼠

It's mid-October and there's a new boy in her chemistry class with Mrs. Edelman. He's sitting near the back, quiet, hands resting on his thighs, head tilted forward with ashen hair falling over his face, hiding his eyes.

"We've got a new student today," says Mrs. Edelman, an open hand directing the half of the class that's not already examining him to do so. "His name is Simon and he just moved out here from the city, so everyone let's show him a bit of country kindness, hey?" She does that strange head-tilt and folded-hands motion that Bliss has always found just a little patronizing.

"Mouse," says the boy.

He doesn't look up when he says it. He's almost frozen in place. If he turned to the side he wouldn't be able to miss Bliss's wild grin.

"Do you mean instead of Simon?"

Bliss's heart does double time. She feels like running over and giving him a hug. He's so like himself, but so much younger, more timid. Mouse had never seemed like a good name for him when she knew him—silent, calm, and powerful. But here, scribbling a note to pass forward to the Chemistry Commissioner, eyes averted and nervous, here she can see where it came from.

"So, Mouse, then?" Edelman looks perplexed, but gives in. "Well, it's a little unorthodox, but if that's what you go by." She takes a breath and moves on, turning to the rest of the class. "Mouse here has obviously missed a week, so can I have a volunteer to help out if he has any questions?"

Bliss throws her hand up, grinning like a madwoman. Edelman, the jerk, pretends not to see it, so just to be sure of things, Bliss draws a little circle on the desk and sends a little will into it, silently dissuading the rest of the class. Ambivalence is a pretty simple thing to instill in a class of teenagers before 10:00 A.M.

The teacher can't pretend any longer and sighs. "Bliss," she says.

Bliss grins harder, until her cheeks hurt. "You can count on me, Commish."

Mrs. Edelman takes a deep, cleansing breath, and begins the day's lesson. Out of the corner of her eye, Bliss thinks she catches Mouse looking.

鼠

Fitting in, in a world not perpetually under siege by the forces of darkness, isn't easy for Bliss. Making up a backstory, "borrowing" a vacant subdivision house—these things are easier with the Knowledge, to be sure.

But having time to yourself.

Being bored.

Not fearing for your life.

Once, before Mouse had come to town, Ginnie had come over to stay, watch movies Ginnie said her parents wouldn't let her watch, and eat junk food until they felt sick. A sleepover. There had been a thunderstorm in the night, and Ginnie had found her crouched by the front door with a kitchen knife, peering out into the periodically-lit darkness through prism-like glass. It had taken her a few minutes, bleary-eyed from sleep, to even pull up the memory of what a thunderstorm was supposed to be like; and even when she had, the crackle of a nearby lightning strike had sounded so like the failing of Mouse's wards beneath the onslaught of the masks' attack that she couldn't sleep alone. There's a reason Bliss puts up with Ginnie's antics.

But there are things that can make up for it. Bacon, on the one hand, and baths on the other. She's soaking in a particularly hot and steamy one when the doorbell goes. She almost doesn't get out, but decides to peer out the window just in case. Mouse is walking away down the driveway.

"Wait wait wait! I'll be right there. Hold on!" She shouts out the window. He's standing by the door when she finally opens it. "Well don't just stand there," she says, and wanders back toward the kitchen.

He comes in and, over coffee, writes her note after note, explaining everything that happened with Anna's ghost and with the man named Priest. He fades fast though, putting his head down on the table and asking for painkillers. She almost has to carry him to "Rain's" room. At first, she'd decorated it as a decoy, part of the backstory to make her more believable. But it was too much like what her brother might have liked, and now she hardly goes in it anymore.

By the time she's pulling the covers over him, he's out cold.

She kneels next to the bed and looks at his face. He's so young. She traces a line with her mind across the top of his ear, a part of him she'd never seen up close. No burn marks creep up his neck. It's like he's still a work in progress; like he's not done yet. She sits back and flips through the notes, his explanation of what's been going on, and says a silent apology to Anna, wherever she is, for not seeing her when she was right there. Then, she gets up and leaves the room, closing the door behind her.

鼠

We're going to try something. It might not work for long, and it's probably going to be a little weird. Probably weirder for me than you. But probably weird for you, too.

It's the morning, and between making breakfast and trying to gauge whether or not Mouse is aware that she might have sort-of climbed into bed with him during the thunderstorm last night, she hasn't been able to find a place in the conversation to explain the sheer weirdness that is the fact that she's from the future.

Why are we friends? he'd asked, and no matter how she thought about it, all the answers she could think of sounded like, *because we were friends, or we will be friends, or something,* or *because I'm the memory-challenged reincarnation of a girl that a previous iteration of your aeon-spanning consciousness loved over the past two millennia.* She'd made up something about knowing he'd fit in and is starting to hate herself a little for it already. She frowns, wondering if she finds it this hard every time through.

Mouse looks at the empty chair, takes a deep breath, closes his eyes, and nods. He stiffens a little, taking a short, sharp breath, and looks up at Bliss.

"Been a while, oneesan," his voice is almost squeaky, and he seems even younger, if that's possible. He claps his hands together and does a quarter bow.

Has it really worked? "Anna?" she asks. "Are you, I mean, is it…?"

"Borrowing it. He said it's okay. Ugh though," Mouse/Anna looks down at his/her arms and frowns. "Bodies are super heavy. And *oh my god.*" They take a deep breath. "*Bacon.*"

Bliss watches as they grab a piece of bacon and talk while eating it. "Oh my god, smelling and tasting. SMELLING AND TASTING, BLISS. Why didn't I do this sooner?" They stop and think for a second. "Oh yeah. Fine, fair enough."

"Is Mouse, um, awake?" It's an awkward question after last night. They stop and think. "Yeah he's here. Oh this is so weird. It's like we're almost the same person. It's like we're overlapping or something. Oh hey, I can see some of his memories, this is so surreal." She's narrating, waving around a piece of bacon while she talks, not looking anywhere in particular, and then her gaze snaps back to Bliss's. "Oh my god! What were you doing in his bed last night?"

Bliss blushes furiously. "I can explain," she starts, but Anna won't let her continue.

"Oh my god! Shut up I don't care if you think she's pretty when she blushes," Anna says, looking up and tapping their forehead. "For a guy that talks so little your brain says *way* too much—"

Pretty? Mouse thinks she's pretty? She shakes her head and tries to interrupt.

"—Anna, Mouse, stop for a second. I need to tell you—"

"I don't care if you can't help it, try harder, geez. And what is it with you and girls in bed? Are you some kind of perv? OH MY GOD! I did not want to think about that when the answers are RIGHT THERE—"

Bliss's eyes widen, but she won't be deterred. "Anna stop!"

They turn and look at Bliss, Anna seeming to realize something.

"Oh my god, that was all out loud."

"Yep, and we'll talk about that later. But right now I—"

"—It's not what it sounds like!"

"—I don't care! Or, I do care, but it's not that important right now and I—"

"—No but it was just this one time, or well a couple of times, but—"

"It doesn't matter! Anna please I need to tell you that I'm—"

The doorbell erupts at a stunning volume and Mouse almost jumps in his seat, before slumping down in his chair, catching himself on the table just as he's about to fall. He puts his head down on his arm and groans.

Bliss sits in silence for almost a full ten seconds, rubbing the bridge of her nose with two fingers before putting down her coffee cup and walking to the door.

Ginnie's standing on the doorstep.

"I brought coffee!" She says, as though she has no idea how much her timing sucks, and bounces past Bliss into the house. Bliss stares out into the street and sighs. She'll try again tomorrow.

鼠

Time, Bliss finds, doesn't like to be altered. After Anna's incarnation, she's too busy helping her friend—who looks now exactly the way she remembers from the future—learn to be a high school student. Anna starts living with her, and the longer she waits to tell them the truth, about the future, about herself, the harder it seems to get. And then Helene is in Mouse's bed, and he's catatonic in his room, and everyone's downstairs arguing about it but her.

She drapes a comforter over the two of them, staring out the window as the snow falls, gentle in the moonlight.

"There," she says, "at least we won't be cold." She puts her arm around him and just sits. "You may not believe me, Mouse," she whispers. "But you're going to get through this. I promise."

She sighs. The snow wafts sideways as a winter breeze carries it past the window. She looks out as she talks.

"I don't know if you can even hear me right now. And I don't want to make things worse, but I have to tell you. And if you don't remember it later, then I'll have to tell you again." She takes a deep breath. "And I'll tell you over and over until it works, because there's too much at stake and I can't do it by myself.

"Thing is, Mouse, I've known you for a long time. I've known you longer than you've known me, which makes no sense I know, but it's the truth. It's *me*, Mouse, not Helene. But she's the one who knows Simon, and you're the only you I've ever known." She pulls her knees up and hugs them. "I'm not making any sense." She puts her forehead down on her knees, closes her eyes and talks.

"I'm from the future. I'm Helene's next incarnation. She's going to die some time soon, during the coming darkness, but we can't stop that or it'll cause a paradox. But we have to do something or else the world will be stuck in a loop forever, and it's all me, going around and around trying to stop myself, or stop you, or stop the guys in masks." Once she starts talking it all starts spilling out, in a long stream of words. She's worried she isn't making any sense, but she continues on, afraid that if she stops talking she'll never be able to start again.

"They're going to use something called an Antiochus Algorithm to break the world, and they're using the loop itself to power it. And you and Anna are going to be the only ones who make it, with the masks and the azazim and the poor human survivors. God, all they want to do is live to the next meal of canned carrots and crappy beans. And then you'll find me, and I'll be a little kid, and my family, Rain, everybody, will be dead, and you and Anna, you're going to be my family. You're going to teach me everything about the Knowledge, about how to fight, about how to keep alive for the sake of whatever world you live in. The survivors, in Cannery and Four Corners and all over the whole godawful world-city of the Fall, they'll call you and Anna the fighting saints sometimes. Or sometimes the jihad. And it's all saints and mundanes, and you'll fight like nothing anyone's ever seen, and you'll save so, so many lives. But it won't be for anything because I'll still see you die and get Verthandi to send me back to save you. Or I'll tell myself I won't and the masks will send me back to preserve the loop to power the Algorithm. Or I'll tell you what I told you last time, that you need to kill me when you find me after the Fall, when I'm just a little kid. And then you won't do that either because you're a good and kind and foolish man who thinks he can fix everything without anyone ever getting hurt."

Her knees are wet with tears. She leans sideways against Mouse, whose frail form still seems so alien when she thinks of the scarred and muscled fighter she once knew.

"And so I have to tell you the last thing you said to me, the last thing you will say to me, because I don't get it. I've been trying to figure it out since I got here, and I don't know. I've tried to find books and look it up, I even thought of asking Priest, but then he disappeared. What you told me, you seemed to think it was the answer. God, I hope it was the answer. You said to tell you to use it. I think. You said, 'Algorithm for arkangel,' and, 'Tell me, use it.' That's exactly what you said. And there aren't any arkangels, I mean, aside from the city in Russia. I checked, and I don't know how you'd use the Algorithm, either, if we're trying to stop the thing that powers it. But you said it, and I believe in you. So please, Mouse...I need you to do this. I need you to fix it. Please."

Sitting next to her, even wrapped in the blanket with her, he's still shivering, maybe even more than before. She puts her arms around him and realizes he's not just shivering, he's shaking.

"Mouse?" she looks at his face, at his eyes, but they're half-closed and he's starting to seize. "Mouse!" she lays him down on his side and bolts for the door. There won't be any future at all if she doesn't get help now.

She tears into the kitchen, which has at least one more person in it than she expects. "Hurry!" She yells. "It's Mouse, and—" She gasps for air, shakes her head. She knows they've gotten through this before. "Whatever you're planning on doing, you need to do it now!"

鼠

Time flashes by in an instant, and suddenly it's March, and they're sitting in Mrs. Dinshaw's Biology class. Mouse recovered that night, but as the days and then weeks passed, nothing he said or did indicated he had any memory of the things she'd said to him. She has to know. She writes a note and passes it back.

I need to talk to you, it says, *without Anna around.*

He nods when she sends back another note suggesting he skip class with him next period. She'll tell him again if she has to.

鼠

They're in the batcave, and Mouse is holding the coffee she got him. She's chewing the rim of hers but not drinking it. He passes her a note. *So what's up?*

"So," she stops, sighs, lets out a disgusted *ugh* noise and starts again. "Look, I don't want this to be melodramatic, but I need to know."

Mouse nods.

"Do you remember the night, your birthday, back in January. I was there with you in your room?"

Mouse puts down his coffee and slides over, closer to her. He kneels next to her and starts writing a note while she continues.

"So, you haven't said anything about it, but I need to tell you again, because if you don't remember I think we're running out of—" She doesn't make it any further.

Mouse does two things, both of which catch her off guard. The first is to put a note, folded up, into her hand. The second is to kiss her, which somewhat unsurprisingly takes her mind off the first. She remembers the letter to herself, and almost smiles while kissing him—she was right, it is a good moment.

And it's at precisely that moment that Anna comes flying around the corner and stops cold.

Bliss pushes Mouse away and shoots up, flustered. "Ann—Izzy!" She corrects herself quickly.

Anna takes a step backward, but doesn't reply.

"This—I can explain this." She thinks she can explain it. Can she explain it? The note sits forgotten, folded in her hand. She looks back and Mouse is facing away, from her and from Anna.

"I was trying to tell you..." Anna manages, staring at their feet. "And you weren't listening." The pit of Bliss's stomach is sinking like a ball of lead in the ocean. "So I came to find you, and, hey," Anna half laughs but it sticks in her throat. "Here you are," she says. "It's totally fine."

"I'm sorry," Bliss says, "this is all my fault, I was just—"

"No, it's fine!" She takes another step backward, wringing her hands. She looks away. "It's, uh. I'm sorry. I didn't mean to interrupt."

"Izzy," she shakes her head. There's no point in the pretense, there's no one around. "Anna wait, let me explain."

"No, it's—it's fine. I just had a thing...and. I have to go."

"Anna it's not like—"

"Yamenasai!" Anna shouts. A tear rolls down her cheek as she looks at Bliss, then at Mouse. "Please. Just stop. I don't need your excuses. It's fine." She turns on her heel, then vanishes into thin air.

Bliss exhales sharply and looks down at her feet, then remember
the note.

She unfolds it, stares at its contents, reads it twice, and then
looks at Mouse, who's sunk back down against one wall like he's been
punched. Bliss walks over and slides down the wall next to him. She
grabs his hand.

"Okay," she says.

He just nods.

鼠

Mouse wakes up to sunlight shining on his face. He's in his own bed.
He remembers fighting the monsters, channeling lightning. Kissing
Bliss. He reddens at the thought, then nearly jumps out of his skin at
a voice from beside him.

"You're an idiot."

He rolls over and Anna is lying on the bed next to him, on top of
the covers. She's on her side, staring at him. Everything hurts.

"Baaaka." She throws in a few extra As for emphasis. "That's what
Priest said to tell you. That, and that you need to use limiting circles
when drawing on lightning."

Ugh. That's why everything hurts.

"And you're also an idiot for trying to take on those things without me."

She's only six inches away from his face.

I was looking for you at the time, he thinks to her.

"Well you should have looked harder," she sits up. "That's what
you're supposed to do when...when something like that happens. A
girl shouldn't have to come back and save your butt after...after that."

Kissing Bliss, he thinks to her.

"Mm." She's sitting on the edge of the bed looking away. "I'm not
prying." Her voice is quiet. "And I know you met her before you met
me, but—" She stops when he grabs her hand.

It's not what you think. He sighs. *It's a little of what you think. But I
can't tell you why.*

"Well. All right. But...I might have, um." She looks away. "I mean I might have told Bliss to back off. A little. After the fight."

When she looks back, Mouse is grinning and shaking his head, half sitting up in bed.

"I also wanted to ask you...how much you remember of the fight."

Ah. That.

I can't tell you that, either.

"It's like I can't...think there. Right near the end of the fight. And I don't know why."

I know; I'm sorry. I'm not going to lie to you, but I'm not going to explain either.

He tries not to think of Bliss's injury, healed by Knowledge she isn't supposed to have. He's had a wall up between himself and Anna for weeks. It's been necessary. Instead he squeezes her hand.

Please trust me.

Anna nods, then pulls her hand away as June walks in, grinning. "Hey, kiddo. How're you feeling?"

He rubs his head and smiles. It's not long now.

鼠

It's two weeks later and he's walking across the bridge from another early morning practice with June. The sun is rising over the far hills, turning the town a shade of yellow that's become familiar on mornings like these. As he gets halfway across it, the hairs on the back of his neck stand up and he swivels, drawing his spear. There's no one there.

No, there definitely is. "Helene," he says, out loud. And then she's there, a veil dropping that leaves her in clear sight.

"How did you know I was here?" she asks.

He shrugs and puts away the spear before continuing on his way. He'd had a feeling. She walks beside him.

"How has your training progressed?"

He shrugs again, keeps walking. He doesn't want to look at her. He hasn't seen her since that night in January, and so much has changed since then.

Helene goes quiet as he withdraws.

"What is it? What has Bliss told you?"

Mouse stops and fishes out his pad and pen.

What do you mean?

"I came here to ask you about her. Who is she?"

She's the first girl I met at school. We're friends.

Helene reads the note, then discards it.

"You're a terrible liar."

I'm not lying.

"Neither are you telling the truth."

Mouse stares at his feet.

"Bliss is me, isn't she?"

He looks away. He's been avoiding this, trying to avoid this. There's a reason he hasn't been to the bar in months.

She looks past Mouse, into the distance.

"How can she be?"

I can't tell you.

"Damn you, Simon." She's not talking to him.

He steps forward and holds her arms, then her hands, together. She looks down, then at him. There's a moment of silence, and she wraps him in a hug.

"Do you know when?" Her voice is soft.

He steps back, and she stands silent while he writes.

I don't know. And when it comes to the things I do know, I don't know what I can say to anyone. Even this might be too much. I don't know what's going to happen. I can't see the way he could.

"But there are other ways of seeing. You told me that."

Mouse nods. Seeing without looking, knowing without thinking.

I wish I knew, but I don't. Not yet, and maybe not in time. But I need you to trust me all the same, because he trusted me with you.

She sighs and turns away, speaking over her shoulder. "Maybe you're not him, but you're a lot like him." She starts walking away, then stops again. "You tell her she'd better take good care of you. Or, maybe I will. I'll be seeing you."

He wants to say she already is.

Mouse watches her walk away, slipping behind a veil as she does so. He's going to be late.

鼠

It all goes the same—the ghost calls in Mr. Wigmore's math class, the power going out, the day turning to night. The events spin rapidly by until they're sitting in Bliss's car, the four of them, pulled over beneath the power lines, the windshield wipers muddily swiping back and forth in the dark.

Mouse undoes his seatbelt and grabs the door handle then stops. Anna looks at him, then talks.

"Mouse has an announcement," she says. He looks at Kai and Bliss while she's speaking for him. "Whatever happens tonight," Anna says, and then stops. Mouse looks at her, confused. Anna almost laughs at him. "Mouse is an idiot," she says. "And he thinks it's all on him tonight." She looks at Kai and puts her hand on Bliss's shoulder. "We're your friends. It's on all of us."

He looks down, smiles, and gets out of the car.

鼠

"So here you are," comes a small voice. Verthandi is standing in the field. In the dark distance the hospital shines like a beacon, if one in the wrong place.

Bliss nods. "You gave him the letter."

Verthandi smiles. "You're not the only one with skin in the game," she says. "I helped where I could."

Mouse bows slightly to the raggedy imp standing before them, and hands her the wrinkled packet of pages as though it's an imperial message. She flips to the back and raises her eyebrows.

"Nothing to add?" she asks.

He shakes his head.

Anna comes over and holds out her hand. "We've never met," she says.

"You're mistaken, but so polite." Verthandi smiles, taking her hand and shaking it. She turns to Mouse. "They'll come for you if you do this," she says, "like kicking a hornet's nest." And then she laughs. "But you know that, don't you?"

Anna looks at him, then back at Verthandi, delivering a message she doesn't fully understand. "He says," she looks back at him, then at Verthandi, "he says 'Pawn to queen is a hell of a promotion.'"

Verthandi laughs, delighted. "You say that like I'm the only one playing." She winks. "Now let's see if you can pull it off." She flickers, fading away. "Hurry, little Mouse. Time's ticking, again." And then she's gone.

Mouse grabs Anna's hand and she turns to face Bliss and Kai. "Let's go."

鼠

"Aren't you glad I stopped by?" Priest wipes his sword clean on his sleeve after slicing something that passes for a head from an azazim set of shoulders. June's rotating barrier flares white as another crashes against it.

"Shut up and fight, Leonard, I'm still not talking to you." She weaves a lance of white light that takes out two more of the creatures. "I should've known you only showed up because you had a thing for nurses."

Priest lets out a deep belly laugh. "Hey now, sweetness—"

"Don't start with me, you old lech." But she's smiling.

He grins back at her, then turns and parries a black-clawed strike that makes it past the wards, before hacking off the offending limb. June is about to fire another insult at her ex when a ball of white light strikes the rest of the creature from behind and leaves it twitching on the ground, a smoking hole where its chest used to be. It's Mouse.

June beams with pride. "Nice one!" she shouts.

They enter the fray.

Kai drops behind June's barrier and pulls out a curved sword.

"Is that Greg's?" she asks.

"Gramps's—his dad's," he says.

June reaches over and traces a finger along the blade, causing it to glow with a pale light.

"That should help," she says, smiling. "Not just anything can get through demon flesh. And try not to swing it so much like a baseball bat."

Kai swipes at another to much greater effect. "I'll keep that in mind."

June throws a twisted lance of white sigils through another azaz, one that expands once it's lodged in the thing's torso. It explodes into a shower of dark purple and grey parts.

"Anyone ever tell you how beautiful you look when you destroy violations of the natural order?" Priest is grinning at her.

"Shut *up*, Leonard."

"What are they after?" Anna shouts.

"Fear," Bliss says. "They want everyone in the dark and afraid."

Then the monsters just stop, like they're waiting for something, and a shiver goes up Mouse's spine. He knows what's coming. He turns and holds his spear forward, willing power into it as the dark lightning crackles and snaps toward him. It branches into arcs on either side of him, which he twists back on themselves and returns to their sender, a figure in the darkness, who bats them away with ease.

Bliss's eyes go wide with a sudden realization, and for the first time that night she has hope. But first they need to survive.

She starts screaming orders, "Fall back, fall back, fall back!"

Having felt the power of the blast sent his way, Mouse doesn't hesitate, and grabs June by the wrist before running.

Helene's pulling up in a black van with Vallis at the wheel, looking utterly confused at the retreat. Bliss grabs Priest and shoves him toward it, before spinning and throwing up a barrier herself. It glitters in shades of gold as azazim thrash themselves against its slow-spinning sigils.

June's eyes widen at the sight. "A fifth-order astral...?" she manages to say.

Bliss catches up and explains. "We're doing things a little differently tonight, sorry to pull rank."

Before June has time to bristle at the idea, Anna has caught up and is climbing into the van while Helene demands an explanation.

Mouse just leans forward, putting one hand on her shoulder and pointing with the other to where a figure with a masked face is literally unmaking the barrier. Even an over-engineered barrier like that requires maintenance, and without someone there to sustain it, it falls in a matter of seconds.

Before Bliss can order it, Vallis is pulling away, with everyone aboard the crowded van.

Mouse's eyes are closed and no one says anything as they drive around the town. The few pockets of light have gone out, all except the hospital, which shines whenever it can be seen between trees and buildings.

"Here," Anna says, and Vallis pulls over. It's a darkened gas station with broken windows. "Turn off the engine, but stay inside. Everyone stay quiet."

Thirty seconds later, a car screams by, pursued by three fast-scuttling azazim. In the dark of the van, everyone waits another minute before exhaling.

"We're good for now," Anna says. "But we need a plan. Thoughts?"

"Just who the hell are you?" June's looking square at Bliss. "And how do you know how to weave a barrier at all, let alone one like that?"

Bliss looks at Mouse, who just shakes his head.

"I...can't tell you yet," she says.

June looks at her son. "Is this your idea?"

Mouse nods, then grabs Anna's sleeve, and she starts talking for him. "We need your experience, all of you. Those people with the masks, they're the ones making all the azazim. Now imagine for a second they have the power and the knowledge to make an Antiochus Algorithm—"

She doesn't even get the opportunity to finish before she's interrupted by three different adult voices, shouting different things at once.

"Hold on, hold on! One at a time. Vallis."

"Impossible."

Bliss looks at Mouse and responds. "I wish."

"Helene."

"Even if they had the mechanics of it down, how would they power it?"

Mouse sighs, and Anna speaks for him. "I guess it can't be helped. Tell them, Bliss."

"A recursive temporal loop."

There's silence in the car, and then, "Scarecrow's eyes, the darkness." Priest is rubbing his temples. "That's what it is, isn't it? Yeah." He lets out a single, sharp laugh. "That could do it."

"But if that's true—" June starts, but Anna interrupts.

"He says he can't explain any more, and that if you have suspicions you should keep them to yourselves. This is one of those weird times where the less you know, the better."

"Timeline preservation," says Priest.

Mouse nods and Anna speaks. "Every change since the last time makes this harder."

Bliss leans back in her seat, thinking, then looks over at Mouse. "Back at the hospital, when that lighting was coming your way. I saw you. You turned as if you were expecting it. How?"

Mouse shrugs.

"He's been getting feelings lately, like déjà vu all the time," Anna says.

Helene almost laughs. "'There are other ways to see,'" she says. "Simon, you lunatic."

"What?" June's losing patience.

Anna explains. "Simon, that is, Simon Magus, he was a master strategist, he could see the way everything was going to go and planned ahead every time. But this time he couldn't make the equations work—there wasn't enough data. So he made Mouse to be the opposite of him—he can't see, but he can feel. He can sense a pattern in the chaos and act right away. His intuition is exactly the opposite kind of knowledge to Simon's. Each time the cycle repeats itself, it leaves a little echo he can feel. But the more things that change the less useful it's going to get."

Mouse, June's son, their friend—everything about him had been planned from the start. The silence that fills the van could smother a fire.

"I see a flaw," Vallis says. "If Mouse here can only feel the things that have happened before—"

"—and of those things only the ones that have happened the most often—" Anna interjects.

"—right. So he can see the most worn down tracks in the tall grass. How is that supposed to help us, who're trying to find a new way through?"

Anna continues, "He has a plan, but it depends on us staying on the same path until right near the end. We have to keep doing the most familiar thing until the very last second, when we swerve."

"Scarecrow's eyes." Priest rubs the bridge of his nose like he's getting a headache. "We're playing chicken with fate."

"Pretty much," says Anna. "And the more we talk about it the less chance it's going to work. We've never had this conversation before."

"I hate everything about this," June says. "But say we go along with it. How do we get back on track?"

"Mouse suspects the hospital was a diversion. We need to know where it's really going down. Priest, how familiar are you with the Algorithm?"

The older man sighs. "Familiar enough not to want anything to do with it."

"Mouse is thinking the best place to run it would be somewhere with a lot of iron...structural steel. Boundaries are important, too."

"The hospital is on the hill at the edge of town," June says. "Sky meets earth, town meets country."

"That's what I was thinking, but Mouse isn't convinced."

Priest nods. "There are too many people around. You saw how the azazim were going wild back there—it's handy for an assault, but that lack of control would be murder for a spell like the Algorithm. Hell, even having them around could be a liability. With just the two of them, I don't see how they could control the things and still set up the equations."

"Three," Bliss says. "There are three of them."

"What?"

"The masks. There are three—happy, sad, and, I don't know, neither."

"There were only two up at the hospital."

"You're sure?"

Anna nods.

Priest shakes his head. "So Sad Sack and Smiling Jack set up a diversion for us, while Not Bothered makes the Algorithm in relative peace and quiet." Mouse is nodding his head in agreement.

"Okay, back to square one, then. Where are we headed?" The van gets ever quieter.

"The bridges." It's Kai who says it.

Priest nods, considering. "Steel rooted in bedrock, flowing water beneath to isolate the mechanics."

"But there are two," Kai says. "The new one and the old one by the rail yard. You can still drive across it, but no one does because it's out of the way."

"What do you think, kid?" Priest says. "Does splitting up seem familiar?"

Mouse nods and grabs Anna's sleeve again.

"Bliss, Kai, Mouse, and me—we'll get out here and walk to the new bridge. June, Vallis, Priest, Helene, you take the van across town—"

Another chorus of dissenting voices cuts Anna off again, but Mouse overrides it by sliding open the door and stepping out.

Anna makes an apologetic expression and scrambles to keep up with him. He's already walking away in the direction of the bridge.

"He says 'Executive decision'," she says, then runs to catch up.

Kai slides out of the van as well, and it's only as Bliss is following suit that Helene grabs her. "Wait," she says. She reaches forward in the van and grabs a walkie-talkie. "Cells are down because the towers are out. We'll use the radios." She hands it to Bliss and exchanges a meaningful look. "None of this is right."

Bliss stares back at her. "You don't know the half of it," she says.

"Right," Helene says as Bliss slams the door behind her. "Vallis, start her up."

The engine roars to life.

鼠

Mouse leads the way, a small sphere of light at the tip of his spear just enough to stop them from tripping in the dark. The air has begun to take on a cold, earthy smell, like the inside of a cave—or maybe a tomb. Muddy water drips from the ground below their feet, through the "sky" above them, and down onto their heads as they steal toward the bridge. They're nearly there.

"There is so much about this I still don't get," Kai says.

"I'm sorry," Bliss says. "I wish I could explain better."

"Crazy monster things, people shooting lightning at us? Sure, okay. June making Gramps's sword into some kind of crazy light saber? Cool, yes, fine—but also insane. And now we've got time loops and Mouse's ESP and what even the hell is an Antiochus Algorithm? Who exactly are we fighting? What do they even *want?*"

"If I had to guess? The same thing madmen who screw with people's lives always want—power." Bliss shakes her head at Kai's expression. "For a while, I thought maybe it was Castlereagh and the Trust behind it, trying to take out Simon Magus and the threat he represents to their power, but I've had a long time to think about it, and I think it's too big and too cruel, even for them."

"Which means—?"

"As below, so above." Anna says, interrupting her brother. "That's what Mouse says."

"Wait, wait." Kai stops walking. "You're saying all this down here, and all the things that are going to happen—might happen—whatever—all of this insane stuff that's going to make a lot of people suffer... isn't even the point? That it's just a power play? For a conflict that's happening on some other, what, like another plane of existence?"

"And that's not even the worst part," Anna says.

Kai stares at her for a moment before realizing what she's saying. "It means the things we're fighting aren't human," he says.

"Gods." Mouse forms the word himself, and they all go silent.

"Bra-*vo!*" comes a voice from the darkness ahead. "Your powers of deduction serve you well." A smiling mask appears in the distance, porcelain white, followed by the sound of thin-gloved applause wafting through the air. "It's only a shame you didn't use them a little sooner."

From the darkness on each side of the street come the clicks and scrapes of azazim, shuffling down driveways and creeping around houses. They're surrounded.

鼠

"Pull on up, I guess," June says. "It's not like they won't be expecting us."

Vallis turns off the van's engine and the sound of groundwater rain on the roof rushes in to fill the vacuum. The muddy droplets strike the old, cracked pavement, lit only by the silent, yellowy headlights. Shadows stretch like ghosts between the upright spans of riveted steel. The old bridge is deserted.

Priest slides the door open. He's about to step out when Helene reaches over him and throws up a barrier, just in time for two arrows to strike it and bounce harmlessly off. In the dim light cast by the golden sigils, a shadow slips down from a point on a girder to the road below. Something glints, and then there's a smashing sound and one of the headlights is out, then the other.

June grunts in the side seat. "Sorry about your ride," she says.

Vallis manages to get a quick "What?" past his lips before a beam of light blasts a new sunroof through the top of the van. A sphere of light hangs like a beacon over the bridge, like a full moon hanging low and dangerous in the sky.

The figure is suddenly fully visible, its dark hood not hiding the white porcelain face it surrounds. It stares at them like a dark-eyed statue, its expression one of nothing but absence.

June climbs out through the hole in the roof, drawing a shield about her that diverts the next two arrows away and into the river.

"Defense at the ready!" Priest barks out the command, slipping into old habits. "Expand that Holzmann, Junebug, we're getting out—agmen formation. We can't fight in here."

June expands the shield until it's a swirling mass of white sigils and pulsating shapes that arcs a fifteen-foot hemisphere above and around the van. They pile out under the defense; meanwhile, the mask angles its head slightly and nocks another arrow. A shield like theirs is two-way; they need to lower it to attack. All their enemy needs to do is wait.

"What next?" says Vallis.

"See any azazim?" Priest responds. He's right, there aren't any of the creatures around. This is the place. This is where they'll build the Algorithm.

"Radio the others," he says to Helene, but she's already at it. She pulls out the black box and twists one of its dials.

"Simon, it's the old bridge, do you hear me?" She waits a moment and asks again, but there's only soft static in response. "Simon, Bliss, anyone, if you can hear me, we're at the old bridge. This is where they're going to do it." Another few seconds of silence and a voice responds. It's Kai.

"Hey sorry sort-of busy call you back thanks!"

June and Helene exchange a look but don't have time to speak before the sigils in June's shield start winking out one by one. Another mask steps out of the shadows behind them, its face frozen in a hyperbole of tragedy. It holds a single arm aloft, the space between it and the shields almost seeming to fold in on itself, an unnatural, stomach-churning motion to watch. A hole in June's defense appears and an arrow whistles through, catching Priest in the arm, and he yells out in pain.

"The shield!" he shouts, pulling his belt off and using it as a makeshift tourniquet.

"I'm trying!" June's shouting through gritted teeth. It's taking all she's got to keep it up.

"On it!" Helene throws up a handful of smaller shields over the holes as they form. In under a minute, the dome is a patchwork of dozens of tiny golden circles with only fading traces of June's silver in between.

June gasps as the last of her workings fail, unmade by the monstrous force behind the mask. It turns its attention to the smaller shields then, taking them down methodically one at a time, with patient, brutal efficiency. At the fall of the first, another arrow cuts through the air. A sound like thunder echoes within the latticework of shields as Vallis fires to intercept, knocking the arrow away with a blast.

"New plan!" Priest says. He ties off his injured arm and starts using his free hand to make shields of his own, inches outside Helene's layer. "Watch it: it can only take down one at a time, even if they're small. We need smaller shields, and lots of them." Another two, three, four shields go up in a shade of iridescent purple. "You okay, Junebug?"

"What did I say, Leonard?" She forces it out, almost too tired for banter; nevertheless, a dozen silver spirals shimmer into life in a third, growing layer of shielding. "Don't *call* me that."

The number of shields grows, then seems to stabilize. "Great," June grunts, "With three of us throwing these up as fast as we can, and Vallis intercepting the occasional arrow, we're not going to be turned into human pincushions just for showing up." Another boom as Vallis makes her point. "Of course, we'll all be deaf before long, and it's only a matter of time before we're all too tired to keep going, but as far as plans go it's not the worst you've ever had, Leonard."

"As the only one of us who's been shot with an arrow, I'm going to ignore your tone and take that as a compliment."

"Take it how you like, just keep working on those shields."

"What about Argo?" Priest says to Helene.

She shakes her head. "The shields alone are taking everything I have."

Vallis grumbles something under his breath, and when the next shield goes down he fires twice in rapid succession. One shot for the arrow, the other for the mask.

He doesn't miss either shot.

The blast tears through the figure's torso, leaving a smoking hole and nearly detaching its shoulder. Its bow goes skittering across the tarmac. The mask looks down, not betraying the slightest hint of pain. It puts a hand to the wound.

And the hole closes.

Ink-black flesh regrows and replaces what was lost, inside and out.

It walks over the bow, picks it up, and nocks another arrow.

"Hnnh," says Vallis. "Would you look at that."

June stitches together another shield and prays the others are having better luck.

鼠

"Simon, Bliss, anyone, if you can hear me, we're at the old bridge. This is where they're going to do it." The radio, clipped to Bliss's hip, blares out.

She throws up a shield, a slow-spinning golden circle in the air, then heaves it with all her might against a pair of reptilian azazim coming at her from the side of the street. They lurch back against a garage door that sends splinters flying, but a third's already advancing from behind. She grabs the radio and manages to toss it to Kai, who catches it just as an azaz with a single long lobster claw lurches into the street from the other side.

"Hey sorry sort-of busy call you back thanks!" he shouts into the device, then pockets it in time to dodge the claw's massive guillotining *snap!* As he's slicing back with the still-glowing sword, he catches sight of Mouse and Anna fighting their way forward toward the mask.

They look like they're dancing. Every twisting strike of Anna's knife is followed by a blast of white fire from Mouse's spear, a cauterizing heat that hollows the monsters out from inside or makes them burst like godawful blisters. She darts forward and he pulls back, and an azaz takes the bait, realizing too late that it's the one surrounded as they close in from either side to deadly effect.

And from the bridge, the mask looks on and laughs.

But it shouldn't.

Mouse feels like he could almost close his eyes. Every move is the way it should be. Every step, every thrust is a moment of focus in a blur of echoes. He feels every blow coming, and so does Anna. Right now, they're sharing everything, they know everything the other knows. And right now they know they only need to wait for an opening.

A minute later, another azaz hits the tarmac with a sodden thud and reveals it: a hole in the line. Another creature moves in to fill the vacancy, a many-tentacled monstrosity, but Anna is already past it and turns on a dime to reopen the way for Mouse with a head-cleaving strike. There's nothing between them and the mask, and they rush forward to meet it.

A bolt of shadow-cold lightning splits and branches off into the sky when Mouse blocks it with his spear, the very antithesis of the ground-seeking power its existence mocks. The masks are creatures of undoing, unmaking—even the things they create are perverse.

A step to the left, a flying leap—they dodge and weave between thunderclaps as the lightning snakes its way along the bridge. Mouse anticipates every step, every duck, every parry. And then he realizes what has to happen next.

Anna doesn't have time to dissuade him, and wouldn't do it if she did. She knows as well as he does what his intuition means. They have to trust it. It's the closest he'll ever get to knowing how Simon—the other Simon—sees the world.

Another icy bolt flashes toward Mouse, and this time he doesn't stop it. It hits him in the chest and he goes down, hard.

鼠

Mouse's heels scuff and bounce along the road ahead of them. The still-smiling mask is dragging him backward down the street by his jacket, eyes closed, limp as a rag doll. If it weren't for Anna, Bliss wouldn't even be able to even tell if he's alive. The three of them are herded behind by slithering azazim, their weapons confiscated by the mask.

"Well now, we're all here at last." The mask's wicked voice is smooth and calm. "You stay off the bridge," an order to the azazim. "You three can play with the grownups. After all, you're a little young to be out without parental supervision, don't you think?" It laughs again and throws their weapons to the ground with a clatter.

June and the others are pinned down beneath a pile of shields, and fading fast. Priest looks like he's bleeding. Meanwhile, the other two masks are in the middle of the bridge, keeping them in check.

"Another step forward and I'll break your friend's neck." It sounds almost bored. "Nothing personal, you understand, but we just *can't* have you interfering, now *can* we? It's such a special night." It twists and tosses Mouse forward into the middle of the bridge.

Mouse rolls and scrapes along the asphalt.

"Mouse!" June shouts, but there's nothing she can do.

With a gesture, the mask erects its own barrier, across the entire width of the bridge. On one side are Mouse and the three masks. On the other, Bliss and everyone else. It's an improbable shimmering of dark mist and whispering shadows, twisted into lines and shapes across the bridge. This is nothing like the Knowledge of June or Priest or Helene or even Bliss herself—patterns of light dancing in the darkness; this has a physicality to it, a solidity, like a wrought-iron fence made from oil and blood, perpetually shifting and changing its form in the air, every movement a swarming, slithering, creeping thing. Its very *wrongness* radiates out like an impossibility, like an Escher painting or a fall through a bottomless pit.

Bliss gasps. She's only seen, only felt one thing like it in her life. "The world-city of the Fall."

Yyyyyes.

From everywhere and nowhere, a serpentine voice grips her heart. It sounds like an echo in reverse, as though each word takes time to catch up with its speaker. Like half a dozen people speaking and whispering all at once.

Aaaand you are the child that allows it.

"Get back!" It's Priest. They've dropped their shields and are backing away as a black string whips free of the pattern and tries to rope him in; he parries it with a quick draw of his sword, but tosses the weapon to the ground a moment later. Everywhere the string touches on the blade it leaves a creeping darkness. He kicks it away and watches as it congeals into a black puddle, then creeps along the road to join the barrier.

The neutral mask stares through at them, then turns to look at Priest.

Vvvvvverdict, Guardian? The voice now seems to speak for the masks.

Priest stares at Mouse, lying sideways in the street, then responds. "Golems. You're sock puppets."

The voice laughs, a vile, rippling sound, as the three figures walk away and begin drawing on the ground in the same black, sticky substance the barrier is made of.

Nnnnot just puppets, comes the voice, *manifested willlll.*

Priest turns to the others. "It's not a barrier. It's something called a subcunary manifold. Less a wall than a doorway." He looks at it, pulling in his sword and transmuting it by degrees into its selfsame tarlike substance. "'Don't touch it' goes without saying. More like 'Don't let it touch you.'"

"Who are you?" Anna asks the puppets. "Why do all this?"

The voice turns angry, as the neutral mask hauls Mouse into the air and shakes his lifeless form.

Bbbbbecause of this! The Diviner! Ssssimon Magus! Simon Aaaaanacreon! Simon the Wwwwanderer! Simon who stood, stands, and yet refuses to stand! Aaaas above, so below! Violation! Unending violation of order! We should be kings! Our right! Us above, Vermin below—He must be stopped. Segregated—Eliminated. No other choice—Only way—Too much threat— Disorder—Inversion—Violation—

The voice starts to fragment, no longer speaking as one but as a crowd of individuals, struggling to shout over one another.

—and you—his witch, Helene—his shadow. Our shadow—how many lives? How many lost—pompous fool—arrogance. Stolen from us—The trade is just!

The voices grow louder and louder, but it's like the sound is in their heads, and covering their ears doesn't help.

The mask drops Mouse, who crumples in a heap, and strides over to the massive circle of swirling black on the surface of the road and to the other two masks.

And then the smiling mask and the tragic one are drooping down, oozing into the same black ichor as the design. Their forms, now grotesque and misshapen, are swallowed, lapped up—in part by lashing tendrils from the ground, in part by the remaining mask. Anna can only watch as they're pulled apart, sucked up, and digested. Then the neutral mask stands—now taller, somehow—and the black lines begin to move. The will of their assailants has amalgamated, power passing between mannequins and machine; the Antiochus Algorithm is coming to life.

鼠

It takes all the willpower Mouse can muster not to cry out when he's thrown. His chest hurts where the lightning hit. His cheek burns when it scrapes the asphalt, his shoulder screams as it tries to dislocate on contact. One of his shoes falls off the second time he's dropped, but he can't let them know he's awake, and so he lets it slam into the pavement with only a thin sock to protect it. Everything hurts, but he must not react.

As the dark lightning had approached, he had known it in every part of him—this was the only way. He had built a tiny wall of barriers inside his chest and let every other defense down. The black and icy power now throbs in its cage within him, a heartbeat beside his own—it couldn't be deflected, but he couldn't let it incapacitate him, either. And so he'd held onto it, the unnatural, the evil, keeping it as secret as his own life. Waiting.

Until now.

As the gears of the Algorithm begin to creak into life, he cracks open his eyes. Only one mask remains, and this secret in his chest is a gift for it.

He slowly angles his head, praying that he won't be noticed, that it's just the right moment. A sudden crash from beyond the barrier catches his attention. It's Argo. No longer needing the shields, Helene's using her power to have him tear the seats out of the van—back row, middle row, passenger, driver—as she uses an unseen force to tear the hood from the front and slam it over a hole through the top that hadn't been there earlier.

"What are you doing to my ride?" Vallis shouts, but Helene ignores him.

"Out of the way!" she shouts. From somewhere she's recovered Mouse's spear.

"But what—"

"OUT OF THE WAY!"

Everyone dives for cover as the van, wrapped in a layer of sudden shimmering silver, slams into the barrier at a great speed. And gets stuck half way through.

The back of the van has been torn off, and Helene strides toward it.

"Anna! Now!"

And he sees it—she's made a van-sized tunnel through the shield. The only thing stopping them is the engine. Anna starts to run. Leveling Mouse's spear, Helene fires three blasts of white fire through the body of the van and tears the front away, leaving a protective steel ring to pass through the barrier. Anna and Helene dive through without hesitation.

And then, still lying on the ground, Mouse sucks in air like he's been punched in the gut. He grits his teeth and bites back an almost crippling wave of regret; realizing only at that very moment what's coming and having no time left to stop it.

There's a crunching sound and a scream of pain as their passage through collapses.

On Helene.

She'd almost made it. Anna's through, but the remains of the van have collapsed on Helene's foot, and although she's past the barrier, the creeping blackness has already started to climb down over the crumpled steel and up onto—into—her leg.

The remaining mask laughs and readies a volley of vicious black lightning to throw at Anna—but Mouse is already on his feet. He summons the darkness from within its cage and balls it into his fist. For this to work he's going to need to be close. Anna knows his plan and acts as a diversion, diving to one side and the other as it tries to hit her. By the time the creature realizes it has another assailant, Mouse is upon it.

As the mask turns to face him, Mouse is certain he sees surprise behind its frozen, empty face.

His open palm strikes the side of the mask and releases its power with a thunderclap, throwing them apart.

For a fraction of a second, Mouse is sure it hasn't worked. Anna steps back as the mask staggers, one hand to its face, before standing again, as if ready to fight. Had it absorbed the tragic mask's 'unmaking' powers along with the smiling mask's lightning? Mouse despairs at the thought. But when it pulls its hand away, they can see the truth: the mask has cracked.

The puppet begins to seize, twitching and writhing like a poisoned cockroach as the cracks spiderweb their way up through its porcelain face, severing the ties that had bound its dark and powerful magic together, cutting the strings that had moved the marionette. There's nothing behind its gaze now—not anger, pain, fear. Nothing. It's simply returning to the emptiness from which it was summoned, like dust to dust. When the mask at last cracks in half, it falls to the ground, every other part of the puppet's substance gone like smoke in the breeze.

Mouse runs to Helene.

She's lying on her side, twisted, looking up at him. She kicks at the van with her other leg, but it's not the wreckage that's holding her anymore. She shoves Mouse's spear away from her, away from the blackness.

They both know what's coming next, and neither can stop it.

He crouches down and holds her hand. Without thinking, he pulls it to his cheek and closes his eyes. But the blackness consuming her is a living thing, and it leaps and lurches over her legs to her waist, hungry. Behind him, the wheels of the Algorithm are grinding into gear. He leans in close and whispers something in her ear, then pulls away.

She smiles, even as her pulse slows, as the vengeful horror steals her life away and gives nothing in return. "That's a promise," she says. "I'll hold you to it." She's staring past him now, looking to a place no one else can see. "I never get used to this," she says, and tenses up.

And then she's gone, her eyes open but unseeing. Mouse steps back and looks away as the creeping absence steals away what's left. He picks up his spear and walks back to the accelerating ring.

The growling voices of the distant gods have lowered to an electric hum of whispers, watching from elsewhere as the Algorithm twists and turns in space, faster and faster in the darkness. A false wind has begun to pick up all across the town, blowing from all directions toward the bridge, toward the single pocket of oblivion it's creating, drawing power from beyond time, from impossibility itself, to create a new, horrifying world.

Then there's a creaking, groaning noise, low and powerful, everywhere at once, as the ground below their feet begins to splinter and crack, pulled down from above.

Mouse stands, stares at Bliss through the hungry, twisting barrier, and wonders how his alter ego does it, how Simon Magus makes changes that affect so many lives. Mouse is going to rewrite only one, and it terrifies him.

He turns away and faces the alchemical machine, its spinning, grinding gears rending the world, pulling it into its most basic component parts.

From behind the barrier, Bliss yells after him, but it's too loud for him to hear. Anna grabs his hand.

"You found your answer," Anna says, above the rising storm. She doesn't need to ask. Everything he knows, she knows. "Two words. Not Arkangel. Ark. Angel." She squeezes his hand. "Go save the world."

And then Mouse is running, spear in hand, dragging a single, golden circle around the circumference of the spinning rings and the perfect, impossible point they're creating at the center. As he completes it, he can hear a change in the voices from the barrier, from anger to fear. He closes his eyes and concentrates, remembering.

鼠

Mouse is standing alone in the white, calm memory. Everything is silent.

He's standing alone, and then not.

The old man is before him, with weathered face and peculiar robes. "You are less of me than any other. And also more. Across the ages, I will never again be so. You stand at the crossroads," the old man says, "why should it be you?"

"Because," Mouse says, "I think it always has been, and I think it always will be. I'm not you, and I won't ever be. But I'm going to need your help, because I don't know how to build an ark. And I don't know anything about angels."

"But?" The old man gives a cagey smile.

"But I know what I'm willing to pay."

The old man laughs a dry, dusty laugh that echoes back through a dozen lives or more. He nods his head in recognition of a gamble well made.

And then he gives Mouse what he needs to know.

鼠

Mouse clears his mind, places his thumb against the roof of his mouth, and releases the charge, just as Priest had done the first time they'd met. White fire lances up through his head making his eyes water, but he ignores it. This is it. He plants the spear point down in the golden circle and begins to speak, reaching into the depths of his memory, pulling words from a pocket of ice within, saved so long and so carefully for just this purpose.

"I, Simon Anacreon, name myself, as the one who stood, who stands, and who will stand. I name the invisible, inapprehensible silence, and call upon the boundless power, the universal root, the tree of all possibility."

The outer ring of the machine begins to slow, and the golden light of the ring he's drawn begins to seep into it. It shudders as it lurches to a stop, lit bright as gold in sunlight, and then starts to rotate in the opposite direction, causing the inner rings to shriek and grind. He shouts above it.

"By the oldest name, I pull a star from the sky and place a living world within it. I divert the stream of fate and reweave the unending. I bind it to the new, and name it everlasting. The song of passing dies and the ancient wind alone reveres her name."

The inner rings begin to warp, the symbols shifting under new orders. The darkness is fading away and a golden glow is replacing it in not just one but in all of the rings of the spinning artifact. The machine is alive, just as the old him—just as Simon Magus had said it would be. Mouse can feel it now, confused, quiet, still vague and empty, and desperate for a purpose. He means to give it one.

"In a lost tomorrow you will have been born—"

"Mind,"

"Voice,"

"Reason,"

"Image,"

"Reflection,"

"Name,"

"Thought."

Each word rings out like a strike on a jubilant bell.

"In the middle distance, the incomprehensible air, you are unmade, and into a new truth I bind you with a name."

The machine is his, only his, and exists now, in this one moment, only for him. In all the time that comes after this, it will think, feel, wonder. It will fight and fail and doubt and, most importantly, it will love. It glows—brilliant—spinning wheels within wheels. It knows what it will be and sings in joyous tones in his head. The light springs forth and hits the barrier with such force that the oily blackness seems to dissolve like mist in sunshine, and dispels the dark will that it had carried.

The others watch, staring at the only dark point for a dozen miles in all directions: the silhouette of Mouse, of Simon Anacreon, the shadow of the scarecrow himself set against the fires of creation.

Against the golden light, June reaches for Priest's hand, and it's already there waiting for her.

Mouse's face is hot as he stands before the blinding flames. His eyes are alight with wonder, and he's smiling, as everything turns to white.

"I move upon the surface of the waters. I name you."

Silence explodes outward like a shock-wave, shredding the collapsing pocket universe, returning the stars to the skies and remaking existence in its wake. Gone at once is the groundwater rain and the ouroboros of a world that had wrapped itself around them, making the dirt beneath their feet hang above their heads as well. It's all being repaired, replaced at the speed of thought by an expanding sphere of normalcy. Anna squints into the light at the center of the world as it begins to fade. There, no longer behind them but in front of them, standing in the middle of concentric rings of ash that drift and dissolve away in the lazy breeze, is a girl plucked from a timeline that will never exist. She will never be born, never grow up in a world defined by terror, never live on Saints' Row or run through the shifting maze beneath the hellish world-city of the Fall. And yet she will have done, and will always have done. The paradox that saved them all.

Mouse smiles and looks up at her, and says her name aloud.

The cicadas buzz and hiss in the August heat. It's sunny as they walk, Mouse and Kai, up the little cul-de-sac to the house where Bliss and Anna live together. Bliss had come clean about her history after the battle, telling stories about times that would never be. It was surreal hearing about their own deaths, Anna had said, and then had thought about it again. Maybe one death would be enough.

"I'm still not sure how Bliss still exists," Kai says as they near the house. "I mean, if the timeline she comes from isn't going to happen anymore, how is she here?"

Mouse sighs and stops on the porch before they ring the doorbell. Bliss's continued existence had always been an impossibility, sustained by the power of the Algorithm, which in turn was sustained by her impossibility. That night he'd taken it all and bottled it up permanently inside a piece of ages old alchemy called an ark. As the focus of the paradox, she'd always been separated from causality, from reality as they knew it, so he flipped it on its head, took the paradox and locked it inside her instead of her inside it, segregating it from the rest of existence. He'd made her what those who knew the oldest Knowledge called an angel.

It was impossible, sure, but given that the whole causal loop was an impossibility in the first place? In a way the loop, the darkness, was a natural part of the universe, a paradox that had always been, the way the moon has always been in the sky. It had taken thousands of years of wondering how it got there to explain the moon. Maybe one day they'd be able to explain the loop. Whatever its origins, he'd taken it and put it in a heart-shaped box and given it to Bliss. He's still not sure what that's going to mean for her, or for the kind of life she'll live, but he knows one thing—the Trust is not going to be pleased. He's already told June to be on the lookout.

Verthandi, on the other hand, he's starting to wonder about. How, exactly, does one of the three Sisters of Fate not see a thing like this coming in time to avoid it? He has serious questions for her, if she ever lets herself be found again.

Mouse notices Kai staring at him on the porch, still waiting for his answer, and sighs. The Antiochus Algorithm had been designed to do the impossible, and it had. But as for explaining it—he just shrugs at his friend. There's only so much impossible one person can do at a time. Everything has a price.

Anna opens the door before they ring the doorbell. She steps out and closes it behind her.

"Come on," she says, and starts walking next door.

Mouse and Kai look at each other, confused, and follow her. She doesn't knock at the next house, but just walks on in. Bliss is right there and puts her finger over her mouth in the universal symbol for *shhh*, then smiles, and motions for them to follow her as she climbs the stairs.

"My neighbors are out," she whispers. "I'm babysitting just for an hour while they go do the shopping. But I wanted you to meet them."

"Who—?" Kai says and Anna elbows him to be quiet.

"Shh," she whispers. Kai rolls his eyes.

Lying in the crib are two babies, just a couple of months old, one in pink and the other in blue, mercifully sleeping. Twins.

Mouse looks up at Bliss.

He knows their names, but she tells him anyway.

"Rain and Bliss," she says. "This is my parents' house."

Mouse stares into the crib and considers telling Priest, but for now there's no guarantee that the little girl will grow to be Helene. And if she needs guardians, then he can think of none better suited to the task than those standing in the room now.

For the moment, they have all the time in the world.

END

完

Richard Ford Burley

Richard is a writer, editor, and graduate student based in Boston, where he lives with two beautiful women, one of whom happens to be a cat. *Mouse* is his first novel.

richardfordburley.com